HELEN PRIOR

Adventures of an Old CxNT

THE THRILL OF LIFE AFTER CANCER

Matador
Unit E2 Airfield Business Park,
Harrison Road, Market Harborough,
Leicestershire. LE16 7UL
Tel: 0116 2792299
Email: books@troubador.co.uk
Web: www.troubador.co.uk/matador
Twitter: @matadorbooks

Paperback ISBN 978 1789015 973
Hardback ISBN 978 1789015 980

British Library Cataloguing in Publication Data.
A catalogue record for this book is available from the British Library.

Printed and bound in Great Britain by 4edge Limited
Typeset in 11pt Minion Pro by Troubador Publishing Ltd, Leicester, UK

Matador is an imprint of Troubador Publishing Ltd

Dedicated to the three men in my life:
to my husband for giving me a good life and supporting me
through many beginnings;
to the man I gave life to – my son – the joy and pride of my life;
and to the brilliant surgeon who gave me my life back – to the
Saviour!

Definition of Cunt

Derogatory term for a woman. Considered by many to be the most offensive word in the English language.

Urban Dictionary

An offensive word for a very unpleasant and stupid person.

Cambridge Dictionary

A very offensive word for a stupid or unpleasant person. Do not use this word.

Longman Dictionary of Contemporary English

'A contemptible person' when used with a positive qualifier (good, funny, clever, etc.) in Britain, New Zealand, and Australia, it can convey a positive sense of the object or person referred to.

The Macquarie Dictionary of Australian English

I betrayed, I lied,
I cheated, I bribed,
I used people, I stole,
I traded my body and soul.
I was a Cunt.
I was betrayed, I was blackmailed,
Was punished, torched and rejected,
I suffered, cried but I survived!
I was resurrected.
Turned into a nicer Cunt!

"There are only two ways to live your life. One is as though nothing is a miracle. The other is as though everything is."

Albert Einstein

It may sound unbelievable that the most exciting time of my life during a few last decades began after I was struck by cancer – but it was! My body fought to recover from all I had lost that had defined me as a woman, and I needed love, sex and fun in vast proportions to compensate for the hellish ordeal. I managed to turn myself from a victim to a victorious survivor. But these great changes whisked me into such a sequence of events that it was often hard to perceive what had actually happened, and what was just a trick of my mind.

Contents

Gynaecologist Is My Life

When you've been around for more than half a century and have survived a brush with womb cancer (I prefer to call it 'Operation C'), you'll find that the most important man in your life will no longer be your husband, but your gynaecologist. It is he, who for the next few years will take care of you and tend to your scared zone, damaged as if by war.

When I met Mr Andrew Kovač I wanted to change the title of the song my son composed at the age of eleven from *Music Is My Life* to *The Gynaecologist Is My life* – because he is. He was. And he will be.

Me
- Popov- Fitzcock, Natalia
- Age: uncertain
- 5ft 6
- Russian-Ukrainian
- Considers herself mostly British
- Art historian, working freelance as a London guide
- Former cancer patient
- Speaks English with a strong Eastern European accent
- Intellectual and cultural snob before diagnosis
- More laid-back post-cancer, at times horizontal
- Opera lover, before and after C

As the train of life passes through the station called *Menopause*, one might assume – as I did – that the problems associated with our reproductive organs are over. They have stopped working, they are dead. Like rusted bicycles, they do not require their tyres retreaded, as they're not in use anymore. How wrong you would be! How stupid I was, even with all my degrees, which my husband Freddie refers to as a PhD in Stupidity! That's when it really starts, the need for constant repairs and check-ups on your outdated canal system from a good pair of hands examining you in depth; the hands of a real deep diver.

He

- Kovač, Andrew Jacob.
- Age: 46
- 5ft 6, nearly bald
- Serbian-British
- Natalia's Saviour
- Considered to be a good man in his circle of friends and family
- Married to a student sweet heart – a proctologist
- He is busy with fronts; she is busy with backs; that keeps the Kovač family going
- Devoted 100% to his job, no time for hobbies
- IQ of 140, which could go unnoticed due to his kind nature
- The word 'adultery' makes him sweat with fear and pleasure
- Nearly never cheated on his wife, he thinks
- Went to the opera only once in his life; it reminded him of his euphoric patients

I've never been considered shy. Shyness was not my virtue, so going to see a gynaecologist shouldn't have been a problem. My first rule was: try to avoid female gynaecologists. They are often like she-wolves and hate other women. If you are younger than them, they hate you for having a bit more time to stride through life, enjoying more rides along the way. If you are older, they cannot hide their disgust at having to venture into your Neanderthal cave for an archaeological dig.

***

A few years ago, when I received a third reminder from the NHS for a smear test, I had no choice but to book an appointment with the she-gynaecologist, Ms Jones. She turned out to be an exhausted, bitter-looking blonde woman, whose age was uncertain – somewhere between thirty-five and fifty – and obviously unsatisfied with her professional life, and possibly her private life too.

"My dear, undress behind the screen, please, and climb into this chair. Are you comfortable doing this?"

What a bitch! She wanted to make it clear which age group I belonged to, I thought.

"Doctor, I could climb Everest and a few bulky guys. Surely, I can handle this monstrous chair."

"No need to be vulgar." She hardened her voice. I think mentioning bulky guys made her feel really jealous.

Then came the question I was waiting for, "Aren't we slightly obese? You need to exercise more and watch your diet."

The 'o' word made me a political enemy of all doctors; they'd use it instead of general greetings. How sharp was Anton Chekhov, the Russian writer, when he remarked, "I'm not a gynaecologist, but I know a cunt when I see one".

As an art historian, I couldn't avoid comparing works of art, paintings or sculptures, with everything I experienced in my life. Here with the she-gynaecologist, I thought about Hans Memling's *Donne Triptych*, which I often showed to my tourists in the National Gallery. Ms Jones would have been on the right-hand side of the painting with the damned, being dragged into the bowels of a volcanic Hell by demons who carried instruments of torture similar to the ones this gynaecologist was going to stick into my cunt. The left side depicted the Gates of Paradise, which were not opened for me either: the angelic choir and orchestra were not for fallen women. Quite the opposite of the pure souls, I was full of the desire to sin, to show the she-doctor my fat ass and tell her that men used to like it, that they enjoyed squeezing my chubby thighs as well. But I had to comply with social etiquette to avoid going to Hell and waiting a month for another NHS appointment. So instead I joked to ease the tension,

"Doctor, whales swim all day, eat only fish, drink only water. They are fat! I eat mainly fruit and veg, supplemented with grilled chicken and organic salmon. My husband's favourite joke is that cows feed on grass and are still getting fatter and fatter."

It was better to stop this polemic – it was clear the doctor would never understand. She was a size six, at most an eight. She had dried out from unhappiness. I bet she wouldn't even allow herself a sweet to relax. Her physique reminded me of Giacometti's anorexic sculptures – an army of bronze aliens, like his *Standing Woman* in the Tate, whose body appeared to have been eaten away. The Swiss artist, a great womanizer, used to scrape away all the flesh and leave the surface coarse and uneven.

I removed my knickers behind a screen. It was a pity she was not aware of what a decent woman should wear under her skirt. I had sprayed my old treasure with cheap Fem-Fresh intimate hygiene product (widely available from Boots) and wiped myself with a soothing relief liquid, marketed as a miracle which could sort out even middle-aged pussy problems. It wasn't that I wanted to help the she-doctor get through the debris of my rusty, unused cave, but I hoped to make her journey smoother, to save myself from unnecessary pain during her drilling. I climbed – no, I jumped – into the scary chair, showing off my agility. I put my legs into the stirrups and waited for her to proceed. The suffocating smell of antiseptic, the miserable grey walls and the hellish chair made me feel that this might well be the end of the road for sinners like me.

The doctor was writing and writing – perhaps it was my verdict. It seemed that she had forgotten about her patient, leaving me with my bare ass looking up to the heavens. She-doctors like to keep you for a while with your legs spread and thrown into the air, like in a prayer, only in an upside-down position. This Maida Vale medical centre was surely taken straight from Hieronymus Bosch's painting *The Martyrdom of St Julia*. The only difference was that St Julia was crucified on a cross, unlike the not-very-saintly Natalia stuck on this chair of horrors. I was praying that the pelvic examination would end as soon as possible and nothing horrible would be discovered.

Jesus, I've made the mistake of having a slightly large number of men in my past. I'd rather not count, nor do I want to remember. Please forgive me, my Lord, have mercy on me.

And he did, I thought. He probably took into consideration that I had paid my penance, as for the last few years I had been a virgin.

The doctor's voice came from down below. "Dear, the walls of your vagina are getting dry and thinning out, but this is normal for women of your age."

She-doctors enjoy reminding you about your age; they feed on it. They like to ask stupid questions, such as,

"When was the last time you engaged in sexual activity?" She made it sound as if she was asking when I had last been to the cinema.

"Do you mean when did I last have a fuck, doctor?"

She blushed, "Stop swearing!"

It took a lot of restraint not to throw the question right back at her. It was waiting to jump out from my dirty mouth,

"How about you, dear? You probably can't remember that solitary moment in your life. It happened only once, in your early youth."

Maths had always been my weakest subject, even making me sweat in horror during the night; I never counted days in hundreds or thousands. I answered her rather politely:

"It was a long time ago. My son was still at junior school."

I always wonder why hairdressers have the worst hair in the world, and why it is that manicurists often have horrible nails – one might intelligently assume that this female gynaecologist owned an undesirable cunt. I think, I guess, I hope.

It was a very different experience when you saw a male doctor, particularly a private one in the Harley Street Golden Triangle. The doctors there were always nice, so sweet; they made you melt. You got a feeling that your purpose there was to experience something mysteriously pleasant and no harm could ever be done. His hands would be so delicate, his touches gentle. He would be like a talented pianist, slightly disorientated, playing on your vagina instead of a pianoforte. He performed his scales and sonatas mainly in two keys, G minor and G major, without any mistakes. He could make them sound quiet or powerful; he would take on his music in lento, dolce, non troppo, and then speed up into allegro and presto. Finally, skilfully using the best of sforzando, he would brilliantly smash all the keys at once in a culminating orgasm. He was an artist and required respect and adoration. You would get anxious and excited before you faced him; it would feel like a rendezvous, an impending sexual encounter. For older girls, it could be the only one of the last decade. Seeing a doctor for the first time might have given you a thrill similar to that of going on a blind date.

Back in Maida Vale, the she-doctor was taking 'real' care of me,

"Are you all right getting out of the chair, my dear?"

The Best of British

25th June 1997
Cobham, Surrey

Husband

- Fitzcock, Freddie
- Successful businessman
- Age: 65, well preserved
- 6'2
- Hobbies: obsessive cricketer in the past, dedicated gardener in his sixties
- Dog-lover – finds it more comfortable to express his feelings to dogs rather than people
- Sleeps with women to help them find self- confidence or fight depression
- Sees it as an act of charity rather than adultery
- Hates opera and cultured people
- Prefers the smell of cow shit to the most expensive perfume
- Reliable when you are ill or in trouble.

My husband, Freddie, never expected or particularly wanted me to adopt guiding as a serious profession. He would have preferred his wife to be at home more, serving him occasional lunches and dinners or making snacks at the cricket club.

"Jane will be scoring today. Can you help with sandwiches?"

I did, for a bit. It was boring for me to watch a bunch of men wander around a field with their bats, trying to do something with a tiny ball and pretending it required enormous skill. For a wild Slavic soul, it felt as though nothing happened during these games *at all*.

The cricket matches started at noon and often lasted until sunset – that's even longer than Wagner's operas! Test matches, which I liked to call 'test-icles' due to the brigade of men running around the pitch shaking their manhoods about, could last five buggering days. Occasionally, when passing Lord's cricket ground in St. John's Wood early in the morning, I would see spectators queuing with their baskets stuffed with heavy provisions to keep their energy levels up and prevent starvation during the endless performances. They also came equipped with big umbrellas – they called them 'brollies' – for rain and sun, whichever was expected, ready to withstand even a storm. These could come in rather useful if you needed to push somebody out of your way. I always wondered where they found the time to watch all those matches, those gents in the straw hats. It's probably the pensioners' favourite game – who else could go, particularly during the weekdays, unless they're unemployed?

For me, the never-ending cricket had neither music nor sex appeal. All guys, eleven in each team, dressed in white as if prepared to be packed into wooden boxes, with long trousers covering them and leaving nothing to spark a fantasy. The only fun was their 'box' – they fixed it to their testicles as protection from the cricket ball. Putting it on their manhood, they would usually forget to remove it until the end of the week, being exhausted from the 'tempestuous' game. These boxes were a good defence system from their wives as well, who were known as the 'cricket widows'. They had to be, as their husbands were absent from family life during, after, and often before the tournament.

I much preferred a rugby match. A game packed neatly into eighty minutes, plus ten for a break, and never short of excitement. Strong guys in tight shorts pushing each other around, pulling at each other's ears, occasionally even breaking the spines and necks of opponents; not at all afraid of the consequences. I would get more aroused watching those lads than the strippers at a Bad Boys show in Soho. Watching rugby was like watching group sex. I'd always tell female tourists that the rugby ground is the best place to find a husband. Of course, only if one had the ability and patience to distract those guys from the ball and each other, and turn their attention instead to courtship.

In this country, we are accustomed to one's gender roles, in sports and in love. Back in public school, the rugby players shared bedrooms at night and spent the days out on the pitch groping each other, and it didn't matter one bit that women weren't involved. Blokes in rugby were happy with this existence with themselves; if only they could impregnate their buddies, they would probably forget about women altogether.

When I came to this country more than twenty-five years ago, players still shared a big bath in the changing room after the match, feeling for soap under the water, or anything else that may find itself in their hand. Health and safety regulations put a stop to that, the best part of the game. Killjoy officers deemed it too risky – instead of soap, something else might be squeezed and injure the player.

The names of the positions in rugby are rather erotic, too. The hooker is a bulky guy who hooks the ball in a scrum. Props, even more bulky – my type – prop the hooker up. Up and down, up and down, like a sex act. But the real warriors are in the second row, tall and gorgeously built, pushing the hooker and the props together. Every player was at least a hundred kilograms of pure muscle, and I would squeal when I saw them on the field in their short knickers and with their hairy legs, unfazed by the wintery chill of -1 Celsius. To be honest, I would have loved to be in this scrum myself as a hooker – under two heavy props like Phil Vickery or John Hayes. And that funny little fast boy, the scrum half, would be half the size of a normal man – I'd call him a pocket chap. He would rush around like mad, trying to put the ball into the scrum so the hooker could hook it. As they say in Russian – *malenkie da udalenkie* – an inch is as good as a mile. Exactly! What a story! A subtle description of soft-core gay porn for public consumption. My husband used to play until he was moved from the second row to the back row, becoming 'a silverback'. For years, he liked to demonstrate his broken cauliflower ears with pride, like a great lifetime achievement.

The crowds at rugby matches were very decent and mostly middle-class – accountants, doctors and company directors. A similar demographic to the Sex Maniacs' Ball, where my husband took me a few times between rugby games years ago in an attempt to revive our fading relationship. Unlike crazy football supporters, rugby fans expressed admiration in a more dignified, often musical way, singing beautiful hymns to the teams they loved and adored so much. They even did it standing in their honour, as if for Her Majesty the Queen. I often liked to show off my vocal talents at these matches. I would inhale as much air as possible into my lungs and support it with my strong diaphragm, resonate it in my tummy as taught during my opera singing lessons, and then blow out as loud and low as I could: *Swing Low, Sweet Chariot*. In those moments I would feel so British!

It was never a problem for me to spare a couple of hours at Twickenham for the sake of a happy family life. By doing this, we could live a thoroughly British life, without having to touch each other or speak to each other for another few months.

British sports were one thing, but it took me much longer to adjust to British people, even with the help of my clever and supportive friends.

"English people put up emotional barriers to protect themselves from everyone, including their wives. They like to keep all their passions to themselves. If you show them any emotion, they'll disappear into their shells like a snail does." I had profound consultations with my friend Ella, who was training as a psychologist, and also in therapy for her own anxious mind and unsatisfied libido.

My Confidante
- Germanskaya, Ella
- Age: 53 & ¾, from the front; 40 from the eye- catching, voluptuous rear
- 5'4 – tall enough to feel proud
- Camden personality
- Brunette with partially grey hair
- Natalia's friend and consultant in the art of soul
- Psychologist and art dealer, desperately trying to be smart and clever
- Fanatically devoted to her dog, which she considers to be the more psychologically balanced of all creatures

"If an Englishman says, 'Maybe we shouldn't do it after all', it means in Russian, 'If you ask again, bitch, I'll hit you straight in your eye'!" She gave me this clever advice too late. It took me a good twenty years to understand the nuances of different cultures. I always did or said something wrong by English standards.

"The best women are Filipino," Freddie would joke. "They say nothing, they ask nothing, are known to be great with their hands and are devoted to their husbands, just as dogs to their masters."

I wasn't like that, which is why I was 'awarded' my lovely nickname.

"Fucking cunt!" A loud howl reached my ear. Freddie was aggressively rushing towards me across the cricket field, while I was reading my book, trying to kill time during the never-ending game.

"You want to look clever! Close the blasted book!"

My husband acted like the master of that place; after all, the club was on his land. He was the managing director of a few companies and liked to call himself *The Chairman*. This pathetic title always reminded me of Chairman Mao, perfectly featured in John Adam's minimalist opera *Nixon in China*.

Freddie loved to serve beer to players and their families, to anybody who would come to watch. He tried to create an image of a Don Quixote, being considerate of the common people. Yet, I could see that they looked at him like an eccentric lord, wanting to show mercy and receive forgiveness for his own sins.

"Who else wants a pint of ale? We're serving London Pride from Fuller's Brewery." I heard my husband's hoarse baritone voice with a clear BBC accent, the product of his private education. The school he attended admitted kids who had failed all their exams.

"I never passed any exam and never went to a university. It didn't stop me from building a successful business. My accountant is from Oxbridge. Whenever you need to make a decision – the higher your grades, the longer it takes to make a choice. Those with top diplomas rarely get it right."

There was no point arguing with the Chairman of the Fitzcock Empire.

I never felt any desire to return to the cricket field, and all other desires towards my husband started fading faster than the flying cricket ball. I would prefer to spend my time learning the streets and museums of London, in sun and rain, in heat and freezing cold when my fingers would refuse to write. I would go with the guiding course to study every detail of this huge fascinating city, write it all down, every story, typing it up later on, learning it by heart, passing numerous knowledge and site examinations for two long years. I became a guide in great demand, able to pick up the best clients.

Venus and I

15th July 2015,
Central London

It was the peak of the season. The telephone never stopped ringing:

"Are you free this weekend for a tour of Neolithic sites for the cosmonaut G? He wants to find proof that Stonehenge was built by creatures from other galaxies."

"Masons and Knights Templar for the government delegation. Mr. Pooh himself! They say that he is a mason…"

"Are you free next week? We have a VIP with his girlfriend, a client with continuously changing partners. He wants a tour of the Tate Modern with a specialist. This time he is interested mainly in surrealists – phallic symbols and their sexual connotations. Last year, when he visited London with his wife, the guy asked for a kitchen interior design style to be examined in depth."

Bastards, I thought. *They want a specialist on phallic symbols but are offering to pay only a normal guide's rate!*

"Katerina," I said to the tour company manager. "Please, add 50 per cent to my fee for talking about this disturbing display, and I'll show them works of Juan Miro overflowing with sexual fantasies – phalluses and breasts of all shapes and designs, floating on the canvas, repeating time and time again. They'll fall in love with Miro's *Head of a Catalan Peasant* and the pubic hair attached to his face instead of a beard."

"Calm down, Natalia! Do you want to take this job? I have a list here with the names of forty Russian-speaking guides."

But I couldn't stop. "Name one who will be able to present the frustrated desires and passions in Max Ernst paintings so that the clients may even cut their tour short. A run to the hotel for a quickie will be needed to satisfy the artistic eruption of passion."

I heard the roar of laughter shaking the office – the girl had probably put the phone on speaker – so I continued, "I'll educate them on the diversity of sexual fantasy and the consequences of the edge of insanity, using his original work *Man Shall Know Nothing of This*. If they double my pay, I'll add in Freud's studies on sexual paranoia and castration, too. They will be so happy... I promise... that this isn't happening to them!"

My usage of sexually-charged words and niche artists did the job – I got my extra 50 per cent allowance. Vivat Mr Freud!

***

"Our tour will last one hour and thirty minutes," I would announce to my tourists, but it was always important to carry on slightly longer. That was a trick of the trade to make the clients feel they have got good value for their money, but also to ensure they have no expectation to see the whole museum in one go – the complete art world for one price.

"This huge cucumber is a traditional symbol of the resurrection. However, you may note the word 'erection' within – the male power. You can never mistake Carlo Crivelli's works – the phallic shaped vegetables are always present." *Was the artist a vegetarian?* This thought often invaded my mind. *Or perhaps he thought that a cucumber could do the job?* I continued with my presentation of *The Annunciation*. "There were lots of discussions at the time whether a Virgin could be impregnated by the Holy Spirit. The provocative cucumber discloses that the artist did not believe in the Immaculate Conception." A few blokes produced a smile of satisfaction – they obviously did not believe in it either.

I led my group to the adjoining room.

"Venus and Mars are having a little rest after prolonged love making." I could immediately spot when I had caught the tourists' interest by the way they looked at me. Single, middle-aged women seemed particularly intrigued by the depiction of sexual acts, as they may not have practised for some time.

"Sandro Botticelli chose a delicate subject for a wedding present. What's even more intriguing is that Venus and Mars are not husband and wife. Venus is supposed to be happily married to Vulcan. He isn't as young and handsome as her lover, as so often happens in real life."

Venus was a cunt, wasn't she? I couldn't stop thinking about my own husband, who was eleven years my senior. He was in good shape though. They say that men age like fine wine – the older, the better – but this was only true to a certain extent. After a while, the wine turns sour. When Freddie's friends came to visit, I always experienced the feeling of being in the British Museum, the Egyptian mummy galleries. I could never properly relate to them.

"The upkeep of this beautiful woman is expensive and requires a lot of money." I was repeating Freddie's favourite saying. He liked to say this to his friends when I was present, implying that I was a kept woman.

"To be able to provide for his beautiful wife, old Vulcan had to work twenty-four hours a day in a hot forge, making armour for the gods of Olympus and Mars as well."

I was talking almost automatically, which left space to think about my own life. I was brought up believing that a man is a provider and that supporting his family with a decent income actually makes him 'The Man'. Then, of course, I should have accepted my husband's favourite saying: 'He who pays the piper calls the tune'. But I did not. I wanted it all my way, just like in Sinatra's song that had become a hymn for me, as it expressed my own spirit precisely.

Freddie hadn't put his hand around my shoulder for years. Our sexless marriage made me feel undesirable, and the ugliest woman in the world; a flawed woman. For some time, I wondered if my husband saw me the same odd way as *The Ugly Duchess* by the Flemish artist Quentin Matsys. Neither of us mentioned sex anymore. This 'scary' word was deleted from our vocabulary.

To fill the intimacy gap, my husband had his own official 'girls', who saw to it that he remained fulfilled and happy. They pulled him out every evening for long walks, they watched sunsets together. Freddie looked like a man in love – with his tetrapods. These hairy bitches would lick him allover just for a biscuit.

His 'girls' were our two dogs, Betty and Molly, whom Freddie the Chairman would personally take for an expensive haircut every three weeks to make sure that they felt loved and cherished.

"The grooming lady will be coming tomorrow. Make sure that your car is not in the way of her van. She needs to reach the electric socket." Freddie had to ensure that all would go perfect for his 'girls.'

"She was here two weeks ago. What is there to cut? Only whiskers, perhaps. There's nothing more left on the poor doggies." I started thinking that my husband was showing signs of early dementia, as he had become rather forgetful. "You spend more time on their hair than on yours." I knew that the expenditure on his hair wouldn't exceed a tenner.

"Just do as you told," he said, putting his hands around Betty's neck. "Aren't you beautiful?"

Thank God, there were no pedicures or massages treatments for his ladies, as their master was not into that stuff himself. However, he would spend any amount of money on veterinary care for his treasured girls. Freddie was a kind chap. He really loved animals, as most Brits do – more than humans. He wouldn't notice my haircut, even if I had dyed my natural golden blonde locks mahogany brown. I would need to shave my head to get any attention.

One day I came back home from the hairdresser and I overheard my Chairman saying something very unusual. "You look gorgeous today, fabulous! I will prepare a special dinner for you tonight." He was looking at me through the window.

I thought, "Blimey me! Is it time for changes? Perestroika!" I rushed to the conservatory. "What did you say, darling?"

"I was talking to my dogs," he answered looking away from me.

I wasn't even upset. I started laughing hysterically. I realised that I wasn't hairy enough for my husband.

"Have you fed the dogs?" I would hear, instead of 'Good morning'. "Have you let the girls out?" That was instead of 'Good night'.

'The Fatty' was Freddie's nickname for our cocker spaniel, Molly. In fact, Molly was a castrated male mongrel, turned into a non-binary creature – happy and jolly. To make it easier to manage them, both our dogs were known as 'girlies'. *'Out you go, girls; bed time, girls'.*

Molly was partly my dog: the fat dog of a fat woman. I was constantly reminded of my weight. I ate to subdue my unhappiness and get some satisfaction in the absence of other female delights. After years of 'idyllic' marriage I ballooned to 110 kilos. I looked solid, like a whole library of wisdom and knowledge. I wished that my weight was a measure of happiness, but unfortunately it was an indicator of the volume of my sadness.

"Ken will take Betty to the vet tomorrow."

Ken was our cleaner, a blissfully married man, who took delight in rearranging the cosmetics in my 'bedchamber', and sampling my expensive creams and perfume. For years, I used to think it was an unknown mistress of my husband, and was relieved to learn it was a middle-aged man exercising his unfulfilled fantasies.

Freddie wouldn't trust me with his English beauty, our standard poodle. Over the years, I had started to dislike Betty. I felt just like a woman jealous of a mistress; the dog was getting all the attention and kindness. I felt delighted whenever she left a piss pool on the floor of our dining room.

"I had to remove the carpet. I can't live in a room flooded with the piss of your lovely elegant sweetie. My Fatty would never do such a thing!"

That was my triumph! He could say nothing. Vivat, fat bottomed girls! You make the rocking world go round! Freddie Mercury obviously admired Montserrat Caballé's ass, which substantially exceeded mine. When we had just met, my Freddie repeatedly sang this song to me. For years now, he had gone quiet.

My first marriage lasted only one year. I was nineteen; nearly a virgin. It was a runaway from my Ukrainian mother. I mistook sex for love. No sex, no love, I stupidly thought. I was disappointed to discover that the connection between thrust and love didn't always work in the way I had expected.

When I married my second husband, I was twenty-six – not at all a virgin. I assumed that he would look after me, and that would make a happy marriage. And he did, but I missed out in my expectations of sex with him – it lasted only a few scarce minutes. And the marriage lasted – only two years and a bit. It was a relief. I would have rather had a cup of tea or read a book instead.

I would lie on my back and imagine him as a sparrow on a wire, with a tiny beak, trying to get some food out of my nest. An anecdote about a rabbit and a she-elephant, that my granny told me before my first marriage, kept popping into my mind.

A she-elephant got into a trap. A rabbit happened to be nearby and offered to help her. He asked for a fuck as a thank you. Time passed by, and the she-elephant got annoyed that the rabbit was in no hurry to receive his reward. She wagged her tail in agitation or disappointment. "Am I hurting you, darling?" the rabbit asked.

That was very much the tale of my second marriage.

When I married for the third time, I was over thirty. I was broody, and dreaming of a son. Subconsciously, I was looking for a good dad for him. In this, I did not make a mistake. Freddie was a father to rival the best, but he hated the job of being a husband. After a few years of marriage I became a complete virgin. My husband was afraid of strong women, like a lot of men are. He would often go elsewhere looking for sex, trying to prove to himself that he could conquer his fears. Eventually he stopped engaging in sexual activities and decommissioned his weapon – at least on my front. He turned it into a tool for gardening. I told him that I was also a flower – not a bud anymore, but the whole bush, all for him, and I needed watering and pumping. It didn't help. Instead of intimacy, I had his money and all the joy and comfort they could buy. Money was supposed to be very sexy. And a lot of money was as good as group sex.

"When a man does not need you in bed anymore, you quickly lose power over him," my granny used to tell me. "But when your husband becomes fairly old," she would continue, "and realises that he requires a nurse, or a driver to help him differentiate brakes from an accelerator, his younger wife might become once again the most trusted and desirable asset."

I have always valued my grandmother's words of wisdom. Her name was Galina, but I called her Gulka from a baby's 'guli, guli' sounds. The illegitimate child of a Ukrainian peasant girl and a Ukrainian count, she was an extraordinary beauty. Men would chase her even when she was in her seventies. Yet her honesty and resistance to using her female assets left her in a communal flat for most of her life – a Soviet reality 'palace', where she had to share a toilet and kitchen with neighbours. I loved to visit her. The dining table in her small fifteen-square-metre room was lit by a beautiful, antique standing lamp, with a delicately painted pink porcelain leg and a matching lace shade. It forever stayed with me as a link to the happy parts of my childhood. My gran was my shelter, my only sanctuary from my cruel mother.

***

I moved my tourists to the room with the Flemish masters. Jan van Eyck's *The Arnolfini Portrait* always caused a stir with Russians. It did not take long before they noticed a very familiar face on this early fifteenth-century masterpiece. Everybody became excited, pushing each other in a burning desire to take selfies with the 'presidential-looking' merchant and his wife.

"It looks like Vlad, your president, forgot to disclose his connections with the Western world of wealth."

My remark immediately provoked laughter and lit up the eyes of the bored husbands, who had initially hated the idea of coming to the art gallery but had to do it, as they were scared to upset their strong-built wives. I read in the Sunday Times about these amazing similarities, and the presence of the Putin's face in the Arnolfini's house, but I was proud that my discovery preceded this respectable publication. That was a few years go. Since February 2022, I don't call that mad monster Vlad anymore, but Pooh-Hitler.

The guys in my group learned the real power of art when we reached *The Rokeby Venus* by Velasquez, widely known as *Venus at the Mirror*.

"Look around – you won't find any other naked woman in this room filled with seventeenth century paintings by Spanish masters of the Golden Age. They served God and King. Their interest was in images of Saints and the Virgin. We are talking about the time of the Spanish Inquisition. Only Velazquez, with his special Royal connections, was brave enough to allow himself to create this, for those times, pornographic picture." The 'P' word aroused a lot of interest among the men in the group and the single ladies. But delicate care was needed not to upset the wives.

I decided to miss Caravaggio – he was a genius but a bad boy, and moved to the room displaying eighteenth century British Art. My choice – Hogarth's *Marriage a la Mode* – was picked up by the hand of Fate, but in the wrong direction. Talking about a cheating husband made me think about my own man.

Once I noticed that Freddie had removed all of our photos from the bedroom. *Why would he do that? Was he removing all traces of my presence? Someone was there to share the bed.* It was the same theme of cheating like in many of those paintings. Luckily, Thomas Gainsborough, whose works were next door, saved me by offering a real idyll in his *The Morning Walk*.

"Ann Boleyn, the lady in waiting to the Catholic wife of Henry VIII, Catherine of Aragon, eventually let the womaniser king into her bed, and divorce was needed to assure the legality of the heir to the Tudor dynasty…" That was the beginning of my explanation of the developmental delay of the British art.

"Wow!" I was interrupted by a teenaged member of my group:

"This is the painting I saw in *Skyfall*. James Bond was sitting just there." And he pointed to the bench opposite the work by Gainsborough. I noticed that my group were now more interested in art, as the cell phones were set to work. Every tourist wanted a picture with the same Gainsborough background as was shown in the popular movie. Despite this great excitement, I had to continue with my job. I decided to drop the explanation of the history of art, and concentrate on the popular painting itself.

"The presence of a dog in the paintings generally symbolises fidelity. The charming, newly married couple in this splendid portrait – Mr and Mrs Hallett – are in their twenties, but their morning walk would last for 50 years, till the very late evening of their life."

What about our dogs – Betty and Molly. Were they also symbols of fidelity, or had they failed to serve the proper purpose? These invasive thoughts were pounding my brain till the end of the tour.

Cultural Taboos

22nd July 1999
Cobham, Surrey

"We have to go! We're late!" Freddie was almost violent with worry about upsetting his friends.

"Give me a minute. I can't find my earrings."

"Who cares about your earrings? It's so disrespectful to be late. Are you coming?" He slammed the front door and rushed to the car.

Usually we were the first to arrive, and that prolonged my suffering in trying to communicate with the hosts. This time it was Marzena and Bryn Farrow – local farmers and landowners, and really good pals of Freddie. I had been blessed to know them for more than two decades – they were boring but kind people. During the twenty years of my marriage, this couple had invited us remarkably often to their house for lunches and dinners.

The beautifully laid table, decorated with crisp, starched white napkins, silver cutlery and three crystal glasses for each guest, made a stark contrast to Soviet kitchen dining. The food, freshly cooked by Freddie's best friend's wife, was always delicious, though I never could understand the British fondness for Brussels sprouts.

Unlike me, Marzena was a great cook, and spent most of her life perfecting her culinary knowledge and looking after the house, Bryn and their two huge Labradors. I still blushed with embarrassment when I recalled how we had returned the favour with a dinner where I served up charred salmon steaks.

Only a few weeks after I met Freddie, I was paraded in front of them and also the entire local cricket club team for approval. My future husband wanted to tell the world that he had managed to conquer a much younger woman than his has-been wife, and was still able to throw more than a cricket ball.

Bryn had lost his first wife a few years earlier and inherited the nurse who had looked after the deceased. That nurse was Marzena. She was a Polish, fifty-plus, pale but kind woman who achieved success in life by marrying Bryn Farrow, the widower of her best girlfriend.. Yet, she found life with the wealthy, penny-pinching British farmer difficult, and discovered her fresh air escape in flower arranging and cooking. She looked typically post-menstrual – her face was swollen, and so was her tum.

"It took a lot of effort to grow this plant. I bought a seed, put it into wet toilet paper, and kept it near the radiator in the loo for a few days, turning it over every few hours…" That was for me the most difficult part of the evening – to maintain conversation before and after dinner, and especially between the courses, when you couldn't escape to the loo with a book. We were 40 minutes into the loo-and-seed story, told by Marzena.

"Another word – and I'll either scream in horror or burst into laughter," I whispered to my husband, not sure anymore which would be best.

"I can't put into words how I feel about your attitude towards my friends! It is so rude!" My Fitzcock turned green, spitting on me.

"It's so funny – a seed resting in toilet paper!" I couldn't stop laughing at the chosen topic. "Marzena could have put some personal touches to it – her own fertiliser!"

"It's funny to you, but not at all funny to me! A fundamental lack of respect!" Freddie was always defensive of his pals.

I made an attempt to change the horticultural evening into a cultural one, "I went to Glyndebourne for Handel's *Rodelinda* a few days ago. It was a revelation."

Immediately I felt a painful kick under the table, and a bulky Clarks shoe on my blister.

"Shut up, Old Cunt!" Fitzcock whispered rather loudly. This expression, together with 'bugger off' and 'bollocks', were the three great favourites in our 'love' poetry.

"Stop trying to show off your nonsense pursuits. Nobody at this table goes to the opera." His whispering was overheard, so he continued in full voice: "I hate opera. All opera houses should be burnt down. The female singer, who is supposed to be young and attractive, is usually celebrating her late autumn, if not winter days, and is nearly always disgustingly fat." He turned his head towards me, trying to compare my body to an imagined soprano on a stage.

"She usually dies, but not immediately. She sings and sings in preparation for her high note, which she delivers as if someone put a knife into her massive ass." He was happy with his detailed description of the opera genre, feeling like a classical music critic from *The Times*. He achieved nearly orgasmic satisfaction from his friends' supportive roars and chuckles.

"Why don't you divorce him?" our son often asked me, having witnessed the physical, cultural and emotional vacuum between his dad and me. My granny used to say, "Never leave for nowhere. Make a move only when you find a new man."

I didn't have time while my son was an adolescent. After fifty, it became nearly impossible. I had nowhere to go. Why would anybody wanted a second-hand ageing item, unless they themselves required some repairs? So, I had to swallow all that was dispensed by my Chairman, in trying to convince myself that lasting love means a substantial compromise.

'A life of compromise' – a fair description of marriage.

The Other Side of the Road

18th July 2015
The Mall, West London

It was a hot and busy summer. Russian travellers were invading Britain. It smelt of business and money. For twenty good years I had been working as a Russian-speaking guide sharing the treasures of London with my knowledge-thirsty clientele. Occasionally I had to answer stupid questions, or tell them some nonsense.

"Why do the British hate Margaret Thatcher? In Russia, she was always our favourite leader." Probably, the Iron Lady reminded Russians of comrade Stalin.

I would not bother mentioning the sinking of the *Belgrano*; I'd just lightly remind them of the Falklands.

"Why do the British ruin tea with milk?"

How the fuck would I know, but I needed to justify the high fees they paid for the highest-ranked guides in London – the Blue Badge guides.

"It makes the guts run like clockwork," I would reply. "Shit freely leaves the body, clearing the brain, thus presenting opportunities for the development of a fair, democratic society."

"What's the average income in the UK?"

They should have asked what was left of the average income in this country after 45% tax. In Russia, they pay only 13% – that's if they pay at all. That's why the first part of my tour was always better. In effect, the second part of the day, I worked to help Indian people with their projects in space. It was even more altruistic than the communist ideas in my Motherland.

"We heard that Charles and Camilla are divorcing. Is it true?" What did I care? It was my third tour that day. In steaming African heat, spiced with the smell of international travellers, I had to walk the group from the National Gallery to Buckingham Palace for more than a mile before the coach would pick them up. My job was to tell them all about the royals: truths and gossip. My fat thighs were rubbing together; it felt like a wasp sting. My feet were hardly moving after a few hours on the go without a break and they were dragging at least twenty kilos of tiredness. My voice was slowly disappearing. In order to discourage my singing career, my mother used to describe it as 'a hair in an ass', very thin and not very clean'. That was when I started to understand her phrase, 'Money doesn't come easy'.

The images of Art Brut were flashing in front of my eyes. I was turned into a character from the Dubuffet painting *The Busy Life*, moving frantically, madly, chaotically with the tough crowd – stepping on top of their former friends and family, crushing and destroying them. The artist went to many asylums to envisage it for himself. I had my own Bedlam here, on the route. My tourists turned me into a worn-out victim, not far from being admitted to the asylum myself. The long-lasting pain in my groin made me worry whether I would be able to conduct my tour to the end.

God, why can't they give the royals some peace? I wasn't sure if I should have sympathised with Camilla – she was a fallen woman of an uncertain age to most citizens of this country and abroad, though recently she had managed to improve her image.

"What is that badge on your chain?" This question I wouldn't miss even if I was about to fall over.

"It shows that I hold the top title in the guiding profession –a Blue Badge Guide."

This title really makes you a professor of guiding. It has

nothing to do with disabled blue badges. I hate being called a tour guide: the words fill me with dread and are more often associated with illiterate creatures pushing their tourists through the streets on foot or on a coach, shouting and pointing with their umbrellas, "Turn your head to the right – you'll see a big white building," is how they describe the Tower of London; "Turn to the left and you'll see a beautiful bridge," by this they mean Tower Bridge, as if it's not clear that it is indeed a bridge and a beautiful one.

"Friends, the coach will be waiting for you on the other side of the road." It was time to wind up my tour. I loved my tourists but one or two of them could be so annoying that sometimes you could almost wish they were dead.

"Where is the other side of the road?" they would ask, after an exhausting stream of stupid questions. That was difficult – I wasn't sure I could answer at all.

Was it them or me who had lost reality? Which side of the road should I take?

I didn't have a guide there to give me the answer.

Suspicions

4th August 2007
Heathrow Airport, London

"Lady, take your boots and put them on a tray for a security check. Hurry up! You are holding up the queue."

I received strict orders from a security guard who spoke with a strong Middle Eastern accent, and reminded me of Emir Faisal, as portrayed by D. H. Lawrence. It was less than a month since the horrifying events of 7/7. The No. 30 bus, which was blown up that day, was the one I usually took from Baker Street station to reach the British Museum. I had been at Heathrow boarding a plane with my son, a young musician, on our way to Moscow. Britain was on special alert. The guard was on the lookout for suspicious persons, and right now, for him, I was one.

"I am not able to open this zip. I can't bend at all because of the pain in my back." I was biting my lip and clearly getting agitated, feeling nearly half-mad. It was obvious that I was raising suspicion by acting strangely.

"Perhaps he thinks that I'm drunk or too ill to travel," I whispered to my son. I turned to the officer, feeling the need to pacify him. "The boots simply won't obey and don't wish to come off, the buggers."

I was sweating, and quietly farting from trying too hard – but no luck! My inflamed tailbone was damaged from years of travel, carrying heavy bags filled with musical scores for my genius. It made me feel disabled or like I was 80 years old. Even just sitting was painful, but being on the move caused flare-ups in my arse, as if someone was sticking a screwdriver straight into my coccyx. I also had more recent pain in my groin to contend with. There, at the airport, I was fighting a battle with my own footwear, and losing.

"Give me your leg." My son was always caring and helpful. His strong fingers, trained by never-ending piano scales, conquered the zip and loosened the chains.

"Off they go," Nicholas laughed. The efforts and money for his music lessons were not wasted after all.

My spine recovered over the years, but the unbearable pain in my groin eventually signalled that I should have an MOT.

An Unwanted Fuck Up

30th July 2015
St Mary's Hospital, Central London

For Londoners, Paddington is usually associated with the railway station, ethnic diversity and St Mary's Hospital, where the royal children of two generations have been born in a private wing. My own royalties were to be examined right there in proper democratic arrangements, with a support of the expensive BUPA Health – an important part of my marital package.

The little Indian chap at St Mary's, who was to conduct an ultrasound pelvic examination, greeted me in a jolly and energetic manner, "Lie down on your back, please, and pull up your dress. I need to put some cooling jelly on the lower part of your body."

This was a rather exciting prospect: to be plastered in this heat with a cooling substance by a gentle male hand. The best part of the procedure was still to come: the ultrasound specialist was about to penetrate me with his phallic equipment. The guy expected full submission during this mission.

"Sir, you have a wonderful occupation!" I exclaimed, not able to quietly enjoy high-frequency sound waves.

"Yes, I do love my job. It's a very important part of keeping the nation healthy," he declared, holding the plastic phallus as a gun aimed at me.

The guy is right! I thought. *Regular phallic penetration is good for the health.*

The radiologist continued his therapeutic mission inside me, using his medical dick. With his unimpressive façade, he seemed unlikely to have such freedom with ladies outside of work. He was skilful with his meticulous movements whilst performing the sonogram. The plastic dick was dancing inside me with delicate movements and lightness in the manner of Mozart or Haydn.

One more minute, then two… nearly twenty… he was still inspecting all my ageing organs. The barricading fatty layers made it rather a challenge to pick up the echoes from the waves and turn them into a moving image on the screen. The guy was staring at the monitor, not missing any tiny change in me, driving accurately through the ancient narrow lanes of my old town. He listened to my body, missing nothing. The musical rhythms were becoming more of a Beethoven style, and then they turned Wagnerian. I was starting to get impatient. Suddenly I saw his pupils – they were unnaturally enlarged.

I wondered if my doctor was enjoying examining me and implementing his little fantasies – my dirty thoughts were trying to distract me from my rising fear.

"It's not cancer, is it?" I joked, trying hard to have some fun. After all, it was a rare occasion to lie on my back in front of a man. I was sure I wasn't the sort of person who could get cancer, but the ultrasound man was not able to raise a smile, or summon reassurance to his face.

"I don't know. I am not allowed to say." His voice trembled slightly. "You need to see a consultant gynaecologist. It's urgent. Don't delay it, lady. I hope you'll get a fast track." Great concern was engraved on his face and I noticed that the words 'a fast track' sounded like 'a fast fuck'. I realised that I was fucked up! I needed to move fast!

The 'C' word was familiar to me. My granny had died from cancer, then my mum. A few years later I had a threesome – not with nice guys but with some ghastly crabs. The first two mother fuckers were probably God's warning – they did not get deep inside. They enjoyed my pretty face and sunbathed on top of it. I discovered the first bugger by accident. For many months I thought it was just a cold sore. By the time it was diagnosed, it had eaten half of my nose. A graft was taken from behind my ear. It took two surgeons to deal with it. The first one cut out the hole as big as it needed to be to make sure that no legs of that crab spread into other parts of my face and body. The other one – the brilliant plastic surgeon – made the repairs, to prevent me from looking like a monster.

When I noticed a similar growth on my left cheek, I knew – that's it, another bugger. I did not want to live. For many years, my face had been my powerful weapon for success in life. I hired a room in a posh hotel and sat on the windowsill thinking to end my life in comfort. It was melodramatic – but I liked opera. Floria Tosca threw herself to death from the Castle of St Angelo! But I did not! I needed to see how my son would do in life. I decided that I could manage to live, wearing something like a burka, and see the world through the narrow slits! It was all before the pandemic. These days it would be easy – just keep your mask on. It can hide all imperfections, prevent infections, and shave off a good decade from your age. You can stay 49 and a half until you pop your clogs.

All of a sudden, there in the hospital, I felt an incredible urge to eat. The hospital shop offered buns, cakes, sandwiches – all the junk food I was trying to avoid. But what did it matter now? I bought a large egg mayonnaise pack, sat at the table, and started consuming it at a disgusting speed. I managed to dig out the last bits from the plastic wrapper and even licked my fingers clean of egg crumbs. It was not enough. I needed more. I bought the tuna one. It went down faster. I was eating up my own fear, trying to run away from the heavy thrum of death surrounding me.

Two sandwiches did the job; I wasn't desperately worried anymore. I wondered if my ultrasound technician had simply freaked out when he'd seen something not quite right. If you have an item over half a century old, you are bound to find that certain parts of it are not working like new.

My Soviet background and survival instincts kicked in, encouraging me to fight for the best outcome from the shitty circumstances I was trapped in. C cells had not affected my brain or energy resources yet. With a bit of a struggle, I managed to book an appointment with a consultant for the next day. All thanks to my private insurance, kindly arranged and paid for by Freddie!

Real British Honesty

5th August 2015
St Mary's Hospital, Central London

The only surgeon gynaecologist available straight away without waiting for weeks, had a typically British name – Chika Chiamaka – and it took me a while to be able to properly pronounce it. I don't know why, but I imagined it was a name with Indian roots. British-Indian people are usually kind, quiet, hard-working and patient. You find a lot of them in corner shops, pharmacies, surgeries and hospitals. I thought it was probably right when I overheard someone saying it's mainly Indians and Jewish people who make it to become surgeons. Five years studying at medical school led into a decade of apprenticeship. Only after that might one become a consultant surgeon and start earning decent wages. "The life is so short, the craft is long to learn", Hippocrates noted.

"Mrs Fitzcock!" a nurse invited me to follow her to the consultant's room. And there he was, Chika Chiamaka, sitting opposite the entrance in his huge leather chair like an African tribal chieftain on a throne. He turned to be a Kenyan man, tall and very attractive, showing his full pink lips and shining white teeth in a welcoming smile. I wasn't expecting this and my jaw dropped in amazement.

"Are you having some problems?" the doctor nearly sang this sentence in his low, velvety voice.

The last thing I wanted was to be considered a racist. I shook his offered hand and replied fast and loudly from nerves, "Oh, no problem, not at all!"

This was my long-awaited chance. For years I had been joking with my friends, even with my husband Freddie, "Am I going to die without ever having sex with a black man?" I had heard the British saying, "Once you go black, you never go back," and it intrigued me. My husband enjoyed massages performed by pretty local girls on our family holidays to Barbados and St Lucia. Those sessions always lasted substantially longer than a booked hour and afterwards, when he slept, he would passionately whisper "Beverly!" This provoked me to begin my own search. Now it seemed that God himself had taken care of this issue for me. Perhaps he thought that I was running out of time and that this would be my last chance for a flavour of exotic love.

"Doctor, there is one problem."

Chika lifted his eyebrows.

"No black man has ever seen me without knickers." And before he could reply, I exclaimed, "You'll be the first!"

Chika was a modern chap. I later saw him in a stylish helmet on his webpage, mounting a powerful bike and discovered that his name actually meant "God is gorgeous". That could refer to Chika himself. He laughed loudly, having real fun. But my day did not come. I was left disappointed. The doctor picked up a set of female display organs – the rubber-made dummies – and started discussing my options, playing with them like a child with dolls.

"I've seen your ultrasound results and it's not such great news – we have found cancerous cells in your womb. Your condition is curable, but only by going under the knife. 100 percent success can never be guaranteed, but decisive surgery is the only chance you have of full recovery."

He looked at me with sympathy, even admiration, trying to distract from the tragedy I faced, and added in a quiet voice,

"We will have to cut out your womb, and both ovaries will have to go, but this should not be so important to you. You are post-menstrual; they sit in you not working at all, unemployed and useless. So we will get rid of the lazy bastards, these rotten fruits that are poisoning your body. You will be fine! With a surname like yours, you are going to live forever."

He laughed, but after these words his facial expression reminded me of the shrunken American Indian skulls I'd once seen in the Pitt Rivers Museum in Oxford, the masks of death, transmitting an overwhelming sense of fear.

The word 'post-menstrual' made me feel like I'd been written off, as if I was second- hand stuff, something from a car boot sale, from a past life. Doctor Chika was trying to make my surgery sound as simple as cutting off a small wart. He talked, but I could only concentrate on how he might look without his suit, out of this office. He was just the type of man I liked – tall, with a wonderful shiny crop of hair, a very relaxed and self-confident professional with a great sense of humour. I was imagining going with him on a Kenyan safari to see the 'Big Five' – the best of Africa's game. *He would make a great gamekeeper. I would love to go with him in a jeep at dawn to search for lions, rhinos and powerful, Minotaur-like buffaloes,* I thought, but all I said was:

"Cool!"

"Are you okay? What are you saying?" He noticed that I had not been following a word of his explanation and could not understand what exactly I thought was 'cool'.

"It's fine." My words meant nothing; at that moment I couldn't identify anything fine at all.

"You are not planning on having more children, so why worry? A keyhole operation will resolve it all. It will allow a surgeon to access the inside of your pelvis without having to make large incisions in the skin – just four hardly noticeable ones. It leaves no visible scars and is less painful but requires special skills. If I do a hysterectomy, it will be a long healing process and you'll be left with a huge scar across your tummy for life."

I wasn't sure how long this gorgeous doctor Chika had lived

in Britain but he had obviously become nationalised – he was so upfront, like a real Brit.

***

It was a week of agonising waiting – then the telephone rang.

"This is Lynn, PA to Professor Jayakar. The professor will see you next Thursday. You need to have had an MRI done by then. I'll book it for you."

"I am very claustrophobic, Lynn. I would hate being squeezed into a narrow tube. It feels like practice for sleeping in a coffin."

"I can try to get you into an open model."

"Please do. I need to move fast. I might be lucky to avoid extra treatment. Wigs do not suit me at all!"

The moment I put down the receiver, an incredible power pushed me out of my apartment and onto the No.6 bus to 400 Oxford Street: Selfridges. They had fine wigs over there; some were even made of natural hair. I knew precisely where I could find them – ground floor, through the central doors, past numerous stands of perfume and cosmetics, round the corner, and there they were.

I had always wondered why anybody would want a wig. I swore that I would never use one, as wearing someone's hair felt a bit like wearing their skin. All wigs in that department store had names – 'Admiration', 'Attention' and 'Celebration' – as if there was anything to admire or celebrate. I tried nearly every one available. To start with, I asked for a blonde, curly wig with a bit of red in it – a Nicole Kidman-type called the 'Voltage' – to match and enhance the colour of my own hair. I remembered that Freddie always fancied redheads. But it made me look like a pig after an hour of cooking. I wanted a radical change to my look, so I asked for the one with black curls on the top shelf. It was called 'The Crystal Wig', though instead of crystals, it was glittered with dust – it had been sat near the ceiling for some time. The sales girl wasn't too happy, as she had to fetch a stool and a stick to get it down.

Mamma Mia! My mother wouldn't recognise me in this!

A stranger peered out from the mirror. The wig made me look like a person whose misfortune was to have been born at all. I started imagining the porters at my Little Venice block stopping me from entering the premises, and my husband calling the police thinking that there was an intruder.

No, I will lose all my identity in this, I thought. *Is talking to yourself a sign of ageing?*

Exhausted, I picked up the next wig with a promising name: 'Transformation'. It did indeed transform me into a clown, but what did I care? Still, I bought it, just in case, in order to cheat my fate. I knew that if I were to prepare for something beforehand, it would probably not be needed. As with an umbrella, you take it with you, and there will be no rain. The moment you forget it – the rain will shower you. My wig in a yellow Selfridges bag was there to safeguard me against a horrible outcome.

No Requiem Allowed

12th August 2015
Harley St., Central London

I struggled, even in the open-type MRI, which I nicknamed the 'Monster of Rare Intelligence'. The gigantic machine launched me into another life, still alive, but no longer fully belonging to a normal environment. I was somewhere in between.

"You have a choice of pop or classical music, what would you like?"

"Do you have a Requiem? Verdi, perhaps, or Berlioz?"

The smart radiologist caught my sarcastic intonation, "I am only trying to help."

They nearly always do, the British.

I was saving my soul by listening to beautiful music through the huge earphones for the whole hour. The coils of metal wire inside the scanner passed electric pulses, producing an incredibly loud banging sound, as loud as 125 decibels, similar to a rock concert being played directly into my ears. It was a sound from Hell, and I had the feeling that I must be descending there on this incredibly powerful and clever monster. Tchaikovsky and Brahms were fighting to not let me be ruined by the painfully loud booming that was intruding into every tiny part of me. It was working hard, taking notice of every molecule and atom, producing full-scale recordings of my body and soul.

This detailed topography fitted easily onto a DVD and was handed to me to pass on to my surgeon. The battle with time had been won so far by moving faster than C.

***

"I want to take a tour around Ireland," I called my son. "I need to stop the anxiety of waiting, it's unbearable – every minute feels like a decade. The bitter taste of Guinness would help."

Son
- Fitzcock, Nicholas
- Age: 23
- 6ft 2- a peace-loving giant
- Son of Natalia and Freddie
- Known as Nick, Nicki, baby, rabbit, genius
- Talented musician – plays eight instruments
- Speaks eight languages
- IQ 143 makes his mother with her PhD feels as clever as a cat
- Fits well with his name – as kind as St Nicholas
- Protects everything, including ladybirds
- Sends money to save donkeys
- An extrovert like his mother
- As reasonable as his dad, on his best days

I had always dreamed of seeing the Giant's Causeway, the book of Kells, the famous Neolithic site Newgrange, and hoped that one day I would be able to follow in the footsteps of Oscar Wilde.

"You probably want me to go as well?" said Nicholas. "But I hate those group tours."

"You don't have to. I'll travel alone."

"Stop being silly, I'm coming along!"

This is the debut novel by fast-rising, critically acclaimed comedian Helen Prior. She put pen to paper as the last years of her life drew out, and dramatic events unfolded, taking her on a different path. Over the years, she has spoken to a number of ladies of an uncertain age, and realised that many of them have gone through relationship difficulties similar to hers, and through health challenges that have taught them, like her, to find joy in every minute of their lives. She writes for them.

Born outside of Albion, she found it a great challenge to put her thoughts and stories into the English language, so begs for the understanding of her forgiving readers.

Adventures of an Old CxNT

I Believe in Fairies

22ⁿᵈ ⁻ 27ᵗʰ August 2015
Comeragh Mountains; Ireland

Every moment on the tour felt like a gift. I didn't feel bitter for this short moment of bliss; I just drifted along on a coach like the ancient Egyptians along the Nile on their last journey. I heard the driver-guide mention the fairies' path, the elves and the trolls – it was so comforting, it felt like being back in my childhood, in the best part of it. I was floating into a world of magic. I turned to my son,

"I should leave the window open at the hotel tonight, so that a fairy may fly in and help me." I was trying to find any means for survival, even if it seemed unreal.

The loud buzz of a mobile phone interrupted the magical story. I realised that the sound was coming from the handbag on my lap. I was waiting for a call from the consultant with the results of my MRI, and instructions on how to proceed further. The passengers on the coach, mainly elderly Americans, turned their heads and made it clear that they had spotted their enemy – me and my phone.

"Hi, Professor!" I said, before hearing whether it was actually his voice.

"Hello, Mrs Fitzcock!"

They struggled in Britain to say Popov, and usually referred to me by my husband's name.

I had been married three times. "Only a lazy person would marry once," I often joked. I could not stand that I repeatedly had to bear someone else's name and change my identity. So I simply added my spouse's surname after my own, creating a double-barrelled title. After I divorced, I would remove all traces of the former male, and then, when the time came for another love, I would tag the lucky guy's family name onto Popov – my constant.

"The tests show that your tumour is small, but growing faster than we expected. It's very aggressive. Unfortunately, my other commitments won't allow me to operate on you next week as planned."

I couldn't believe what I was hearing. I felt breathless as if there was a lack of oxygen on the coach.

I probably didn't catch his pronunciation; he's like me, British, talking with a strong accent from his home country. I held on to the hope that what I was hearing was a misunderstanding.

"You aren't saying that I am in the worst position, with a more aggressive cancer and you won't operate, are you?"

There was only his silence as an answer.

"You promised!" I spoke so loudly that most of the coach passengers probably heard what was being discussed. They turned their heads towards me, but this time their eyes looked sympathetic. On hearing the 'C word', people seemed to soften.

"This tumour has been in your body for a while," he said, "so another few weeks shouldn't do much more harm."

His words felt like a punch below the waist.

"How can you fail me?!" If he had been near me right then, I would have launched my heavy fist at him.

My son wanted to hear the conversation and pressed his ear to mine, squeezing my arm in support.

"Don't worry, we will find you someone else who can operate. We'll take you to a Swiss clinic if we need to," Nicholas said, full of kindness and compassion, trying to calm me down as much as he could. But that was impossible; I was in a rage, and my voice was rising,

"You know, Professor, I could have found another surgeon by now if I was not assured that you would be available next week. If the cancer cells escape from my womb because of your delay, I'll have to go through chemo and radio. I promise that I'll take you with me, just pull on your long moustache so that you too can try the bitter taste of these poisons."

I felt like Cadmus, needing to devoured the dragon. For a minute I became part of the sixteenth-century painting by Dutch master Cornelis van Haarlem, perfectly depicting the human fear of predation.

"You'd better find me a good surgeon who is able to perform the procedure right away!" I hung up and the whole coach reacted with murmurs of support. Professor Jayakar – he was like an evil maharajah from an Indian fairy tale for me.

Our driver broke the silence that hung heavy in the air after the distraught call,

"Those who want to see the magic bush can leave the coach now – walk around it three times and ask for a wish to be fulfilled."

Before my diagnosis, I would have probably ignored a magic walk, thinking that it was the usual crap and the complete nonsense sold to tourists. But for the last few weeks I had needed the wonders of the world more than most.

"Nick." I turned to my son. "You are coming with me! You can make a wish to the magic bush on my behalf!"

"It's complete folly…" he began, but he was kind enough not to dash my hopes and played the game of Celtic beliefs, "Of course, let's go!"

My son jumped off the coach first. I took his strong hand and he led me around the hawthorn-wishing tree like in a dance.

"Let's ask the fairy to send us a real magician who will cure you, and very soon."

***

While still on the tour of Ireland, I received an e-mail from Jayakar's PA. I guessed that she was afraid to talk to me over the phone after my heated conversation with her traitor-boss.

Dear Mrs Popov-Fitzcock,
> *Mr Andrew Kovač has agreed to operate on you on the 1ˢᵗ of September. He needs to meet you tomorrow as he is going on planned holidays this coming weekend. He does not have any other time available. He has to examine you before the operation; otherwise he won't be allowed to proceed.*
> *Yours sincerely*
> *Lynn White,*
> *PA to Professor Jayakar, MD FRCS FRCOG*

That was good news, and I needed it. There was one problem – I was in the middle of a tour, miles away from the airport. Even if I left the group and hired a private car, I wouldn't make it on time for Mr Kovač. My heart was pounding. My newly found hope for survival would vanish, unless I found a way of getting back within the next eighteen hours.

I believed my fairy was also thinking of how to help me, as another squeaky phone call broke the silence of the coach. This time all the passengers were eagerly watching. One leant over and told me, "We made our wishes to the magic bush for you".

It is a well-known joke that doctors are great as long as you don't need them. I learned that they are even greater when you need them, and they come, descending as angels.

"This is Pamina, PA for Mr Kovač. Natalia, when the doctor returns from his holiday on Saturday, he'll come straight to the consulting room. You don't need to change your travel plans."

The magic had worked! Her name was like the soprano from Mozart's The Magic Flute. Another arty world, the opera one, had supported me! I looked around the coach with a happy smile. Though my companions didn't know exactly what the call was in detail, they understood from my radiant face that things were working out for me so far. The whole coach erupted into applause. I burst into tears.

During dinner at the hotel I searched the Internet to find out who this angel was, so ready to divert his travel arrangements for me. I found him straight away on the web – he had a long list of degrees, skills and achievements. I couldn't see anything striking or heroic in his appearance – just a very intelligent face: rather soft and even feminine. A tiny moustache made him look a bit exotic. He didn't fit the saying that a man becomes bald when he leaves his head on too many different pillows. That was not Andrew Kovač. He was not about excessive testosterone but looked more likely to have donated his hair to ease his patients' pain. Death was part and parcel of his professional life.

Whenever I saw someone in glasses I always assumed they were intelligent and reliable. But it was his academic credentials as a Cambridge graduate that made me feel particularly confident and reassured. That's all.

I headed to London to meet Mr Kovač.

Sex under Guarantee

29th August 2015
Queen's Hospital, Central London

I flew at a cosmic speed through the glass doors of Queen's Hospital into the lobby to the astonishment of the security guard. The lift taking me to the second floor was exceptionally slow. My heart was pounding – it felt as if I had biked at least ten miles along curvy mountain roads. That's what Freddie and I had done in the Italian Alps when we'd just met, more than twenty years ago. I was in love and ready to conquer any peak for him, despite my fear of heights. I used to find tall, wealthy men irresistible.

I was five minutes late for my appointment – well, five minutes or so. Precious time was lost while trying to find a parking space for my Merc, which simply wouldn't squeeze into the bays marked out by the generous Westminster Council.

"Mr Kovač is waiting for you," the receptionist announced politely, but still delayed my appointment by asking me to fill out endless forms and insurance details.

Upon reaching the consultant's room I was breathless.

"Sorry, doctor."

"No worries." He gave me his hand. "Please, call me Andrew."

There he was, Mr Andrew Kovač, very short, no more than five-foot-six, standing behind his desk with an expression of slight irritation or perhaps surprise, at my impolite delay. I understood. With all the efforts he had made to accommodate me, changing his own travel plans, I should have been there earlier and waited for him, not he for me, as had happened. His colour-less suit made him look rather undistinguished. It was difficult to say how old he was: ageless, as doctors often are.

Usually, I do not wear a lot of make-up, but that day, I tried to look my best. I put on some toning primer cream, a little mascara and used hardly visible lipstick to avoid looking vulgar. My face was nearly free of wrinkles, but my puffed eyes filled with frozen tears didn't help me look younger. My light-blue Basler dress, decorated with red flowers, painted the picture of a softer woman than I was in reality. It also made me feel rather English, in spite of the German make of the dress. That gave me hope to appeal to Kovač. I needed him to like me. I was quiet and pensive, not really me. I was listening to him, not my usual non-stop, chatty self. He projected a strong energy, and I was transfixed by his magic.

The doctor positioned himself comfortably in a big leather chair that smelt like new. Straight away, he felt like a guy you could trust, like a friend that you had known forever. Or perhaps, someone you've been with in another life.

"I just came back from my holidays, so I'll be fresh … especially for you." He rubbed his hands, looking at his fingers and nails as if checking that they were indeed at their best for me, as he'd said.

Of course, it wasn't for me. He didn't hear about me before he booked his holidays. *He cares*, I thought. I knew it straight away. He wasn't a robot of surgery. He was a person and so was I to him, not just another C patient. I noticed how delicate his hands were – gentle but strong, with blood vessels pulsing on the skin's surface. We stared at each other for a while without a word.

"Will it be difficult to operate on me because of my weight?" I felt a desire to break the heavy silence.

"You'd be surprised to know that, although abdominal operations are indeed more difficult for larger people, particularly in their healing, in laparoscopic procedures a big body will help avoid injuring your internal organs."

I could hear a recognisable Eastern European accent. One was hardly ever able to get rid of it. I looked at him with curiosity, trying to guess where he was from.

"I was born in the former Yugoslavia, in Croatia," he said quietly as if he read my mind and was ready to deliver the answer straight away.

I should have guessed it from his surname! I thought.

"Go home and rest. I want you to come back on Tuesday early." His voice was full of compassion but not in a sentimental or pathetic way.

"By nine?"

He paused, assessing whether or not I could drag my ass out of bed that early, and then replied quietly,

"By seven – can you manage that? You would need time for admission, an hour or so, then some preparations for the procedure. I only have one patient before you. Just a small operation, to warm up for you."

Surgeons are like musicians. Their fingers need practice to perform 100 per cent without mistakes. He smiled, and his eyes were so reassuring.

"It was nice meeting you, Mrs Popov-Fitzcock." He was able to pronounce my name in full! His Cambridge degree did not fail him. The doctor got out of his chair and his body language told me that my time had run out, I had to go, and he had to move on.

"After the operation, sex will be the same. I guarantee it." The words spilled out as he tried to hurry through what was obviously an uncomfortable task.

I jumped out of the chair.

"What sex, doctor?" I was frightened by even the whisper of that word. I had forgotten what it meant.

What did he say? "Guarantee? Surely, he couldn't guarantee it on behalf of my husband?

How was I to know the extent of this truth when I first met Mr Andrew Kovač?

Theatrics and Sympathy

29ᵗʰ August 2015
Cobham, Surrey

I had always loved opera, and a bit of extra drama had always been in my blood. Like a real woman, I was ready to use anything to capture attention and sympathy. Back in the country house, the sounds from my bedroom in the middle of the night were powerful and dramatic.

"Mother, you have to control yourself. Every third person in the world has or will have cancer." Both my son and I were night owls. I had forbidden Nicholas and his dad from telling anybody about my illness. I did not want any pity, and hated the idea of being looked at as less fortunate. Yet the mental pain scalded me, and I needed to sooth it with some reassurance and sympathy. *Isn't that what a family is for?*

"Why me?" I asked, in a slightly theatrical tone, gesturing like an ageing provincial actress.

"These days medicine can work wonders! You are in the best hands. I'll take you to the hospital," Nicholas said.

"There's no need to accompany me. I'll stay in London Monday night, at the apartment, and will go alone. My will is on the bookshelf, just behind the door in my bedroom. Don't cry, or bother spending money on an expensive gravestone. Just get on with your life."

"You are not going to die, for Christ's sake! Why are you so pessimistic?" Nicholas diminished my illness to flu.

"When there is an opportunity for drama, your mother has

to make the most of it!" Freddie could not stop criticising me, even in front of my son. He turned to me and whispered hysterically, dripping saliva, "You bloody do!"

I didn't attempt to protest.

"All will be fine." Nicholas gave me a hug on behalf of his dad. The door of my husband's bedroom squeaked in a minute. Freddie appeared, looking like Saint Nicholas on the paintings of the Old Masters, ready to perform his miracles for kids.

"Let's do something nice together tomorrow or on Monday evening. What would you like?" The Chairman already felt guilty for shouting at me and, as usual, was ready to serve a penance, I, as usual, was ready to accept.

"Dinner at Sketch, the famous restaurant in Mayfair!" I screamed with happiness, as if I'd made a discovery that would change the world. "All my VIP tourists have been talking about it. Let's go there on Monday night. We'll not get in tomorrow. Sunday is going to be too busy."

"Book it. I'll come straight after work with Nick. Text me the address and time." Freddie was ready to spend the whole evening in London! A great sacrifice for a countryman, he probably thought.

I was ready to make my last journey before the C operation like a fairy tale, entering this wonderful place steeped in mystery and blessed by God for good fortune.

I had no fear of C that night. All my pain was blocked. God took care of the Old Cunt's soul. He and his disciples had good practice with Mary Magdalene.

Reaching Up to God

30th August 2015
City of London

It was my last working day before the C Execution: the London Panoramic tour ending at St Paul's Cathedral followed by the city walking tour. The tourists pay for the full day tour, often not realising that the coach has been hired by the company for only three hours and the rest of the day they will be on their feet. And on mine.

"Please, check all your possessions carefully before leaving the coach. The driver has another job straight after us and it will not be possible to find lost property. Do not leave any litter, take it with you." I had no idea whether our driver would be going to another job, but I had to use some tricks of the trade to ensure a smooth day. Disembarking the group of fifty people from the coach required good training. Most of them were in London for the first time, spoke no English and needed a nanny, not just a tour guide.

In spite of all my warnings, there were nearly always forgotten phones, bags filled with souvenirs, and even passports left behind. This misadventure would be followed by an attack on me, with numerous calls from the company, demanding that I assist the unfortunate traveller. That would be real hell and beyond my responsibilities as a guide. But if you want the job, You gotta serve somebody. My Chairman often cited this part of the song to me, from the collection of his favourite troubadour, Bob Dylan.

I had to look not only after my tourists, but after my driver as well,

"Friends, Marcin was with you for a few hours. It is considered to be good manners in this country to express your gratitude to him." I was not too comfortable saying these words, but if you wanted to have decent relationship with the driver, assuring that he would stop when and where you asked him to, and not a mile away from the place you needed, '*You gotta serve somebody*' and do it for him. I never took or shared any tips – I was too proud – but I always fulfilled the expected duty.

Entry to the cathedral was free on Sundays, and a lot of tourist companies used this opportunity to enrich the itinerary of the day without any financial cost. That provided a great opportunity for their clients to look inside the magnificent building, to hear an organ, an angelic boys' choir, and have a piss in the crypt's loos. And all for free! Thanks to the generosity of British taxpayers.

"Look! There are graves and monuments next to the bogs. You can shit and eat in this holy place – not a Christian tradition." Russians could not stop commenting on the ridiculousness of this 'convenience' set up from their point of view. It would not be possible inside Russian Orthodox churches, for sure. It did not stop the commenting tourists from freely using the 'heavenly' facilities in the crypt; although across the road they could relieve themselves in a far less holy place for just 50 pence.

"You have 30 minutes for your break," I announced loudly. "If you're lucky, you'll hear the boys' choir during the service, one of the best in the country. You need to go up the stairs through the main entrance. Enjoy!"

After these instructions – followed by hundreds of questions – I was usually able to find some peace with a skinny cappuccino in the Crypt Cafe. But that Sunday I was prepared to skip this freebie. I felt a strong desire to go in and have a chat with God.

Not being completely convinced that I believed in God, I looked at churches and holy images like an art historian rather than a religious patron. I became particularly skeptical after overhearing a clergyman sharing his thoughts with his old friend. "You do not need to believe in God to be a priest", he admitted. That was not a joke – it was a revelation. I recalled how twenty-two years earlier, when I went to Israel on a tour, I came to the famous mysterious Western Wall that had been standing in Jerusalem for nearly two thousand years by Temple Mound. All the tourists were putting notes and letters inside the cracks with their most sacred wishes.

"Such nonsense!" I said, and laughed at them. "Who gives a monkey's about all this?"

I was brought up as an atheist – an obligatory requirement for a successful life and career in Brezhnev's empire. However, as I had paid for the tour, I thought I might as well continue tradition and stick my written wishes there too. I scribbled fast, just three short words: *I want a son*. This decision changed my life.

Back then, I was not unable to conceive for a whole year, in spite of multiple attempts per day. Freddie was randy like a stag injected in the dick with horse steroids. Miraculously, the same month I returned from Israel to Britain I became pregnant with Nicholas. I was heard by the Creator and allowed into the world of the fifth dimension where all was possible. And now, a couple of days before my C operation, this old story turned out to be a great support in bringing me to God.

The west of the cathedral was adorned with two huge Greek Orthodox icons of the Virgin and Christ the Saviour. I always trusted men on important issues. I looked at him, at the Saviour, deep into his eyes. I begged him to spare me, just this time: *I've been a cunt but I promise you, I'll make a better use of my life. Give me a chance.*

I was sure he heard! He kind of winked at me with reassurance. He was well aware about Mary Magdalene, and trusted a woman who was ready to repent.

A Sketch on Sketch

31st August 2015
Mayfair, London

It was rather relaxing to get away from the overagitated tourists, away from the intrusion of their questions about directions, shops, exchange rates and even very personal ones – how to find a British husband. A day before going under the knife – what did I care?

Walking from the National Gallery, I strolled up Haymarket, passing the yellow Bath stone building of the famous theatre, and quickly reached Piccadilly Circus, illuminated by the light of the huge advertising boards, and turned into Regent Street. I slowed down and looked at the historic Café Royal, recently redeveloped into a modern five star hotel, still retaining its historical interior and the flavor of a special place. It made me shiver that I was walking in the steps of D. H. Lawrence, Oscar Wilde, Bernard Shaw, Winston Churchill, James Whistler, Jacob Epstein – a long list of writers, artists, politicians, who used to gather in this stunning place. I was a happy ghost walking next to them towards what might have been the last of my earthly enjoyments.

I reached Conduit Street. The Vivienne Westwood shop immediately caught my attention, though there was nothing in there that I would dare to wear. It was all beyond the borders of my life with my Chairman. Deep down, I admired this controversial designer for her liberating personality, and her ability to not worry about what people would say. Most of her life, she did what she wanted.

I saw Freddie's blue Saab parked further up the road – my guys made it before me. That was amazing on its own. My Chairman was known to be late – but mainly on his journeys to London.

"Hi, Mum, they found our booking!" My son greeted me in the restaurant lobby with an embrace. His dad looked rather uncomfortable, as he should have followed suit but did not know how. He'd been out of practice for nearly a decade.

We were seated at a small round table decorated in pink cheerful colours. I quickly realised why the place was called Sketch: the walls were plastered with art sketches, creating a special atmosphere like you would find in an art gallery.

"Let's try a really good wine." My Fitzcock was feeling generous, perceiving that it might be the Last Supper.

"Australian Shiraz would be my first choice, depending on what we're going to eat," I said. I love medium-bodied, elegant red wine. My mood was improving and I felt happy, surrounded by a son and husband both willingly doing nice things for me.

"It's a French place. I hate those Frogs!" Freddie would not miss the chance to stick a needle into our neighbours. "France is a nice country, but it would be better without the French. French women are fine; the problem is French men."

"You hate racists but you mimic them," I poked, only because I often received the same criticism from my husband.

"Bollocks!" And the real Brit waved the waiter over.

I often quoted his views to my tourists while passing the French Embassy in Knightsbridge. It was a killer – the whole coach would burst into laughter, particularly when I demonstrated how Freddie, after expressing his patriotic views, started to sing Rule Britannia, often in front of the astonished French.

Six o'clock was too early for dinner, but it had been the only available time at short notice. This trendy place was not busy yet – just a few rich Arabs with their flock of wives and kids were nesting around the tables covered with fine white cloths. Only they could afford this place with its rocketing prices.

"Excuse me for a moment." I left the table in the middle of the meal, and headed to the loos.

The polite waiting staff pointed me in the direction of what turned out to be a real shitting heaven! The cabins, designed like capsules or rockets, were ready to shoot your piss and crap straight to the moon. Their shiny pink colour made them look very sexy, like women's private parts with full and juicy clitorises sticking out. The wealthy clients of the restaurant were wandering around taking selfies and family photos.

"Freddie, Nick, come here!" I ran back to the table. I wanted them there, in the wonderful Land of Fairy Loos, for the last family shot before my C trip. The waiter was ready to help with the iPad. It was obvious that he knew the location we had chosen – it was the Mecca and Medina of Sketch. I radiated such happiness in that glamorous shitting place – the best and most entertaining loo I had ever seen in my life. I felt my expectations on Mother Earth had been nearly fulfilled, and I was ready to hand my fate to my doctor – Mr Andrew Kovač.

Pop Your Clogs in Comfort

1st September 2015
Queen's Hospital, Central London

Tuesday morning, under the order of 'nil by mouth' – no tea, no breakfast, nothing – I walked to the hospital on my own from my apartment in Little Venice. I did not want any witnesses to my approach to the Day of Judgment. Still, I wanted to look nice and had chosen very elegant and comfortable clothes – a Marina Rinaldi dress, blue with fashionable-that-year dots and a light, matching jacket. It was unusually warm for the first day of autumn, even at six-thirty in the morning. I was pushing along a beautiful Louis Vuitton luggage bag, which I had carefully kept for a special occasion. Today was one. I thought it would be unfair if this exquisite piece of craft never got the chance to be taken outside and shown off. I stuffed the bag with a few books, hoping that they would help me pop my clogs as a much wiser girl.

On the first day of September, children in Russia traditionally start their school year. They come nicely dressed: girls with beautiful bows in their hair, boys in starched white shirts, all with flowers for teachers. A wave of these childhood images passed in front of my eyes while I walked for a good twenty minutes along Marylebone Road, before I entered the Harley Street Golden Triangle. Probably before I was to die, God had given me a chance to see the film of my life for the last time. I enjoyed spotting red double-decker buses – they were from a normal life. The plain trees with a bit of gold in their leaves made me feel part of the circle of nature, and turned the idea of dying into more of a fun trip to eternity. I was warned at school that we all come to Earth to die and feed the trees and flowers. The road was uneven and my expensive bag was jiggling and jumping along behind me, but I cared about nothing except making it to my appointment by seven as I had promised Mr Andrew Kovač. It looked as though I was on time and that made me happy.

On time for The Last Judgment! Ha-ha!

Entering the private hospital was different from going into an NHS one, where people were usually running chaotically along endless corridors. There, in Queen's, I was hit with dead silence and a feeling of emptiness. It was sterile, just like the famous installation *Pharmacy* by Damien Hirst, whose works were mostly preoccupied with themes of death and life.

"This room is so noisy and has no view!" I was fussy in choosing possibly my last chamber in this place of dissection. I wanted to walk in comfort under the knife.

After being kindly resettled two floors up, I stepped into a lovely room with a view, a view of Marylebone Road. The green crowns of plane trees behind the windows reminded me about the joy of life beyond the hospital doors. As it happened, Forster's novel *A Room with a View* was in my bag for re-reading. It was Freddie's favourite novel. I could never understand his taste for such subtle books, but his lack of interest in any other types of culture. He was, in many ways, a man with a split personality, like Doctor Jekyll and Mr Hyde in Robert Louis Stevenson's novel. A lot of us are, including me.

Changing into a hospital gown made me an integral part of the place. It was like an actor's costume, helping me fit into the role of a cancer patient. My mind was still denying that it was me. It could have been Magda Cordell's *Figure (Woman)* from the Tate Modern, inflated by illness and rotting flesh. She needed this operation. With me nothing was wrong.

My doubts were soon diminished as a long pre-admission assessment began. They wanted to know my blood pressure, my heart condition – I was all wired up to an ECG. My finger was pricked in order to establish my blood group in case complications developed and they had to refill my tank. I just lay back and let it be. Freddie had taught me time and time again the 'British way': lie back and relax if you cannot control or change anything.

"Do you have any allergies?"

"I do get very red after eating broccoli."

The nurse carefully wrote that down; something was definitely wrong with that girl. "Does it matter for womb cancer?" I found the courage to ask.

"Just give me an answer. Are you on any medications?" The inquisition seemed to last forever.

"What is your weight?"

That question brought me to a stop. I stayed silent for a few moments. Usually I would have supplied a false answer to that question, cutting at least a good ten kilos off the scary figure. But that day the lie could cost me rather dearly – my life.

"110. No, not pounds; kilos."

Soon after, a tall, handsome man in his mid-forties approached my bed.

"Good morning! I am Philip Goodman, your anaesthetist. I want to examine you to evaluate any conditions that might affect the kind of drugs and dose I am going to use. May I look at your neck?"

"I'm afraid I do not have one."

I knew mine was so short that my head was sitting straight on my shoulders. Years ago at school, I was teased, "Head on the ass, head on the ass". Showing my tourists a portrait of gorgeous

Consuelo Vanderbilt by Sargent at Blenheim Palace, I used to make a joke. She was nicknamed 'the Swan' for her long neck.

"A wife of the ninth Duke could easily put a sixteen-string pearl choker around her long neck. I would struggle to fit one."

"Great sense of humour! Actually, a shorter neck makes it easier for me."

"Better give me some morphine for sedation. It works well with me, makes me feel good."

I acquired that taste years ago, when it was administered during an abortion. I was just seventeen. It was murder. We all have to pay.

"Thank you for telling me," Mr Goodman pronounced, and walked out of my hospital room.

The door closed. The door opened. At last, Kovač, my surgeon, came to visit.

"Doctor, did you come to say that I would be fine without a womb, ovaries and lymphatic nodules, that all will be the same? Should I still consider myself the luckiest girl in the world?"

Kovač sat on the bedside chair near my head. It felt as if I was lying on his knees, like we all do in our childhood, holding onto our dear ones and seeking protection. After a minute of silence, he moved his arms. Was he trying to pat me on my head? I wanted him to. Like a little girl, I was ready to submit myself to a responsible, caring adult. Instead, he produced a piece of paper.

"Now comes the most difficult bit. I need your consent for the operation. I can't proceed further without it. I have to explain the benefits and the risks of potential complications." The word 'consent' sounded like a court order – as an official permission for death.

"Just give it to me. I don't want to know how many people have died during or after such operations. I trust you, Mr Kovač. There is something about you that makes me feel at ease."

"You are still young, and you can live through this."

"How kind of you to call me 'young', but it's not true. All my life, I've been running down narrow, zig-zagging corridors. I never expected to reach the end not in a beautiful garden but here, in this hospital."

Kovač squeezed my hand. "It hasn't ended. And it's not going to. I promise, you will see some light." And with this he disappeared behind the door, leaving me to journey solo into hell. Doctors are also afraid to face death.

They came for me. Two male nurses loaded me onto a trolley and wheeled me to the operating theatre. The extreme cleanliness of the place gave the impression that all your past, all your real life would also be wiped away with a strong anti-bacterial gel. I was thinking about cows and the way they are brought in for slaughter. I was grateful to God that my thoughts were growing numb. I was observing my present and past without any emotions. I was remembering my mother being put on a similar trolley against her will two years ago and taken for the operation in a Moscow hospital.

"Please, do not leave me. I want to be with you, I trust only you. I never thought that I could have such a wonderful daughter!"

Those late words of compassion and reconciliation still brought tears to my eyes. My mother never regained consciousness, and never returned to our world. Now it was my turn. Perhaps I would be rendezvousing with her later in a hotel called Hell in Heaven. That felt like a normal plan for the day.

I performed the holy cross on my shoulders and forehead. "God, forgive me for all my sins and the wrongdoings I've done, and the many more I've considered doing." I usually only did this when landing on an EasyJet flight or another cheap carrier. After receiving God's blessing and the reassurance of a place in his housing estate, I asked the nurse curiously:

"Where do you put the dead bodies? You probably have a huge refrigerator in the hospital? What brand is it – Neff, GE – or does it have to be a specialised piece of equipment to store frozen human meat?" "You do not need to worry about it, Miss," the nurse replied. He sounded like a Methodist, with a typical melodious intonation and a kind facial expression. "The freezer will remain empty."

He stuck a needle into my left arm hastily, so as to no longer be disturbed by my death-wish talk. A little prick, a mosquito bite, and I did not have time to reply. My dark sense of humour was put to sleep. I remembered nothing that followed.

The Hole

Everything was so slow. It was slowly that I opened my eyes. Slowly that I breathed in the air. Slowly that I started to think. *Am I watching a horror movie in 3D about myself? I am the horror. But I am alive; I'm still here. I think.*
I was not sure if this was good or bad. A large bag of fluid was fixed above my head, and endless tubes with catheters inserted into my veins were hanging around – just like Rebecca Horn's *Overflowing Blood Machine* installation, which had red tubes filled with blood, wrapped around her body, slowly pumping from a glass container underneath. My body was encased in multi-coloured equipment and I was transformed into a piece of art, with red tubes filled with my own blood, yellow pipes with my piss, and the blue ones with death, the colouring agent. I hoped that this was a mirage or a dream and it might disappear.

Doc had forewarned that my face, my arse and my wee would all be blue for a while after the operation. Even my shit. He explained that the paint moved with the blood flow and would allow him to see if any cancer cells had managed to escape. He seemed to be worrying about it a lot but tried hard to make it sound like a game with soap bubbles.
C cells – they travel, they are my tourists, tourists inside my body, unwelcome ones.

It turned dark outside. I could hear the door being opened. I turned my head towards it – Kovač had come to see if I was still alive. He had white scrubs thrown over his shoulders. My gaze stopped on a huge clock on the opposite wall, above the TV set. It was half nine, more than twelve hours since my operation. He must have been working all this time, seeing his other women – wounded, dreading their fate.

"How are you doing? You look very blue." He seemed concerned.

"Maybe my husband will see me with a blue death mask and will fire his 'charming' secretary." I could hardly talk but was revealing my secret wishes and worries to this perfect stranger.

"Doctor, all that made me a woman has gone under your knife. Do I still have a gender?"

Kovač came up closer and pulled the blue tube towards himself. It was intimidating. But he was in charge.

"Don't be silly. You are a woman. Nearly a perfect one. I did my best with the reconstruction."

He gave me a demonic smile, this little bald man, as if slightly flirting with me. It was he who had saved my life and my look, inside and out. He had managed to pinch everything through four tiny holes. If I ever undressed in front of him, the scars wouldn't be seen at all.

"The operation went very well and you're free of cancer. Of course, we will have to wait for the results from our pathologist. I've sent him a gift of your womb and your ovaries – I feel like Jack the Ripper." He giggled gently as if afraid I could misinterpret his joke and it might scare me. "Based on these results, my team and I can make a decision whether you'll need further treatment."

"You mean I might lose all my hair and my ability to work after receiving chemo – a poison which not only destroys cancer cells but the rest of a human as well?"

Kovač was looking straight into my eyes with a stare full of sadness and compassion. He was nearly hypnotising, imploring me to calm down and to leave all worries behind.

"Let's take things step by step. You don't need to think about it right now. Try to feel comforted by the fact that keyhole surgery was possible. There was a lot of bleeding, and, according to the regulations, I should've proceeded with an open operation. I stopped it by using two suction drains, so you will be perfect. All has worked out for the best so far."

"You are a magician, doctor!" I was absolutely sure of it.

"You need to go home to your family. It's very late." I could hardly talk – I whispered, but actually I did not want him to go.

"Now you're my family, too – well, part of my extended one," Kovač whispered with some sadness in his voice.

This hospital's cancer ward was his real home. Kovač used to spend occasional nights in the hospital's accommodation, to be nearer to what he called his 'extended family'. It was a long time ago when he had made his choices, limiting his own life for the sake of prolonging others. His words brought tears to my eyes, tears of gratitude. He was happy to stay in my world of horror to make it better for me, trying to guide me out of pain and loss for the sake of redemption. His name was listed in the Bible as *the Saviour*!

Kovač was not in a hurry. He looked around the hospital room at everything that was possible to notice – my Louis Vuitton bag, my mobile phone, iPad, a few books on art. One with Titian's naked Venus on the cover, definitely captured his attention. All doctors deep down, I had been told, wanted to be artists, or at least wanted to exist in the arty-farty world, one so far removed from their own.

All these thoughts were going through my mind, or whatever was left of it. I felt my brain shrinking; it did not belong to a human being any more. I was existing in a different form and in a different dimension.

"Doctor, have you seen Francis Bacon's paintings of mutilated human bodies, *Three Studies at the Base of a Crucifixion?*" I attempted to think about the subjects I usually talked about before I had been stripped of my parts. "I could be exhibited next to them as an installation on the same theme – the inhumanity of humankind."

My mind was invaded with the works of Germaine Richier, who modified all humans and eroded the surfaces of their bodies, making them scarred figures. She was also diagnosed with C, while creating her *Chessboard* stuffed with characters composed of human and animal features.

I am a real workaholic, aren't I? I'm lecturing on my arty stuff. I was present in that world, wandering among them, talking to them. I was hallucinating.

"Dear ladies and gents, look at this painting," I said, pointing at myself. "It is a contemporary work by Natalia Popov, called *The Hole*… this is just a cavern covered with skin. You do not see it, but it is there and nothing more."

By my hospital bed appeared the mirage of Lucio Fontana, a crazy Argentinian chap adopted by Italy and famous for his *Spatial Concept, Waiting* series – sliced cuts in a canvas that looked like vaginas. He waved at me,

"Hello, dear! Your doctor is a great artist. He makes perfect *Tagli*, like me. His cuts go beyond the visual surface, just like mine do, beyond time and space, into eternity. My cuts only look spontaneous; they are in fact carefully planned, just like the ones on you. A good surgeon knows how to cut; a great surgeon knows how not to."

He laughed madly and he pushed his knife through the canvas. And again and again. And the next one into me.

I opened my eyes. Kovač was still in the room, standing next to the door, touching the wall to keep his balance. I wondered what featured in his nightmares. The wounded cunts he examined every day? Wombs, where human life begins, shielded from death by his hands? Women with stretched legs and blood gushing out of their holes? Or did he dream of many grateful smiles? And I smiled, trying to give him the best possible dreams.

"I want to return to my work. I want everything back to normal." I wanted to scream but my voice could hardly rise. It sounded more like a sigh.

My exhausted surgeon looked at me but said nothing. With his bald head and piercing eyes, which reflected his high IQ, he reminded me of a creature from another planet. He entered into my mind, sending reassuring impulses that all was fine. And I drifted into nirvana, walking through sunflowers with Van Gogh. The Dutch artist was not a happy fellow, but he tried hard to be one. He surrounded himself with colours of joy. Vincent and I talked.

"Your doctor is an artist. You are lucky to be looked after by this guy."

"Why do you call him an artist? That's just what Lucio Fontana did."

"It's a great art to love people!"

Yes, I read those words by Van Gogh in my earlier life; they did indeed belong to him. My world and mind were going around – Vincent, Lucio, Kovač – all swinging on a merry-go-round. Was it a dive into childhood, or was I circling with high speed on Mark Gertler's *Mary-Go-Round*, surrounded by wounded people covered with masks of death? It was not clear. I was in a space where present, past and future blended together. These visions made me shiver. I woke up.

Kovač was slowly walking through the door in a heavy silence, still focusing his eyes on me until he disappeared to finish his ward round. In his dark colourless suit, he did not look like an angel who had saved my life, but rather a tired demon who held people's lives in his hands and executed his judgement. Kovač knew better than anybody that it would take a long time before the world would return to normal for me, if it ever would. He obviously tried to ease the healing process for his patients. He loved them all, but some more than others.

Fart for Life

2ⁿᵈ September 2015
Queen's Hospital, Central London;
9ᵗʰ October 1995
Queen Charlotte Hospital, London

After a night under sedation, I woke up to reality. Still alive, I had to accept new aspects of my existence, and follow positive thinking to find happiness in different pleasures, perhaps.

It was definitely a great joy to have the longest luxury foot massage of my life. Special mechanical kinky boots were put on my feet to prevent blood clots from destroying my already much damaged body. The rhythmic soft movements made my chained-to-the-bed existence just about bearable.

I felt real joy when all the pipes and attachments were taken off the next afternoon. I was set free. Freedom! I wanted to enjoy it. But it did not take me long to realise that the best things in life could be very trivial: a fast progression of your own shit on the way out; a hope to turn it into a sprinter. This need was sending alarm signals through my brain, marked as *Attention! Emergency!* It was holding me hostage, mind and body.

The doctors had inflated me up during the operation, pumping five litres of CO_2 into my fat belly. It was needed to provide extra space for the surgeon's manipulations, to avoid any damage to my internal bits, the remaining healthy parts of my body. After the cancerous monsters had been removed, the stupid intestines, like impatient tourists, immediately moved into the vacant space. They took priority position and ignored the fact that this could cause a stoppage, a stoppage that came with a glamorous title: constipation.

A nurse arrived with my lunch and placed a tray on my bedside table.

"I don't want to eat! I can't even think about food or anything that should go into my body! I am stuffed and filled with gases like a thousand party balloons ready to float up to the ceiling." It was degrading to even talk about my farting business, but the subject dominated my thoughts at that moment.

"I'll ask your doctor to prescribe you candles; they will definitely bring some relief."

I wished she had been talking about Christmas candles or the ones lit during Hanukkah, but she meant Arse Fest fireworks.

"You mean Doctor Kovač?" This blabbermouth was ready to discuss my farting problems even with God himself!

But, at this point, what did I care? I cared about one thing – performing a long everlasting fart and getting rid of shit, which was causing a very severe traffic jam in my bloated relics. I felt as though I'd been impregnated – it was a constipation of body, brain and soul.

I dreamed of being as lucky as Piero Manzoni, the Italian artist from the 1960s. The bugger managed to make an incredible profit out of his own ka-ka. Unlike me, he had no problem with delivery of the matter. He declared that this human substance, represented in a minimised form, was the essence of the human soul and spirit. He beautifully displayed his shit in 25 tins, each containing 30 grams of the stuff. The Tate Gallery went crazy and paid £745 per gram of his faeces, proudly named *Merda d'artista – The Artist's Shit*. That significantly exceeded the price of a tin filled with 24-carat gold. That's when I realised the real value of contemporary art.

As for me, I was ready to give away my triple-barrelled Ukrainian-Russian-British shit for free. To be honest, it was getting to the point where I would pay that money myself to remove all the crap out of my desperate butt. I started to understand the miraculous wording: to *relieve* oneself. I needed a fucking relief, big time.

I couldn't stop thinking about how wonderful the sounds of wind orchestra instruments were – horns, trumpets, trombones and tubas. I turned on a tap in the loo and left the water loudly running to soundproof what I hoped would be a blast of ten Wagner tubas. But mine refused to play – my orchestra kept solidarity in silence, like in John Cage's masterpiece. Not even a piccolo squeaked. My chamber did not resonate at all under the powerful demands of its conductor, despite the pressure I heroically applied.

"Mrs. Fitzcock, you should move more, be active, try to walk in circles around the room." The trio of ward nurses liked to bombard me with advice on my relief issue. I was in utter agony and – God forgive my ungrateful feelings – they reminded me of the three prophesying witches from *Macbeth*. Shakespeare's words would be just right to describe my troubled state of mind.

Walk? Being the determined achiever that I was, I outperformed their advice by a mile. I was nearly running in circles around the room. Like a wounded animal, I was holding my huge belly with both hands. I tried desperately, with Olympic fervor, to make that stony stuff inside me move around as well. The tiled floor was slippery. If I fell, I would probably have bounced like a big ball.

"Do some breathing exercises. That should help," suggested the enthusiastic nursing team with the combined expertise of the EU and friendly Commonwealth.

I puffed warm air in and out, breathing deeply. Fast and slow, slow and fast – I was recollecting medical articles and images from TV programmes fed to the public to help us die in a wonderful state of health.

Nothing!

It was stuck inside me like a granite monument to my lost womb and ovaries. I walked into the bathroom and, sitting upon my porcelain throne, I asked God for help in the great hope for deliverance. Kissing the toilet with my arse for hours, I prayed and prayed to all the gods in the universe, including the pagan ones, "I will make any sacrifice, just help! Send my shit into a travel trip out of the Fitzcock's bottom."

They did not! I hadn't served my penance, yet.

I started to understand why some wealthy and healthy fashion-conscious people paid upwards of £11,000 for a special loo. I could have used one of those state-of-the-art privies myself at that moment, with magic remote-control cleansing functions and a water jet, which I would've fired on maximum power towards the shitting target.

I decided to give myself intellectual support by googling for more information on the painful subject.

Why can't Silicon Valley come up with a computerised and personalised enema to remove human waste? I thought. *Fuck, they are all young over there – the whizz- kids are far too preoccupied with their frontal genitalia to worry about back door problems.*

Perhaps, it was all too high-tech for my old rare. I resigned to a traditional remedy from my parents' generation: I took a book to read on the loo, just like in my childhood.

Years ago, in my old Soviet life, I would lock myself in the toilet to hide from my brutish mother. That time was not completely wasted: I managed to get through thousands of pages by Charles Dickens in this solitary confinement. We did not have any toilet paper in the USSR then, but we had *The Pravda* newspaper – which means '*The Truth*' in Russian. It was a daily collection of lies about everything in our society and abroad. We loved to use it for wiping our Soviet asses, displaying the true value of this repeatedly bended 'truth'. The loo was turned into a High Court chair and it was up to you to choose whom you were going to execute in your own arse. It was so relieving! A hard experience for our backsides, as it was for our brains – the paper was far from silky.

Here, in the hospital cubicle, locked in a struggle with my painful bottom, I managed to get through two chapters of *The Picture of Dorian Gray*. A mahogany throne with big armrests or a cute Edwardian blue and white porcelain bowl would be more suitable for this genre. I wondered whether Dorian was ever as concerned about his bum as with his pretty face. I ended up too emotionally invested in his plight to concentrate on the success of my own business. The result was the same again – nothing!

Even in such an uncomfortable situation, my high professional standards wouldn't allow me to avoid thoughts associated with my job, and I was reminded of the time when I had to explain the word 'loo' to my tourists.

"In the Middle Ages, shit was thrown out of the window and, to be polite, the lucky shitters shouted to people below: '*Gardez l'eau!*' which means, '*Beware of piss and shit!*'" That was why decent gents used to walk in the middle of the street, protecting ladies from the droppings; and that was why big hats were in fashion – to shield them.

I, on the other hand, had nothing to throw out. *Gents down there, you can remove your hats – no danger, guys!* Even without the organs that used to define me as a woman, I was feeling pregnant, with a baby in breech position. It reminded me of my traumatic experience with childbirth.

***

"I'd like to give birth in The Portland," I had begged my husband more than twenty years earlier. I had no doubts that with his big, successful business Freddie would be able to afford private care for his family without any problems and hiccups.

"My first wife had all three on the NHS! Our son will come out one way or another. They all do! You'll be fine! The Queen Charlotte is known to be the best maternity unit in the country." My Chairman would not spend his money on what he classed as 'luxury' – the birth of his son. He was not a mean man at all. For many years, he had been paying high-rate taxes, believing that the NHS should work well. It was strange though that his extra money flew so easily into the cricket club. Freddie defended this decision in a democratic way, "This is a game for people." And I wasn't one.

On the way to the hospital, Freddie drove through red lights.

"I always dreamed about doing this. And now I've got an excuse; the police can't do anything to me!" he exclaimed happily.

My Fitzcock loved to break rules occasionally. He hated many establishments, and rebelled against those who represented them. He eventually ended up departing from most of the official organisations connected with his multi-purpose business. We lost most of our invitations to the corporate Paradise – there were no more VIP boxes at Ascot: no chance to show off, even a bit; no invitations to balls and galas, and many more magnificent freebies were cut out of our lives.

To Freddie's delight, the police eventually spotted him speeding. As if rehearsed, he cheerfully announced without a hint of anxiety, "My wife is in labour." My Chairman wildly enjoyed being let off with no consequences. My loud moaning on the back seat helped him to fulfil his dream.

What followed was not all that fine. I was howling like a helpless animal brought to slaughter,

"Help me! I'll burst any moment. I'm torn apart."

"Let's put her in a hot bath. It's an old-fashioned method,

but it should do the job," an exhausted midwife suggested. Frustrated with my wild screams and moans, she tried hard to ease my pain using this 'sophisticated technique' from one of the best maternity units in Britain.

"Here we go!" Freddie helped me to undress and step into the hot water. After an hour of desperate soaking, it became clear that 'the best method' wasn't going to help much in my battle. Neither had it pacified my heart-wrenching screams. I was given a gas mask to shut me up. I knew I shouldn't use it – it was bad for the baby. But the excruciating pain blocked all channels of senses; I just needed relief. I was promised an epidural injection, and the hospital guaranteed to supply my choice of anaesthetic. I wouldn't believe a verbal promise in Russia, but in Britain's moral society, I stupidly thought that lying couldn't take place. The truth was somewhere in the middle. There was no specially trained staff available on duty.

The gas loosened my inhuman agony for a short while, but my baby turned into the breech position and started tearing me apart. The tiny creature was fighting for life and trying to find his way out. His head was like a hard rugby ball, forcing out of my backside, pushing hard but in the wrong direction. My son's heartbeat was failing. The little miracle was starved of oxygen. I saw my husband's frightened face – it went white for a while. Another few minutes and my son's brain would be dead, or suffer irreparable damage. Thank God the NHS still have some brilliant consultants, like Kovač, who spared a day or two a week attending to the normal citizens of Great Britain. Our consultant at the time was brought in when the situation reached a critical point – when lives, baby's and mine, were at stake. He did his job miraculously well and managed just in time to save my boy.

There was not an entirely happy ending to that fairy tale. Freddie's tax contributions to the NHS sadly did not benefit me. Not that time. I had to face the enormous Kielland's forceps. They should have been called 'the killer forceps' – that would have been a much more appropriate name for those monsters. My first thought was, *There's no way they can enter me! They'll rip me open!* Luckily, I lost consciousness after one glance. The monsters were the size of a golf club, or an old witch's rake. In medieval times they used to punish prostitutes by sticking similar instruments inside of them. I had seen equipment like this at the Tower of London in a Chamber of Torture.

My son was pulled out of me with a deformed head and jaundice but, thank God, alive. Nicholas escaped brain damage. I've never stopped thinking that, with his IQ of 143, had he not been squeezed during labour, he would have turned out to be a pure genius.

I could empathise very well with Queen Victoria's advice to her daughter prior to childbirth, "Don't be alarmed for the future; it can never be so bad again."

When an old nurse saw me later, she shook her head and whispered with compassion, "Oh, dear, dear! It's a miracle that you both pulled through. In my day, you would be dead."

I survived, but I soon discovered that I had sacrificed sexual stimulation for my boy's life. I was cut front to back, and all pleasure points on my cunt went into a deep sleep for years – they became numb. I had to use all my theatrical talents to generate passionate sex scenes and create the illusion of G-spot perfection. In fact, the letter G was wiped from my vocabulary, and changed to P for 'performance' or 'pretend'. I learned to skilfully fake orgasms. It worked. To get ready, I just had to watch a lot of Hollywood movies about sexually hungry wives. *Gigolo* with Richard Gere was my most helpful case study.

On top of this, for years I had to cope with post-traumatic

stress. Those four letters – PTSD – affected everybody near me. Freddie suffered, too.

***

Back to the Queen's Hospital. "Nurse! I need to have some help before I burst like an atomic bomb."

"Are you alright?"

What a pathetic question! She probably thought that it was the sort of potty humour so popular in the UK, not an embarrassing problem of defecating impotence. The only positive effect of this suffering was that it took my mind off the bigger picture of what had actually happened to me.

"I think I may need a pencil to excavate my backyard, or even a knife."

Judging from the look on my nurse's face, my words had formed a disturbing image in her mind.

"I read that pencil excavation is a tradition in this country. Don't you believe me?" The nurse stared back at me with a smile accentuated by ton of horror, before rushing away to fact-check this cultural novelty.

As a last resort, I tried to help myself with singing. I took a lot of air into my lungs and pushed as hard as possible, "Vincero!" The famous aria from Puccini's famous opera *Turandot* turned out to be the best remedy for my backside matter and truly helped me to win the battle against my own shit. As if a talented conductor waved his magic wand, the Wagner tubas started playing, accompanying my voice. My chorus of wonderful, tootling farts brought me more pleasure than any opera!

Don't Think Twice, It's Alright

3rd September 2015
Queen's Hospital, London

"My name is Ingrid. I'm a Macmillan nurse. I'm here to help you. Do you have any worries or concerns you'd like to talk about?" A heavily built middle-aged woman landed on the chair in front of my bed, the chair in which my surgeon had previously been seated. Kindly worrying about my state of mind, the hospital had sent in this dark-haired fairy.

"You're not alone," she continued. "Many people struggle to cope."

"I should have tried sex in a group. For now, I'm not interested. Don't waste your energy on me! We only have so much of it per day. It's rationed." I hated myself for being rude, but my mind was occupied with thoughts of death. To survive, or not to survive. It was a pity they didn't have daisies around the hospital rooms.

"Mummy, here I am." My big boy was pushing through the door with a big bunch of flowers, gorgeous lilies. I was saved from the merciful Macmillan woman! She delicately lifted herself from Kovač's chair, and dissolved behind the door.

"We've brought you cherries and a juicy watermelon," my Methodist squeezed into the room with a basket of fruits and a huge exquisite and expensive bouquet of roses.

It was a surprise. He had obviously called on a good florist's shop to get these exquisite and delicate pastel pink shades. Was it really him? My husband usually handed me a pot of geraniums for £3.99 – at most a fiver – from Sainsbury's. He would plop it down on our expensive dining table without thinking of including a surface-protective saucer under the licking pot. That always drove me mad. I had to be constantly on guard to prevent thoughtless damage in the house.

I expected to feel joy over my family visit, yet my guys looked like strangers to me, people from a life to which I no longer belonged. Ten minutes of talking about nothing, including a 'hello' from Freddie's hairy girls – our lovely doggies – all seemed irrelevant and trivial. I was waiting for Kovač and only Kovač. My dependence on him was growing like raising pastry.

By size, Kovač could only play the position of scrum half, but in my eyes, beyond my wishes, he had already grown to a hooker.

Perhaps, I was with him in another life, I said to myself. I was trying to find an explanation for this closeness I felt to the man who had rescued me from the claws of the C dragon.

Has he forgotten about me? I thought, as it reached 8.30 in the evening. Freddie and Nicholas were still with me, but I was gazing out the window. Rush hour had passed. Traffic was slowing down. Lights in the residential building opposite were turning on as people returned from work.

Maybe my doc went home and I won't see him tonight? I was sincerely worried. My son's and husband's words were muffled through my thoughts. I was waiting and listening. Steps in the corridor, a laugh – just visitors to one of the nearby patients – and then the door opened. I quickly licked my lips to give them a little shine and ran my fingers through my hair to create some volume; thankfully, I'd done all the colouring before the doc performed his witchcraft on my body.

"You look better today. Much better!" Kovač walked in with footsteps too heavy for the petite man he was. He looked tired and obviously carried all the weight of his patients' troubles. It was a long day for him, one of many.

"You have the whole support team here! Hello, Freddie." He turned to my husband. I was amazed that he knew his name. "The operation was very successful! Pity we don't have wine here to celebrate." Amazingly, Kovač was able to joke. He looked satisfied with his performance on me, seeing me smiling too.

"That's my son, Nick. He's a classical musician." I tried to play hostess at my 'glorious' hospital estate.

"Wonderful!" The doc had to look up at my son. Nicolas was nearly a head taller.

"I've not been to concerts for years and to the opera only once in my life. To be honest, I don't even remember what production it was."

I hoped my saviour did not notice that my son looked at him with contempt, as at some uncultured plebeian. But Kovač switched his attention to me. He took my hand.

"It's so blue," he murmured, inspecting my nails with a furrowed brow. "Oh! It's just the polish," he laughed with relief. Then he turned to my husband, "Your wife will be even better off at home, I think. I will tell the head nurse to prepare all the paperwork. Tomorrow, Natalia can go." Kovač had probably decided that I was a closed chapter for him for the time being; he'd done all he could and wanted to pack me up.

"Look, boys! Please go. I need to talk privately to the doctor." Kovač looked at me as if he knew that this would follow. He was so short next to my guys – Freddie and Nicolas appeared like two giant Vikings beside him.

"She does," the doc added quietly. The Vikings obeyed without question. Kovač waited until the door closed behind them and asked, "How are your bowels working?"

That was not the topic I hoped to discuss. These words confirmed that all that mattered in my life for now was shit. I was, for all intents and purposes, a piece of shit.

"They're still under anaesthetic, the lazy sleeping bastards!"

I repeated the words I'd heard from the Kenyan doc. Kovač detected my anxiety, and did not indulge on that theme anymore.

"Please, come and see me in a week's time. Pamina will book your appointment. I should have the pathology results by then and it'll be clear if any more treatment is needed. And we will remove your stitches. In few months' time, you'll be wondering where on earth the incisions were."

So I had to go, and the magician had to stay in his cancerous kingdom. He opened the door back into a normal world for me, but he was not allowed to follow. He was needed here, to continue his service in Hell.

"Doctor, I am so scared of what these results might be. I can't bear to think about radio or chemo. I'm dreading losing my hair."

"There's a good chance you won't need them. At present, you are cured. But, even if you do, you have the best team there could possibly be. Please, don't worry. And…" He paused for a few seconds, a little too long. "Well – good luck and see you soon." Kovač cast his eyes on the flowers. "Wonderful roses." He pronounced these words with pensive admiration as if they reminded him of something or somebody.

"*Ring a ring o' roses, a pocket full of posies…*" I was not sure why this nursery rhyme fell out of my mouth with tears streaming down my cheeks. The song was connected with death. The plague with a P was as bad as cancer with a C.

"*A tissue, a tissue…*" Kovač talked to me like I was a little girl. He gave me a tissue and continued, "*Don't think twice, it's alright* – do you know these words from Bob Dylan's song?

"It's my husband's favourite. He worships Bob Dylan – he is his god of music." I answered through sobbing. My pain began to melt with my tears.

"You don't need to cry and you definitely won't need any

posies." He took both of my hands and squeezed them into his delicate fists like my dad used to do.

"After all you went through, it's no wonder that death is on your mind. *She aches just like a woman but she breaks like a little girl...* Perhaps these words are about you. You know a lot about British culture and traditions." He was impressed with our song game. It was, probably, one of the rare moments of fun he could allow himself.

"How can you cope with this difficult job? It could drive anyone insane – piles of tragic stories every day."

"Yes, it's often very hard. But the satisfaction is very high, too. Look at you! Tomorrow you will be at home."

It was ridiculous: I didn't want to go home. If I had seen a fairy, I'd have asked her to impose a duty on him to keep checking on me every evening in his white scrubs, at least for a little while longer. Sadly, my fairy wasn't around and, for Kovač to get satisfaction from his work, I had to say goodbye.

Back to Life

4th September 2015
Maida Vale, London W9

5th – 7th September
Cobham, Surrey

"Good afternoon, doctor! It looks like you had a great time!" The porter at my Little Venice apartment noticed me walking unstably, as if heavily drunk. On account of my PhD, the porters called me 'doctor'. I found it really funny that Kovač was only a mister – the mister treated the doctor!

I had learned on a guiding course that these understated titles were connected to the fact that doctors used to be in the same livery company as barbers. Centuries ago, barber surgeons with their razors used to leech patients, and even amputate their limbs to save lives, but they were not trained doctors. So both sides of the same guild took the title of Mister.

"Yes, I did!" I tried to squeeze a smile. That was a fucking 'good time' under the knife, a dream of a masochist. Yet, I was happy that my mischief went unnoticed.

"I always wanted to ask you – what kind of doctor are you?" He was relatively new, that guy. He had worked in my block no more than ten years.

"I'm a gynaecologist, dear. I wouldn't be able to help you with your neck, back and premature ejaculation." I had to keep my humour on a level with my 'drunkenness'.

Being back at home helped me to feel normal. Kovač was right, as usual – I was much better out of the hospital.

I have to water my flowers, – that was my first thought as I opened the door. I rushed straight away to the kitchen to fill the watering can. My flowers had noticed my absence; they were getting dry and seemed relieved at my return. I inspected some new brown leaves, which made it look like my plants were ageing badly. I violently cut them off with huge clippers, restoring them to a younger and healthier look. I couldn't bear seeing anything ageing or dying around me.

A beautiful melody broke the silence. My son was playing piano. We had strict rules in the block – noise was forbidden after four in the afternoon, and the piano was considered a nuisance by our wealthy neighbours. Nicholas broke the rules to perform for me, welcoming me back into a world filled with music and all sorts of pleasures.

"Mum, fresh air will do you good." Nick much preferred the countryside to London. The next morning, I was ready for a drive. Kovač told me it would take four weeks to mend and return to my normal physical state, but even he might be wrong. I was a star patient and in a couple of days I was already ready to prove that something was still left for me on this Earth.

"Let's go for a cycle ride!" I told Nick as soon as I arrived. I needed to prove that my body was still in working order and I could carry on as normal.

For a minute, my son looked a bit hesitant, but he decided to support my act of bravery. We took our bikes out of the garden locker. I slowly started to push the pedals around the endless fields. It was still a bit painful on my tummy, but what did I care?

I spotted a few gorgeous butterflies, a lot of bees, and watched a few rabbits grazing on dandelions. All of it appeared like a real fairy tale; it had always been there, but I used to pass it by without noticing anything. Now, they were talking to me,

You silly goat, you lived for years blindfolded. You were dying long before you were diagnosed with C. This unexpected connection brought me to an amazing conclusion: the near-to-death experience condenses the beauty of the world, and makes you a happier person.

Leading the Charge

11th September 2015
Southampton

Just a week later, a huge cruise ship was moored at Southampton and we, Blue Badge guides with many different language skills, arrived from London to pick up our disembarking tourists.

"God! It is only five!" I switched off the alarm on my mobile phone. It was still dark. It was definitely worth a heroic struggle to start the day so early, as the job paid extremely well. At that time, it was not the money that mattered; being back at work was far more of a reward.

Working with private clients, often VIPs, was considered to be a more prestigious job, often embellished with gourmet dining and other small perks. Working with the groups, I was the boss – always in charge. If you tell your tourists to sit – they do it. You tell them 'time for the loo' – they all feel an urge to piss and crap in unison. I was like an orchestral conductor, showing tourists when to pause and when to speed up. I even told them when they should take photographs, what should they like, and what they should ignore.

My group was the last to pass through customs. No doubt, the British border guards considered Russians the largest security threat to their 'holy' land even then. I had to train my patience at these jobs and wait, and wait, and wait. All European groups departed, the trusted Chinese and the Indians passed by, and all my colleagues waved me goodbye. Then I saw from afar – my guys! It wasn't difficult to spot them. Russians often joked – 'the smell of Russia betrays its citizens from a distance'. That said it all. The cruise crowd was pushy and demanding – they had one day in Britain and they wanted the maximum possible, as the cost for the out-of-port-excursions could leave anyone on edge.

"Here's our guide. Our coach is number thirteen, what a fucky-lucky number!" A family of four approached me, displaying their rather rude demeanour. Russians liked to dwell on the negatives and suck them in.

"Please, come on board. Don't worry – thirteen in Britain means good luck." I wasn't sure they believed me but I continued regardless.

"Traditions are different here. The British, they don't mix hot and cold water in a tap. They have it running separately. They never have tea with cake. First comes cake, tea come after. The British devour their cakes with a fork!" My words definitely added some mystery to the country and put smiles back on the often gloomy Russian faces. When people laughed – they were pacified.

A long time ago, I had accepted the number thirteen as a sign of luck, a black cat crossing my path was a good sign as well. These beliefs helped me to avoid the fear of something bad approaching me.

At Southampton, one subject should never be touched upon – *the Titanic*. She sank after leaving this port. Cruise tourists preferred not to be reminded that something similar could happen to them during their long journey across the pond.

"We have everybody on board. Let's go!" I gave my command to the local driver.

The job helped me push C to the back of my mind. I told myself I could do it. Talking about English Kings and Queens diverted me from thinking about choosing wigs, the poisons of chemo, and possibly more cuts. *No more Lucio's Tagli on my body* – the thought of them numbed me.

I had built up a huge store of knowledge that enabled me to talk about history and life in Britain for two long hours on the way to London. Russian-speaking tourists were the most demanding – they would not allow you even a short break; they wanted 200 per cent value for their money. To survive that day, I had to choose the British way of guiding – the way we were taught on the guiding course – pausing every now and then, in between talking for ten to fifteen minutes. It was good to give the tourists some time to digest the avalanche of information and enjoy the pastoral views. For me, it was a chance to refill my energy.

Spiritual energy teaches you how to turn your desires and wishes into reality. A few days before my operation, I received a book in the post called *The Secret*. There was a small note enclosed: 'Read it – you may need it.' I recognised my friend Ella's handwriting. The book tells us that everything around us is filled with energy. If you send your wishes and desires through the flux of energy into the cosmos and they will come back to you in real substance.

No secrets were there for me. Even prior to reading this book, I believed that my subconscious mind could influence my physical existence. The book confirmed what I had already experienced myself when I'd been heard by Him in St Paul Cathedral. But *The Secret* provided the scientific name for this undertaking – *manifestation*.

Thinking about magic energy, I realised that we were passing not far from Stonehenge, one of the most powerful energy spots. The mysterious ancient stone circle still holds a lot of secrets. *Why did ancient people pull those heavy stones from afar to this particular place? Did this place have special qualities that helped them to communicate with other worlds, to come through into other dimen-*

sions? *Could they do it all on their own, lifting and erecting 50 tonne stones so precisely that a ray of sun could accurately pass through every pair each month of the year for 4000 years? How could they achieve perfect symmetry, being in possession of only stone tools?* I started sharing my thoughts with my tourists, telling them everything I knew about this mysterious place, and even quoting from *The Secret.* That caused a lot of excitement.

"The first time I took tourists to Stonehenge was more than twenty years ago; I just had started my training in guiding. Not many were interested in visiting this place then. One of the first I brought here was Georgy Grechko, the famous cosmonaut." My statement caused a sensation.

"We heard about this amazing place," they said. "The next time we come to England this will be our first stop."

"I'm from Magadan," I heard an excited voice from the back seat. "We also have mysterious megaliths, in the form of altars."

The word 'Magadan' still causes shivers in people of my generation and the elder one. The area was famous not for these ancient monuments, but for the Stalin's concentration camp known as the *Gulag,* where all the best intellectuals and talents of Soviet Russia were either shot or left to rot in the Arctic Circle, an unwelcoming place.

"There are a lot of prehistoric monuments in my country, in Armenia. Those huge dolmens and stone labyrinths are all over the place, some dating from the 4th millennium B. C. We even have an Armenian Stonehenge – Karahundji. *Kar* means stone and *hundji* sounds remarkably similar to your *henge.*"

"And on Kamchatka – they call them megalithic portals." I was also learning from my guys. To achieve an active interaction with clients was a sign of good quality guiding.

"Quiet, quiet, guys. Incredible information! Thank you for this. One day I will quote you to the next group, as I did with Grechko. He seemed to know much more about this mysterious Stonehenge than I did at that time. In fact, Stonehenge is a part of a bigger complex – thirty miles to the north there is another Neolithic monument – Avebury circle, which is even bigger than Stonehenge. Grechko believed that local people were helped by another civilization. He was sure that they would not be able to align all of the structures on their own. He, of course, could not avoid talking about UFOs. 'When you are in the cosmos,' he told me, 'you can clearly see all those ancient monuments – the pyramid of Giza, Teotihuacan – the sacred complex in the valley of Mexico – where according to the myth, the Sun was created; you would see Aztec pyramids that were built much later; Stonehenge and many more amazing creations. They all were constructed along the leylines – the energy meridians. It was not possible to align them from Earth.' I had laughed at his words then but not anymore, as more and more unexplained features were discovered."

My story was well received, and most people were asking me to continue. Yet gliding along the motorway eventually turned the coach into a cradle. A big group of the passengers, mainly middle age male, departed from reality into the dimension of their dreams.

Talking to my tourists about this mysterious matter, I realised that there was a strong connection between the ancient monuments, the Wailing Wall, my personal communication with the Creator at St Paul's and *The Secret* book. The possibility of a small break from talking was a blessing – it allowed me to concentrate on Manifestation. I put my energy flux into action, focusing on the outcome of the verdict.

I thought hard.

I knew what I wanted it to be: to be free of cancer.

I told myself – I would get it!

My break did not last too long and I was brought back to guiding duties by an awakened tourist.

"Why do cars in Britain have different colours on their number plates – some are white and the others are yellow?"

That was a very sophisticated question. Even the Blue Badge Guides course could not prepare me for it. But my PhD did.

"At the front, it's white, at the back – yellow." I was so pleased with myself. The coach burst into happy laughter.

I am worthy! I was sending positive energy out. I was leading the charge.

The Verdict

11th September 2015
Queen Anne St, the consulting rooms

We arrived ten minutes early to the appointment. Freddie was holding my hand. Since C, I had regained some closeness with my husband. It was typical of him to be kind and supportive when I was ill or in trouble. These minutes of waiting felt like a good hour, an hour of mind-crushing tension. We sat in silence, shoulder to shoulder, like two prisoners awaiting our verdict.

Anxious thoughts crept up on me in the waiting room: *The people waiting in the hall – are they also C patients? Are they like me, and left without a clear gender? Are they lucky ones or will they have to grow accustomed to wigs? Who will make the decision for me and for them? What does the word 'fate' actually mean?*

Professional habit pushed my thoughts towards Ancient Egypt. Working in the British Museum, I often talked about *The Book of the Dead* and *The Judgement of Osiris*.

> *The soul of the deceased was placed by him (Anubis) on the golden scales. The highest god of the afterlife would balance it against the white feather of Ma'at, representing the truth and harmony. If the heart were lighter than the feather, their soul would be admitted into the wonderful blissful world. Should the heart appear to be heavier, it would be thrown to Ammit – the Devourer of the dead,*

the god with the face of a crocodile and body of a leopard and a hippopotamus, who would swallow it whole. So, nothing would be left of the soul.

Nothing – it was a scary word in a scary world. Judging from my behaviour in the past, my heart would be tonnes heavier than any feather. Not because of my body weight, but because my sins could flatten a truck.

"Apologies for the delay. I'll see you in a few minutes." A quiet but cheerful voice delivered the message I had been waiting for. It was Kovač. He was able to detect my anxiety even at a distance. He stood in the doorway of his office for a minute, looking like a provincial Jewish tailor in his colourless suit. But his eyes! They were shining with happiness. I could not be mistaken! My kind messenger quickly shuffled back into his office and shut the door.

"Freddie, I think all is fine! Have you noticed the doctor's eyes? It was a clear stream of energy with a positive message. For me!" I squeezed my husband's hand in a spiritual wave of positivity.

"Probably." Freddie did not want to deprive me of hope completely, but he was a pragmatic guy. "Let's wait until we hear it. I hate false assumptions."

It did not matter. I knew that my wig was going into the bin; I was fine and free of cancer. My doctor had communicated with his eyes – he wanted to share the good news as soon as he could. He possibly considered it unfair to make me wait longer. He rushed to reassure me, even if briefly, saving me from a flood of dreadful thoughts in my disturbed head.

"Please, come in. The doctor is ready to see you," a nurse eventually invited us to the consultant's room. Kovač was sitting at his desk, writing something with his head down. Then he stood up and threw us a welcoming glance before shaking hands with my husband and me.

"Sorry again for the delay. I had some complications with a previous patient. For you, Natalia, I have great news – I can confirm you're cured. The cancer cells hadn't spread outside the womb. We caught these bandits just in time. You will need to come back for a check-up next month, then every three months, so you'll have to put up with me for a few years. And then…"

"And then I'll die," I buckled with relief and laughed joyfully. I was happy that I would be seeing him again. I didn't grasp from his instructions that there was a danger of C reoccurring in me for years to come.

Kovač smiled, happy to be a bearer of good news. His little moustache made him look like the little rabbit from the pages of Beatrix Potter. Yet he had to deliver a nasty warning.

"The most likely reappearance could be in the form of vaginal cancer. It is treatable, nowhere near as dangerous as it was. We would just put a special capsule inside your vagina to destroy the cancerous cells." He spoke so casually and sweetly that he could've been offering me a mint chocolate, rather than a radioactive object, to save my pussy.

"Oh God! And everything between my legs will be burnt! I will be useless forever with a damaged cunt." I should have said 'unfuckable', but Freddie's presence did not allow me to express what I truly meant. The word 'cunt' shouldn't have been a problem as it was commonly used by the Chairman himself. He had dismissed me as an undesirable object years ago, and was, probably, surprised that I was even concerned about this 'irrelevant' issue.

I was slightly distraught by this awful prognosis, even if it was not a very likely outcome. But I wasn't able to absorb any more threats, warnings or troubles. I needed to believe that all was fine.

"Thanks, doctor. I owe you so much." I didn't want to see

Russian roulette in my future, a wheel of fate spun by Moirai. God became my croupier and helped to spin the wheel.

"This is my job," the doctor modestly added.

Did Kovač mean that he was spinning the wheel?

My gratitude was jetting madly. I stepped forward with the intention to kiss his hands. In fact, I did – I grabbed one but dropped it quickly, as the doctor retreated from my grateful advances. He stuck himself in the far away corner, looking rather scared. He obviously wasn't accustomed to such outbursts of emotion, and was worried I'd go further. My husband's presence did not ease his fear.

"Doctor, if you ever need anything, please, let me know. There is nothing I wouldn't do for you. I will be forever indebted to you."

Strangled by the General Medical Council's regulation to avoid any physical contact with patients, and overwhelmed by my larger-than-life presence, the little doctor stepped back closer to the wall, trying to protect himself. He suddenly squeaked out, "Sex after the operation will be the same!" He looked at my husband, as if begging for assistance. I decided to cool my passionate 'thank yous', and increase the distance between our bodies by a metre or so.

"That's the last thing you need to worry about, doctor. I haven't practised sex for God knows how long. I told you at my first appointment. I've been a virgin for the last ten years." I sensed my Fitzcock standing behind my back feeling uneasy.

He butted in, "She needs to lose some weight first." My husband was trying to say that my fat body put him off my cunt. That was Freddie's reflection on our sex life. I stupidly thought that my excessive eating was a substitute for achieving some satisfaction denied to me in the bedroom. My husband's words removed all the radiance from my face. I was back to normal existence, where the truth was often merciless and difficult to accept.

He is right, I thought. *The only creatures interested in my body are flies and mosquitoes. I just have to accept it and live with it.*

"It's easy to say but so difficult to achieve."

It was the little doctor! He was not lecturing me on how dangerous it was to be obese, and not even recommending gastric band surgery. He was defending me from my powerful, and often insultingly hard, husband.

"Actually, doctor, my husband is capable of being nice to me – he's just promised to buy me a new car." I wasn't trying to protect Freddie, but I wanted Kovač to know that my life at home was not so bad after all. "Now that I am cleared from the worst…" I paused, not sure if I should continue.

"You mean, the make of the car can be downgraded?" The Doctor was stealing my words and worries, which I was about to express through my never-disappearing black humour; always on guard to protect me like a shield made of steel.

"Let's go." Freddie was being rigorously judged by both sides, and had had enough. He expected to be perceived as a respectable man and a decent, caring husband. A wave of great sympathy from the doctor made me blush. I noticed that he blushed, too. We were in a silent dialogue.

***

"I'm too tired to walk. Let's have lunch. There are plenty of nice little restaurants around this area," I suggested to Freddie. I was not hungry, not at all but I desperately needed to hang around, closer to Kovač. *You don't meet many people like him, and when you do, you want to stay closely connected.* These thoughts run through my mind, engraved there for a long time.

An Italian waiter was pleased that we brought some business to the almost-empty restaurant. The absence of people and sounds

99

was healing for me at that moment. It was much better to not say anything, unless it could improve on the silence.

"I'm going for the halibut." Freddie had chosen the same dish that I was thinking of ordering. It amazed me that, as the years passed, our taste in food became very similar. I even started liking Brussels sprouts, after years of being revolted by them.

"And two glasses of Sauvignon Blanc," my husband added. We liked the same wines, too. Yet other things kept us apart – we appreciated that in many aspects of our life we were very different.

"How old is the doctor, do you think?" I asked Freddie, while looking through a menu..

"About 46, 48." My husband was surprised I'd asked. I was, too.

"What a job, to save people every day!"

"What a job to peer inside sick ladies' holes all your life," Freddie sneered, demonstrating his contempt for the job of a gynaecologist. Then added, "Someone has to do it, I suppose."

I was upset on my doctor's behalf. I tried to enjoy my food, but it had already lost its flavour.

"A man would only want to become a gynaecologist if he was immune to women's powers. He probably must be a queer to dig inside their cunts without wanting more." Freddie spoke as if he possessed the wisdom of Solomon and the fairness of David. He was never wrong; so he thought.

I wondered if a magician could appear, pull out a hair from his beard and say "Abracadabra!" and there my Chairman would go, disappearing through the window without a trace. I finished my lunch quickly without really tasting it. It was a lousy celebration of sadness that my life had not come to an end.

Doctor Knows Best

16th September 2015
Cobham, Surrey

"Tomorrow we can go to the garage and choose your new car. Do you still want a four-wheel-drive Mercedes?"

Freddie was competing with my doctor. Kovač had given me a new life, and my Chairman? A new vehicle to drive smoothly through it. He always found the way to my forgiveness by offering payment, a kind of barter for his 'sorry'. I gained intimacy through an expensive flat, jewellery and clothes – I had discovered lots of equivalents to love in my life.

"The same."

"Okay…" Freddie pronounced it with an intonation that demonstrated his generosity, to cough up nearly £60,000 for several tonnes of metal. He was rewarding the piper to silence the ugly tune.

***

Only a month prior to my C verdict, I had had a car crash, which wiped out my previous silver Mercedes. My first ever car accident – it was a mystery. I was driving back from London in the afternoon, after rising early for a demanding job, and had nearly reached our country house. I dropped off at the wheel for just a second, and that was enough – I came off the road. My silver friend was left deroofed and badly smashed, but miraculously, there wasn't a scratch on me! I was paralysed with shock, but managed to place a call to Freddie.

"I need you!" I whispered into my phone. He would always come when I was in trouble.

"I knew you were a lousy driver. Looking at the state of the car, I can't believe you're okay! The car is fully insured, so no worries." Freddie laughed in my face – the accident reaffirmed his belief that we women were not to be trusted.

I should have known – I had been warned! Yet, I missed this sign and His caution. It couldn't be just coincidental that the accident occurred in this particular place, near the Mecca of my husband's ex. For many years, Freddie's first wife, whom he divorced after he met me, was closely connected to a charity that owned the car park I had vandalised.

Was it a revenge she wanted to impose for the theft of her property – her husband and father of her kids – but did not have enough nastiness to complete? Did she manifest her energy too? After that, I started believing in the unbelievable. Could the mysterious coincidence of events like this be a prediction of my illness?

"Have you been drinking anything?" A policeman was filling out a damage report.

"No, not even a cup of coffee. I had just water and tea."

"These things happen. If the road was straight, you'd have just jerked, woken up and continued. Unfortunately, there was a bend." He was trying to calm me down and reassure me that I wasn't a criminal or a dysfunctional person; not yet anyway.

"We won't prosecute you. I've written that this wouldn't be in public interest." He was obviously taking into consideration my husband's charitable work around the area.

***

Freddie kept his word, so on the Saturday morning we went to the local garage to choose my new car. I did not even need to remind him about his promise. That was, in itself, a special event.

"I like this one." I pointed at the muscular vehicle. "It's exactly the same as my old one, but it has fine, black, leather seats. I love the smell of leather." I jumped inside, still experiencing pain in my tummy from the stitches.

"Let's get the paperwork done. It'll be registered to my company," he told the saleswoman, avoiding facing me directly. Then he turned to me and whispered gently, "It is better this way. You don't have the capacity to think about so many issues, particularly now when you're slightly disorientated after the operation. Repairs, insurance – all will be done for you."

Freddie's generous present was downgraded as my doctor, a real magician, had foreseen. The make was the same, but the car was not mine. It was only for my use. I smiled and tuned into positive thinking – surely, *even better for me.*

The Meat in the Sandwich

20ᵗʰ September 2015
Cobham, Surrey

"What would you like for dinner? I'm going shopping." Freddie was trying to be nice to me, his damaged girl. His daughter Denise was visiting from Australia, and my husband wanted to gather us all around the table for a 'happy family' scene, like in a children's book. For many years, he had persistently kept me and Denise apart. We hardly visited his three kids from his previous marriage. 'The less the better' was his main motto. "I don't want to be the meat in the sandwich," he would say. Nothing more.

"Buy two containers of cottage cheese, please, and four chicken breasts for me. Free range, please. I need to keep up with my protein diet."

I answered automatically, as I was busy with something very important. "I'm writing a letter to the head of the hospital about the wonderful service I have received." I couldn't hide from Freddie my admiration for Kovač's brilliant skills, and his compassion for his patients. And why would I?

"We paid for it," Freddie said. "I've being sending cheques to BUPA since I was twenty-one and used it for the first time when I reached forty. Even after all the discounts, it is still incredibly costly."

I was grateful to Freddie. I would never have been able to afford this life-saving treatment myself. It was far more attractive than using the NHS and waiting several months for a 'fair' distribution of hope in equal micro-doses – often too late. The best treatment costs money and lots of it. You learn that very quickly, especially when your life is under threat.

Freddie was about to leave when Denise came down the stairs. She was in her mid-thirties, a petite woman, who never had time to look after herself and always appeared exhausted by her three daughters. She greeted me with a compliment, a rarity.

"You look great!" She stared at me curiously, as if I had descended from another world. I was sure she knew about the C. Freddie wasn't cut out to keep secrets; it was like incontinence. His daughter probably thought that I deserved my fate, as karma for her parents' divorce.

"Well observed. I have survived!" I glanced at my husband and he looked like a wetted schoolboy, who had lied about his marks and been caught out by his parents. To avoid becoming the meat in the sandwich, Freddie was happy to self-destruct. He disappeared into thin air, using shopping as an excuse. He was going to spoil us and spend a lot of money as his 'get out of jail free' card.

"My step-children have been bloodsuckers for years," I would complain to my son.

"Mother, don't you understand them? If Dad had left you for a younger woman, I'd also hate her."

"When we met, your dad told me that his first marriage had been dead for a long time. There was no sex between them. He called it 'a brother and sister relationship.'"

My own words nearly choked me. Perhaps he now described our relationship the same way to his friends, or his secretary. Maybe, I had been a sister for him for the last ten years, too?

My son was perfectly aware of our no-touch family ways. No sex means no marriage, I had thought twenty years ago. These days, our lovely newspapers regularly inform us that we are not alone in being celibate, and should not worry about it too much. Apparently, a good third of couples, even in their thirties, do not remember what sex is about. Even millennials put a stop to sex – they probably think that it is connected to slavery.

It was strange, but even without sex, I still felt properly married. Every first day of the month, my account was credited with a decent amount. A salary for a job: the job of a wife. That was the best way Freddie could show his appreciation. No sex? What did I care?

An hour later, my Fitzcock emerged through the front door laden, with Waitrose shopping bags.

"Daddy, when are you going to celebrate your jubilee? 65 is a serious milestone. You were planning it for this summer, but because of Natalia's illness it was postponed till…" Denise trailed off and then changed the subject:

"What a fantastic cake! I'll have another piece." She had turned her attention to the rhubarb pie, which she nervously called a cake. I had bought this homemade dessert at a farmers' market and presented it as my own creation. My son smiled behind my back.

"Mother, what a lovely pie you have baked today! It's not even burnt," he winked, and kept our secret for the sake of the family honour.

Freddie never bothered to ask whether I'd made them or someone else had baked them – as long as they were edible and not too expensive.

"We'll do it in early November," Freddie said, "before the Christmas parties start booming. We've already sent out most of the invitations: 200 just this week." As he spoke, he was looking at me across his shoulder, nervously awaiting a punch.

"Already?" I asked. "And have you issued these invitations on our joint behalf?" There was no need to ask the Chairman. I suspected that it wouldn't be the case. 'We sent out' referred to him and his PA.

"Does it matter?" Freddie wouldn't consult me on most of the family issues. He knew how to manage it all by himself.

He continued, "I've written a script for the event. You remember that wonderful film with young Dustin Hoffman – *The*

Graduate? I've done my own interpretation of a few scenes." Freddie was obviously in possession of a great literary talent. After sponsoring a Hollywood movie years ago, the Chairman had always wanted to be involved in the arts in some way.

"Which scenes? You're not really a teenager anymore who can be seduced by his mother's friend." I stared at my 65 year-old spouse. He looked decent for his age – tall, slender, without a beer belly. Though he was betrayed by a couple of missing teeth. His white hair stuck out in all different directions, not only on his head but – what was worse – from his ears and nostrils. I saw similar hairstyles in the London Dungeon. I tried endlessly to cut these ghastly invaders off, but he never allowed me close enough to succeed in destroying his relics.

"For your *The Graduate* role you need to change your hair-style, at least. The present one adds a few decades to your high-school age. Why don't you go to a better, trendier place?"

Freddie had been having his hair cut for a fiver at the same local barbershop for years.

"I'm helping my barber's business. He's sort of an old friend!"

My Fitzcock would buy a bad-quality TV from 'a friend' running a local shop; he would use 'friendly' builders for house re-decoration and would not dare to ask them to redo a crappy job.

"You don't harass friends! Stop complaining!" I would hear as I pointed out the running paint on the walls or the gaps left after the floor-fitting job.

"Just put up with it!" That was another manifesto of my Man of the People.

***

My son was four years old when all three of us flew to Vienna. After having been locked for thirty years in the Soviet cage, I perceived any trip abroad as an achievement. Visiting the capital of the waltz was simply magical. It was winter and very cold. I was wearing a short skirt and still remember the touch of the frost on my thighs. In spite of the brutal weather conditions, my little Nick wanted to visit the zoo. It took ages to catch a taxi.

"Here you are." The driver stopped his car along a big stone fence with no entrance to be seen anywhere.

"Where's the zoo?" I dared to ask.

"Just around the corner, five hundred metres, no more." The driver closed the window and was about to take off.

"Please, take us nearer to the entrance, it's so cold!"

"Cunt!" Freddie shouted. "Why are you torturing this person? Can't you take your fat arse there yourself?"

He took off his hat, the mink one I'd bought him as a gift from Russia, and threw it fiercely to the ground like a mad man. He disappeared in an unknown direction, leaving me alone with a crying son. I couldn't work out what my fault was. Only much later did I understand that it was his insecurities. His nervous outburst was not just against me. The Chairman had no interest in Vienna or any other cities; he couldn't stand Mozart and waltzes, and being brought up on a farm meant that he hated zoos, too.

"The high fliers and heads of big companies often score highly on the psychopathic spectrum to be able to do their jobs. You need to be a psychopath to rise up the ranks." My friend Ella Germanskaya was reassuring me over the phone.

"But he called me 'cunt'- the most offensive word ever."

"Are you sure he didn't say 'he can't'? You are very emotional, Natalia."

"You must be joking! I wish!"

"You know, 'cunt' has many meanings. For the ancient Indians, it meant 'queen' or 'knowledge' – it was a very positive word. Look in the Australian English Dictionary – it's often used with a positive meaning there, too. It shares the same root with the word 'country'; it can mean 'funny' or 'clever' – and that's what you are." Ella, the aspiring specialist, thought she had delivered a brilliant therapy session.

"Do you know that play, The Vagina Monologues? I saw it off-Broadway some years ago, and there's this whole section on reclaiming it, the word 'cunt', as an empowering word. I really love it, listen…" She almost started to sing the word. Ella surprised me – she obviously didn't find this 'dirty' word taboo.

Well, she's lived longer in the West than me, I thought.

"No, I don't know it. But this is too much. It sounds disgusting. My husband is possibly ancient but he is not an Indian; neither is he an Australian, as far as I know." I knew perfectly well what Freddie meant to say.

My Chairman returned to our hotel late at night with a damaged forehead. He was known to practise knocking his head against a wall to demonstrate that it was less painful than living with me. He might have damaged his frontal lobes where social behaviour was organised. That could cause him to have sudden outbursts of violence and irrationality. *Perhaps it was a sign of male menopause.* But that clever thought only occurred to me years later.

"Let me take your coat off," I offered to help Freddie out of his heavy sheepskin as an olive branch.

"Get lost, old cunt!" That definitely wasn't intended as the Australian definition. Since then, I had felt myself very old. An old cunt.

***

"I have arranged a huge marquee out near our lake. It's in the shape of a wigwam. The theme of the night will be the Wild West. We're going to have great fun!" Freddie got very excited by masterminding this big event. "I'm hiring two different costumes – a cowboy, and an orangutan who will be carrying ladies around. I know a few light ones, easy to lift." He looked at me, making it clear I wouldn't be one of those 'lucky ballerinas'.

I hadn't suspected that my husband would turn into such an extrovert at the age of 65. It had taken him a while. I found the strength to smile and withhold a mocking laugh.

It was early for bed but I could not find any better excuse to hide my tears.

"What about our dinner?" Freddie looked frustrated.

"Wouldn't it be better for me to skip it?"

My husband realised at last that he had said something offensive. But it was not a habit of his to apologise. Not in front of his daughter, that was for sure. His defence was always in the form of an attack.

"Is this your idea of emotional blackmail? I'm leaving!"

I was not sure where he was going to go, but I went upstairs to my bedroom and locked the door. I curled up in a big armchair and picked up a paperback of Amado's *Dona Flor and Her Two Husbands*. I tried to read it, but I wasn't able to concentrate. I couldn't stop thinking how good it was in the hospital with Kovač. I could hear his voice – "Especially for you ..." he'd said. I felt the touch of his gentle hands.

I moved out of the armchair, dropped my skirt, pulled off my jumper and stretched my hand under the pillow to find my nighty. I threw myself on the bed. It was cold in the room, cold everywhere, all over my body. I rolled myself quickly under the thick duvet, hiding from the world where I was a Fitzcock. Kind touches of the silky pillow made me close my eyes. A couple of minutes of silence – I was tuning in. I found his energy wave. There he was – I held Kovač in my arms.

"How was your day, Andrew?"

In Fatties We Trust

22nd September 2015
Maida Vale

The next morning, I drove to London. A splendid gilded Georgian mirror was hanging in the entrance hall of my London apartment. I believed that every decent woman should have a full-size mirror. It records your wrinkles, your bloated shapes – all your imperfections – and alerts you, if necessary.

The subject of reflection bothered many artists from Van Eyck to Rossetti, Millais, and Holman Hunt. Twentieth-century genius Michelangelo Pistoletto, who used a lot of real mirrors in his mixed-media works, attempted to see through the looking glass to the Other Side. After my operation, I tried to by all means to avoid this huge antique marvel. But I needed to observe my shape, whatever was left of it. I could only hope that facing reality would not increase my desire for self-destruction. That was what I saw in Louise Bourgeois's works. Her installation, *Cell (Eyes and Mirrors)*at the Tate Modern, showed huge eyeballs carved in marble, surrounded by mirrors of different sizes, enclosed in a cage-like structure. According to the words of the artist, this work reflected pain, both mental and physical. I had known enough of both. I justified my hatred of mirrors after C, while understanding that they were often a symbol of vanity. *Keep some sanity,* I would think to myself, *and completely ignore your reflection.*

A Russian fairy tale that my granny used to tell me immediately came to mind. It was a story about a wicked queen, who interrogated her mirror demanding it to reveal the truth, only the truth, and nothing but the truth about her looks. Of course, she expected to be admired as the most beautiful creature in the world. Thankfully, her mirror knew how to lie. Mine, unfortunately, was not in possession of such a talent.

I wasn't expecting a ballerina to be staring back at me, but I still wasn't prepared for that view. I was a chunk of rubbish. And a big one. I looked as if I had walked out of Rene Magritte's painting *Rape*. It shocked me when I saw it in the Met. The face and the naked body were squeezed together and crowned with pubic-like hair; no waist, an overhanging, extended stomach; and only the tits showed that it was an image of a woman at all.

It was possible that my reflection was accurate as a surrealistic image, but it wasn't pleasing, nor was it inspiring, nor alluring in the real life. It looked like a cow and an elephant were put together, by a mistake of nature, to create an *Elecunt*.

My sexuality was buried in a grave of fat. It was dying inside, unused. The fat, like a social and physical barrier, would be there to secure my solitude. It wasn't what I wanted to see on a portrait hanging on the wall for public observation. Even though *the Fat Sue* by Lucian Freud had been sold at auction in New York for £35m … for myself, I would not give a fiver.

***

In Soviet Russia, we didn't trust thin people: a fat man was a boss; a fat woman was trustworthy. Success in children's development was measured by weight gain, particularly after the holidays. If, during the summer time, you put on a couple of kilos, it was considered an achievement. If you lost weight, that was looked upon as a failure. Soviet Russia had been bringing up generations of fatties since their kindergarten years. Communists probably wanted us to look big and scary and frighten the rest of the world.

Our main meal for breakfast was semolina porridge. After consuming my portion, I would raise my hand and ask for seconds. Teachers would say, "Look at Popov – she is the best example of a healthy child." Their compliments were so important for me, even then, at only five years old. I lacked any emotional support at home. I wanted to eat more not because I was hungry, but because I wanted to hear something nice about myself. For many years, the huge amount of food I consumed was associated with positive achievement. If I could outperform kids in eating, then I was considered to have the potential to break records in other fields.

My mother used to lock our fridge, leaving just enough food on the cooker to keep me going. She didn't give a fuck about my look; she simply did not want to waste anything on me. On weekends, my granny would compensate for all the missing calories with her generous Ukrainian borsht, delicious duck stuffed with poached apples, a variety of pies, endless pancakes and homemade jam. All of these were a real treat. Granny was showing her love mainly through food. When we talked about how women could achieve success in love, we used a Russian proverb – 'The way to a man's heart is through his stomach'. *Food, glorious food!* If this song from the musical *Oliver!* had been known then in Russia, it could've become a second national anthem.

In Brezhnev's time, in the seventies and early eighties, only our communist elite had a special supply of food, but for most people, shops were empty. You needed special skills to be able to get hold of food, enormous determination and good contacts to find it. It kept our people busy for most of their free time, not leaving any energy to think about what the hell was going on around them. The main slogan of our society was, 'You give to me, I'll give to you'. We used to barter anything we could for food: our position, our services, our conscience, or simply pay for it at a much higher rate – often five times more than retail value. Food was a trophy and a symbol of status and wealth. These presumptions started to fade only after Perestroika, when Russia took a more Western approach.

My first husband loved to cook, just like Freddie. We often had his relatives and friends over at our flat.

"The Olivier salad is a real success!" It took him a few hours to prepare a huge portion of the favourite Russian starter. This salad was a combination of everything we had in the fridge, topped with a generous dollop of mayonnaise to the delight of any guests at the dinner table. We would invest much time and money to provide a generous welcome.

"Put it here. Smoked eel goes to the other end of the table. Let's put the jar of black caviar in the middle."

I would help with laying out the table, making sure that my favourite dish would land next to me. That was my best contribution to the dinner.

Caviar on the table would give the impression that we were doing just fine financially and in other aspects of life. We Soviets would have loved to go out much more – though there weren't many places to go, but the main reason was that we did not want to demonstrate our financial stability to the world. People wouldn't forget Stalin's regime. Many suspected their colleagues and neighbours of being informers.

Our preparations could last for the whole week – five days hunting for food, and two days for cooking. In one evening, we would eat everything that should have been consumed in a week. After a successful reception, guests were expected to crawl away from the table. A litre of vodka per person would be the norm in those days. This magic liquid would work with food like oil on the rails, helping the train to pass smoothly; with vodka, you could consume an unlimited amount of forage.

Having fought with fat cells all my life, I tried to keep my spirits up, and I often thought about the 30,000 year-old, curvy figure of *The Venus of Willendorf* in the Vienna Natural History Museum. She used to be an aphrodisiac for the Stone Age men. Even now, people from from all over the world come to look at her chuby figure, simila to mine, and admire it. Her body is so different from the delicate Venus painted by Botticelli. His elongated beauty looked as if she went on a strict diet and was shaped at the Reformer Pilates sessions.

Unfortunately, fat cells never disappear – they just shrink. Anything I threw into my mouth immediately made itself at home around my belly or thighs, and wouldn't budge. Freud was right – it's nearly impossible to get rid of our childhood's inheritance. My fat was a dowry from the Soviet past.

Transformed into Sunflowers

28th September 2015,
Battersea, London

The intrusive thoughts about Kovač pushed me to make some efforts in improving my historical facade. "You can't do it on your own. This matter requires professional knowledge." My mind nurse Ella suggested that I should seek an advice from the well-established Image Consultancy.

"After a few hours with the Black Leopard, you will not recognize yourself. They will create a star out of you," and she handed me a card with the relevant contacts. I wasn't prepared to wait even for a day, visualising the impact of my new starlight on Kovač.

I was met at the company's entrance of the Battersea Headquarters by two elegant ladies of an uncertain age. The image consultants looked like film stars from the cover of *Vogue* magazine. They themselves were the best advertising for the services provided.

"We are so glad you made it. I know that you'll benefit enormously from this visit." Maria, the stunning blonde, scrutinised me with her eyes, probably trying to find something good in my image, something she did not need to improve.

The Battersea loft, serving as their work place and living accommodation, occupied the whole top floor of a former warehouse that had recently been transformed into expensive apartments. It was like walking through the setting of a Hollywood production. The stylish interior, lavishly decorated with contemporary art, added confidence that I had chosen the right place for my image revolution.

I had not lost my professional touch after C, and immediately recognised Damien Hirst's early *Spot* paintings. Simple red dots on the white canvas were for some reason considered to be great art, and were amongst the most recognised creations of the artist, together with the infamous shark and sheep sunken in a tank with formaldehyde solution; a severed cow's head that was eaten by maggots released into the cage-like container, and thousands of flies' bodies glued onto the canvas. Hard working Damien managed to sell more than a thousand of these *Spot* pieces, mastering the joy of colour without any requirement of the craft of art. If some 'great' experts – a cartel of greedy gallery owners, art critics and dealers – would not decide that those creations were masterpieces, probably after investing quite a few bucks into Hirst's art, I would consider those works to be a production of sex-deprived teenagers on drugs. As office decorations, they were fine – the random and infinite colour canvas complemented the essence of this consultancy business.

"Do you know that people make up their minds about you within the first ten seconds of the meeting?" The dark-haired consultant was helping me with my jacket. "This means that first impressions have never been more important."

The charmers directed me into a small room packed with colourful draperies, exotic shawls, all shapes and sizes of scarfs, loads of accessories and a small mountain of cosmetics. I was put in front of a round mirror – this time, not just to observe my reality but to create a new one.

"We will help you to discover your most flattering colours and style. We aim to achieve the best possible look for you." For four long hours I was wrapped and unwrapped into different items in a quest for 'the best for me'. At a price! But what did I care?

"The cold shades are not complementing you at all." The use of colour charts gave an impression of a modern scientific approach to this exploration. "Compare it with the light brown, orange and yellow – warm tones. Can you see? You're already shining, and shedding off a whole decade of your face," the brown-haired Anna proclaimed proudly, happy with the achieved results. She obviously loved Van Gogh and wanted me to look like his *Sunflowers*, draping me in the positive colours of life.

After magical manipulations, this small but exquisite team of enchantress-experts came to an interesting conclusion,

"Forget about grey and all its shades. You have to change all your wardrobe of clothes entirely – colours and shapes. No geometrical designs – concentrate on floral, soft, natural lines. From now on, you're buying everything only in warm, autumnal colours. The sparkles of orange, yellow and red will compensate some…" The blonde stopped for a second and then bravely added: "…small imperfections. We all have them, but the secret is to learn the art of hiding those undesirable features." The Black Leopard found the way to present me at my best and even better, to the world, in case the world gave a fuck.

The Finest Instrument for Men

28ᵗʰ September 2015
London, Knightsbridge

I had always preferred Selfridges to Harrods. It felt more intelligent, more sophisticated and less flashy. But the Knightsbridge store rewarded devoted customers with points that could be redeemed and used for various treats! They were my beloved freebies that aroused me like good foreplay.

My hands were full with the distinctive green Harrods bags. They were just right – serving as the leaves to my yellow-orange dresses, my sunflowers, that I had managed to pick up in three morning hours. This rich crop added a good number of points for me, enough to spend at St George's Cafe on the fourth floor of this exquisite place with my friend Ella. The steaks there were really good, and tasted even better being freebies.

The place was unusually empty. That gave us a good chance to talk about very private matters.

"I can't stop thinking about this good guy, my surgeon. What would be appropriate to give him as a 'thank-you' present?" We Slavs have our traditional way to show gratitude. "I need to do something special for him."

"In this country they don't do it, and it's not always expected. Perhaps send him nice flowers or a bottle of good whisky, if you feel you have to."

Ella turned to the menu and ordered the beef tenderloin. She obviously valued her advice very highly.

"No, flowers are more suitable for a woman. For any other doctor I would buy a bottle of good stuff, Black Label, and that would be sufficient. But for Kovač, he is remarkable; I have to do more than that." I felt a strong bond connecting me to my little doctor. "Let's have half a bottle of Merlot, goes well with beef," I generously suggested my own preference.

"That would be lovely. I love this kind of red wine, the earthiness and aftertaste of berries – it's delicious! Tell me more about how you are feeling."

Ella liked to help emotionally damaged people, and today I was her patient. Surprisingly, she couldn't help herself with her broken, twenty-two-year marriage.

"I'm bursting with an enormous gratitude to Mr Kovač and an overwhelming need to see him. I talk to him every day as if he is with me. I see him everywhere. My life makes perfect sense when he is around. Do you remember that song – *Everything I Do, I Do it for You*? I would add – *I Do it with You* – that's how I feel."

Ella took a long sip of wine, "This is actually a song about love. Does he know about your feelings?"

"Not yet. And it's not *love*. He's not my type: short and bald. I fancy tall man."

"Like Freddie?"

I just sighed instead of replying to that question, and continued with my thoughts on Kovač.

"He is simply an amazing person, who possesses qualities I don't have around – kindness and compassion. He is so clever and subtle – he simply reads my mind."

"I think you are deeply in love. It's common for grateful patients to fall for their saviours. Be careful it doesn't grow into an obsession and turn bad – maybe go and see a psychologist."

"I'll be fine. I don't need any shrink! I can talk to my friend. That's enough."

"As your friend, I am not allowed to have proper sessions with you. I have contacts for an extremely good specialist. Just try him. You'll feel the difference." Ella was clearly concerned about me. Since my operation, whenever she and I met up, I was constantly crying. Tears had become an accompaniment to my life.

"Okay, maybe later. Sometimes I feel that I'm losing the balance between dreams and reality, but the dream world seems to be much more attractive." *Recognising your weaknesses shows your strength,* I thought. "Text me his contact details."

"I will. And believe me, your doctor won't accept anything expensive. It's not ethical in this country, especially in the medical profession."

"But he isn't English, he was born in the former Yugoslavia."

"Well... listen... I have to run now. My husband's away tonight and I have to take my little darling Harry on an evening walk."

After three free glasses of delicate wine, Ella had forgotten to tell me that her husband would be away tomorrow, and the day after tomorrow, and the day after that. She rushed out of the door for a harmonious stroll with her spaniel. He was much easier to handle than her own husband, who had fled to a younger woman, leaving behind his ageing wife and an ageing dog.

I was not going to accept Ella's advice on a 'thank-you' gift. I had my own views on what I should do. I'd always thought that Cartier was a mark of something special and distinguished, and could express the highest appreciation and gratitude to the recipient. Possessing Cartier brought you into the world of the powerful and the mighty.

The Cartier boutique in Harrods demonstrated its exclusivity with a set of double doors and a bulletproof glass wall separating it from the rest of the world. A well-dressed security man looked me up and down as if estimating my wealth, trying to work out if I could afford the cosmic prices in his department, or had simply lost my way crossing the road from Zara. My Louis Vuitton handbag acted as an entrance ticket, and he held the door open for me.

Firstly, I glanced at the watches – much too expensive. I set my limit at £500 – full stop. This was enough for a decent gift, and, in any case, it would be the most I'd ever spent on anybody working in the medical profession. The Cartier pens were the closest to my price range. They first seemed to be too insignificant for the great feelings I had for my doctor, but their smart description – 'fine instruments for men' – made them more attractive.

"May I look at this one, black with silver?" I asked the assistant to show me the *Diablo de Cartier* optical illusion fountain pen. *Diablo* made me think it could correspond with Kovač's magical talents. The sales assistant, probably a Japanese lady, whose age was not possible to guess – she was young and old at the same time – rushed over to me. It was clear she worked on commission and knew her subject well.

"This is a new model – beautiful, black composite body, black lacquer and palladium-finish metal."

"How much is it?" I asked with worry in my voice, as this description implied a very high price.

"850 pounds. A Cartier pen is a signature of unique taste in fine accessories. It is worth every pound you'll be paying."

"And that one?" I pointed hopefully to the one looking a bit plainer. "With the gold band."

"Three thousand."

"Is there anything under five hundred?" I started to worry that I might be walking out with the only modestly priced item in the department: the wrapping paper.

"Nothing you'd like."

"I'm looking for a gift for my surgeon, the man who saved

my life. I think he might be embarrassed to accept a gift worth thousands." I already felt I was being selfish for setting my allowance so low for a saved life. My life!

"Look at this. This wonderful pen is solid silver. It will make a very unique and memorable gift for a special person." She knew how to sell. "Do you want to try it?"

I took the 'fine instrument for men' into my hand. The shaft and top button, which was decorated with a blue cabochon, shone like a rare piece of jewellery. It definitely gave this pen an erotic edge, similar to the head of a slick, circumcised penis. And, of course, a 24 carat-gold flexible knob added some extra points to the value of the exquisite model. I pressed it gently to the paper and wrote, 'Dear Andrew'. It left beautiful lines. I thought it would be just right in the hands of my doctor – a special pen for those special hands.

The word 'special' secured the deal. I paid £650. Not cheap. But it was for the best doctor in the world. The pen was beautifully wrapped – that was on its own a performance, like a Japanese tea ceremony. After layers of wrapping, the gift box became five times bigger than the pen itself, making the present look substantial.

With my pen and my new autumnal wardrobe, I was fully equipped to see Mr Kovač. But there was a hurdle to get over first.

I went straight to Harrods' seafood bar to finalise my plan and recuperate from the shopping trip. I went there from time to time for light meals, trying to convince myself that sushi was not fattening. I occupied two seats: one for my arse that felt barely supported by the narrow bar stool, and the second for my Louis Vuitton bag. The trophy bag was probably supposed to last forever. It was a relief to be able to shed its weight for a moment.

I ordered two eel rolls and, before even touching any food, I typed out a hasty e-mail to my surgeon's PA.

Dear Pamina, I would like to see Mr Kovač. I want to thank him for the great job he's done. Do you think it is possible for me to meet the doctor for a few minutes at a convenient time to him?

There was no reply. Pamina guarded the gates to His Majesty, the doctor.

Have I done something wrong? I wondered. I was never sure how gratitude was supposed to be expressed in Brittan. She probably thought I wanted to waste this medical genius's time for a box of chocolates from a petrol station or, at best, Waitrose.

It didn't take me long to realise that the only way to deliver the gift to my doctor was to once again become his patient. That felt painful and unfair, but there was nothing I could do. I sent another e-mail in desperation, feeling like a helpless outsider in this reserved British world,

Should I book an appointment?

Perhaps BUPA would have to squeeze out another £200 to make it possible for me to say 'Thank you' to the doc.

The reply was e-mailed straight away.

Yes, please do.

Walking Tall

28th September 2015, late afternoon
Mayfair, London

As soon as I knew I was about to face Mr Kovač, a panic started growing beneath my breasts, which actually protected a gentle, aching heart. I wanted my doctor to feel that he hadn't wasted his time on saving a plain, 'hormone-fed turkey', but had used his brilliant hands on a worthy, 'free-range', branded woman.

I loved my flats, and I hadn't worn stilettoes for a long time – ten or more years at least. But I wanted to appear slender and glamorous in front of the doc, and a bit of friendly heel-lift was needed.

The first task was to minimise my scary voluptuous size. Three-inch shoes, not quite Louboutin, helped reduce my width and stretch my body in height towards the heavens. There was a price to pay – every step was a struggle. I conducted a short rehearsal at home before stepping out onto the busy streets of London. With every step, there was a risk of a big fall. I really hoped I didn't resemble a clown on piccolo stilts.

My black and silky Basler atlas skirt made my arse look more compact, cutting off an inch from my derriere, unfortunately only as an illusion. Basler had been my favourite shop for years because there you were always elegantly catered for as a size 22. At a price! But they couldn't compare with the crappy granny stuff you get at M&S, or even worse in Evans: a shop for fatties who feel awful about themselves. An out-of-fashion Spandex control panty – my secret weapon in the war of looking good – squeezed another inch back into my body. These devices packed my fat into a smaller shape, sucking me in, cladding my modesty in a smooth shell, hiding cascades of extra layers and curves in the wrong places.

A tigress print on my jacket was rather appropriate – it conveyed my incredible emotional range and passionate personality. The high waistline made my legs look longer, though still not long. I spent time finding matching jewellery. My Marina B semi-circular gold earrings, encrusted with diamonds, and a huge, emerald-cut aquamarine were simply splendid. Diamonds were the hardest stone, possessing spiritual power, known for its properties of protection and healing. The aquamarine complemented my blue eyes and was considered good luck, a promise for eternal youth and happiness – all the qualities I desperately needed.

Not too much! I was warning myself. *Less is more!* So many people had said these words to me during my life, including Freddie, the Methodist.

Maybe I shouldn't wear the two sets of earrings, but nobody could stop me putting two Chanel rings on my fingers. They looked just right to me. Each hand was decorated to assert that a vintage woman of substantial significance should have the real thing. Though when two young girls complimented my Louis Vuitton bag, saying how splendid it was, I replied that I'd love to exchange the designer-label-shit for their young age, and use a plastic bag from Tesco instead.

My final task before the meeting with the doc was to do something about my hair; a fresh cut could nicely deflect attention from my ageing face.

I parked my car at Grosvenor Square; a tenner for two hours would be nothing compared to what I was about to spend. I crossed the square and headed to the Nicky Clarke salon. Expensive, but you get what you pay for. Cheap and skilful was not a combination readily available in Central London. I liked

the red carpet and golden railings by the entrance – it made me feel rather special and even grand from the moment I walked in.

The receptionist greeted me like an old friend, "Good to see you again, Natalia! Your stylist is ready for you. Leave your jacket with Julie and she'll take you straight to the wash."

I hated any procedures involving water at the hairdressers because the youngsters did it, the trainees. My neck was too short for my heavy head, which was filled with a PhD's worth of knowledge, to comfortably hang backwards over the rim of the sink. I dreaded the feeling of hot burning water steaming my brain, cooking it. The 'guys and dolls' doing the washing wore gloves and hardly felt the water temperature with their hands. The head massage they offered with their rubber-coated fingers was far too rough for me to appreciate. I was glad when my hairy jar of brains was wrapped at last with a soft, harmless towel, and I was led to my favourite stylist, Chris, for a miracle transformation.

Chris was twenty-nine and looked gorgeous even without his front teeth, which I liked to think he lost in the battle for the title of the 'best sucker in the hair businesses. He was very cockney, very gay, very lonely and very lovely.

"Chris, darling, cut and blow, whatever you need to do – I want to look at least three days younger! Use all your talents, babe."

Chris could transform me, an old Elecunt, into a phoenix, in thirty minutes or less. The wisdom of life is to die young and beautiful but, of course, to delay that as long as possible. You learn it with age.

"Natalia, my love, where are you going? Anywhere exciting?"

Chris could listen for hours to any nonsense from his lady clients, who all adored him, never mind the great haircuts.

"I'm not sure about exciting. I would call it significant," I replied, then turned the topic to him. "How was your weekend?"

"I went to a fashion show with my girlfriend, then for dinner with a few of the anorexic models."

"Runway models remind me of Alberto Giacometti's sculptures – he liked to chisel away all the flesh from their bodies."

"Giacometti? Sounds familiar. Is he from the model agency?"

"He was," I lied, not wanting to disappoint my barber by revealing that the sculptor was a dead artist.

"They don't eat. I left hungry."

Chris kept telling me about his life with his girlfriend, who was twenty years older than him. He was a kind chap and wanted to convey that older women like me still had a chance to attain a much younger companion. Chris wasn't aware that his colleagues had already informed me that he was not a women's man. It was fine with me – he was a women's friend – compassionate, creative, cheerful – and had a brilliant pair of hands. He made his living helping women, just like my doctor, but working on a different floor of their departments.

"Shall we cut off a little more off today, darling? I would recommend a full recut for my lady." He actually said "'ecommend a full 'ecut', as he'd lost his 'r' sounds with his teeth.

"If it's possible to trim my age as well as my hair – cut it all! Shave me, darling!" I caught myself speaking differently in this posh salon, adopting a vocabulary filled with 'darling' and 'dears', like in TV soaps about rich, ageing wives.

"Oh yes, shorter hair will make you look much younger."

Chris's scissors were traveling fast along my neck. Click, click, click and click.

"What other delights are on offer, darling?" I asked. "Keratin, *spermatin* – any of those?" After my operation, I could not miss an opportunity for a sexy, twisted joke.

"Keratin blow dry will make your hair smoother. Shall we go for that?" The hair-master was trying hard to sell some expensive products and services.

"But spermatin can make my privates smoother." I knew it was vulgar, but I couldn't stop.

"You can't find that product at the hairdressers," my stylist replied automatically. *That was honest!* Chris was right; the guys in this profession took no interest in my gender. But even without this absent, rare substance a younger woman was emerging in the mirror. My hair looked shiny, stylish and expensive.

"Darling! You made it just right. I feel 39 and a half – like I still haven't passed my seduce-by date! It will be some time before I have to blow out the candles on my 40th birthday cake. I am flying off, I have to go!"

To Chris's delight, I squeezed a note into his hand, an amount equal to the number of years he managed to knock off. I picked up my Louis Vuitton bag in one hand, not forgetting about the package with the gift in the other.

Before leaving the luxurious hair palace, I couldn't resist the pleasure of popping into the glamorous toilet, decorated like a royal privy. With all the money I'd spent, I allowed myself a small souvenir from Nicky's, a token of appreciation as a customer – a soft and fluffy white napkin. It would make a wonderful duster in my London apartment. A glass of water with fresh orange, on the house, saved me £2 off my heavy bill. These little freebies gave me a higher degree of satisfaction with the services provided in this heavenly world.

I headed to the appointment with my doctor happy, fully equipped and groomed. I looked like an art installation, like a big, glamorously clad woman stretching up into the sky with her killer heels and volume of hair. It never crossed my mind that this contemporary, costly creation could scare, rather than impress, the petite doc.

I Like You, Too

28th September 2015, later in the day
Queen's Hospital, Central London

I found Kovač sitting at his desk in a simple blue shirt with a huge, unfashionable collar, writing notes in his journal. He looked tired and sweaty from working hard throughout the day. My 7.30 appointment was his last. He had worked a twelve-hour shift as usual. It seemed that he would always try to accommodate everyone who needed him without delay, even if it resulted in an inhumanly long day. I saw a different man from the one who had come to see me in the hospital room. This one was softer and younger. His cheeks were slightly pink and looked very gentle.

"It's so nice to see you, doctor." Kovač nodded a polite greeting.

"Here's my little 'thank-you.'" I handed him the gift and hastily added, "This is a Russian tradition."

I always felt uncomfortable giving gifts to people I did not know that well, which is why I decided to get rid of it straight away.

"That's very nice of you but you shouldn't have done it. I mean – you don't have to, you know that," the doc said, placing my gift under his desk and moving it further away with his foot, probably to save me from further confusion.

"How are you feeling, Natalia? Is anything bothering you?"

"No, all is fine, as much as it can be in my circumstances. Thanks to you, Mr Kovač."

"I thought we were on a first-name basis now?"

"Yes, Andrew."

The guy in front of me was so familiar; I felt like I could talk to him about any aspect of my life. I wanted to touch him across the table, hug him and tell him that he was a good boy. The aura between us was so warm and comfy. I had a feeling I had known him before, for a hundred years perhaps, in a previous life.

"Doctor, I like you so much!" Overwhelmed by his presence, I announced passionately to my own surprise. These words simply jumped out of my mouth. This 'so much' sounded like a whole choir of women's voices in a Greek tragedy. I had almost frightened myself. Having lived for many years as a Wicked Wife, it was strange to suddenly see myself as a Juliet. I wasn't expecting much in return, and definitely not what came next.

"I like you, too!" Kovač blushed. No, he went red all over! He pronounced these words within a sigh. It seemed to erupt from his mouth spontaneously and he looked just as surprised as me.

My heart raced. I wished he had said it with his arms around me but he kept his distance. Then our eyes met. We gazed at each other for a minute. His were so blue – like the sky. I just wanted to fall into them and jet into a flight together. Shakespeare expressed all my feelings: "*I do love nothing in the world so well as you*".

***

It was the second time in my long existence that I had made the first move in revealing my feelings to a man. The first occasion had happened many years ago, in a different life. I was sixteen; he was forty-four – my father's friend and colleague. Victor was the member of the Soviet Academy of Sciences, with a bright international career. He was a tall, good-looking man, locked in a childless marriage with an unattractive biologist, eight years his senior. He had been desperately suffocating in this relationship for a long time, so I'd been told. From the perspective of my younger teenage self, his wife was an old witch who kept my prince in chains.

We used to go out – my parents, Victor and me – sometimes even with his 'wicked old bag' walking somewhere behind. I loved to feel his attention that I was lacking at home. Fellow schoolmates were of no interest to me; they were sixteen-year-old idiots. I adored my dad, and for a big part of my life I was looking for someone like him.

Victor would often stare at me and wouldn't be able to take his eyes away for a long while. As a young teenager, I was an ugly duckling. My stunningly beautiful mother never missed a chance to remind about it, "What a pity, you haven't inherited my looks, but at least you have your father's brain." She would repeat this many times with a smile, often in front of other people. To her surprise, by the age of fifteen I started to blossom. Victor was the first man to notice and admire this change.

"You are so beautiful, Nata!" he told me, and that created the fatal attraction. The next time I saw him, I put a small note into his hand that read, 'I love you'.

My parents, busy with their high-flying careers, never had time to talk to me much. Victor was using every minute to teach me about the world, including his own – his work, his interests, his friends.

"Read this book by Thor Heyerdahl; I bought it especially for you. I met him personally. This book tells all about his great adventurers and discoveries." He awoke my mind and made me feel good about myself and worthy. That's mostly what we love people for.

There was a short, scribbled note hidden inside the book, 'I will be waiting for you at six pm on Tuesday.'

Below this, he had written the address of his marital home. I felt thrilled and excited. I wasn't myself for the next two days. I couldn't concentrate on anything at school or at home. Everything was slipping through my fingers, literally.

"You've broken my favourite vase!" I heard the ear-splitting scream of my mother. She lifted her hand and was ready to give me a slap. I had received these lovely 'kisses' since I was very young; an unfortunate consequence for any trivial mistake, or even if I had to go to the loo at night. "You woke me up, cunt!" And slap, slap, slap. She loved pulling my long blonde hair and pushing my face against the wall, as it didn't leave a physical trace. Much later in life, guiding at Tate Modern, whenever I saw Sheela Gowda's work *Behold,* made from 4000 metres of human hair, a shiver would run through my body.

Once Victor appeared in my life, I was not afraid of her anymore. With the broken shards of vase around us, I caught my mother's hand about to slap me and squeezed it.

"If you ever touch me again, I'll hit you back."

She did not even try to resist me. She noticed the change in me that I now spoke with conviction, and surrendered. She never again threatened me, and while I wished this meant a happy ending, she instead resorted to more subtle psychological torment.

I took a taxi to Victor's apartment – my father had spoiled me secretly with pocket money. During the twenty-minute ride, my heart was unable to cope; it felt like it was about to stop.

Victor met me by the entrance doors, shivering in the winter evening. It was dark, very dark – darkness on white snow – I remembered that day very well. With many shadows around, stretching up the street.

I had been in his flat with my parents. But this time, it was different – just him and me. Victor wasn't in a hurry. I learned that his wife was abroad at a biologists' conference, delivering an important report about mammal embryos. They didn't have children together; she was too preoccupied with the reproduction of other species. We walked up the stairs to the second floor. His flat was number thirteen. Since then, thirteen has been my lucky number.

"You are so cold – let me make you a cup of tea." He went to the kitchen. I followed like a shadow, afraid to lose sight of him for even a second.

We Russians loved having our tea and meals in the kitchen – it was the traditional place to gather with friends. But Victor wanted to stress that my visit was a special occasion. He took out expensive, rarely used porcelain tableware – cups and a teapot, loaded them onto a tray, and brought it into the dining room to the big round table.

The tea was left to get cold. He came from behind and kissed my neck, then turned me, shivering, to face him, and my lips were immediately sucked in. I still remember the taste of his mouth and the sight of it closing in on me. Victor pulled me out of my chair and led me to the bedroom. The zip on my dress got stuck, I remember. We struggled with it in silence for a while. He put me on the bed and I saw him naked. It was a shock, as I'd never seen the male tool in reality, so close to me. It felt very scary, like jumping from the thirtieth floor.

"Have you ever done this before?" he asked, covering me gently with his body.

I lied, "Yes, a year ago or a little more." I was worried that he wouldn't want me if at the age of sixteen I was still a virgin. *If no other man was interested, he won't be either*, I thought.

"You're all mine now," Victor whispered as he entered me, sending a jolt of pain from my cunt to my heart. "I'll do anything for you." He couldn't find enough loving words; he realised I'd lied. He was a responsible man.

It was my mother who ruined our blossoming relationship. Somehow she found out, probably from our housekeeper, who would notice how often Victor used to call.

"He is a cheat, a fake!" She told me that the man I loved so much was having an affair with her at the same time. I never found out if it was true, but I overheard her talking to him on the phone, flirting and arranging a possible rendezvous. After that, Victor simply disappeared. His name was no longer spoken of in our family. I was made to believe that he had betrayed me.

It took me years to recover from the wounds and heartbreak. Decades later, I still had the traces of a razor on my wrists. Victor spent at least a month in a sanatorium after a nervous breakdown. As a result, he developed horrendous sores all over his face, head and body. I went to visit him.

"Go! Go away!" That was all he said, without even looking at me. For him, I was a cunt who had brought disaster into his life. Everything beautiful and happy between us had disappeared. I never saw him again.

A few years ago, I read his obituary in a Russian newspaper, which grieved for 'the distinguished Russian historian'. For many years, I tried to find a man who looked like him, falling into the trap of much older, intellectual and powerful personalities.

After this traumatic breakdown, I grew a thick skin shield over my heart, and tried to take revenge on men. Granny used to tell me, "In a relationship, only one is in love – the other only allows themselves to be loved. It's never equally balanced. The one who is in love always suffers. The one who accepts the partner's love is the lucky one, who would be spared of the heartbreak."

With all my men after Victor, I managed to stay the cool one – I just allowed them to love me and lavish their generosity on me. I followed my granny's joke that the best exercise for your spirit was counting money. It dissolves all pain and improves one's appetite, wardrobe, appearance and living conditions.

I was a cunt.

***

With Kovač at his desk, everything was moving in slow motion. He was pretending to scribble something, hiding behind his job. He closed his eyes, slowly sinking into his thoughts, probably analysing his feelings. Then he licked his dry lips and whispered without daring to look at me.

"But we are patient and doctor. We can't have any relationship other than that."

His unexpected confession made me feel for him even more.

"Would you allow me to do anything for you? Maybe drive you to work or iron your shirts?"

He sunk into his chair, unsure of what to say, and hid his face back into his papers.

"Or maybe you are involved with some charity? I'd love to contribute as much as I can."

"I'm a very busy man, Natalia."

He sounded sombre and very uptight. It was clear that my doctor was already regretting his moment of weakness. He looked uncomfortable and was closing up. But it was too late; the door to my well of feelings had already been unlocked. I wondered whether I would have fallen for him so deeply had he not pronounced those few words.

Kovač held his head down, hiding his eyes and not wishing to show me any more than he should. A few beads of sweat rolled down his forehead and landed on his Charlie Chaplin-style moustache. I wanted to lick them off, but he quickly wiped them away with his handkerchief. He stood up and stepped towards me as if pushing me to the door.

"Come and see me in three weeks. You will need a proper check-up then." My doctor was giving me the cold shoulder. I felt alienated and alone. I had to go.

I heard him exhale heavily; I heard his heavy steps, as he walked back to his desk. I could visualise him sitting down with his hands on his temples, unsure how to deal with this difficult patient of Russian descent. I knew he was angry with himself for his emotional slip and he, probably, considered it unprofessional. But with his nice sensitive nature, he clearly couldn't bear to hurt his patient after they had already gone through hell. He knew that these wounded fairies, desperate to believe they were still women, needed magic, which only love could bring into their lives.

I nearly fell out of his room. The door was shut in my face. I turned around – a nurse was standing just a few steps away. I could see that she was perfectly aware why my visit had lasted so long, almost like a full movie, a 1950s Hollywood melodrama. She was trained to assist and protect her adorable doctor from his patients' nymphomaniac passions.

"What a nice doctor!" I uttered on my way out.

"He is indeed!" The nurse looked happy that we agreed.

Things I've Never Done Before

3rd October 2015
Cobham, Surrey

"Kiai!" I shrieked, together with the other participants of the body combat class half my age. I repeated this word like a ritual prayer, going through that hard physical drill. The word helped me to increase intensity and focus my mind. In a way, it protected me from the painful real world.

"Kiai!" – *I need to survive!* That was my translation. I was whacking and whacking the empty space in front of me. I set my target, thinking about C cells and fat cells as well. Murder – I was training in martial arts.

My next appointment with my consultant was three long weeks away, so I spent my time counting, crossing off each day as it passed. I regretted that maths was my weakest subject at school, and it didn't help that, when you're in love, weeks count like years. I had to keep myself busy and that was not easy.

Ella diagnosed me straight away,

"Natalia, all your big emotions are the results of a hormonal imbalance and post-operational shake-up. It'll calm down with time. But you need to be careful. It is so easy to slip into a deep depression." My clever psychic friend was giving me a lecture over the phone. It was handy to have a friend who could scientifically explain the state of my mind and soul. "Instead of crying for your doctor, transform yourself and fast!"

She was in a rush as she had to take her beloved spaniel out. Her dog always stood in the way of our meeting in person. Yet our brief conversation made an impression, and I felt compelled to indeed transform myself; to remould my big chunk of flesh into a woman. A woman Kovač might like.

Task Number One was to lose the shitting weight. I was off to a decent start – I'd come out of the operating theatre two kilos lighter. Black leggings and a black t-shirt made me look slimmer, and attending an evening class helped to skip an evening meal. Before C, I used to do Pilates and Body Balance, but after the op, I had started to call those classes 'lazy bums workouts'.

After my conversation with Ella, I switched off the TV and dialled my club's number. It was late afternoon, but I hoped that it still would be possible to enrol for the evening class.

"Boxing is full. There is one place for a weightlifting class at half past seven. Can you make it?"

"Fine! I'll do my best." It felt adventurous to try something new, and I did not like to spend the evening eating. *Let's see what I can lift.*

I hung up the phone and saw Freddie listening in, clearly suspicious of my new activities, which were so contrary to the elements of my previous lifestyle.

"Are you sure this is suitable after your operation?" he said, then turned to our son and sneered, "Your mother is going mad or has bipolar."

My husband expected me to serve him dinner when I was loading my gym bag into the car. Through the window, I saw him stood in the light of the open fridge, searching for an appetite quencher with a rather disappointed face. If I stayed at home, I would have neither the company nor entertainment – my Chairman enjoyed friendship with his telly and the company of his gorgeous hairy girlfriends, who would stare at the screen for hours watching all the programs together with their master. My absence would be forgotten a few minutes later.

At the gym, I loaded weights on a bar: twenty kilograms! I lifted it, then rested it on my shoulders and stared at the huge mirror on the opposite wall. I did have the look of a professional weightlifter, as you see them at sports events with more than two-hundred kilograms on their shoulders. Fat thighs, hanging belly, substantial tits – a Chinese mandarin, no less.

"You can add more. You'll be fine. Over time you should increase the weight." My very masculine, gay instructor was ready to help.

And I did, indeed! Three obsessive weeks of intensive training brought about a very unpleasant outcome.

The Big Reveal

15th October 2015
Cobham, Surrey;
Central London

They say 'no pain no gain', and yes! I gained that pain! In my rear end! Wiping my bum, I felt that there was something unusual and terrifying sticking out down there. I panicked. I didn't tell anybody about it to start with. I just couldn't face discussing my backside problems again; I was still mentally recovering from 'constipation-gate'. Talking about my equipment around the front was always okay, but I wanted my backdoor to stay taboo.

"Not again!" I screamed so loudly that if someone happened to hear me, they would think it was the roar of a wounded bull, a Minotaur!

"Not this C disease!" I was afraid even to pronounce all six letters together.

I attempted to explore my treasures using a big mirror in our conservatory. A big wooden pot with a palm was in the way and I moved it to the side to get a full view. I squatted but I could see nothing. I used my fingers, aiming to touch the bump and evaluate the extent of the damage. It felt like hardened grapes adorned my butthole. I tried to push them back in. Hopeless! They kept popping out again and again.

Through the windows I caught sight of our gardener – a handsome ex-policeman in his late forties – taking interest in my pursuit, staring with a smile at my naked bottom. I waved at him, pretending all was fine and nothing was out of the usual.

"Do you want a cup of tea?" I mimicked with my lips and hands. He pointed to his watch, indicating that he was busy. Naturally, he had to attend to the garden as he had lost some time on admiring my backside manoeuvres and manipulations.

In order to cause no further distractions, I moved upstairs for more in-depth research of my unpleasant condition. I lay on my side on the bedroom floor and twisted my rusted hip as much as possible – I could see nothing – my bum was too far away. I resorted to calling my friend Ella to give her a full report, though I knew that backside was not her subject.

"Perhaps it's only haemorrhoids?" she said, surprisingly-knowledgeable in the butt-hole problems. "Just wait a day or two and, if it doesn't go back to normal, see a specialist." Then she hung up, leaving me to figure out the rest on my own.

What the fuck are these specialists called – the butt saviours?

I couldn't remember the word 'proctologist' straight away, but later it did come back to me. Occasionally losing my words scared me even more than my backside problems. I hated the thought of going gaga, and didn't want to fall in love with a neurologist.

The receptionist at the proctologist's delivered some bad news over the phone,

"The next appointment I can offer you is in three weeks' time."

"This is not the NHS! I am on BUPA."

"I know, dear. But the doctor is very busy."

It was reassuring to find out that you weren't the only one with cherries in your arse.

"I had womb cancer surgery two months ago and I think it may be cancer again, this time in my backside."

The word C worked immediately.

"Oh! You should have said. I do have a cancellation tomorrow morning at ten. Can you make it?"

I would have preferred an immediate consultation, but the following morning was acceptable. I took some sleeping pills and set my alarm for eight in the morning.

I arrived at the hospital ten minutes early, but with appointments running behind, I had a twenty-minute wait. I had to spend the whole time in a standing position!

"Hello, Mrs Fitzcock!" A handsome Indian man in blue scrubs eventually approached me. "Call me Vimal!"

He went to shake my hand, but at the last moment changed his mind and just pointed to the direction of his consulting room. Perhaps he remembered that his hands were inside someone's bum just a few minutes ago. I wondered why such a handsome guy would like to spend his life digging inside sickly bottoms.

"Please, sit down!"

"Doctor, I wish I could! But the chair looks hard. I'd much prefer to stand if you don't mind. And please, don't start asking me about my age. I provided all that information at the reception."

"If you can't sit, can you lie down?"

"Doctor, I can lie down but you probably want me to demonstrate my bottom?"

"Isn't that why you came to see me?" the arse doc said, joking with me. He was right. My previous visit to the gynaecologist now seemed like a trip to the cinema. This was a real act of bravery.

"I've gone to a great length to preserve my arse. It's never been subjected to an inspection or anything else; I have kept it private."

He laughed. "Perhaps the time has come for the 'big reveal'. I just have to call the nurse."

"What? Someone is going to witness you probing into my backside?"

"It's important to always have a third party present during

these procedures. My medical tutor told me that this is the only way to protect your career. I follow his advice."

"Nobody will be interested in penetrating my old arse for pleasure! At present it's simply impossible – the entrance is barricaded by a bunch of bombs."

"I understand you, but either we follow procedure or I won't be able to help you."

"This is so degrading." I said. It was hard for me to comply with these arrangements, even after going through my horrendous operation. "Can you sedate me at least?"

"Mrs Fitzcock, this doesn't make sense. Most patients in your position accept this policy and are happy to go ahead with the examination, no matter how many people need to be present in the room."

"Fine – I'll allow this group expedition into my arse," I sighed, defeated.

"Good decision!" the butt doctor victoriously pronounced, standing above me like Perseus, who turned Ariadne to stone. Doctor Vimal was obviously entertained by my resistance. He took a few minutes to stick something metal into my backside.

"It is definitely not cancer. Just a haemorrhoid. We can book you for an operation -"

"No!" I screamed like a wounded wolf.

"– otherwise it will probably dissolve on its own."

I wondered how Vimal took his tea breaks – if I was in his shoes, tea and coffee would remind me of diluted shit. Ironically, Vimal is a Hindi word meaning 'clean' or 'pure'. This lovely name probably helped him eat and drink without much concern for where his fingers had been all day. I needed to give my butt some TLC after that 'delicious' visit and decided to stop lifting heavy weights. I moved on to a new trimming activity.

Slimnastics Drills

17th October 2015
Cobham, Surrey

"Shake it, shake it, shake it harder!" The Zumba class teacher, a rather heavy middle-aged Asian woman, was throwing her big breasts from side to side like two heavy melons. She was sweating from trying to inspire us, thrusting her Rubenesque body with great fire.

The loud music I used to complain about before my operation didn't bother me anymore. I actually enjoyed how it knocked all negative thoughts out of my head for a while. The melodies of rock and pop corresponded quite well with the younger and sexier me, emerging out of the sweat. The word 'sexy' did not seem frightening either; all the movements in these passionate dancing drills were rather seductive.

My Zumba shaking was particularly impressive. It had some unique qualities – I had never worn a bra in my life. I kept my tits up naturally, without any supportive cloth, and they were impressively flying in different directions, exceeding even the teacher's span. I noticed that my 'darlings' attracted a lot of curiosity from the other Zumba participants. Slim, young girls with their breasts ironed, so that no one could notice them, observed me with jealousy. I could see an unmistakable expression on their faces – 'What is that fat mamma doing here? She forgot to put her bare necessities on'.

It was my mother who gave me advice when I was a teenager, repeating it for many years with a demonstration as a follow-up, "Never ever wear a bra. It will ruin your breasts. The bra will weaken the natural muscles and they will hang like a goat's udder. We, the Popov women, do not need it. Our breasts stand up and hard on their own without any support."

And they did! Indeed!

The dancing instructor promised that we would burn 800 calories in this 'shaking hour' if we pushed hard during these 'slimnastics' drills. Looking at her baroque aesthetic and apple-shaped body, I was not sure if she herself was doing enough. We were both 'big' girls, Delilahs and Venuses from Rubens' paintings. When I showed his works at the National, I could not avoid thinking that my GP would describe all the ladies on the canvas of this seventeenth century master as heavily obese, and would threaten them with soon being struck with diabetes. With my slightly protruding belly and the fat deposited on my hips and buttocks, I had so much in common with those baroque beauties.

I tried my best to reach my calorie goal, and frantically copied the teacher's movements, while dreaming about my dinner, particularly vividly during the last ten minutes of the class.

It took me no more than twenty minutes to get back to my country house. I reached the front gates and they opened slowly like in a Hollywood movie from my childhood. I could often spot a fox crossing the road to our house – it lived nearby, it was our neighbour. The full, bright moon stared from the sky, giving the countryside a dusting of magic and mystery. It was looking at me, pushing me to think about the past.

Saved by Rottweilers

Twenty five years earlier,
London

When I came to this country, I was over thirty. I was broody, and longed for a baby. I needed to find a suitable dad. In the early nineties online dating wasn't in existence. To achieve your happiness, you needed to do a lot of hard jobs with your own hands. For the whole year I had to commit myself to a boring and exhausting search through the numerous love-seekers posts, and writing endless replies. In English! Not an easy task for a newcomer to Britain.

These days, if you use dating apps, you would receive numerous dick pics with all sorts of mickeys (from the Mikey Mouse to an elephant trunk). But at my time, I used to receive the whole novels with unsolicited descriptions in writing of all sorts of male appendages. It was a 24-hour job to select the best of British.

At first, to save time, I used carbon copying paper and just changed clients' box numbers, provided instead of their names. It didn't take me long to realise that a handwritten letter would add a personal touch and create a much better impression. I transformed my approach and fully committed to it, changing the list of the hobbies to match the requirements of a particular ad. If a gent was interested in museums or the opera it was easy to find a common interest. I would write:

Dear whoever, a 30-year-old glamorous blonde, medium build (you needed to bend the truth to achieve your aim), *an art historian, looking for a long-lasting relationship and maybe more.*

I love opera; I am a keen theatre-goer and wouldn't miss any exhibition in London and beyond.

Deep down, I'd have preferred to meet a guy whose main interest was his job. That would allow him to afford our future son's education and a decent home to raise him. If a bloke turned out to be too arty, there would be a great danger that he wouldn't meet my parental expectations at all.

If an ad stated that a desperate guy preferred the country life, I would have to lie a bit, stretching both my knowledge and imagination, and ensure he envisioned us hand in hand on our future walks in the Chilterns or the Cotswolds. I drew on my knowledge of art.

One of the valuable resources was Gainsborough's *Mr and Mrs Andrews* painting, which depicted an idyllic pastoral scene with a happy couple surrounded by their dog and nature. Everything a country guy would fall for.

My substantial experience in art research helped me to prepare myself for a meeting with each suitor. Some nasty bastards ignored my intelligent approach and dared to ask what size I was. Stating size twelve was a lie and a half as I was size fourteen in my dreams and sixteen in reality. It was a twenty-four-hour job to meet with a selection of the best of British. My Soviet discipline helped me organise the day and fit in endless lunches, dinners and afternoon teas – the proper ones, even occasionally at The Ritz or The Savoy. It was a 'no' to the Yates' wine bar clients, or the dukes of the Wetherspoon.

"If a man invites you to a cheap venue or just for a drink, it means he's arranging these rendezvous often, maybe daily, and does not want to spend a lot of money," my newly acquired friend Dasha, with ten years of husband-searching experience still in a progress, was teaching me over the phone. "It's unlikely that he would focus his attention on one particular lady. For such species the process, rather than a result is of interest. Those guys will, probably, never stop in their explorations of the un-known."

In fact, she was bloody right, even though her own search for happiness had never successfully ended.

When Freddie first contacted me, he was happy to take me for a dinner straight away. Clearly, it was a special occasion for him. I thought, *Even if the guy is shit, at least the steak will be good.*

Freddie's ad in the Telegraph read:

Company director, 40 plus, 6ft 2, looking to have the wind back in his hair.

I wondered if he was prepared to have the wind in his pockets soon.

"Choosing to advertise in this newspaper and not in the Time Out already indicated a person of wealth and status." I received Dasha's approval to reply to this ad. I asked her to keep me company and join me for dinner.

"Well, that's sounds like a good choice! Let's help the desperate company director to have his hair perk up again. Will he be ok with another diner?" I took it as a 'yes' from her. I knew she wouldn't pass up a chance to a freebie meal of quality.

"Who gives a monkey's?" Thirty years ago, I could command men and submit them to my desires and necessities.

Freddie was already waiting inside, occupying the entire large round table all by himself. I spotted him straight away. Tall and attractive, with curly dark hair, my new acquaintance looked prosperous and confident. Yet, he was in demand of urgent help with his bursting desires, which obviously caused him a lot of inconvenience. As soon as he saw me, he immediately stepped out. At that time, I did not need to twist my information too much – I was recognizable. A little lie about my parameters did not put Freddie off.

"Hi! My cousin Dasha came to visit me today. Would you mind her dining with us?" I asked.

The guy produced a happy smile, "No problem at all." – He obviously was not worried about a heavier bill.

I buckled with relief. Later I realised that, as a shrewd businessman, he probably estimated the increased value of a double offer: two ladies for one exhausting trip to London.

My future husband was direct with his intentions and expectations – he was looking for stable hanky-panky outside of his marital bed. 'Having the wind back' should have been translated as 'having a good fuck'. According to his pitiful stories, the bed had stayed empty and cold for many years.

"My wife has denied me sex for the last few years," Freddie informed us during the first course of the dinner, trying to justify his choice to advertise. "If she'd only lie on her back for a few minutes for a quickie, I wouldn't have started looking for someone else on the side."

"No joy with the other women in your life?" I was surprised that he needed an advert to meet somebody; he was tall, wealthy and healthy. An attractive company boss!

"Pretty secretaries are usually ready to do little extras," Dasha added. It seemed that she appreciated not only the food and expensive wine, but took a great interest in the guy too.

"Out of the question! It's wrong to mix pleasure and work." Freddie clearly kept his morals at his work place. Desperately trying to subdue the bulge in his trousers during board meetings, he had started this little 'Lonely Hearts' adventure, like an ambulance coming to the rescue.

After a glass of wine our host felt relaxed and told us that the first reply to his ad had come from a twenty-year-old girl.

"Bugger, she was younger than my daughters. I threw her letter into the bin."

After this honest revelation I noted that my future husband definitely was not a pervert. He was a decent man, who wanted a comfortable fuck with a comfortable person.

The second letter he received was from a thirty-year-old (so she said) German lady with a beautiful name: Janelle. That was where her beauty ended as this frau looked like an old crow. Yet Freddie couldn't afford to be too fussy. He never asked ladies for their photos beforehand.

"Every time I went on a blind date," he confessed, "I told myself that looks could deceive." After meeting Janelle, he deeply regretted this decision.

"She was much older than me! A completely unfuckable person; only when blindfolded could you have sex with this creature, punished by God." He shortened dinner with the frau to half a starter, and made a quick retreat.

Freddie, the shrewd businessman, was trained to overcome difficulties and disappointments, even on such a big scale. He intended to wade through all the candidates to the bitter end.

The next object of promising love was an English rose, Joanna, who spoke in a posh manner, hardly moving her upper lip. From the moment she said, 'Hello', Freddie was ready to do a runner. Our host, the Methodist, started to hate her and all that her South Kensington postcode represented to him. Yet, the pressure building below his belt pushed him toward the bedroom. The lady, the English lamb, screamed during sex as if being screwed by a team of rugby players. Freddie needed to save his eardrums and his manhood from permanent impairment.

Amazingly, this episode did not encourage him to become a Catholic monk. Only three days later, he was back on the trail of adventure, and drove to Ealing to meet Mariam, a thirty-five-year-old dog lover.

Dear Freddie, she wrote to him, *I live alone, with my lovely pets.*

The dear lady forgot to mention that 'lovely' translated to two huge studs: Rottweilers. During Freddie's visit, these beasts became rather jealous of a new man in their mistress's bed. That substantially lowered my future husband's sexual appetite for the evening. He wasn't comfortable unzipping his trousers in these hostile surroundings.

The last blow to Freddie's stiffened rifle was the presence of the strangers in the bedroom, as six little puppies crawled and shat on newspapers plastered all over the carpet.

"All I remember from that night was the fear of my mickey being bitten off, and the 'pleasure' of cleaning up a pile of shit…"

After all Freddie had gone through in his search for a sexual marvel, he didn't give a fuck about a few extra pounds around my arse.

"You're a fairy compared to the witches I've met."

So he said.

The Boots Adventure

25th October 2015
Central London

After my childbearing organs were removed, a huge shake up of my hormones launched an obsessive invasion of hunger upon me. It did not affect my stomach. This time it was my damaged cave, which wanted to be fed and speedily launched into action. I simply couldn't stop thinking about sex in all its forms and variations and couldn't cope with keeping my knickers on. All I wanted to do was ride anything that stuck out of a flat surface. It was like the paintings of *Zips* by Barnett Newman, who saw life like I did at the time – in phallic verticals. I sexualised everything – objects of art, words, actions. All my dreams turned into one long thrusting affair. *For God's sake! Did I need to have cancer to discover my loving relationship with sex?*

I was rather curious as to whether there was something new inside of me. *Did Kovač insert some kind of Perpetuo Mobile into my cunt-hole before he made the necessary repairs? Or was I given some libido enchanting pills by mistake instead of painkillers?* I felt a great need to explore this further and to get the truth out in volumes – enough for a second PhD, this time in Kinetic Studies of Sexual Capacities after Full Hysterectomy.

I didn't dare look to my husband for help. Our sex life wasn't exactly sizzling. It had seized up. As soon as my bum had recovered I had to take matters into my own hands.

My trip to Boots on Sunday was an adventure all on its own. It was a blind date with something unknown or something I'd completely forgotten. I walked into a Marble Arch branch like a petty thief looking behind my shoulder. It felt that everyone was watching me and judging as I scanned the shelves for the right items to bring me happiness, one for a recreational use by a seasoned woman. On the way, a few bottles of lubricant soon flew into my shopping basket. They had the responsible job to perform the unlocking of the rusted door, which had been left in a poor condition after the operation.

I was aware that my sexual appetite wouldn't be quenched solely at home by myself, so I had to think about proper protection. Not against attacks from wild beasts or prevent pregnancy – the latter being less likely, but against bugs and viruses, the ones which existed outside of computers.

One brand attracted my attention – Love Sex by Durex. The packaging looked promising – 'ribbed & dotted for extra stimulation'. It sounded comforting, like an old knitting pattern and aide for 'shag and go' chaps to stop their needles dropping a stitch. The box held six condoms – this quantity, obviously, was not sufficient. I had to put six boxes in my basket to feel comfortable and be prepared for my sexual pursuits; I hoped that this would be just about enough. I was in the market for a brave explorer, ready to bury deep into my greedy cave.

Then I spotted it on the next shelf: the Micro Wand Vibrator. Nice and compact, with three adjustable speeds. I took this sex-tech item out of the plastic box and put it gently into my palm. The size was just right for my damaged equipment.

This could be my stairway to heaven, I thought.

It was a bit on the small side, but for the first time after all these years on a strict sexual diet, spiced with the Kovač's knife, it would be sensible not to overestimate my capacity. The three different speeds would allow me to customise my reintroduction to this lost experience. I wondered if this miniature dick might ease the sexual insecurities of the country's male population. The huge dildos I saw in Soho could emasculate most British gents, who wouldn't be able to match up to that grand scale.

At the checkout, the cashier, a young girl – eighteen, no more – looked with surprise at the items I was paying for.

"Do you have a Boots card?" she managed to squeeze out.

"Thanks for reminding me. With the extra points, I'll be able to get an extra pack of lube for free."

The sales girl turned red. If she followed contemporary art, I wonder if she might have linked me to Sarah Lucas's sculpture *Pauline Bunny*. Instead of a head and a brain, a provocative female torso dressed in black stockings had two long ears, looking like monstrous phalluses.

"Is there anything else I can help you with?" That was all she could muster. The youngster probably thought that I was there to collect my medicine on a free prescription and had used my senior citizen Oyster Card to get to the store. To cheer her up I 'penetrated' her with a question. My turn.

"Dear, I was not able to find a larger vibrator. Do you think you can help? You see, at my age they become like an aspirin – a medicine for all sorts of diseases – depression, rejection, life disappointment, lack of libido, early impotence. Have you heard of those? They fuck you up for years as soon as you reach my age. Do try to stay 49 and a half for as long as possible. The half-a-century border is a real scare. Don't you agree? I think all these goodies in my basket should come as a complimentary gift to all couples when they get married, and as a birthday present to all spinsters older than 25. With this vibrating *medicine* in their pockets, British men would feel much braver to engage with women. This eventually will increase the British population." I was so proud of my speech. I put my geometrically shaped, heavily loaded Prada bag in front of the counter – a great statement of confidence. I felt almost like Margaret Thatcher.

The girl was frozen in shock, but I felt no shame or guilt. I believed that I had lectured her well and given her good, motherly wisdom for life, worth a ton of gold.

***

On the drive back to my country home, I was in a happy mood, looking forward to the start of my sexual awakening. As I stopped at the traffic lights, I noticed two nice guys in a blue Ford Sierra next to me. They flashed their eyes at my chest, obviously finding something interesting there. I remembered that I did have a lovely pair of tits and immediately straightened my back, pushing my chest forward. BBC Radio Two was blaring out: '*If you got it, flaunt it*' – the right song for that moment. I was giving those young testosterone-soaked riders a better chance to admire my assets. Out of the spotlight, my gorgeous hills faced a boring existence. Adrenaline rushed through my blood vessels and I pressed down hard on the accelerator, alive to the distant smell of male hormones. I felt aroused by everything around me; even the orange cones along the M25 looked phallic and tempting. I thrusted into my car seat for the remaining fifty minutes of the journey, filled with surreal and filthy dreams – what a wonderful ride! I even hoped for a short traffic jam to be able to extend it.

A good part of my journey was illuminated with the recollection of a most exciting event.

A Very Unusual Charity Do

12ᵗʰ September 2000, Cobham, Surrey
14ᵗʰ September2000, Soho, Central London
16ᵗʰ September 2000, Didcot, Oxfordshire

My friend Tamara mentioned an exciting event which she described as a *Love therapy for the over-macho couples – The Sex
Maniacs' Charity Ball.* That was handy.

For some time, neither of us had been getting enough sexual
fulfilment. It went speeding down after our child was born. Sex
experts advised aging couples to substitute sexual penetration
with simply lying in bed together, stretching and having a cud-
dle. In that case, I could have had sex with my cat every night.
The beautiful animal did not worry about mortgage or apoca-
lypses but simply enjoyed the moment being with me; and he
stretched so well. I hoped that going to a ball, with a twist of sex,
would work as a spiritual detox, to revive our deflating attraction. But there was no way I could even pronounce word 'sex' in
front of my husband, who was brought up as a Methodist. But I
was right to presume that the word 'charity' would work.

"A splendid charity ball is taking place next Saturday in Didcot." I didn't dare to mention the name of the event to my husband, trying not to frighten or offend him with 'dirty' words.

"It's for the benefit of shy, disabled people, deprived of sexual
pleasures. The organisers want to ensure that the less fortunate are
comfortable with their sexuality. They are invited to the event to
explore it." I gently popped in the *sex* words, preparing my Methodist husband to the full blow. "It's a great fundraiser like no other,

this Sex Maniacs' Ball, the reputable well-established charity!"

I expected a burst of anger or, at least, rejection, but Freddie replied supportively, even with a twist of excitement, "We have to help them, those that are less advantaged." The charitable side of the Sex Maniacs', obviously, appealed to my man. He took the bait.

"What is the damage?"

"Hundred and fifty." I did not specify that it was per head.

"We need to buy some accessories for the evening, some kind of special equipment." I was carefully choosing the words I used.

"Equipment?" Freddie became alert and looked even slightly scared.

"The theme of the ball is domination. I was thinking about getting a leather skirt and a whip for myself."

"You know I hate cruelty." He meant, of course, cruelty towards animals, but I managed not to mention it, and that was an achievement on its own.

"I'm not going to use it on you. It is simply for decoration." I didn't want him to fear the unknown, not yet, not prior the event.

"I'm going to borrow a nice oriental dress from my Egyptian friend Fatima. It will look splendid on you. You may put my bra on and my stockings with suspenders; black will be the best. We'll have to buy some artificial boobs to plant inside the dress. We'll create a stunning lady out of you."

"Where can we get this stuff? I imagine France will be the right place." My Chairman was joking. It was a great sign – he wasn't resisting and he wasn't upset with the future perspective of changing his gender for the evening.

"Surely, we can find all we need in London." I googled a few addresses and all roads pointed to Soho. To justify his trip to central London, my Fitzcock combined it with a visit to the company solicitors. Perhaps he wanted to take some advice about the legalities of a family man attending the Sex Maniacs' Ball.

The shop named 'Coco de Mer' sounded too French for Freddie. Luckily, I spotted the place with the English name 'Harmony', just across the road. It didn't sound dirty: more like a therapy place or a counselling centre.

"That'll do." I quickly undid the safety belt, indicating my intention to land. Freddie was lucky to find parking in Soho, right by the shop. After several attempts, he managed to squeeze his red Mercedes into a 'generous' space, a gift from Westminster Council.

Our son was with us; Nicholas was at the tender age of five.

"Mummy! Look how many beautiful fairies are around!" Our little boy was admiring the revealing window. "There are mermaids coming from the water!" He took the tiny thongs for bathing suits. "So many magic horns are here. A unicorn probably lives in this place." And he pointed with his finger towards the phallic toys he could see through the opened door.

"Sorry guys. Nobody under eighteen is allowed on our premises." A colourful gent with the voice of a ten-year-old girl and a blond crop spiking out on top of his scalp, stepped out of the shop and defensively covered the 'fairy-tale' characters and attributes with his anorexic body.

I turned to my husband, "Go back to the car with Nicholas. I'm sure I can deal with this." I wouldn't allow someone to deter me from our exciting plans. I walked in on my own to face all sizes of dildos, shameless thongs and pictures, leaving nothing to the imagination. It was like stepping into the Underworld.

"Madam, how can I help you?" The sex shop assistant seemed to cool down, and presented me with a nice, charming grim.

"I need a leather skirt for myself and a pair of big boobs for my husband. No small cherries, please. I'm a complete novice in this field and will be grateful if you can suggest anything else for a party with a domination theme."

The guy had a good look at my body, inspected it and finally pronounced his disappointing verdict: "Madam, we wouldn't have anything in your size. Nothing at all!"

I had almost foreseen that – it was an issue in most of the shops I went to, even out of Soho. "I still would like to buy a whip. This leather one would be just right." I pointed at the one with a beautifully decorated handle.

"Wait a minute! I have an idea." The sex-gear-seller disappeared through a small doorway covered with a red cloth. The provocative colour was there to remind the customer that throughout the 20th century, Soho was the red light district, London's sex industry hub, and still partly remained one. In a couple of minutes, the enterprising man returned with a black leather skirt in his hands.

"This stunning outfit is tiny, nowhere near your size. But no worries! I can detach the leather easily and make two halves from this skirt. Voila!" And, in a second, I saw two separate parts of the skirt in his hands.

"Blimey!" That was all I could squeeze out in astonishment.

"Now you have two small aprons that can cover your front from one side and your lovely back from the other. I can use these chains as a connection between them. Later on, when we get a similar item, it will be possible to add more pieces and stitch them together into one skirt. What do you think?" The guy looked so happy, even triumphant, with his cleverly invented solution for my big rear.

✳✳✳

The Sex Extravaganza was taking place in the middle of a field, in a huge marquee. A lot of posh cars were parked alongside the grounds and more still were approaching – Mercedes, Saabs, BMWs, luxurious Bentleys, Land Rovers and, Jaguars, in all shapes and colours. I had not seen such a variety even near the

Royal Opera House on opening nights, with world-class singers performing on that famous stage.

Classy couples, looking quite proper at a first glance, were piping out of their filthily expensive transport in rather plain clothes. At the entrance, after careful inspection of their tickets, they were quietly directed towards small screens. It was amazing to see them a few minutes later, emerging completely unrecognisable in their provocative gear, already experiencing feel-good benefits of the event. We followed them and they soon emerged looking like proper participants of this staged charitable game.

In a short time, the whole place was transformed into Watteau's *Fête Gallant paintings,* filled with sophisticated, elegant people getting together for the business of love. The participants were full of gaiety, playfulness, seductiveness and shamelessness – just like on the canvas of Boucher or Fragonard. *Perhaps this spectacular event is being staged by an art historian,* I thought.

A few pairs of eyes were watching me lustfully. Two tiny parts of the former leather skirt revealed a huge proportion of my voluptuous body. Packed into the red and black corset, complemented by black lacy stockings attached to the erotic suspenders, I expressed a wild call for male attention, arousing their amorous instincts.

Feeling attractive gave me a burst of energy. As soon as I noticed a big metal construction hanging from the ceiling like in a circus, I mounted it without hesitation, displaying my eagerness for a provocative game. With arousing magic I turned into the main character of Fragonard's famous painting *The Swing.* I often showed this eighteenth century masterpiece to my tourists at the Wallace Collection. Here, at this unusual charity fête, quite a few artsy-educated men obviously knew this masterpiece of the Rococo era, too. They were eager to mimic the composition, observing my legs and taking deep interest in my sacred possessions from below. To make it closer to the settings of Fragonard's brilliant creation, known also as *The Happiest Accidents*, I threw off my left shoe into the air in a theatrical manner, demonstrating my superior understanding of art.

A few minutes later when I moved deeper into the centre of the love-therapy events, the rococo style elegant beauty started to fade away – it turned into a bacchanalian bonking spree. Another hour, and I found myself surrounded by the Gothic horror, spiced with the surrealist world of Dali, Magritte, Duchamp and Breton – a complete madness recreated by charitable people; only Dali's ants were missing from the scary mise- en-scéne! A few disabled people in their wheelchairs were wheeling around rather confused, adding to the madness of the atmosphere.

It was a bit uncomfortable to see an old man in his nineties, squeezed into a tight leather bodysuit, pulling a twenty-year-old beauty by a leash, attached to her heavy chain collar. I held my breath – it seemed he was about to break her gentle neck. Probably, that was the only way he could achieve his feel-good state at his respectable age.

Just a few meteres ahead, a semi-naked man was screaming joyfully, as hot wax droplets from a burning candle were poured onto his bare back. He was being attended to by a woman who looked like a samurai in her horrifying gear, similar to the kind you see in the British Museum or V&A.

The centre of the marquee looked extremely crowded. *Something interesting should be going on!* With these thoughts I rushed forward, pulling my hesitant husband along. A large number of people were gathered around two big, metal cages. The writing on the board attached to them was intriguing – *explore the unknown*. Some guys in this very special congregation looked excited, others – indecisive or even ashamed.

"Freddie, come here! If you stick your hands into these holes, you may get into a juicy cave through a hairy mane, or possibly catch precious Fabergé eggs, or even a wet gold fish."

That was too much for my Chairman. He could not recognize the great potential for the whole new world of pleasure; he wasn't brave enough. My disturbed husband turned away, heading to the bar for 'spiritual' relief.

"What do you want?" The Chairman was trying to conceal his excitement, fighting with his Methodist modesty. He looked gorgeous, as never before – or she looked gorgeous – Freddie was transformed into a passionate Oriental lady with a prominent moustache, underlining her southern sexual spell. The shiny Arabian dress displayed his slender body and showed off the boobs acquired by me in Soho. Fifteen pounds of artificial front extension turned out to be a real treasure. I noticed that my 'sexy lady' with moustache was rather popular – a few pairs of eyes were gliding along Freddie's/Brigitte's cleavage and backside.

"Gin and tonic will be fine." I didn't really care about what I was drinking. I just wanted to have something in my hands as an accessory to support my confidence.

"Get away!" I heard my Chairman's powerful baritone. *He should have been a singer,* I thought. A huge crowd turned their heads his way. Freddie was using the purse I'd lent him as a lethal weapon to stop an attack on his masculinity, disguised under a shiny female outfit. With his strong arms, he pushed away a short baldish man, who was trying skilfully to attach his front to my husband's rear, and to explore less orthodox sexual desires.

"Fuck off, motherfucker!" Freddie obviously wasn't ready at all to enjoy this 'wonderful' moment of male intimacy.

"I'm sorry!" The bloke looked really frightened. "Something got stuck to your bottom, to your beautiful dress, I mean. I just was trying to remove it."

Freddie tended to trust people, or at least to give them a chance for self-defence. He stared more peacefully at the little gent.

"You look familiar. You're a lawyer, aren't you?"

"I'm a Thames Water solicitor." The man gave Freddie his hand.

I wondered if a lot of the sex 'maniacs' around were representatives of the legal profession.

"Cheers!" We all shared a drink.

Substitute for Love

25th October 2015
Central London

My chubby legs moved incredibly fast to reach my room upstairs, reminding myself of a fat, juicy centipede running for its life. I didn't want to wait until bedtime to start using my new toy, but I decided to pretend at being civilised. I was in possession of a British passport and wanted to prove to myself that my citizenship qualities were in place: like a real Brit, I was able to control my sexual appetites as long as necessary, and even longer... Yet the Slavic side in me hoped that the wait wouldn't last too long. I kept myself on a short lead to add some romance to my filthy pursuits.

Of course, an arousal balm was an unnecessary extra – since the operation, I was aroused non-stop anyway. I looked at the description of my Pleasure Wand, and loved every word of it. 'Discreet and powerful for enhanced pleasure whenever you choose' meant that I could slip it into my handbag, make-up bag, or even keep it in my knickers most of the time, in case of any urgent desires on the go. It had a battery-life of four hours, which perfectly matched the duration of my Windsor Castle tour. What would the Queen think if she knew that the guides on her premises could combine work and pleasure nicely and harmoniously? Of course, that luxury should be reserved for the highest echelon – the Blue Badge guides, exclusively.

The Pleasure Wand instructions had been developed by actress and author Julie Peasgood, who wrote about sex for many magazines. Lucky girl! I hope her activities in this field were not limited exclusively to writing, but that she also had a chance to take extensive practical research on the subject of female pleasure. I felt the need to explore her book, *The Greatest Guide to Sex*. Her job description as a resident sex and relationships expert on ITV1's *Alan Titchmarsh Show* gave me hope for future career possibilities in media. With such a sex drive, I should have been bombarded with propositions in this delicate and highly important sector.

I'd hidden my new toy behind my bed for the time being. It was time to go back to my well-paid role at 'Fitzcock and Co', to my unsexy country reality. The only sexy creature on our farm was the ageing bull named Horatio. I often watched him grazing stress-free in our fields – he obviously had a preference for big bottomed girls, but I was always afraid to come close. He was a real gigolo, who earned his comfortable living by fucking cows all day. I observed him in action, mounting his muscular ginger body on our Lincoln Red farm girls with his huge manhood – a rare relic in Britain – and I'd wished it was me out mooing in the fields.

Caught up in all the dildo excitement, I had forgotten to shop for food on the way home. I jumped into the car and drove to our local Waitrose. Since the supermarket had introduced a free cup of coffee and a newspaper if you spend a tenner, it had turned into my favourite shop. I would never miss a freebie. I registered my husband and my son too, so three cups of coffee a day was a great start to a caffeine-rich diet. Three newspapers a day presented the whole world from *The Telegraph* and *The Daily Mail* conservative point of view. *The Guardian* reflected the socialists' ideas, and produced the best reviews on culture, while *The Independent* reflected the liberals' views, with their high IQs and top education, but low income. These free goodies from Waitrose brightened my day – of course, I knew that Tesco and Sainsbury's were cheaper, and I was actually paying for everything that was pretending to be 'free'. As I was sipping a 'free' cappuccino in my car, I felt that nothing could spoil my sense of achievement. £2.25 per cup multiplied by three-hundred-and-sixty-five days gave an encouraging result, helping to fight my depression. Free coffee offers were stopped during COVID, and newspapers followed suit, probably to never return.

My stepdaughter had gone to Cornwall for a couple of days. It was very quiet in the house. Only the sound of sports presenters and cricket supporters could be heard from Freddie's end. There were two halves in our house: one for Him and for Her – Yin and Yang, the contrary forces, – very much like in ancient Chinese philosophy. I walked through a set of rooms towards the roaring sound.

"What would you like for dinner?" I asked my husband, who was deeply engaged in the TV.

"Anything will do."

Freddie wasn't a demanding man when it came to food or sex. He would eat the sole of a shoe, if it was soft enough for his teeth. Or, perhaps, as a shrewd businessman, he knew that there was no point in asking anything of someone who could not deliver. I could do only what I could do, and that didn't include much range or variety.

"I'll make you a nice salmon steak. I can grill it for you, or cook it in the oven." I usually bought good quality stuff, which would be difficult to ruin.

"That'll do," my man answered, not even looking at me. There was a cricket match on. No way could I compete. We never used words like 'darling' or 'dear', as they would sound pathetic or even ironic between us. If I wanted to ask anything, I needed to exercise patience and wait for the right moment to pop my question. I put his dinner on the table and settled with mine in the armchair next to the sofa. I looked at the screen, pretending to watch the game with him, and trying to play happy families.

"Who's leading?"

"India," he said, irritated by being disturbed. Freddie's gaze retuned to the screen. The profile of his face suddenly reminded me of Clark Cable, and for a minute, the scene of seduction from *Gone with the Wind* splashed me with a hot wave of sexual desire. After all, my husband was a handsome man, though indeed quite a bit older than Rhett Butler.

My granny used to say, "Men are like good wine – the older the better." Taking this into consideration, I moved from the chair to the sofa next to my Methodist. I had forgotten how to flirt and was acting pretentiously, like a 1950s star on a film set – breathing heavily and launching my profound chest into action. I was screwing Freddie with my eyes, trying to send a telepathic message of my desire for intimacy. That was the most I could count on. My husband seemed not to notice my manoeuvres at all, or tried hard not to. The seats on the sofa sank under my weight, and Freddie jerked a bit towards me. Yet he applied all his skills to avoid getting close. My husband bounced back and held himself frozen on his left buttock. He tried to merge with the TV screen with all his might.

I gathered all my courage and stretched my hand towards his arm, exposing my beautifully manicured nails. His hands were rough, adorned with dirty unkempt nails. *But they are the hands of a real strongman*, I thought. *Freddie looks after so many of us.* I wanted to hug him; I thought of dropping my face to his knees and reintroducing him to the wonders of my mouth and tongue. But as soon as I touched his skin, the cricket lover pulled away and reached for his cup of coffee. Out of respect, I did not want to force myself upon a scared, vintage man. Freddie coughed uncomfortably.

"I'll be away for the next two days. Can you look after the

dogs?" Freddie made it clear that any physical connection was out of question, but I was still considered to be a useful household item. I should've been content with a sophisticated task, very humanitarian – babysitting the dog. With a British husband, I had learned that even the simplest question or statement could descend into a row. I retreated back to the kitchen. *He's lost the taste ...* I thought.

On many occasions, my virgin friend Tamara tried hard to reassure me that celibate relationships demonstrate even stronger love. She was an expert on celibacy, which she had fiercely protected for more than half a century. My granny would say, "Count your blessings! You need to appreciate what you have". I counted all my blessings, admiring them with fervour, watching them accumulate in my bank account. Deep down, I knew that there was also some fault on my part for the growing gap between Freddie and me.

"Have you seen Betty in the local newspaper?" I was glad that my husband talked with me about something, even again about the dog.

"Was it the dog cruft show?"

"No, I was giving an interview on climate changes and I thought that Betty should stand next to me. Can you let her out?" Freddie was going up to his bedroom, reserving his last thoughts of the day for his hairy treasure. He was obviously in love with his four-legged girlfriend. Always believing that it was wife who should stand next to her man, I was left paralysed.

"Good night, dear!" I kicked the dog's plate, and sent it bouncing out of the dining room into the kitchen, in an emotional rage. My husband fed her all the time in our dining room, so it had become her territory, where she allowed herself to eat and piss.

"She is old," my husband was defending Betty, when she had an accident.

"The carpet on the floor she watered is also old, in fact antique. I just had to throw it away as it had been soaked in our 'lovely's' urine." No answer followed. It didn't bother Fitzcock. There was only one girl in the family that was allowed to do anything and stand next to her man. That girl was not me.

***

That night, I was so exhausted by my defeat that I forgot about my new little friend from Boots. I jumped into my bed as if into a safe haven and fell immediately asleep. But a strange sound woke me up and forced me out of bed. I stepped into the bathroom, trying to detect the source of the disturbing noise. *It might be the boiler or the water pump perhaps?* I thought. My husband always hired the worst builders and plumbers. He paid them by the hour, so they were encouraged to come back and take as long as they needed, with never-ending cups of tea and coffee. "Can't you put up with it?" he would say. But this noise stretched my patience to its limit.

I switched on the TV – it was *Inspector Morse*. This usually worked well, and I'd often fall into a deep asleep after watching it for only ten minutes. But the mystery noise drowned out even Morse – it was more authentic than a Celtic Carnyx, the war horn. The thick goose-feather pillow I wrapped around my head helped a little; the noise was drilling like a dentist into a nerve ending. I looked at my watch. It was nearly one in the morning. I had no choice but to wake Freddie and alert him to a problem, in what I guessed was the loft above my bedroom.

It felt strange to enter my husband's private chamber at that time of night. It had been years since I last crossed that boundary. Luckily, the door to the room was already ajar. His 'girlfriend', our poodle Betty, had probably climbed into his bed to warm up her tail.

The smell of medicine mixed with aging body sweat nearly diverted me back to my room, but the drilling sound was more powerful. I had to find courage and intrude on the privacy of my husband and his favourite girl. I could hear his breathing – Freddie was deep asleep; the gentle snoring duet resonated nicely in the room.

"Fred," I whispered, worrying that he may die from the fright of seeing me in his bedroom at night. Fortunately, Betty was almost deaf from old age and did not hear my invasion.

"What is it?" The Chairman nearly fell out of bed, terrified that his wife, me, might have besieged his chamber on a sexual quest.

"There's a suspicious noise above my room. I'm worried that there's something wrong and we may be blown up or burned down tonight," I blurted out in a rush to let him know there was no need to be frightened and it was only a household matter.

My Chairman was relieved and followed me to my room. His loose pyjamas did not flatter his body, unlike the blazers and tuxedos in his wardrobe. He listened with a smile, ready to debunk my theories and eager for proof that his thoughts about me were fair. But the vibrating noise continued, confirming to all that I was of sound mind, and had potentially saved our house from an impending disaster.

It sounded that the noise was coming from somewhere above. Freddie rushed to the corridor, took a long stick and tried to open the door to the loft. But the door did not budge. Freddie was knocking against the ceiling like mad. I started worrying that he would bring it down on himself.

"I'm not a plumber, not an electrician, not a handy man!" He was hysterical. "I'm helping everybody, I'm looking after everybody!" He screamed and screamed, winding up himself and me.

"You don't need to look after everybody. Just look after me!" I smiled, trying to project some charm.

"Do you think this is funny? You'll have to put up with sleeping in a guest room tonight, I'm afraid." He held the stick towards me, ready for my refusal.

"That's fine," I accepted without fuss, mostly to annoy him, so he'd miss out on screaming at me even more and using his stick as a piking weapon.

"Saturday night, Mike will be staying with us."

Freddie hated thinking about the possibility of me spending any time with his friends. Mike was my husband's comrade, with similar ideas on how to change the world. He was old, and his face reflected the rich deposits of his spite. My husband always treated me badly in front of him, trying to show off his own importance and power.

"That's okay; I'm working that weekend and will stay in London." I couldn't face being screwed by the eyes of someone, who loved the world in general, but was blind when it came to real people.

"Yes, that'll be much better."

The Chairman obviously preferred me to be absent – and so did I. Every so often, we held the same opinions and these rare occasions helped save our family. I wasn't worried anymore about his indifference. If I didn't come home for a few days, my husband would barely notice. Even if I lost all my hair and looked like Kovač, it would take Freddie a long time to spot the change.

I climbed up the steep stairs to the other part of the house. The place had a touch of neglect, and the guest bed was narrow and uncomfortable. But still, it was better than the drilling noise in my bedroom.

I woke up at eight in the morning, feeling tired and broken with a pain in my right shoulder, which had served all night as a pillow. With my positive mental attitude, I hoped to return to my room and discover that the noise had stopped and I could have a little nap in my own wide, cosy bed. But, alas, the noise was still going strong.

It was only then that I realised: the Pleasure Wand from Boots, which I'd pushed behind the bed, had mysteriously gone onto automatic, vibrating hard on its highest speed setting. It was a real hard worker, creating all night this horrendous noise amplified by the carpet. The packaging had guaranteed only four hours of power, but I wasn't too upset about this misjudgment. I switched off the crazy gadget and the blessed silence confirmed that my Pleasure Wand had both ruined my night and nearly given my spouse a heart attack. There was no way I could confess to Freddie about my stupid mistake. It would simply confirm his diagnosis of my diluted mind.

"How is the noise, is it still going?" my caring Chairman asked in the morning, forgetting his nocturnal hysterics.

"Miraculously, it has stopped," I reported without hesitation.

"I've asked Graham to check the plumbing and the boiler. He'll be here in a few minutes." Just as he said that, the doorbell rang.

"Graham!" I proclaimed, beaming. "So good that you came. We've had horrendous sounds all night from above my bedroom. Once you've sorted the problem, do come down for a cup of tea."

Granny used to tell me, "Sometimes a lie can bring about a better outcome than truth. Never confess to stupidity, cheating or lying". My wise old woman knew it all.

***

I had to wait till the next night to get up courage and arrange some time alone with my hard-working sex toy. It was exciting to know that it was modelled on the most joyful male organ, but yet wonderfully detached from men. I was ready to start my deep exploration of the result of the C operation. I locked the door, took off my clothes and inspected my damaged body. The four little holes left after the surgery could hardly be seen. The fat around my stomach had definitely started to melt, like an iceberg on in the sun. That put a sparkle into my eyes. It was time to see the doc as soon as possible and surprise him with my new look.

I stood in the shower and let the running water soak my body, closing my eyes and imaging myself in an erotic movie. I removed the hose from the hook on the wall and aimed it straight between my legs. It created an incredible sensation. I imagined someone kind and tender next to me. Kovač, with his gentle hands, was perfect. A few minutes under the water took me away from my life as a wife. I was a witch riding a broom with Kovač as a passenger. I stepped out of the shower, wrapped myself in a big fluffy towel and gave one to my doc,

"Let's go, Andrew."

We both squeezed under the duvet and I took out my new vibrator. I needed all the help I could get from the moisturising balm to ease the virginity-breaking process. I was nervous about sticking this alien piece of plastic inside me, so I used my hands first to ease me into it. It felt warm, soft, smooth and very young inside. *My doctor must have removed all wrinkles there!* I liked what I felt. An act of bravery followed – I slid the vibrator inside. My entire body was aching for this penetration.

It's not always bad to get screwed, I thought.

Come closer, Andrew.

***

Warm October sunlight woke me up rather late in the morning; it was almost nine o'clock. I had a V-pillow between my legs. I had bought it a few years earlier to help with my back pain, but last night it had given me the chance to do whatever I dreamed about. But it was not enough.

Another two weeks! That was my first thought. I was due to see my doc two months after the operation. That seemed unbearably long – more like a life sentence. Hating the empty side of my bed, I stretched my arm to the phone and dialled the clinic.

"Pamina – I have a problem – inflammation. Some horrible stuff is coming out of me. Help!"

I lied so naturally, I even surprised myself. That talent was part of my Soviet background. From a young age, many of us experienced our grannies 'dying' a few times a year, whenever we were late to school or missing Komsomol's (young communists) meetings.

"I can give you an appointment for this Thursday at four?"

"Do you have anything later? I'm working during the day."

I wanted to be the last patient, ensuring that my meeting with Kovač could develop without time restrictions.

"I have one cancellation at six-thirty."

"That'll be fine. Thanks!"

I hung up and pushed my body back into the V-pillow between my legs. My mind and aching body melted while I recollected last night.

This is just the beginning of our romance, I concluded, and a blood vessel started ticking in my temple.

Preparations for the Doctor

28ˢᵗ October 2015
Central London

My upcoming appointment was going to come at a cost, but what did I care? I would give my last penny for the sake of looking good for the doctor. I only had a few days to fit everything in and restore my antiques to a presentable level. No face alteration, no Botox or fillers – I was too old for the Barbie doll illusion. I wanted to keep my own expressions, not a mask; just light 'tweakments' – straight stuff for looking loud and proud. I started this marathon from the head down.

First: hair colour, which cost £100. Expensive, yes, but I didn't want to risk going to a cheaper place and coming out with green streaks or orange feathers poking out of my scalp. Then, Nicky Clarke's blow dry with lovely Chris and his youth-summoning haircuts came at £120, but it took ten years off and upgraded me from a car-boot-sale piece of junk to a respectable Sotheby's collection item (contemporary sales, of course).

Second: eyebrow shaping, which was an absolute necessity. At Nicky Clarke, Mayfair, it was costly at £60. But if done on the cheap, it would look like two caterpillars had fallen on my face and were kissing my nose. One glance at that 'lovely' face would cause impotence in any man.

Third: my saggy face had to be electrified by CACI Microlift and StriVectn Labs Facial Toner – the anti-ageing electrical wand. The spa treatment cost £95, but it removed hanging fat

176

from under my chin and firmed the jaw line. You needed at least six sessions to achieve noticeable results.

Fourth: hair removal – it was necessary to get rid of the beginnings of a beard and moustache: both the products of a testosterone increase following my operation. It totalled £60, plus a lot of pain. I was always taught that looking good required sacrifice. My advice on the procedure: wipe your tears and dream about love. It may come.

Fifth: a manicure and pedicure at a cheap Chinese place for £35. They are not too friendly there with hygiene, but you have to put up with it to stay within a budget.

Last but not least: a visit to a podiatrist. To keep my feet looking nice for my doctor, a lovely Indian guy on Wimpole Street shaved off two good kilos of dead skin and blisters – worth £60. He made me feel like a butterfly after only thirty minutes with his skilful scalpel. I didn't walk out of there; I flew.

Total investment: £840.

I saved money on pubic hair trimming, which I saw as a do-it-yourself job. I hated even thinking about having my bikini line waxed in a spa or, even worse, at the local beauticians! I could not trust this sacred land of mine to some young girls – what did they know? I had to ring my friend Tamara. Since Ella had got lost in her own divorce, she took premier position as my personal adviser in matters of soul and body.

My Celibate Sister
- *Ilias, Tamara, known also as Tamrico*
- *Age: 56*
- *5'2 in height and width*
- *Very colourful brunette*
- *Natalia's good friend and adviser*
- *Russian language teacher*

- *Works twenty-four hours a day paying off her mortgage, which miraculously only grows in size, as does Tamara*
- *No time for either love or sex*
- *Her favourite foods are cheese and chocolates; before, during and particularly after dieting*
- *Spinster, loved by so many but at a distance*

My devoted friend could listen to me on the phone for hours, and she always gave me a great advice.

"If you really want to impress your doctor, you should shave your pubic fringe into a heart shape. My A-level students told me that's how it was in the latest Vogue." Tamara took their words on sexual trends as gospel. Her senior students passed on all sorts of knowledge about the affairs of the heart and below, which my friend then generously delivered to me.

Since I had heard about these heart-shaped pubes, I couldn't stop wondering whether women I passed on the street managed their hairy business themselves, or enlisted the help of a barber to sculpt a heart for them. What was the percentage of heart-shaped pussies around the world? That question bothered me from time to time.

My drastic preparations were going well. I took a razor to the hair on my front – it had to go. It felt a bit like going to war with an enemy, just like Saint Michael in the fifteenth-century painting by the Venetian artist Carlo Crivelli. The fearless Prince of Archangels led God's army against the rebels seduced to sin by Lucifer, and in the painting he's standing victorious over the defeated enemy. With him as an ally, I could not fail. Cut off! Done!

Unfortunately for me, my pubes refused to order themselves into the shape of a heart. In fact, the aftershave resulted in an abstract painting – Malevich's *Black Square*, perhaps, though in different, lighter shades.

I recalled the pubic hair of two nudes by Pablo Picasso at Tate Modern, London. The first, *Nude, Green Leaves and Bust*, on loan from a private collection, was painted in 1932, and depicts the artist's young lover, Marie-Therese Walter. She is seventeen; Picasso was forty-five. He painted her with a strong sense of tender love. She is laying in a beautiful pose as a concubine, waiting with naive desire to submit herself to her master. Some years later, the artist betrayed his young mistress, the mother of his child, pushing the young woman to commit suicide. Her pubic hair in the painting is nearly non-existent; it's clean-shaven, smooth, like the marble of an antique sculpture. No wonder this piece of art sold for £66m at Christie's.

On the opposite wall was the second nude, painted 34 years later: *Nude Woman with Necklace*. Picasso was 86 years old and the subject was his last muse and second wife, Jacqueline Roque, who was half his age. Their marriage lasted for 11 years, till his death. He made 400 portraits of her, far more than any other of his lovers. The artist completed this canvas in one day. It was a statement that he was not prepared to die, but was desperate to live, love and fuck; a dirty bastard. Jacqueline's body on the painting had been twisted around and mutilated by her husband. Picasso painted her as she expelled a huge fart, the smell of which drifted straight through the canvas. Perhaps she had been trying too hard to stimulate the old man's instrument. Jacqueline's pubic hair takes up a big proportion of her lower body. It is black, very black, and thick like a shield. He breaks through it, throwing his sperm over the canvas like a white fountain of erotic dreams and desires, a gift given by many women to enable him to propel his art to unreachable heights. Gertrude Stein once said that Pablo was a real monster, but insisted that we should love him for his genius.

If the artist's subjecs didn't have heart-shaped pubes, it doesn't matter that I can't achieve it, I thought. The most important thing was to ensure clean, tidy presentation. So, off it all went. My pubic off-cuts looked like tiny ostrich feathers. They felt silky and nice. Perhaps I should've kept them in a locket as a souvenir. They contained the smell of female mystery, though occasionally they stunk like rotting fish. At least my doctor wasn't going to have these prickly 'flowers' sticking into his face. I did take care with members of the medical profession. I was ready to face my gynaecologist for a proper internal check-up.

I took the late appointment, aiming to be the last patient of the day, so that the doctor didn't have to be in a rush, and could get to know me better. I found a loo and tidied up my ground-floor chambers. The worn knickers went into my Prada bag. A flow of warm water, backwards, forwards, forwards, backwards, with long visits to the backside, restored my privates to their native freshness. That precious back passage became drawn in as well; I needed to make sure that no toilet paper was left stuck there. Luckily, my haemorrhoids had since disappeared. I would not dare to offend my doctor with that nasty dozen.

I had a little hiccup with my preparations. Hoping to finish with a spray of moisturiser to beat the post-menstrual dryness, I accidently used glitter spray, multicoloured sparkles that I'd bought for the forthcoming Christmas festivities. Thank the Lord, I noticed my little mistake straight away; otherwise the site for the examinations would be too joyful, and rather spectacular. I used a spritz of Agent Provocateur perfume to give my doctor a nicer working environment. The choice of knickers was decided beforehand, slightly erotic but also respectable. The balance could be achieved by neutral colour spiced up with provocative lace. The toes had to be perfumed, too. After my long working day on the streets of London, a Vivienne Westwood 'poison' granted those little stinkers the tang of glamour and lust.

I wouldn't dream of arriving to my appointment empty-handed. I turned to my wise friend for reassurance:

"Tamrico, I want something really solid."

"A clock would be perfect. He'll keep it on his desk, and each time he looks at it, he'll think about you. He won't be able not to!"

I agreed. My friend should have been a doctor of philosophy.

The table clock I chose, displayed the extra time my surgeon had given me by stepping into my life and saving me.

Love Makes Us Shy

29ⁿᵈ October 2015
Queen Anne St, the consulting rooms

"I'm here to see Mr. Kovač," I informed the receptionist at the consulting rooms. It was the same woman as last time, when I had come to hear my verdict a few weeks ago.

"Yes, Mrs. Popov. Please, take a seat in the lobby. A nurse will call you soon."

Everything looked so familiar. The polite silence of the place re-assured me that I had stepped into a different, more caring world, one where I was at peace with all diseases and disasters. I sank into a comfortable leather armchair. Yet it was hard to relax – the anxiety nearly suffocated me. As I waited for my appointment, I tried to sit in the most attractive pose, artistically rearranging my legs all the time in case my doctor might pass by and see me. The newspapers on the clinic's coffee table were very handy – they made good props as I pretended to read. *The Times* was the best choice – not too big, and allowed me to be seen behind the pages, that were filled with the usual Tory cheer. My impatience meant I could only focus on the headlines; everything else was white noise.

All of a sudden, my breath stopped – I saw Kovač walking along the corridor with a young female patient, talking to her flirtatiously. He was telling her something about a colposcopy, a detailed examination of the cervix, in such an excited way that he could've been asking his patient out to a Michelin-starred restaurant.

I disliked the woman – she was much too young to be liked. A wave of jealousy splashed my face with rouge. But Kovač obviously did like her. He was engaged with this youngster for another twenty minutes, overlapping the time of my appointment. "Mrs. Popov, the doctor is now free and can see you. Follow me, please." The nurse then glanced at me and added with admiration, "You look beautiful and young!" It seemed sincere enough. Or was it a sarcastic comment, as she'd noticed me engineering my postures and presentation?

My heart thumped like a giant pendulum clock – tick tock, tick tock. My legs softened, and walking turned out to be extremely difficult. I moved as if trudging over sand, while trying hard to keep in the style of a catwalk, by swinging my hips and throwing my legs forward to extend the line.

The door to the room was open. It was a different place from the one where I had last seen him. This room was situated on the other side of the building and was bigger, lighter, with a small, private annex.

Kovač's simple v-neck, probably Marks & Sparks, complemented his green eyes enormously. I hoped that he had chosen it especially to look nice for me. The doc appeared unexpectedly young. *Just a boy*, I thought. He did not look any more like a magician or a judge delivering a death sentence, but someone from a simple and joyful life.

"Doctor, my apologies!" My behaviour during my previous visit was rather explicit." I wasn't planning an apology, but I needed to say something to distract my doc from his desk. He kept his eyes on his writing, as he had before, avoiding meeting mine. My breasts, nicely framed in a new bra, were moving up and down as if I had an engine inside. It was very much like in old silent movies, where the heroine's bosoms would heave with passion for the leading man. I didn't want to convey anything, but just could not control my body language. I underestimated how much my cleavage could reflect my internal love.

"You don't need to apologise." He probably wanted to say: *you patients are all mental to some degree.* But he had to put up with a lot of nonsense and be polite in order to reach the position of a consultant, which promised an income exceeding the prime minister's.

I was grateful that Kovač did not push me away. He was such a dear.

"I may not see you before Christmas," I said, placing the beautifully wrapped gift on the free chair. I went pale, thinking about spending Christmas without him.

"You didn't need to do that."

"It's nothing. Just a little 'thank you' for all you have done for me."

"It's my job."

Kovač stood up from his desk and, without looking at me, kissed me on both cheeks! I still wonder if it was a real kiss or whether he just air-kissed me. He took the gift and returned to his desk. He didn't ask what was in the box, but clocked the Cartier logo on the carrier bag.

"Any pain or discomfort?" He looked almost hopeful I would say 'yes', so that he could help.

I should have shouted, *Yes! Pain in my heart and soul; it's unbearable without you!* But I went numb. I dropped my body onto the chair and stared at him, hoping to catch his gaze. The moment came when he had to lift his head to break the awkward silence.

"I need to examine you and make sure all's healing well."

The doc approached the small annex, with a narrow couch looking rather like a place for a quickie. My emotions spiralled out of control, overloaded with recollections from my Soviet past, which I preferred to forget, but it kept coming back to haunt me.

***

It was a similar annex and narrow low couch, where I had to spread my legs nearly thirty years ago to obtain permission for a one-way trip to Britain. I was supposed to go to America for a two-year study programme, planned by the Soviet government. But the project grounded to a halt.

"Aren't we friends? Let's have a drink. Your place… tomorrow, at noon." An old friend of a family, a famous children's book writer, well connected to all governmental forces, including the infamous KGB, promised to help me out. Not for nothing. Not for a smile – I had to give this 80 year-old Soviet giant's apparatus a glorious return back into virility. I had to make him feel once again a man.

The Soviet giant was a decent man to some extent – at least he fulfilled all his promises. Straight from the 'sucking sofa' he dialled his top KGB contact. I lifted my ear to the phone line and overheard the conversation.

"It was her father who asked us to stop her trip to the States," a hushed voice, trying to please the giant, shared this shocking fact.

"She's thirty, what does her father have to do with this trip?"

It was my own dad who had prevented my exit abroad! He suspected that I was not going to come back to our chaotic society of Perestroika. He was not worried about my future, but instead dreaded that my move would affect his own career in the virtually dead Communist camp.

My honourable bugger ordered the secret agency to eject me from the country as soon as possible. He took a sip of my expensive brandy and swallowed a blini with black caviar – a real aphrodisiac – and turned to me.

"Tomorrow you will see the deputy minister of culture and your problem will be sorted."

The deputy minister looked like a nice man, of around my father's age. I respected the unwritten laws of our society, and did not come empty-handed to this important meeting. As it happened, that was not enough.

"Come here, my darling." And the grey-haired cultural mandarin pulled me into a small annex room with a narrow couch. He kneeled down and unzipped his fly.

"You are so beautiful. We have wonderful cultural forces – there will be something to show the capitalist world."

Before showing the capitalist world 'my beauty', I had to show him my 'talents' and spread my legs 'culturally wide' in the annex room. It was like a casting couch, not for film stardom, but for a one-way ticket to the free Western world. Nobody cared what kind of specialist I was, but my *cunt* happened to be of a great scientific and cultural importance.

Unfortunately, by that time, the study vacancy in the US had been already filled by another art historian. She was obviously a real sprinter to reach the magical annex room before me. I was directed to the UK instead, to bring our rich culture to the enchanted land of Dickens and Byron, and ease the tension between our two nations.

A disgustingly positive outcome – two Wise Men and my pussy won the battle against my dad. My freedom was the prize. It made me forget the traumatic experience and consider those fuckers as my saviours.

If you look into world history, you may discover that the fates of whole countries were often determined by three holes – one on the face and one down below, and for the full Monty – one at the back. These history lessons helped me to accept the annex events as a cultural pursuit in the safe, secured-by-KGB surroundings. It was nothing to be ashamed of.

***

"I need to call a nurse," Kovač said, afraid to be left unsupervised with my damaged pussy and high voltage emotional state.

"*No!*" I screamed. "*I can't!*" It sounded more like "*I'm a cunt!*" I felt sick and dizzy from the thought of opening my legs in front of him with a stranger present, witnessing the damaged funnel exploration. I didn't feel that embarrassed at sixteen when I lost my virginity. That felt more natural. Now it was an ageing woman's shameless cunt on display – a threesome – my doctor, a nurse and me.

"Why do we need anyone present? This is all just between you and me, isn't it?"

"The nurse is for the patient's protection," he sighed, not even convincing himself that this statement could serve as a good reason for such a degrading act.

"I don't need to protect myself from you!"

Kovač moved towards me. I felt his hand on my elbow. He was careful where and how to touch.

"You need a check-up. You do!" His eyes were so loving and his voice so calming – the voice of a very special friend.

Did he say 'darling'? He may or may not have. Romantic thoughts swirled all over me, body and soul. I had prepared myself well for this kind of intimacy, equipped with nice knickers and toes mastered to perfection. I was still on the heavy side and not that young, but nobody could take away the fact that I was a classy, pampered female, and had something impressive to offer. Those points were the reasons that I agreed to submit myself to such ridiculous, undignified arrangements.

"Call the old girl, please," I said. It was easier for me to accept a granny-type nurse to observe these intimate relations. Just like in the painting by Rubens, *Samson and Delilah*, an elderly chaperone had to be present to prove that the trust was betrayed with the assistance of seduction. The thought of a young woman staring at us revolted me.

"Dear, you can remove your underwear but leave your skirt on." The nurse was giving me instructions on how to prepare myself for my doc. Her blue headscarf made it impossible for me to guess her age. I shook off my Versace shoes, removed my tights, and positioned my lacy knickers beautifully on the small chair. The blood-red colour of the lace was aimed to seduce – a modest attempt to make my doc notice what was left of me woman-wise. I sprayed my thighs once more with Agent Provocateur to make sure the doctor's starting and landing points wouldn't smell of piss and rotting fish. But the bloody nurse managed to spoil my romantic preparations, as she threw some tasteless white clothes in the gap between my opened legs. She tried to cover as much of my mystical cave as possible and informed me that she was going to continue her supervision through the opened door to the annex.

The bright ceiling spotlights blinded me as I dropped my body on my back in preparation for the examination. I had to cover my eyes with both hands to avoid loss of sight. And then time stopped – I realised that I was not able to go through with this public inspection. I jumped off the couch, picked up my knickers and dropped them into my bag without wasting time putting them on again. On my way out, I pushed away the startled nurse, who was blocking the exit. I flew through the door, not even looking at Kovač. It took me seconds to run down the stairs, sliding my hands along the railings. The security guard shouted out, "Are you OK?" His question was left unanswered, and the hospital doors closed behind me and reality.

Even Doctors Make Mistakes

29th October 2015, later in the day
Central London

Fresh street air filled my lungs and made me slow down. I was walking along the pavement towards my car, when my mobile buzzed in the handbag. It took me a while to fish the phone out as I carried around a house-worth of contents on my shoulder. The number was listed as unknown. *It's probably Nick*, I thought. I answered, ready to hear, *"It's me!"* – those words had become a traditional greeting between us. Instead, I heard a voice I was not expecting.

"You need a check-up, Natalia." It could only be Kovač! He sounded overwhelmed with concern about me; not very typical for an Eastern European man. "Where are you now?"

"Walking towards my car," I answered, not understanding why he was asking.

"Is it to the right and right again from the exit?"

"Yes."

My heart started pumping like mad, and my mouth became disgustingly dry. By then, I almost knew what was to follow. It was like déjà vu. "Can you wait for me down there, in your car? I'll be with you in a few minutes." His voice sounded as if he was whispering from afar.

"Of course," I said as if his call was expected.

I reached my Merc and regretted not sparing a tenner for the car wash offered in the car park this morning. I quickly moved all the rubbish out, collected some personal stuff from the front passenger seat and tucked it into the boot, which now looked ready for a car boot sale. Multiple tubes of foundation and sun cream didn't want to fit into the central console, so I shoved them into my purse. I refreshed my mouth with chewing gum found in my pocket. My lips needed attention, so I circled them with a touch of bright-red lipstick – the colour of seduction.

My car was facing away from the hospital. I was using the wing mirror to keep an eye out for Kovač's approach. I was always known as a person very able to multitask, though not always delivering the best results. I carefully watched the road from my seat, not missing anyone who was moving towards my car, and at the same time, sprucing myself up with a fresh touch of powder and a layer of lip gloss.

It was approaching eight o'clock and getting dark. I was his last patient of the day. One of ten, twenty, thirty? How many cunts had he examined in one day? I turned the key and switched on the sidelights to become more visible, and then put on a Sinatra CD. It was playing my favourite song, *Fly Me to the Moon*. I felt like I was about to be launched over there. I forgot that my passionate love for Sinatra revealed my age. My heart always missed a beat when Kovač read those four digits aloud from his notes, forcing me to face the horrible reality.

Another fifteen minutes passed before I spotted his black long coat and heavy leather briefcase in his right hand – a look of mourning for those that he couldn't help. Filled with his patients' horrendous stories, this heavy bag dragged Kovač down and made him visibly bent to the left. He stopped near my side of the vehicle, then went around and opened the door. He began saying something as a doctor, but our eyes met and we just stared at each other. If you've ever seen films about creatures from other galaxies you might have noticed how they often talk without any sound! His powerful eyes were capable of conveying two messages simultaneously: *How can I persuade you to come back to the hospital?* And at the same time, his eyes were asking if he could jump in. My eyes were saying: *Never mind the hospital. It's nice and comfy on my leather seats.* Their smell gave away that the car was very new and created a dizzy feeling of prosperity and freedom.

Kovač caught on to my telepathic invitation. He quickly and nervously looked around wondering if anybody could see us, and climbed in, moving his heavy luggage deeper inside towards my seat. He stayed quiet and gave no instruction; he left the initiative to me. I turned the key and started the car, breaking the silence with the roar of the engine. My heart was pounding so loud – I believed that Kovač could hear every beat. I held the air in my lungs not able to breathe it out. Eventually, I did! And with this exhale, my life seemed to start rolling in a different direction.

It was only a twenty-minute drive back to my apartment, but my preoccupied mind made me divert through Regent's Park, making a short circle. Even in the dark hours, the journey had a romantic touch, and each new Sinatra song seemed especially composed for the moment. We did not utter a word. We were both possessed by the power of fate.

I parked the car along the canal, a short walk to my block. Kovač tried to put his case under the seat but then changed his mind and took it out with him. He probably knew all his patients' stories by heart, but couldn't bear to part with them even for a short while.

It was nearly nine when we approached my Edwardian mansion. The head porter was still on duty. Dressed in his uniform, Colin looked well-groomed, sharply fitting into the Rembrandt's *Night Watch* masterpiece. He winked at me, letting me know that he understood what was going on and that he approved, or at least didn't mind.

We crossed the entrance lobby towards the lift in a zombie-like state. I spotted Kovač throwing a glance at the decadent red carpet and the huge crystal chandelier hanging heavily from the ceiling. All those luxuries would not be his favourite scenery – far too extravagant for the taste of a Labour supporter.

Just as I pressed the sixth-floor button and the lift doors closed, it all started to roll. Not started, just burst. Kovač dropped his bag. He pressed me against the wall and without any hesitation or resistance, our lips met and melted in one long kiss, a kiss which never seemed to end. It felt electric, like three thousand volts. His lips were so soft. The metallic scent of blood filled the inside of my mouth. He had bitten my lip. But what did I care?

We turned into one creature breathing in and out together, not able to get enough of each other's smell and taste. The lift jolted, indicating arrival. My key did not want to let me in, as if it knew some wrong-doing was going on. I turned the lights on and he walked in – into my apartment and into my life. I shut the door between us and the rest of the world.

Kovač hung his coat on the hook, turned sharply and pinned me to the door, covering my mouth with his, this time gently. I returned his kiss. His right hand took my head from behind, pulled my hair down and towards him. He wanted more of my lips and I wanted everything that he wanted.

"Let's go."

His voice was hushed and low like a bass-baritone. He was no longer a shy British doctor. He was someone who knew how to seduce and how to possess. He guided me to my bedroom as if it was his own place. His trousers were off and on the floor. In complete silence, he unzipped my jacket and released my bra. He was so skilful – nearly artistic. I was unable to take my eyes away. I felt my nipples growing harder, and Kovač saw it too. He bent down to reach my bosoms, paying professional evaluating attention to my prominent birthmark. His gentle yet firm hands were removing my skirt. He pulled me down onto the bed and towered above me for a while, taking off his tie. He stretched his hand up ready to pull my knickers off, but had to retract, realising that I was going commando; my lacy lingerie was still in my purse. He looked down at my navel – a surgeon's look – he had been inside there during my operation. He put his tongue in and circled it down my belly towards my pubic hair. His touch brought a shiver down my spine, which worked on me, as if he had a key winding a fully wound clock. His head was moving lower, towards my cunt.

"Andrew! Oh, Andrew! You don't have to!"

I wasn't sure if I wanted his mouth down there with his tongue and lips. Kovač understood, as he always did. He lifted my duvet and rolled behind me, covering us both. I was glad that my far-from-model-type body was hidden nicely from his eyes. My self-confidence was returning. It was clear that the doc had not been in a gym for a long while. His skin was much too soft without the hard definition of muscles, nearly feminine, without a sign of a hair on his chest – it was bald, completely, like his head.

Kovač tipped my head back, took hold of my hair, and started kissing my short but very sensitive neck. I felt his manhood press against my hip. Surprisingly, it was rather big, considering his height and very delicate hands. I'd love him at that moment even if he would not have anything in his trousers at all.

I was a bit scared – it was my first time after the operation, excluding a little dildo action. His hardening penis had gone between my thighs. My body was pulsating, producing visible waves. It felt so wet and juicy down there. I was pleased by the miraculous absence of middle-aged dryness. When I read about this problem in *The Times*, on the pages of *Body and Soul* with sex counsellor Suzi, it always scared me.

Kovač took his weight on his left arm and used his right to position his penis next to the entrance of my vagina. This was the moment I had been waiting for and had fantasised about for weeks, as I lay alone on this same bed. This breakthrough, this breaking of the ice, this blast of the cave entrance… I'd dreamed of these images time and time again. But Kovač collapsed before he could penetrate me. His head was on my tummy.

"Sorry! I just can't!"

It was another 'can't' from so many that made me feel a failure through my life. Perhaps he knew the map of this wounded field of mine too well, and that stopped him in spite of his own will.

The doc jumped out of the bed and headed towards the bathroom. I stayed still among the bedsheets and listened to the drops of water in the shower and the sound of the pump cutting in; it was a disgusting melody.

Something went wrong. I'm a failure.

"Is it okay?" I heard his voice from the shower. "I've used this towel."

I blinked. What did I care about the towel?

"Andrew," I whispered, trying to hold on to the dream.

Kovač walked over and sat on the edge of the bed. The huge towel was covering his hips – very much like Roman togas. He looked at the paintings above the headboard. They were two nudes in a Japanese style. He put his head down and I caught the look in his eyes – he stared at the photo of my husband carrying our little son on his shoulders.

"I have to go."

I knew that he felt guilty. It was dark, so I lit the candle. I was amazed by how pale his skin was – he probably hadn't seen the sun for many years, hiding himself in his cancer ward.

"You don't like the sun, Andy?" I touched his silky pale arm.

"What did you call me?"

"Andy. Don't go. Just stay next to me".

"I'm out of practice. My job drains me."

"I love you for what you are."

I put my hand on his thigh and squeezed it gently. I felt blood pulsing through his body, filling him from top to bottom with desire. I noticed movement under the towel as his penis grew full again, erected by the volume of my feelings. I wanted to lick his marble body all over, but within a second he was on top of me. Just hop, hop – he was there. Another moment and I felt him filling me with his gentle passion.

"Ah!" This was the moan not of one woman, but of the entirety of womankind.

He looked at me, possibly checking whether I was in pain, but saw a different sensation reflected in my eyes. And then we both flew away. I'm not sure where – was it to the moon like Sinatra foretold, or the sun, or passing through Hell? I wanted to enter all of his body and merge into a two–headed creature. It was a symphony of great passion – Kovač became part of me. He squeezed my buttocks, lifting them and entering still deeper, as if hooked on the taste of my nectar. And then it came – the moment of climax. He fell on my chest and my thighs hugged him back. I squeezed my legs, my cunt. I learnt this trick in my younger years, not so much from my husbands, but from the men who were in between. I could even smoke a big cigar, puffing in and out with my ground floor grasp. I wondered if I could still do it, and Kovač moaned in affirmation. He was not in a hurry – he tried to squeeze out what was left, like paste from a tube into me.

"That was great, and I don't have to worry that I could get pregnant," I joked, stupidly. He rolled off me and took the left side of the bed – the man's side – stretching his arms across a pillow.

After a long silence, he asked, "What are we going to do?"

"Whatever you want." I was surprised by my submissiveness. I'd never been that way inclined.

"I want some water for now," he said with his typical charming smile, hiding his eyes from me.

"I'll bring it for you." I started moving my body towards the edge of the bed.

"No," he intercepted my action. "I'll get it myself. I'm still able to do it."

He looked so happy, and you can bet – I did too. We smiled like two idiots, two happy kids. I fished out the towel he dropped and wrapped it around myself.

"How about a glass of wine, doc?" Kovač pulled a corner of the towel and looked under it, like a kid looking into a peep hole or spying on a friend. He brushed through my pubic hair with his delicate fingers, trying to catch some of his own traces, and brought them up to his nose to enjoy the scent. He kissed my belly button, just like my granny did when she bathed me half a century ago. I noticed some blood on the bed sheet. Kovač's eyes followed – he saw it too.

"Did you have any pain?"

"Nope. But otherwise I felt as a virgin."

"My Virgin Mary! It's been only eight weeks since the operation – we've been a bit impatient."

"What did you plant in there, doc? You lied when you said that sex will be the same."

He was kissing me, "I knew what I was saying."

"But it's not the same. It's *so* much better!"

His face spread with happiness, as if he had been waiting for these words all his life. "I'm glad." He poked his nose into my cheek and rubbed it affectionately. "Now I'm hungry, like a wolf. Woof!" He was so charming and childish, clearly enjoying being away from his death ward.

How could I miss this? I was angry with myself. I'd even planted roses in a beautiful Japanese pot in the hope that Kovač would see. But food?

"I'll check the fridge and see what I can do."

"It's chilly; shut the window, would you?" Such simple words were delivered by a voice radiating calm and happiness beyond belief. I knew he'd always belonged here, and my apartment was his place as much as mine. I'd completely forgotten that Freddie bought it for me.

I rushed to the kitchen barefoot and stood on something sharp – but what did I care? Trying to shape myself for Andrew, I hardly kept anything in the fridge. A pack of smoked salmon turned out to be my saviour. I hoped Kovač would like my pretty Royal Albert plates with little roses, a similar pattern to the dress I wore when I first met him. I laid out two big pieces of salmon, decorating it with a slice of lemon, cut a big avocado and positioned it in a circle around the fish, creating something like a sunflower – a flower of happiness. I fetched two beautiful serviettes from a drawer and fixed them on the dining table, took out my silver cutlery and Doulton Crystal glasses, and pulled out a chilled bottle of quality Sancerre 2008 from the fridge. I lit a candle. It looked exquisite and romantic.

A CD went into the player – who else but Sinatra? I threw a glance at myself in the mirror and saw a reflection of happiness, albeit in great disorder with smeared mascara all over my cheeks. I wiped the black smudges away and gave my hair a quick brush. I returned to the bedroom ready to invite him to the table, but then heard his heavy breath – he was deep asleep, my Andrew.

I sat on the side of the bed. My weight sank into the mattress and woke him up. He looked surprised and glanced around, not sure where he was. He took a look at his watch that he'd left on a side table. "My God! It's already eleven-thirty!"

"Your food was ready some time ago. But I didn't want to wake you up."

"Thanks," he said and sat for a minute on the edge of the bed with his head sunk into his knees. "I have to go. Sorry!"

Kovač started dressing in a hurry. It was obvious that he was uncomfortable and tried hard to avoid looking directly at me.

He woke up from fifteen minutes of sleep into reality. The doc looked around the flat, scanning all that he could see – my paintings and portraits that revealed some of my colourful past. He clearly wanted to go, but felt impolite to ignore the beautifully laid table awaiting him through the arch in the main hall. He stepped into the dining room, took the plate into his hands and started to shovel salmon into his mouth. He looked like a different person.

"Would you like some wine? Try – it should taste really good."

I must have said or done something wrong! Like in my childhood – at nursery, at school, at university, I was always pointed at when something bad happened; as if everybody knew I was the trouble.

"I have to go!" he repeated firmly.

Kovač came up to the big bay window, facing the opposite block. He was looking into someone's life. And thinking.

"Please, forgive me for leaving in the middle of the night. I feel like a thief. He probably wanted to add that he shouldn't have been here but didn't dare to upset me that much. He looked at himself in the hall's mirror, checking for any traces of our tryst.

"I'll call you," he said, apologetically. He put his heavy coat on, picked up his dark brown case, uncomfortably pecked my cheek with his nose, and off he went. Without even looking at me.

"The lift is on the left," I said, as I saw him heading in the wrong direction.

"Oh! Thanks."

It was a different man. Not my Andrew. His mind and his body were already somewhere else. My Cinderella ball had come to an end.

The telephone rang. I jerked and discovered that it was morning and I was lying on my sofa in the dining room. It felt strange, as I never slept in this room. There was nothing on the dining table except a wine glass and an empty bottle of Sancerre. I got up slowly and went to the bedroom. In the pale light I could see the bedcovers neatly spread, completely untouched. I looked in the bathroom – all the towels were carefully hung on the rails.

No traces of Andrew, I thought and felt sick. *Did he or I tidy up, or did we meet in another dimension? Could the cancer have muddled with my brain and twisted my mind to such an extent?*

I looked at my phone and called the number back.

"Mrs Fitzcock?" It was Kovač's PA. "Doctor insists that you book another appointment, preferably this week."

This bitch is not going to take away my doc! I will not let my dream go.

Perestroika

31st October2015
Maida Vale, London

For the next few days, my phone kept ringing like mad, much more often than usual. All of a sudden, a whole bunch of people whom I hardly remembered wanted to get in touch, but not the one I really hoped to hear from. I needed a big, comfy shoulder to cry on. The largest I could get belonged to Klava, my old friend. I had known her since my late teens, when we'd attended the same school in Moscow. Being November scorpions, we had both loved and hated each other throughout our lives. We'd been planning our meeting for some time, to catch up on news and gossip.

The Scorpion Next Door
- *Kalina, Klavdia, known as Klava*
- *Age 55 going to 69*
- *5ft 8, looks like Everest*
- *Weight – a tonne and a bit*
- *International lifestyle – only in the direction of lower tax*
- *Busy practising the role of a wise woman*
- *Cancer survivor*
- *Despises most people*
- *Can scare with her love as well*

"Your flat looks like an old lady's place – an antique boutique or a car boot sale. All these pictures, vases – remove it all. Too many things, much too busy. It's old ladies who usually keep everything they have and never let it go," Klava started lecturing me, as soon as she stepped into my apartment. She was always ready to give her harsh but honest verdict on the spot. "You need more space, more light, more air. Get rid of half of your paintings; just leave the best ones."

She took some time removing her boots, bending over her prominent belly with obvious difficulty.

"No one really needs boots in London. Here you can walk around in slippers during the winter. But these are my old friends."

Klava eventually conquered her zip and walked rapidly into my dining room. The floor was trembling under her feet, reminding me of the Giant's Causeway in Ireland. Next to her, I was a tiny Red Riding Hood.

"I'll make you some coffee," I said, trying to encourage her to soften towards my lifestyle, and me in general.

"Forget about coffee. I need some brandy for a start." She walked straight to the trolley that was filled with bottles of all sorts. "You have Courvoisier Five Star, right? I need it. I'm really concerned about you."

Klava grabbed a bottle opener, the new one I had just bought for serving drinks to my Andy. She filled up the glass and it over flowed. She was obviously too absorbed in her concern for me to pay attention.

"Fuck! Please excuse me. Give me a cloth to wipe it up. Let's toast to happiness. I'm here to put things on the right track for you." She was obviously on a mission.

After tidying up the mess on the table, my super-sized friend dropped her body onto my three-seater. I was worried that the twenty-year-old sofa may not be able to accommodate her rear without damage. Klava gave it a judgmental look.

"This furniture is too old and out of fashion. It's been here as long as I can remember. It's time for a change. Go fresh and modern."

"It's nice. It was really expensive, from Harrods." I was trying to defend my property.

"Yeah! You are right – it was! When we were in our early thirties." Klava found a comfortable position, sinking her arse deeper into my 'junk'. She was helping herself to some Russian chocolates given to me by my grateful tourists, and stared at my portrait, painted by the famous Russian artist years ago, when I was twenty-seven.

"I cannot believe it – it's been more than twenty years since we moved to Britain. I remember you like you are in this portrait. You were at your best. No man would pass by without turning his head. You need a good shake-up. And for Christ's sake, get rid of this hoarding habit. I can assure you this change will shake off your age as well." She looked at her fingers, clad with a variety of diamond rings, caught me looking at them and sighed, "For our disappearing beauty, we need at least an attractive frame to divert attention. I use these diamonds like armour – a protection from being invisible. It helps. People can ignore me, but they rarely ignore my jewellery."

Klava looked so happy admiring her own collection, feeling younger and twenty kilos lighter just by staring at them. She was absolutely sure that other people around her saw it the same way.

"It wouldn't worry my doctor if I had any diamonds or not."

"It would. He likes Cartier, does he not? Try to give him cufflinks with diamonds, for sure – he'd love them like a father loves his twin sons. They all do, those men from Harley Street and similar." And she burst into laughter so powerful and demonic that I already knew – I had to follow her advice to escape her dissatisfaction.

Klava was also from the C brotherhood. She had recovered slowly after gall bladder cancer, and had been taking life at a lethargic pace, piling on enormous weight and shuffling around at the speed of a tortoise. Yet, she was confident in herself and didn't give a fuck what others thought about her. She was a queen who took no notice of the laughing common faces, tickled by her 'spectacular' figure and controversial personality. Nothing, not even her cheating husband who she caught red-handed, was able to destroy her solid happiness – so long as she was provided with enough funds to finance her Chanel bags and an expensive car with a private chauffeur. It was therapeutic to know that I was not the only one accepting an unconventional marriage arrangement. There were a lot of us out there, struggling to enjoy life beside a husband who had lost his memory and affection for his wife, unsure even of the original colour of her hair.

"Natasha, forget your doctor, trust me on this." Natasha is a Russian equivalent of Natalia or Natalie. "You're worrying he did a runner? Are you sure your tryst had indeed taken place?" I shared with her the full story of my after-hours encounter with Kovač. Her questions confused me and I started to wonder.

"It's a miracle that he actually came here at all, if he did. Count your blessings." Klava was loudly drinking my expensive matcha-powder tea and swallowing her third home-made bun with jam. She had brought those delicious looking fantasies of gluttony, well aware that I did not keep anything fattening at home – not anymore. To deliver good advice, she needed sugar to keep her energy resources up.

Looking at my big, voluminous friend, who had a cup on top of her chubby fingers, I couldn't avoid comparing her with the main figure in the painting by the Russian artist Boris Kustodiev – *Merchant's Wife at Tea*. There were some differences – an extra thirty years in Klava's passport, less choices of still-life on my table and an absence of the Samovar.

"Doctors live in such fear in this country. In Russia, gynaecologists often sleep with their patients, and even victoriously discuss it with their colleagues. Here, they are afraid to shake your hand. They wake up sweating in the middle of the night, afraid of being struck off the register if any female patient or her suspicious husband were to report gross misconduct."

It was a monologue. *She would have made a good barrister,* I thought, biting my nails. I did it to keep my temper at bay. There was simply no chance to respond for a long while. Eventually she paused to take a breath, and I had a chance to pop in a few words,

"But he's not like all doctors! I know that he is, or at least he was, in love with me, too."

"Loving a patient could destroy him completely. If your doctor reached your apartment, he's a brave soldier, surely deeply in love. The stakes are so high: his entire career, his job. After my operation, I was full of gratitude for my surgeon. Not just gratitude, I confess that I harboured some feelings for him. After all, he saved my life, like your doctor." I could see that she was getting emotional as her iron voice softened. "I wanted to thank him with all my heart and give him, a lovely antique sculpture as a present, really valuable – an eighteenth-century patterned bronze Venus. And you know what? He didn't turn up to our meeting. I was very upset for a long time. He spat into my soul."

I could see that Klava felt wounded, but had tried hard to bury her pain.

At least my doc didn't spit; he accepted the presents, I thought and smiled.

"Oh! I remember that piece from your collection. It's fabulous!" I wanted my friend to feel better, too.

"Well, now I can enjoy this marvellous piece of art myself. Whatever happens – it's for the best!" Klava was always capable of finding a positive spin to her shitty situation. "I knew that he would appreciate it, but fear had prevailed," she added. "Doctors here are in the chokehold of a horrifying burocracy and its rules." Klava took another sip of brandy to strengthen her tea, before she could pronounce the word 'GMC' – the General Medical Council.

She was naive to think I didn't know that the stakes were high for my doc. The GMC was a real chamber of horrors for all the doctors of the land. This powerful organisation brought more fear than MI5 and MI6 together. It kept many doctors up at night from haunting nightmares and the fear that something inappropriate could be discovered about them and their practice.

The lucky Dr Samuel Jean de Pozzi was the first chair of gynaecology in Paris in 1884, back when there was no threat from this organization. He had affairs with many famous patients, including the French actress Sarah Bernhardt, the opera singer Georgette Leblanc, the actress Rejane – the widow of George Bizet, the famous composer. Knowledge of his extra services attracted even more patients. He eagerly helped them all, in different ways. His portrait by the Anglo-American artist John Sargent perfectly showed his love for cunts and the erotic skills of his multitalented personality.

"You should be prepared that he won't come back. He'll sit tight for years with his ears glued to his head, afraid to even sneeze, ignoring his true feelings. And not only that… " Klava enjoyed giving me some pain, presenting it as a 'caring' truth. "I wouldn't be surprised if he bans you from being his patient and reports you as a hazard case."

"I'm regretting telling you about Kovač ." I started getting nervous, and nearly all my nails had been gnawed away.

"I bet he's no Casanova in bed," interrupted me Klava. "The job he's doing must have brought on early impotence or turned him gay."

It was all too much to take in. But after Klava's visit, I knew I had to fight for my doctor. The number one priority was a transformation of my apartment, to encourage Kovač to seek sanctuary in a fresh, airy space, away from the heavy, cancerous atmosphere of the hospital. I needed a Perestroika of everything.

"Paul," I called my block manager, a very colourful former electrician, who had been promoted to run our palatial place. He was a decent bloke, in touch with reality, who had managed to not fall prey to the corrupting forces of power. Not yet.

"I want to redecorate my flat – bathroom, shower room – to the highest standard."

"When do you want to start?" Paul was obviously interested in my ambitious plans.

"Yesterday."

I hoped he would understand that there wouldn't be time for tea and biscuits for his builders. I needed to create an elegant, smart and comfortable place for my dear doctor, somewhere he'd dream of returning to. He deserved the best. My place was only a short drive from the hospital, and I imagined that Kovač could come and spend lunch breaks or some evenings here with me. I was well prepared, and even popped into Harrods to buy him silk pyjamas and woollen slippers. That was certainly not in my dreams, as my very real bank statements confirmed.

Klava was right: my apartment was indeed overloaded. It was full of antiques, and an enormous numbers of books; every wall was plastered with paintings, like in a museum. I had been collecting all this stuff in Soviet Russia when the rouble was worth nothing, yet antiques and paintings were a kind of currency.

***

Years ago in Moscow, I would regularly receive a call from the director of the antique shop on Smolenskaya Embankment.

"This is Vitaliy Borisovitch, Natasha. I've reserved for you a couple of Khlebnilov's wonderful salt cellars. Silver – great stuff! Come as soon as you can."

In Soviet times, all valuable items were distributed among a well-known clientele. Despite often paying double, it had been money well spent, as over the years they had appreciated in value and helped me feel more independent here in the UK.

My granny used to say, "Money in your bank account helps to keep your head up and your man on the hook." But she would also repeat another wise doctrine: "If a man spends a lot of money on you, he values you more than if he had gotten you as a freebie. You become his investment and that makes it difficult to leave you."

That's what had happened with Freddie and me. In the early days of our relationship, my future husband wanted to guarantee my exclusivity for himself.

"I will buy you a flat. It'll be registered to my company and you'll be a company director. You can live there as long as you wish."

What he really meant was as long as *he* wished. He thought he had offered me irresistible arrangements, which I would accept with gratitude after living for a few months in a tiny, cold bedsit in London. But I wanted more: a family, a child and a husband, and a house – my house.

"What? I'm not that kind of person. I don't want to be treated as a kept woman!"

I couldn't believe that I was capable of rejecting such an attractive proposition. The different moral forces inside me were fighting with each other. I found the courage to say 'no' to Freddie's comfortable offer. In response to my words, he wrote out a five-figure check to put down as a deposit on a flat in my name – I was rewarded. I couldn't believe my luck, until the next morning when I cashed that check at the local bank. Freddie later paid for the flat in full. Since then, he has found it difficult to leave his investment – me. My granny was right!

***

The building work distracted me from the invasive thoughts about my cryptic night with Kovač and his sudden disappearance from my life. I was calm and absolutely sure that my doc would be back as soon as the flat was ready. I let the builders disassemble my shower so that it could be recreated big enough for the two of us to enjoy it together.

"Don't trust your builders," Klava continued sticking her nose into my affairs. "You need to watch them closely; otherwise a few of your best things may disappear. I had a bad experience with my workmen and my designer... with all of them. It was a few weeks of Hell."

I wondered if she had ever had a good experience with anyone.

All the time during the great renovations, Kovač was neither seen nor heard.

Fly Me to the Moon

6th November 2015
Aero Club, West Oxfordshire

I was always afraid of heights. Even looking down through the window of my apartment made me dizzy. And it was not a sky-scraper. I also hated moving at speed on the road or anywhere else. When driven by Freddie, I felt uncomfortable on narrow, winding country lanes. Thirty miles an hour seemed more like a hundred, and each turn carried the danger of a head-on collision. Freddie enjoyed those frightening trips and, instead of reassuring me, he'd always try to add more of a thrill by turning the steering wheel with bravado. That's how it was before my operation. After C – my Chairman was scared to sit next to me in my Merc. He thought that I had turned into a crazy driver. I started enjoying fast rides – it made me feel rather erotic. Every wheel-screeching turn gave the sensation of gaining back control of my zigzagging life. Yet, driving fast wasn't enough for me – I wanted more from life. I had always dreamed of achieving something incredible, against all odds, to prove my mother wrong when she told me as a young girl that she regretted not aborting me.

"I've decided to take up flying," I informed Freddie. I was sure that this would make a big impact on Kovač. My husband looked taken aback by my sudden revelation, being well aware of my previous issues with speed and heights.

"Don't be ridiculous," he said. "You'll bring the plane down… or it'll never take off."

That was rude. But what did I care?

Joining the Aero Club seemed like an exciting prospect. It wasn't only about piloting, but also about meeting the club's fearless male members – guys of substance and grit. I put a call through right away to book my lesson,

"I want to fly." That was all I said.

A lovely female voice replied, "It is 180 pounds for two hours. One hour of theory, the second is for a flight."

"Theory?" That was not exactly what I wanted to spend my money on. "I'm a lady of practice. I learn as I go."

"Learn as you go is fine, but not when you're flying a plane." The answer was firm, and there was no chance of bending the rules.

"Fine. That'll do for me."After my operation, I had stopped counting money. "Life is for living, not for counting," – I lived by my granny's words. It became part of my own philosophy. Freddie always used to spoil the pleasure by adding, "Only when you have something to count."

"When would you like to come in?" I was asked by the club manager.

"Today!"

"I'm afraid the weather this afternoon isn't good for a first flight. But the forecast for the next few days is promising. Shall I book you in for tomorrow?"

The lady took my credit card details and everything was set up.

"I want the best possible instructor. Who would you recommend?"

"All our instructors are excellent and very experienced."

"I don't want them to be *too* experienced. Give me someone under thirty, please."

After a little silence, the lovely voice answered with understanding, "I'll book you in with Scott, our Australian tutor."

I knew that I was understood.

***

It was a frosty but sunny, clear November day, reminding me that winter was not too far away and that late autumn could be truly beautiful. Before C, I would never have noticed this subtlety in the changing of the seasons. It reflected my new lease of life, keeping my spirits high.

The club's car park was almost full, and a lot of the cars looked posh and rather arousing. Passing through the bar, I saw a few old guys. *How charming! Probably dads*, I thought. *They've come to see their kids in action, or even grandkids*, as some of the guys appeared to be in their eighties.

"These are our members," I was introduced to the group by the club's manager, who was showing me around.

"Members?" This word nearly gave me a heart attack. I knew that all of the planes in the club were for visual guidance only. It was unlikely that those guys could hear and see much, not only in the air but on the ground, too! "It's a suicide club!" I squeaked.

It was probably rude to say that, but I was concerned for my well-being. "What if they don't see me and my plane in the skies?"

"You don't need to worry. This is your instructor, Scott. He'll teach you all aspects of being in the air."

I was introduced to a very tall, very handsome young guy. I perked up.

"Great! My name is Natalia."

I gave him my hand. I wanted to check if his was warm or cold. It turned out to be very warm. I gave it a little bit of a squeeze, trying to indicate my approval.

"This is how I visualise pilots. I can tell that you'll be definitely able to teach me how to fly."

"I'll do my best," he said, blushing slightly. He must've understood that I was appreciating his aesthetic.

"Let's go and see our eagle."

"We will in a minute. First, we need to register you in the

book and complete some paperwork. It's important we do this before every flight."

"I understand – someone needs to be aware that we'll be in the air, and if we don't come back, they'll know that we found a better life." I pointed to the sky and laughed. It was encouraging to see that Scott also smiled at me in return.

"That's right!" He took my remarks as humour and didn't take any offence, or perhaps, as a part of a different, Eastern European culture he had yet to explore.

Twelve planes were lined up on the airfield just a hundred metres from the club building. The fresh grass tricked me into thinking that it was safe to walk over, but as we proceeded towards our plane, my lacquered shoes sunk into the quagmire of earth below.

"To reach the right target, you need to pass through shit," I recalled my dear granny's wisdom. Her saying turned out to be a programme written into me, including during my encounter with C.

We soon stopped near the tiny plane.

"It looks like a toy. Can it fly heavy cargo like me?"

"Don't worry. It manages much heavier loads! Appearances can be deceptive – though small, it's actually very strong, built to a higher standard than a car."

"Does it have a parachute?"

"Not this one. The one on the edge of the field does. Can you see it?"

I peered across the field and saw a far superior plane.

"That one costs 300.000 pounds, and a lesson would be double the price."

"And how many lessons will I need to get a licence?"

"A minimum of 48 but for you, with your humour, I would say at least 100," he laughed.

I decided not to comment on his estimation of my flying talents until I had shown him what I could do in the air. And actually, being in the sky with a guy like Scott - you wouldn't catch me complaining about a huge number of hours! The only obstacle was the cost of having him on board!

"Our plane is a Piper Warrior, 1960s model," my tutor started his pre-flight briefing.

The date made me jerk. It was not too far from my age. I knew well that at my age not everything works perfectly. Some parts got loose. Occasionally you couldn't get on time for landing. Scott caught on,

"Don't worry. It was recently refurbished and supplied with a new engine."

"Just like me - I was also recently refurbished. I ..." and then I stopped. I decided that perhaps he did not need to know the exact details of my reconstruction. *He will probably think about Botox and fillers or a face lift. Let him.*

My lovely instructor continued his educational duties,

"It has dual controls and also many duplicated systems - duplicated flying control, two fuel tanks, two ignition systems..."

"I wish I had something duplicated in my engine. That would make my life much easier - two pairs of boobs would attract double the guys."

"Actually, it's only a single engine."

"What do we do if..." I did not want to say 'crash', following my belief that your thoughts could materialise.

"We glide."

"Not with me in the cabin. It will be too much for this little chick."

Scott looked at me nervously, unsure how to handle my questions. He seemed to have trouble telling whether I was joking or being serious. At least he could bear me - that was an achievement on its own!

I hardly took any notice of those features he showed me on the plane, though noted that the two fuel tanks were full. That was enough of the technical side for me. I could not stop worrying about how I'd climb up and get into the cockpit through the narrow door that looked like a pigeon hole.

"Do you have any steps?" I had to pop in this 'delicate' question.

"Use these handles. It's slippery – be careful." My handsome instructor probably realised that I was a bit older than it was desirable for learning to fly.

My arthritic hip and lack of stretching practice made it highly unlikely that I could make it without any help. But since the operation, after my womanly organs were removed, testosterone, the male hormone, prevailed in my body. It made my face hairy, pushing out black moustache hairs around my lips and chin. I had to get the little beasts threaded every two weeks and go through agonising pain to avoid looking like Salvador Dali or Good Soldier Schweik, and actually match my photo on the driving licence. But this hormone also filled me with incredible determination and fearlessness. To my own surprise, I climbed up the wing of the aircraft as fast as a young scout.

"Hey! Let's take a photo together. It's so cool to stand on the wing of this dragon!"

It looked like Scott was well accustomed to the photo demands of his crazy 'pilots'. We were lucky to spot an engineer passing by and he was entrusted with my iPhone.

"That has to go on Facebook. I want the entire world to know!" I shouted to Scott. By the entire world, I meant Kovač. It was for him that I needed this gorgeous young man to be with me in the shot, hugging me and getting ready to take me to the skies.

There were no helmets or goggles, no oxygen masks, no evidence of a parachute – none of what you'd see in the movies. All I was offered was just a huge headset, so that I could carry on the conversation with my lovely instructor in the air. Fitted with many mysterious dials, the control panel looked a bit scary. Scott talked and talked, using some strange words like 'altitude indicator', 'altimeter', 'turn indicator'. I remembered hearing some of those words at school during my physics lessons.

***

I was always a humanitarian-minded pupil. Back in Soviet Russia, science and maths lessons induced frequent nightmares.

"Popova, go to the blackboard. What's your chosen topic for this term?" Our physics teacher, a fat baldish man, Yaakov Isaakovitch, obviously fancied young, fat girls. He loved my big thighs, sticking out very provocatively from under my school uniform. I gave him a good chance to observe and admire them in full. Not for nothing: I needed a decent mark to avoid a hysterical attack from my mother.

"The vocal waves," I replied. I sung in a choir and had a pretty good understanding of how voice sounds worked. Yet, at that time, my speech was filled with a lot of stammering and long frustrating pauses – the result of the psychological terror that I went through. Thank God, I had a helper – a small pencil. I kept dropping it on the floor and kept bending low to pick it up, exposing the tops of my thighs to the sweating teacher. Judging by the strangled sounds that followed, the poor man was clearly unable to cope and was restraining himself from orgasming in front of the whole class of sixteen-year-old students.

"That's... that's good enough. You can go back to your desk. Four."

Four was a good mark, equivalent to a B in the UK. Bending over ensured my acceptable academic result in this complicated subject.

***

"Ok, first we need to roll the aircraft to the holding point. It's over there where we will start," Scott pointed to a big red sock, fluttering two hundred meters or so away. "Let me ask the air traffic controller if it's clear to go."

I wasn't sure what exactly we were told, as the radio message sounded like a stream of verbal nonsense. I couldn't understand a thing, but Scott's expression confirmed that we were allowed to make a move.

"This is a control panel," he explained, as if I didn't know.

"They are the same as in a car," I was quick to note.

"Nearly," Scott sounded sarcastic. "Both elevator and ailerons respond to the movement of the control column. To release the parking brake, you need to pull this handle."

"It doesn't want to move," I answered after a good try.

"Pull it harder – harder – harder!" This command shifted my sex drive into its top gear, making my brain malfunction, and preventing from dragging our plane into the right position.

"The throttle should be fully opened."

I wondered what he meant. The word sounded very erotic: throttle – ha! It was all too much for the ageing beginner – too arousing, too complicated – as if I was back at university and studying an engineering course for a change.

"Darling, let's fly. Leave this for later," I shouted into my mic, making sure I would be heard. Scott looked at me with understanding, and after a short pre-start check-up we began taxiing our bird across the field.

"I want to do it myself. I can! It does not look difficult at all."

"You can steer on the ground using the rudder pedals. They are connected to the nose wheel."

But my pedals were faulty – I wanted the plane to go left, but it was going to the right. I tried to push it to the right, but the bugger was carrying to the left.

"For the money I paid, they could have given me a better plane."

My instructor did not reply to my comment; he simply took full control with his hands. It was bumpy for a short while but soon I felt we were in the air, higher and higher. It seemed very easy – just letting the bird fly.

"How can this heavy bird stay in the air?"

"The forward movement of the aircraft produces upward thrust on its wings, and that makes it go."

"Thrust – another nice word," I smirked. It looked like my lesson fee included the full service. "A good thrust would make me fly, too. And a few good thrusts would turn the clock back and take me to the heavens. We are in the heavens, aren't we?"

The guy enjoyed our little off-protocol entertainment. He blushed but continued, "Thrust opposes drag."

"There're drugs here as well? Lovely! We can get high in all senses of the word!"

"It's not difficult to sustain the same altitude. You need to watch the line of the horizon. Applying pressure on the control column means we can keep it up on the right level. The back pressure makes the nose pitch up and the aircraft starts to climb." The Australian guy was naively hoping to pique my interest in the technicalities of flight.

"Yes, that sounds familiar. I had to put pressure on all my three husbands to sustain a decent altitude, so we could fly beautifully."

I felt all my comments and jokes were horribly vulgar, but I wasn't able to stop. Sexual images filled the hole in my wrecked body. It was insane but at the same time magic, all these provocative lessons with this handsome and relaxed pilot. Of course, it was a blessing that he was Australian and had good training in tolerance. An Englishman would probably have thrown me out of the plane straight away.

"My turn," I held firmer to the control column. I was eager to try it myself, feeling confident at that height. Even if something went wrong, there would be enough time to put things right before we hit the ground.

"Wait, watch my demonstration first. When we reach twelve hundred metres, we'll be more stable and then you can try on your own."

I was watching the altimeter – 1200 meters! Now! I pressed the right rudder, the pedal by my feet, and the plane skidded to the right. That was a bit rough. I remembered that there was a left one too, which would straighten up my Piper Warrior. I probably pressed slightly hard, as I noticed Scott turn rather pale. Obviously, he did not trust women much, just like Freddie.

"More gently, please," he begged quietly, not to scare me and make it worse.

"You men are all the same. You want to look brave on the battlefield, in the air, in bed. All three of my husbands asked me to be gentler. My current one, the Chairman, barely allowed me to make a sound. And, if my passion left scratches on his back, he'd consider it an assault."

My conversation probably aroused the veteran engine – the plane started going up and up and up.

"What should be done to put it right?" Scott was trying to question my new knowledge on navigation.

"Nothing can make my man right. My navigational skills are not needed. It's just one way – down."

It was a pity Freddie failed to realise that the occasional hug around the shoulder wouldn't have aggravated his blood pressure. This painful thought chased me even higher in the air.

"I'm not sure if this is funny or sad and I don't want to know so much, not here anyway. Move the control column away from yourself."

"Column? I just call it a steering wheel," I said and, as I pulled it gently away, a miracle happened: my airborne dragon did exactly what I wanted him to do. "He is a good boy! I wish the men in my life would be as obedient."

"Well done. I'm impressed. It's actually you who's flying the plane." I heard the supportive voice of my instructor. "Look below – Didcot power station and nuclear research centre. We're not allowed to fly over it. Take to the left."

"Fuck! What would happen if one our club veteran pilots landed his plane over there? Not sure if those aviators I saw today have good sight."

"It's very unlikely. We don't need to discuss it here, do we?"

Looking at his beautiful brown eyes, I thought he was right. *Another place should be better.*

"Didcot? That's where I attended the Sex Maniacs' Ball with my husband. The energy there was atomic, and now I know where the supply came from."

"What's a Sex Maniacs' Ball?" The astonished guy asked me, though quickly regretted it and turned beetroot-red.

"Stick with me, my darling, and you'll learn a lot of things you're missing out on in life. Next time I'll bring a Sinatra CD, so we can fly with music."

"I have to say you're a very unusual pupil."

"My granny used to say to me – 'The best woman for a man is a new one.'"

"I have a girlfriend," the Australian pilot revealed in haste, looking scared that I might want to take her place.

A voice through the headphones interrupted our studies. I thought it was something in German or even Danish, which I was not fluent in at all. But Scott obviously was.

"The air traffic controller wants us to come back. Dark clouds are moving towards us."

"Well, all wonderful things have to end sooner or later. Surely, later is better but, as my husband likes to say – 'The best is the enemy of the good.'"

We turned back towards our airfield. Soon after, I started to make out three lines of planes in the distance. They looked tiny, like kids' toys.

"May I do the landing?"

"No. That's the hardest part. Most people think that take-off is difficult but landing is far more dangerous. Can you look out for other planes, please?"

"You are making a third circle…"

"Yes, there are other aircrafts that have priority for landing. I need to hear 'all clear' from the controller."

And then I noticed one plane that seemed to be coming straight at us.

"He can't see us. Look! What's he doing?"

Scott sharply raised our altitude to avoid a collision. "That was close," he said, exhaling loudly.

"I told you: those blokes lost their sight a decade or two ago. I'm sure they're not able to hear commands from the controller either. I knew it was a Suicide Club the moment I saw that lot in the bar!"

"Yeah! But it's not always like this. Today is Friday and the veteran team likes to get together and fly to France for lunch. This is the time they return."

"They probably, couldn't resist the French wine," I said, then noticed another plane coming in to land. It veered uncomfortably close to us. My sweating instructor had to make a fourth circle at a very low altitude.

"We're so close to those houses. I thought we'd touch their roofs. Just a couple of metres above them!"

"It was actually eight."

"How do they live there? They are always at risk from 80-year-old pilots and crazy ladies like me. Makes me think of *Whaam!* by Roy Lichtenstein. It was painted in 1963, about the time those brave suicidal aeronauts started their flights."

"I'm trying to be very careful to avoid the *Whaam!* pilots." He knew the painting – I was impressed.

Scott gave me a charming smile and we gently touched the ground. Rolling on the field felt even rougher after our 'smooth' ride in the air. It was so nice to fly with such a fun-loving cultural tutor. But I decided to never take my flying lessons on Fridays anymore.

"Tamrico," I called my friend from the club's bar. "I can fly a plane! Well, nearly. Just landed. I don't feel like a victim anymore. I am a victorious survivor! And there, in the skies with my handsome tutor, I didn't think once about Kovač."

"There's no limit to what you're prepared to do to impress your doctor. The only thing left for you is to fly straight to the moon."

I've just been there! I thought, but I kept it to myself so as not to make my friend too jealous.

The Elderly Graduate

It was a Saturday in November, a fine day – still warm, green and quiet before the Christmas madness. The huge wigwam-shaped marquee had been erected a couple of days earlier on our farm grounds near the lake, ready to accommodate a substantial amount of people. It was time for the Chairman's milestone birthday celebrations.

"Tamrico, my husband recreated the Disneyland he missed in his post-war childhood." I was again on the phone to my dear friend, thanking Alexander Graham Bell for his wonderful invention.

"We all want a fairy tale at some point in our life." Tamara always took a fair position.

"280 lucky fellows were invited to celebrate my Chairman growing old and mad. I need you to be there for support. I can't face it all on my own."

"If I come, it will only be for a couple of hours. Then I have to go back to London. I'm working the next day from eight in the morning. You should understand why he's organising this event. He simply realised that he's reaching the winter of his life. That's surely pushed him to throw this massive extravagant party."

"You're right. It's sad in a way. But his crazy ideas about *The Graduate*… it's unbearable even to think about!"

"Why? You are interested in your doctor – he wants young

girls. You want to be a pilot, he's chosen to be a graduate. You are both equally unsatisfied with reality and are trying to invent it in your own way."

"I thought you were going to be on my side."

"I am. But you need to understand the reasons for his actions, and then it'll be easier to accept."

Tamara was the gift of my life. It was a pity that her good judgement didn't help my clever friend to organise her own life. She asked too much from herself, wanted perfection from others, and as a result never got married, never had a family, and never even had sex.

The cowboy outfit the birthday boy had hired for the evening made him look like the star of a 1940s Western – John Wayne, no less. Freddie spent a few extra bucks on good gear to really look the part in his own fairy tale. Tamara was right: like most of us, he wanted to believe, even at his respectful age, that he deserved a happy ending with eternal love and life.

In charge of the preparations for this extravaganza was Freddie's PA, a single, childless woman in her mid-forties who looked like a little girl. For me – a book-lover – she looked more like a Lilliputian: a small body with an ageing adult face.

"Hi, Natalia. What a day! Everybody looks so happy!" she said with a cheerful smile. I knew that she disliked me; perhaps she could sense negative energy towards her, and the hatred became mutual. The woman was pretty sure that I wasn't over the moon about the events about to unfold.

"Ha-ha! Ha-ha!" I sniggered and pulled a plastic gun out of my belt. I'd found it earlier in an old trunk stuffed with my son's toys. I pointed it at her like kids do when trying to eliminate their enemies. But what looked like an innocent joke was a real desire to shoot. It made me think of Niki Saint Phalle and her *Shooting Pictures*, where she would shoot a gun at a bag of paint attached to the canvas. Just like her I would take great pleasure in pulling the trigger and creating some art of my own, albeit with a rather messy outcome.

Miss Lilliput looked at me as if I was mad. And she wasn't wrong – I probably was going mad under the pressure of the Chairman's World of Westerns and his complete disregard for my existence, both in this adult play and in life generally.

The guests were arriving in their chaps and jeans, overloaded with the pistols and whips they too had borrowed from their children. Or perhaps from their grandchildren. Every second attendee had a cowboy hat pulled over their balding head or hanging down their back. We were invaded with a lot of odd-looking guys – Jack London's stories brought to life.

Some faces expressed amazement at the grandeur of the setting, or even sincere surprise that they were worthy of an invitation to such an extravaganza; some just looked amused; others, after stepping into the fairy tale, were sadly realizing that they would have to increase the scale of their own forthcoming celebrations or simply skip them completely.

At the entrance to the wigwam was written, 'Welcome to the estern Fantasy World', but the letter W was missing, changing 'Western' into almost 'Eastern'. That was probably God's doing, to reflect a diverse reality more accurately: a lot of guests were of Indian and Pakistani origin – Freddie's cricket club members. This 'English' game at the local club had been transformed in the last few years and now represented more of the Commonwealth. They may have disregarded or been unaware of the cowboy theme, as many were dressed in national Pakistani shalwar kameez, mostly black or grey wool, appropriate to the season.

The majority of this crowd were people I'd never seen before. I hadn't been invited into this part of Freddie's life. There was also a strong presence of local farmers among the guests. Some seemed rather familiar. On the whole, this macho team did not give me any tickles.

"There can't be two 280 friends. Who are all this lot?" I asked Nick.

I didn't get an answer.

"Nice to see you. Oh my! You've grown so much." A huge tall man in his late fifties approached us.

"I remember you as a little boy." He was addressing my son. It was Joel, not quite a farmer. Joel used to coach Nick in tennis when he was seven or eight years old. During those years, I had to put up with his complaints that my son was far from the most able kid,

"I throw him a ball but he always misses it! He sings and sings all the time. He was belting out something about Nessun Dorma. Little Pavarotti; full stop."

Joel was right – Nicholas missed all the balls – tennis, cricket and rugby to the grief of his dad. But he never missed a note in his music scores. Joel used to be an attractive guy but he had fattened up over the years. His bust had grown to a full C cup. I would never have recognised him if he hadn't addressed us himself.

"Are we still throwing balls?" My words were just a polite greeting. I hugged Joel and was done with him for the evening.

This picturesque mass of people made me think for a minute about William Firth's painting *The Derby Day*, presenting a broad panorama of Victorian life moved forward 150 years to Surrey.

The Wild Surrey birthday scene looked even more theatrical, covering all genres – from comedy to drama, as if it was staged for an outdated theatre production.

Besides the farmers and cricket-goers in attendance, there were also former business acquaintances, windsurfing club members and local residents, all of whom Freddie had come across at some point during his lengthy life.

"It's much too lavish!" an old ruddy-cheeked man finished his words with a good sip of expensive wine.

"He is such an extrovert!" added his wife, sticking one of the many decorative cacti plants into her purse as a souvenir.

I knew for certain that Freddie wanted to give his guests a nice time, but it became clear that many saw this event as showing off or even as an opportunity for bragging.

"Hello, Natalia!" Two familiar faces entered the wigwam. It was Marzena and Bryn Farrow, local farmers and landowners, and really good pals of Freddie. I had been blessed to know them for more than two decades – they were boring but kind people. It was Marzena's prolonged conversation about the seeds in the loo that had driven me mad and away from Freddie's parties and friends. One thing I noticed was that Marzena was never happy. She smiled all the time but with an expression of sadness or disappointment.

"Well, it's hard for her," my husband would comment on Marzena's state. "Bryn used to chase a lot of women into the family bed and would unfairly compare Marzena to them and his first wife. The old man always been cruel to his second wife. He still lives with the past in his dreams."

"I wonder if his first wife died prematurely because it was nicer than living with Bryn." I simply could not keep my mouth shut, though I was perfectly aware what might come after such a comment. That was years ago. Since then, I had learned to breathe in and count to ten before saying anything. I thought that made me very British.

"What an amazing party!" Bryn and Marzena exclaimed in unison. I wouldn't exactly call them Bonnie and Clyde – they seemed a far cry from a wild outlaw couple in spite of their carefully chosen outfits.

"This is just the beginning," I said, playing the role of the hostess. I put on my granite shield to be able to do it.

I noticed that a lot of guests were staring at me. They had heard that Freddie's wife landed in Britain from the dying planet, the USSR, but had never seen me before. Now it was their chance to take a good look and deliver their judgement. It was even harder to bear when others passed by not noticing me at all. My Chairman didn't make any effort to introduce me to his friends and acquaintances. He was busy showing off his costume and occasionally disappearing behind the stage to prepare for his *Graduate* showcase. I was so glad when I saw a vast ball rolling towards me – I knew it was my Tamrico. She was carrying a huge bunch of flowers.

I rushed towards her with warm greetings,

"You're my saviour! I feel like I'm being stripped of all my clothes in the middle of a circus. How did you get here?"

"I took a cab from the station and gave him the address you texted me last night."

"You should have called and I would've picked you up."

"I'm glad I didn't. You clearly don't have a free minute. You were right – it's like Disneyland in here – busy, glamorous and pretentious." She was wheezing heavily after a short run from the cab. "You need big ambitions to organise an event like this."

"And money!" I added.

"We don't need to mention this. The English don't talk about money, they spend it. It's been ages since I last visited; Nick was still a young kid. I love it here. I hardly have time to enjoy nature – work, work and work."

"He's a big guy now. He'll be very glad to see you." I knew she mostly made the effort to come here to meet Nicholas, to whom she taught Russian years ago. They were very fond of each other.

"Where's your Wild West costume?"

"Here it is!" Tamara smiled and gave me the flowers. "They're for you and Fred."

"Freddie would prefer a banana as he's getting ready to perform as an orangutan. Don't worry, I can dig something out to give you a touch of the Wild West."

"I was thinking of bringing a toy gun like yours, but the kids at my school play different games, involving condoms and drugs. As far as I know, that's not in practice at your place."

My dear friend worked night shifts with troubled teenagers on top of a full day's work. She needed it to pay off her ever-growing mortgage.

"I can find you a hat and you'll look like most of the other guests. And you can give the flowers to Freddie. There he is," I pointed towards my husband.

"Hello, Freddie!" My jolly virgin stepped forward and tripped. She was short and round, like a ball. It was both sad and funny. I was glad my husband didn't notice, as he was busy with his guests. In his eyes, this would be the typical behaviour of two fat Russian women.

"Tamara!" Nicholas was running to help. "What happened? Are you ok?"

He lifted her up from the grass and they hugged tightly after many years of not seeing each other. I collected the dropped flowers and we, a team of three against nearly 300, headed into the huge tent.

Guests were making the most of the open bar and slowly proceeded to the tables with filled glasses. Endless wooden tables were decorated with a variety of cactus plants in small ceramic white pots. A few fir trees would have been more appropriate of course, since we were not that far from Christmas. I wondered if it had been a present from the British Commonwealth or from Uncle Sam, perhaps, from Arizona. Or was it the Lilliputian's idea to stick my arse with those exotic 'beauties'?

The prickly cacti indeed reminded me of the painful stings of life, like Freddie's rejection of me as a woman that came with a similar warning: *Do not touch!* It made me think about *Noli Me Tangere*, do not touch – the title of the painting by Titian. It depicts Christ appearing to Mary Magdalene after the Resurrection to comfort her. I could have benefited from the Holy Spirit giving me some peace of mind and strength to withstand the event. Or maybe Tamrico was my angel? Angels come in many forms and shapes!

"Attention, friends! Attention!"

Freddie looked stunningly odd in his wide cowboy trousers and wide leather belt, taking the celebration into his own hands.

"I've written a script based on the old Dustin Hoffman film *The Graduate*."

The Chairman had always dreamed about being a writer, but only now had he discovered the literary talent within himself. I knew what was coming next. I also knew that I should not have done what followed, but anger and jealousy prevailed and I shouted across the room with all the power my belly could give to support my voice,

"The guy in Mike Nichols' film was 16 and you are 65!"

"Calm down," Tamara pulled the sleeve of my denim jacket. "Let him enjoy himself."

My husband ignored this remark and signalled the start of the show, putting life into action. A woman appeared on the stage, and I recognised his friends' daughter Lacy. She was in her early thirties, but was aged with heavy make-up to look like the actress Anne Bancroft when she came to seduce her friend's son. Here, in front of everyone, it was Freddie who was trying to seduce her – his genius script had an original twist and was presented with passion, and rehearsed rather well. Even Stanislavsky, the inventor of the famous Method, would say "*I believe!*"

I turned numb. I was not sure what to do and how to behave. My 65- year-old husband lifted the 'actress' in his arms and carried her out of the room backstage. I started to laugh hysterically and, like a supporting wife, demonstrated to all around me that my husband's disgusting and degrading actions were actually enjoyable and witty. I pushed Tamara with my elbow, inviting her to join in the applause with me. Nicholas teamed up with us, clapping with his huge hands.

"I'm impressed with the scale of dad's literary and acting 'talents," he whispered in astonishment.

Freddie appeared to take all the cheering as a sincere compliment. His confidence was growing stronger and stronger. He disappeared backstage and came out a few minutes later dressed to impress – in an orangutan suit! I hadn't imagined that our local fancy dress shop was that diversely stocked. The face of the ape reminded me of the *Guerrilla Girls* poster at the Tate. Pity, that the girls Freddie were aiming to pick up were not naked as on that famous piece of art, which presented a strong gender statement.

We moved from the movie to a circus. My husband, a company director, a father of three, was running around the wigwam and filling it with what he thought would be the sex appeal of a real male monkey.

"She's the best!" My husband approached Bryn's daughter, thirty-year-old Jessica, a pretty redhead and lifted her up into the air.

I knew Freddie adored redheads, including even the Duchess of York, who he had always considered to be the most normal of the royals and a victim of their intrigues. The toe- sucking scandal made her even more attractive for him.

"Wow!" We exclaimed simultaneously with Tamara, and I froze in disbelief. It was not clear if the Chairman was more excited about the girl or about his own ability to lift her from the ground. He was thrusting his hips 'artistically' like a sexually super-powered ape. He played the character well, but he could not fool me.

The anticipation was growing among the audience, but it looked that something went wrong with the planned production. Jessica managed to free herself from my husband's passionate embrace and slapped him across the face in front of everybody. I felt triumphant. At least he got what he deserved. It was rather unfortunate that the guests didn't really notice. The line of waiters appeared at the same moment with plates piled spectacularly high with lamb, which produced a narcotic aroma and caused the interests of their stomachs to prevail over the delicate drama. Still, that was a firm setback for the Old Man, but I had another one ready to go into action.

As a birthday gift, I had bought him an impressive sculpture by my son's friend, a struggling yet hopeful artist. It presented an old man, perhaps an aged Bacchus, absolutely naked, proudly displaying his male trophies, constructed out of a Kalashnikov bullet. This image made a lovely postcard too. I had printed exactly 280, one for each guest, with the added text: 'The real face and essential features of Freddie Fitzcock'. I took them out of my purse and started handing them out to all guests as a keepsake of this important artistic debut, to make it indeed unforgettable.

At that moment, Freddie's deputy, Steven, a bulky guy with a crop of short hair sticking up like spikes, embarked on a long speech praising my husband and his life achievements.

"It can take me a long time just to mention everything that Freddie Fitzcock has done to help our community!" The life of my 'dearest' seemed to be so important and grand that the overexcited bloke was unable to fit his entire list of my Chairman's wonderful qualities and charitable generosity into a 40-minute speech. At that moment, I realised that I lived with a local saint.

The local councillor, slightly drunk after a bottle of brandy, took over from Steven and continued the tribute.

"Freddie and his wife's enormous contribution to our society attracts great respect and gratitude." The applause rocked the Wild West marquee, accompanied by the sound of empty glasses. In fact, most of the long list was true. The Chairman supported many local charities.

"You see! They mentioned you in the speech!" Tamara was trying to focus on the positives of the evening.

"The wife they mentioned was not me. It was his first. They cheered the deceased one. I'm not of any importance in my husband's life – just a useless piece of furniture, an old, deserted cunt."

"Mother, but you didn't take any interest in Dad's life," Nicholas joined in.

"When could I? For twenty years I was busy with you – first your education, then helping to build your career in music." I knew I was partly guilty but I had the excuse for giving all that I could to my son, all that I never received in my own childhood. It started from choosing the right father for him.

"Thank you, ladies and gentlemen," The 'graduate' gushed, cutting the speeches short to clear the hot air in the wigwam. "I want to thank my PA for helping me to organise this party and get you all together."

Miss Lilliputian grew at least two inches taller in front of everybody from pride! She climbed up onto the stage and grabbed a huge bouquet of flowers from my husband, not forgetting an envelope with thank-you vouchers. She kissed my old man with the passion of a woman who had received at least ten thousand pounds. *It was no more than a hundred quid*, I guessed.

"Bitch!" I whispered loudly into my son's ear. His presence next to me at the table helped to prevent me from breaking down in tears. My whisper sunk under the storm of applause.

"I want to thank my daughter, who came from Australia especially for me!" A big palm tree was brought to the stage for Denise.

"Of course, there are no palms in Australia, are there? Or not enough to feed kangaroos. She'll take it in wrappings to Qantas," I said to Tamara dryly. I hated myself for starting to be nasty, sniping with all these ugly remarks.

"I want to thank my nephew for the wonderful present, a stunning sculpture of a walrus. Have you all seen it?"

In response, multiple voices piped up, "Yes" and "Fantastic!"

Freddie glanced towards our table and added, "We're now surrounded by creatures with large forms." He laughed, enjoying his own joke. My son squeezed my hand under the table. We both perfectly understood what the Chairman meant by these words.

"Just ignore it!" Nicholas cheered me up. "We both know Dad is going gaga."

I thought I was invisible to my husband. The reality was even worse – I was his target for humiliation. And so was my fulsome friend, Tamara.

"I also want to thank Natalia," Freddie stammered. I felt he was not sure what he should thank me for. "She's been through very hard times, but she is still here with us." He wiped his sweating forehead, looking happier that he had finished with me.

"I asked him not to let anyone know about C," I whispered in my son's ear.

"You know Dad, he can't keep secrets, they gush out of him."

"He didn't even call you 'my wife'. He simply listed you among the other women," Tamara looked very upset for me.

My husband did not invite me up to the stage. He handed a small, slightly tired bouquet of yellow roses to his youngest granddaughter, five-year-old Cathy, and pushed her towards me. The words about death – *ring a ring o' roses, a pocket full of posies* – were pounding in my ears. I felt like my heart was going to jump out of my chest. This time there was no Kovač to stop my scary thoughts.

"Darling," I was approached by Susanna, a 90-year-old local physiotherapist who had treated Freddie's injuries since his adolescence. "Another few years, and time will eliminate all your differences and forgiveness will cement your loving relationship. Look at our Queen and Prince Philip. All his adulterous and stupid behaviour has been forgotten, and the royal couple are now like two palomas." Sadly, the wise Susanna couldn't help Freddie with his head injuries, as that not quite her field of expertise.

"She's right," said Tamara. "You just need to have some patience. I have to go; the cab is coming to pick me up."

With that she left, reassuring me that she could find her own way out from the Wigwam of Hell.

A jazz band set up and started to play, possibly trying to black out the pain and embarrassment of the event. Strangely, Freddie decided to approach me as his first partner on the dance floor. It was time for his guilt to come out. With my lighter figure after training in Zumba, I didn't feel too bad there, in the middle of the stage. My emotional state produced a powerful, fire-like dance. It was not a dance – it was an eruption of my soul. My 65-year-old 'graduate' could hardly catch up with me. He seemed surprised by a burst of passion in his wounded *old cunt*.

"I'm amazed by your ability to pick yourself up from broken pieces. You're a master of survival," he yelled through the music. I realised that Freddie had tried to break me into even smaller pieces, and watch if I could rise again as a phoenix.

I stopped in the middle of the dance and looked around at this mad, now drunk crowd. After a couple of bottles, the guests had forgotten whether it was a birthday or a funeral. I knew that at some point in your life you have to let go of what you thought should happen and accept what is happening. Yet, I was not ready to accept this ridiculous extravaganza. For me, it was a feast in a time of plague, nothing else. I started walking away, faster and faster, until I was nearly running back to the house. I wanted reality my way, and for that I needed Kovač. I had to get him back into my life, whatever it took. I ran up the stairs to my bedroom, put a big, hard book on my knees, and placed a piece of paper on top. I paused for a minute and slowly began my letter, trying to make it clear and understandable.

Dear Andy, I've missed you so much...

It took me hours to produce ten pages of love – at the end, my heart and body felt like it was covered in ten litres of tears. I used the special, expensive paper my son had bought for his CVs. The thick, yellow pages could hardly fit into an envelope. When sealed, it looked rather pregnant with my feelings. I felt drained and needed to escape from all thoughts, dreams, hope, pain. I sank into the darkness.

A Personal Delivery

16ᵗʰ November 2015,
Queen Anne St, the consulting rooms
Central London

The first thought that entered my brain upon waking up was the fear that my precious letter could end up in the wrong hands. I decided on the spot that I couldn't send it by post, so I set myself a mission for the day: to hand it to Andy in person.

I carefully chose an outfit for this important handover – a black leather jacket with gold studs that was supposed to reflect my adventurous soul; and high boots, purposefully kinky ones, which were able to knock off a few days of my age, at least at first glance. I headed straight for a manicure; a necessary activity as my fingers would be seen during the letter exchange. I also popped into the Indian threading parlour to sadistically pinch away my little moustache, in the hope of communicating my gender more clearly. I hopped into the car to begin the hour-long journey to London.

My Merc, still saturated with the fresh scent of new leather, conjured up an image of a financially independent woman. The drive gave me time to think about the logistics of the task ahead of me: how to catch my doc off-guard. I knew he operated on Monday mornings at the Queen's, and about lunchtime he would be moving from the hospital to the outpatients rooms nearby.

"Hello, I have an appointment with Doctor Kovač today but I am not sure where. Is he at the King George consulting rooms?" I gave the receptionist a call to confirm the doc's location.

"Yes, he is. His first patient appointment is at 2.30. What's your name, madam?"

My name? That was something I did not want her to know. I hung up.

Stupid cow! No security for doctors. They happily divulged all this information to a perfect stranger. At least I had obtained useful information as to where and when to expect Kovač. I was ready to step into action.

I found a convenient place for my car a few yards away from the entrance of the clinic, where I could see all who were approaching the consulting rooms from both sides of the street. I became extremely agitated whenever I noticed a bald-headed man. I never realised before that there were so many hairless guys in this country, nearly every second one. I was exhausted counting all those UFO lawns. Had they had chemo after cancer? Were they stressed too much at work? I preferred bald male heads to hairy ones. They were smooth and shiny, and you could imagine the size of the brain underneath. They made men look like people of substance and success. Dwayne Johnson, Bruce Willis: both great looking guys. I couldn't stop thinking about Nikita Khrushchev, a Soviet leader in the late fifties, early sixties. He was the butt of many jokes regarding his hairless head; the suggestion of giving him a hairbrush as a gift was particularly popular in Soviet Russia. He was the first leader since the revolution of 1917 that Russians dared to laugh at without the fear of being arrested.

It was the sight of a heavy, dark brown case that made me shiver. I knew it was him. The short figure was in a black coat as if he'd come straight from a David Lean movie. The doc moved fast from the hospital towards the door to the centre. Omar Sharif had a wonderful, pampered crop on top of his head appropriate for the movie. Kovač had a haircut appropriate for the cancer ward. I was a bit of an ageing Lara who wished to look like Julie

Christie. I managed to put on a last touch of lipstick the moment I recognized my doc. I elegantly jumped out of the car like a skilful horsewoman in a circus show, and appeared straight in front of the unsuspecting guy.

"Natalia!" he almost whimpered, his cheeks turning pink. "I'm on the way to my shift and here you are… for an appointment?"

I found myself staring at him foolishly. I was a bit confused by his assumption that I'd coincidentally arrived to see another consultant at the start of his shift. He should've realised that I was there for him. Yet, Kovač behaved as if nothing had ever happened between us. He appeared so pure and innocent – no traces of blood after surgery, no cancer shadows, no trace of sins, nothing at all. He looked like a young boy who was successfully lying to save his day.

"I'm here to deliver this letter to you," I uttered and quickly handed him the thick envelope. I was amazed by how swiftly he hid it inside his coat, dropping it into his portable safe as if expecting it. And with this, Kovač disappeared through the doors without a word.

The Twisted Mind Escapade

My mission was complete. I returned to the car but couldn't leave. I was glued to the seat and my brain went into a neutral mode, even my power of manifestation was disabled. I was frozen. I sat there for six hours, without moving, without the need for a drink or a piss. All bodily functions switched off completely.

It started snowing. Snowflakes, beautiful magic crystals, turned grey as it grew darker. The lights in the clinic's windows allowed me to see a few faces who were observing me in return. One middle-aged man with a perky beard – I decided that he was the manager – kept staring at my car through his office window.

But what did I care?

A lot of women entered the centre. I wondered how many of them were Kovač's patients? I was playing different scenarios in my mind of how he felt after reading my letter.

I saw a few dirty spots on the window of my car – they had to go; some dust on the passenger seat was carefully wiped away. This was a place ready for a special man in my life.

Then I noticed an enormous bag nipping out of the clinic's doors. Behind was Kovač. He looked elfish with his head sunken into his body – half the size of the already-short man he had been before. His cheeks, formerly pink, were now ashen. He looked frightened, as if he himself had seen a consultant who had given him a prognosis of just a month.

"Jump in, Andrew!" I pointed straight to the cleaned seat next to me. I expected repetition of the first time, when he had taken this seat and we'd driven to my place.

Kovač did not share my excitement. "I'm working. Go home,"

he whispered to me in response. He pronounced the word 'working' with a triple R – his inheritance from Eastern Europe. Kovač was heading back to the hospital to check on those whom he had operated on earlier that day. I followed him in my car.

"I've read your letter and I've written back to you," he said on the go, looking around to see if any colleagues or patients had spotted us together. He seemed scared, very scared.

"Andy!" I moaned, trying to soften his cold, estranged demeanour.

"I'm working!" He turned away and sped up. I kept following him for a while. My foot was pressing the accelerator more and more and I was nearly touching his heavy bag with my Merc. It was so close... I had seen scenes like this in thrillers. I turned the wheel to the side and let him go. I drove away.

***

I checked my mail every day, but it took ten days before I spotted his letter in the post: a cheap white envelope with a hospital stamp. It burned my palms. For me, it was a pivotal moment of my life – to be or not to be. The letter had an official header with his titles and degrees, the same as the one I received after my operation assuring me that I was cured. For now.

With trembling hands, I opened it,

Dear Mrs Popov-Fitzcock,

Thank you for your letter. (As if he really felt like thanking me for anything at all!)

I understand that you are euphoric having had your cancer treatment. I think it is important to understand that I am unable to guarantee 100% that you will be cured. (He obviously wanted to point out that I was mentally ill.)

I always think that it is good not to tempt fate and

not to make any assumptions, but just to proceed in a cautious manner. (He was trying to say that I was the destructor, not him.)

As such, I do think it would be appropriate to celebrate the success of your treatment so far. (He implied that I may still need him as a doctor and my C may reappear. He tried to scare me with bad prognosis.)

With both my capacity as a doctor and my settled family life I am not in a position to ever have relationships with patients, nor would I wish to. (There was no need to add this last part of the sentence. That was really cruel.)

It is my pleasure to look after you and help you with your illness, but this situation will never progress any further into anything on a more personal level. (He obviously forgot that it did. Did it?)

Yours sincerely
AK – Andrew Kovač
Consultant Gynaecologist and Gynaecological Oncologist MBBS BSc (HONS) MRCOG

I dropped down on the sofa, the new one – it had just arrived from Harrods, bought for the benefit of the traitor. I took out my iPad and googled the word *euphoria*. I knew its general meaning, but wanted to understand the full nuance of what he may have meant: 'A strong feeling of wellbeing or happiness. It is sometimes used to mean an abnormally exaggerated feeling of elation'.

You got it wrong, doctor! I thought. *I'm mostly unhappy these days.*

I'd kept the roses fresh in a Japanese cachepot for weeks, in case he would come and visit. I wished them dead after the horrible letter. I re-read it many times.

My verdict: *I was betrayed!*

A Top-Notch Therapist

28ᵗʰ November 2015
Maida Vale
September 1993
Moscow

"Pull yourself together and stop crying." I was being comforted on the phone by my friend Ella, who managed to turn her life around by getting a second dog. She sounded unusually bossy.

"You clearly can't deal with this *love* of yours on your own. However much you ruminate about it, it will never go away. You need professional help to cure you from your emotional hang-over."

"His letter was a poisoned dagger." I was consumed with guilt, shame and self-loathing.

We had been on the phone for hours before Ella reached her conclusion; all the while I had wept like Medea over her children. She gave me the number of her friend, the well-known psychologist.

"Promise me, you'll ring this guy. His name's Malcolm. I mentioned him before. He helps top sportsmen and artists find their peace of mind, to regain confidence and self-esteem. He deals with their concerns from receiving too much money and paying too little tax. He's held in very high regard in those circles."

The circles of the mentally unstable like me – that's what she meant, I thought.

"A few sessions with him and you'll forget your little doctor.

Your dear chap probably lives in a small Victorian house with a tiny pool in the middle of his garden. He accidentally dipped his medical dick into unknown waters and little did he know that it would come with a tsunami wave of consequences. He simply hasn't the foggiest idea of how to cope with it." Ella should have been a Wise Witch.

"Your own arse is always more important than others'. To save his career he needed to push another person down, even a vulnerable and wretched person like you."

Her words terrified me. *Was it a fair description – a wretched person?* That's what I wanted to hide so much from the entire world.

"I understand the position he's in – his job is his life. But he could have dealt with it differently. Why couldn't he have rung me and told that he had to do this official letter? I would completely understand. Instead, he simply disappeared. I'm now not sure if I love him or hate him."

"Hatred and love are linked, connected to the same part of the brain. They're both active when either feeling is experienced. Don't worry! Malcolm will help you recover your confidence – you'll be able to laugh at this soon enough."

"What is there to recover? I don't have anything left. I'm crushed."

"You need to find ways to get over it. Try him. There'd be no harm, except to the pocket. He is fucking expensive!"

I always believed that nothing good came cheap, particularly in Great Britain. The word 'expensive' spurred me into action. A few minutes later, I was dialling the number to the magician hopefully capable of retrieving my happiness. For 150 pounds an hour, Malcolm was indeed positive, confident and eager to fit me into his busy schedule.

"I can come and see you tomorrow. Or even later today. I'll fix you! Wait and see!"

I didn't need to wait for long. The doorbell went off only a couple of hours after our conversation. And there he was! Malcolm was a sixty-plus-*plus* guy, slightly heavy, with dyed, cropped hair to disguise the traces of grey. I had been tipped off that he happened to read *The Guardian*. With the Whig's liberal approach to life, he wasn't going to appreciate my apartment's interior cluttered with paintings, sculptures and all sorts of antiques. Upon entering, Malcolm remarked that my collection was 'unnecessary for happiness' and 'complete garbage'. He obviously couldn't hide his contempt for those types of dwellings and thier hedonistic owners, who surrounded themselves with unnecessary riches.

I was about to snipe, "But your fellow *Guardian* readers might not be able to afford your fees". Instead, I politely asked him to put the guest slippers on, to spare my newly lacquered parquet that had recently been renewed.

"Shall we sit in a quiet corner, where no street sounds can disturb us?"

Malcolm strolled into my dining room without an invitation. He landed heavily on my new, exquisite armchair, still with the Harrods label attached. It was big and comfortable, arousing no fears or anxiety. The price however was big and *un*comfortable. It was there for Andy! This thought nearly made me scream, but I had to quell my anger – I needed the psychologist on my side.

"Tell me what bothers you and what you want to achieve in our sessions," he began, embarking on his professional quiz and making it clear that one session wouldn't be enough. I would have to dig deeper to further fund his magical services. But the very thought of investing in my peace of mind started the healing process. I looked into his eyes, trying to weigh up how much I could tell him. They were brown, intelligent and neutral. He carried the aura of the Wizarding School, with similar features to Harry Potter's Dumbledore – or the actor Michael Gambon – both in shape and sophistication.

I started telling the therapist my story. Listening to myself, I found that my sufferings might sound rather funny to him: a vintage woman with a PhD weeping over a little chap who didn't come back for a second fuck. My Whig therapist let me speak for nearly fifteen minutes, and after taking everything in, he gave a scientific explanation of the state of my heart and mind.

"You need to understand that falling in love with your doctor is a classic story, Natalia. It's taught to medical students. The knight arrived on a white horse and saved his patient. She dreams about him for the rest of her life. She comes to his castle – hospital – and waits for his kiss."

"It wasn't quite like that."

"That's exactly what happened. It has nothing to do with love. It's an illness, an obsessive attraction. The pain of lovesick people and the disturbing pattern of their behaviour can be as severe as a serious psychiatric illness."

The psycho-guy is saying I am probably mad. I wasn't at all surprised to hear that.

"What bothers me is that your doctor knew but didn't behave accordingly. Even in his letter, in which he was covering for himself, he talks about you like a woman in love, not just an ill patient in need of help and guidance. Something doesn't fit together. Or is there something I don't know?"

"He fell in love with me, too, but then chickened out. He's human; I understand. He had to save his job."

"He isn't *just* human. He's a d-o-c-t-o-r. That's against their ethics. Though the Florence Nightingale effect can happen. It's when the carer falls in love with his patient. But it's unlikely. I link this excessive passion to another more infantile love. Everything in our life is an imprint from our early days. I'm now thinking you had a trauma in your young years. Your state of mind is identified as transference. Have you heard about it?"

"A little," I murmured, not wanting to delve deeply into my

past in the hope of sorting out the present. Though I supposed for 150 quid I should be entitled to get a detailed explanation of my shitty situation.

"This phenomenon, first described by Freud, is characterised by unconscious redirection of feelings from one person to another. Often, it can be a repetition at the present time of a relationship that was important during your childhood."

"That was so long ago. I think of it as another life." I wondered if he could have guessed about my cruel mother.

"People can suffer agonies for years and decades because of rejection, particularly at a young age."

I wasn't ready to accept any connection between the horrors of my Soviet past and my failure with the doc.

"It could even be a more recent event that provoked it. Like rejection from your husband."

I decided not to scare him with the tale of the orangutan event. He'd probably want to make a double appointment to treat my Chairman as well.

"The redirection of feelings and desires – especially of those unconsciously retained from childhood – towards a new person, can be strong and also painful, as they usually go only in one direction. It could be a reproduction of emotions relating to repressed experiences and the substitution of another person. Often, it's a doctor who saves your life and then becomes the most important person in the world. That's a classical transference case."

After his clever speech, I felt my pain had some sort of scientific significance. He was bloody right – all my childhood was a trauma. Without any planning, I started sharing with him the painful stories about my past life. He knew how to listen. After I finished, he simply concluded with his recipe to ease my sufferings.

"The first step to your cure: forget your doctor. After that letter, there'll always be a catastrophic lack of trust from your side. As for him – he's scared and will never come back. If there is anything to come back to." He looked at me with doubt in his deeply penetrating eyes. "His letter indicates that he'll avoid any private contact with you. He'll have a deep thought about how to maintain an appropriate degree of professional distance – it'll be increased to a marathon length. He'll think twice the next time he wants to see what colour the eyes of his female patients are. He might even change his medical profile to urologist to deal with men instead." Malcolm finished and burst into laughter, proud of the depth and power of his conclusions.

"I think about him all day, even after his insulting letter. He should feel the energy flow."

"I'm sure he does feel it, and I imagine it burns him with terror. I'm not even going to discuss this. The solution is simple: you need to transfer your affection to someone else. Exchange it, if this is more understandable."

"Malcolm, may I be completely open? I have some awful things to say."

"Of course you can. That's why I'm here. May I have a glass of water?" he asked, eyeing up the armchair trolley beside us, loaded with beverages of a different kind.

"Perhaps, you want a glass of wine or…?"

"Whisky and soda would do."

He'll need it once he hears what my problem is, I thought. I generously offered him Johnnie Walker Black Label, and watched until the wizard had taken a good sip from his goblet before I continued.

"Something has happened since my operation. More than food or water, I want sex, and not only with my doctor. I can't control what my body wants. I dream about sex, talk about it and pray for it. It's so overwhelming that I went to see my GP for help. But he dismissed it; he took it as a joke and wouldn't even discuss it with me."

I wasn't sure if my information was met with sympathy or if my therapist, quite possibly, took my cravings for sex as me being completely crazy, quite possibly like my GP. But I wasn't ashamed of my words, no. I had always been considered slightly eccentric. I had a strong view that complete mental stability never really contributed to history. The best achievements were made by loonies; they produced the most interesting things in any fields of life. It also wouldn't scare me if my therapist decided to sign me up for an intensive sex addiction therapy. Perhaps he could place me in a clinic with his male sports clients.

"Well, we call it an *excessive sexual drive*." The Wizard looked at me with surprise and with a definite evaluation of my facade. "It's simply a consequence of the operation. Firstly, a psychological compensation for the loss of your female organs; and also fluctuating hormones are the cause of your big appetite. I wish I had it!" And he burst into laughter, his eyes sparkling with mischief. From that moment on, I knew for sure that all psychologists were crazy, sexually obsessed creatures, starting from the great Sigmund.

***

In Soviet Russia one year in the early nineties, I received a call from my friend Tatiana who was the head of the Psychiatric Department at a leading Moscow hospital.

"I'll come to you after work. I need to talk, I need your advice!"

It was nearly ten in the evening when she arrived, extremely exhausted.

"Nata, sorry I'm so late. My shift felt never-ending today. I simply couldn't face going home to another Bedlam."

My American cocker spaniel, Derby, met her with cheerful barking. That spoiled pet also had fluctuating hormones. He didn't mind my lady friend paying a visit during the late hours, but if my guest was of a different gender, he'd become aggressive and would try to bite off the competitor's valuable tool. Derby believed that he was my master and the head of my household as well.

"A cup of tea would be good. I need a few moments to pull myself together."

We used to talk in our small Soviet kitchens. The electric kettle didn't keep us waiting too long, and in a short while we were sipping Ceylon tea, which was a rare luxury at that time.

"The bastard wouldn't give me any money for our kid. We live in our flat like bad neighbours, not like a family. Our marriage had crumbled long time ago." Tatiana was talking fast and smoking Dunhill, a grateful gift from the young patient she was treating. She described him in official papers as slightly madder than he really was. That helped the guy avoid the draft into the Soviet army. A tiny change in professional opinion provided a respectable business for psychiatric doctors in Soviet Russia; a good half of the young male population was labelled mad.

"I'm working day and night; I'm supporting the whole family. But there are limits to what I can do. He's the father after all. He should contribute to his son's upbringing."

"Do you still sleep together?"

"You're joking! He is 100 per cent impotent."

"Anxiety is a huge libido-dampener."

"He doesn't worry about anything. He drinks like a pig. You'd need a crane to lift his little cretin even a centimetre! Just sitting next to him makes me mentally ill."

For some reason, I thought that she actually was deluded. I qualified her as my mentally unstable friend in need of psychological help.

"Perhaps, the lack of a sex life makes you nervous?"

"Nata, do you have anything stronger than tea?"

"I can offer you a gin and tonic."

"What about whisky?"

"Nothing left. I had a private guest yesterday."

"Who?"

"One literary genius, an ancient reliquary. I'll tell you later."

"Give me some vodka. I'd prefer a stronger drink; I need it. We dilute medical spirits for personal use. That helps us survive in our mad-house."

"I gave my last bottle to the plumber earlier today – I had some problems in the loo."

"What? Shit? Why didn't you just flush it away? Aren't we all covered with it? Give me gin if you really don't have anything stronger." She finished the full glass in one go and continued.

"I'm about to present my PhD to the board. There are a couple of important people I ought to have sex with before the big date. My success or failure depends on them."

"I never realised you have to go through that. I didn't have to."

"You have your powerful father as a shield in fights with all sorts of Gorgons; your men took care of you well. I have only my *cunt* – for protection, satisfaction, benefaction, for all – one small hole."

She poured more gin in her glass, this time without tonic, and tipped it down her throat.

"Psychiatry is such a delicate matter that, if you don't have close people who care, it's unlikely you'll win. And I need to win. My degree will add extra bucks to my salary."

"Instead of sleeping with the whole brigade, why don't you find one quality man who can stand by you? You are fucking beautiful." And she was. *Perhaps too slim, and that's why she was so nervous and unstable*, I thought without spitting it out.

"Sergei Malakhov is assisting me with my exit visa, helping me say goodbye to the Soviet way of life. Shall I introduce you to him?" I was happy to share the old motherfucker-saviour with my suffering friend. "He's a man of his word. He may help you as well."

"You mean the famous writer for children? Is it really him?"

"You got it! He's a very powerful man with connections in important places. Surely, he will appreciate some medical treatment from a near-PhD woman of stunning beauty."

Tatiana looked at me with adoration and great interest, "I knew it – you are a real friend!"

***

My meeting with the therapist was coming to an end. I didn't want to overrun into a third hour; two hours of soul-and brain-tuning were expensive enough.

"You can deal with this by going online. This will distract you from this negative state. You'll be occupied with a joyful activity – a search for people looking for sex. There are so many good apps – Stay Anonymous, Casual Encounter, Glamour, Tinder. They help their subscribers to conduct perfect affairs. You should remember that infidelity is only natural for human beings. That's how we are made. Even good women cheat."

Did he mean Mary Magdalene? That was a comforting thought. The psychic pronounced his speech so convincingly; it felt the right thing to do.

"I believe that, on some of those sites, membership is free for women." Malcolm continued.

I wondered if a registered psychologist was allowed to recommend such a controversial treatment.

"Of course, the best for your purpose would be Ashley Madison, but some time ago a huge scandal shocked the world. Hackers released their members' personal data to the public."

I felt horrified.

"You don't need to worry. It was more about VIPs – top bankers and politicians, UN officials and Vatican employees. They also wanted more to their life."

"The Vatican is not a novice in sexual affairs, I know. When I talk to my tourists about the portrait of Pope Julius the Second by Raphael, I like to mention that he died from syphilis. In the Sixteenth Century nobody suspected how the disease was spreading, so he died as a saint. We now know that he was not one." My professional background helped me to recover from the shock.

"That's interesting. You learn a lot through art." It seemed that Malcolm took a real interest in the arty subject. "The artist also had a hyper libido, and not only Raphael," he added. I was surprised by such a broad knowledge, that Malcolm demonstrated in this field.

"My clients have also shared their experiences with me. Rather fruitful. If you can't get a fuck from those sites, you must be a ghost," he giggled, trying to disguise it as a cough.

He is an exquisite psychologist, with a modern approach to treating mental conditions, I thought. *I am so lucky to meet a top-notch specialist.*

"Go online as soon as I leave, and in less than a month you'll find a man. I met my previous girlfriend through *Guardian Soulmates,* and the present, on a dating site. We've been together for two years now." It looked like my adviser had a lot of practice to embellish his craft.

"I feel lucky to have met you – you really understand sex and its connection to a suffering heart and ageing body." I needed to convince myself that the money was well-spent on this session. The 'friend of Freud' smiled acknowledging his excellence.

I was indeed blessed with his acquaintance and his session. It changed my life – I felt 180-degree rotation. Yet, his suggestion to look for other men for casual sex frightened me.

"I'm too old, too fat. And I'm married."

"Come on! You look fine! Most of my female clients are over fifty – that uncertain age! And you're forty-nine and a half, right? Not too bad! You need to shock yourself into feeling alive – that will knock a good decade off your age. Threats of death push people to celebrate life. Having sex is a part of it. " Malcolm completely ignored the married bit. He obviously was not a marriage counsellor.

"Another piece of advice," he said, wanting to give me good value for money. "Seduce your own husband. You can do it at the same time, like a double act. It's possible to have multiple romantic relationships."

"Oh! He is unseducible, I've tried. I'm not hairy enough – he loves his dogs."

"Add a bit of Viagra into his beer." *That was a rather innovative suggestion, probably based on folklore and fables from the wizard's childhood,* I thought. *At least he is not suggesting I use polonium.*

"But if your husband doesn't have any sexual feelings towards you, he is actually contributing to your actions of infidelity; he is an equal player in a game of cheating. Women sleep with random men mostly when they are sad and lonely. You have a great defence, knowing that many illnesses are the result of repressed emotions and the lack of sex. This should make your husband the guilty one."

Those words, spoken by the top professional, immediately killed all my moral culpability.

"It's a hard job to be married for many years and not to be bored with the same sex routine with the same person." I was surprised that I was defending Freddie.

The Wizard interrupted me, "It's up to you to make it to be not the same. It's great that you've made a big effort to lose weight, but it would be good if you're able to shave a few extra kilos off for a successful dating start. I can help you with this through hypnosis."

A few minutes later, Malcolm asked me to close my eyes and listen to him before counting to three. A hypnotic beat filled my ears. I melted into a complete relaxation, hearing his faraway voice. The Wizard was programming me – telling how little I needed to eat, that no sugar or bread was allowed on my plate, that no food after seven in the evening was permitted. He was promising that soon I'd feel good about myself and would forget my doctor.

"It'll be an interactive process – you'll find a right partner, who will quench your sexual appetite; meanwhile, your husband will rediscover how wonderful you are," he summarised, before lifting his huge body out of my armchair. I couldn't miss that the expensive piece of furniture had moulded around the shape of the wizard's bottom, but his words brought my mind back.

"You shouldn't have mentioned your last prediction. I have no intention of rediscovering what's irreparable. My granny used to say, 'You can glue a broken cup but would you like to drink out of it'?"

"Remember – infidelity helps marriage to survive." The top-notch therapist looked at me with his special, penetrating glance, planting this message deep into my mind.

When wizard had gone, I felt it would be stupid to spend all that money for nothing, so I simply had to stop eating.

After a small piece of Wild Garlic Yarg, I will go on a diet.

There was no way I would deny myself the last drop of heaven.

The Fucking Marathon

28thNovember 2015, later in the day
London

Parting with a substantial sum paid to the top-notch specialist pushed me to accelerate the use of his professional advice. I did not waste any time, and began delving into his unusual prescriptions.

"It's unbelievable! I just wanted to check the websites my therapist had recommended, but before I even managed to register, I started to receive a huge number of offers from all kinds of male species." I was on the phone to Ella.

"That'll keep your mind off your doctor. Be careful – you are a married woman, after all."

"Of course! I gave a false name and used a different email address. It's all rather adventurous. I like the motto of one of the sites: *Life is short, have an affair.*"

"I'm glad Malcolm improved your spirits. You sound so much happier than during our last conversation. Enjoy the adventure! It is much better than having an embroidery kit in front of the telly and stitching the name of your doctor."

I couldn't believe that Ella was so modern and didn't consider it a failure to look for sex with a complete stranger. She viewed it as a pretty acceptable event.

"I'm bombarded with photos of guys longing for sex," I exclaimed triumphantly. "The offers are flooding into my inbox day and night. I already have an impressive collection of male appendages. The 'suitable' candidates range in age from 26 to 70. There must be a shortage of women on this site as I didn't need to pay anything to register. It's a win-win!"

"Lucky you!"

"I called myself Wildfox49 to indicate that I haven't passed the untouchable fifty, not yet."

"That's clever. And no need to feel guilty for joining a dating site. All sorts of people go there, those who want more in their life than misery, that's all." And my friend sighed – as she herself had chosen misery.

Ella was right. In fact, I didn't see joining the world of online dating as an act of infidelity at all. For me, it was more like a friendly gesture to help my husband with something he couldn't cope with himself. I was acting like an altruistic charity worker, saving our family life that was stuck in the doldrums. Freddie himself hadn't been an example of monogamy: by his standards, he was 'reasonably' faithful to his first wife and then to me. Ha-ha! I was mirroring him in his adventurous search for extra-marital affairs years ago when he met me! I didn't feel a pang of guilt.

"The site suggested that I say 'hello' to all my matches! I haven't seen their faces yet – they're all half-covered to hide their identity. What I could see didn't look too exciting."

"Come on! If we put a photo of your Kvach on that site or what's he called – Kovač? He wouldn't look desirable either. You need to meet those guys in person," Ella shared her views with great passion. She really wanted me to dive into the business of fucking.

"They're such perverts. Just listen to their laundry list of interests: someone is calling himself Mentalsex50. I suppose he is fifty. Then he states that he is in a happy relationship, just looking for a daytime adventure. He likes 'light kinky fun'. And this is what he calls *light* fun – *submission, blindfolding, domination, experimentation!* I'm a bit scared!"

Ella didn't respond. I could only hear her heavy breathing on the other end of the line. Was she worrying or jealous?

"To add to that, he wants to experiment with tantric sex. Do you know what that is?"

"Yes!" Ella shouted into my ear with a great enthusiasm. "It's an ancient Hindu practice that's fashionable now. It's a slow form of sex that's supposed to increase intimacy and lead to powerful multiple orgasms." My friend surprised me with her deep knowledge on this subject. "It means weaving and expanding energy. I believe good vibes can do a lot of good. Negative energy can cause malignancy, cancers."

Does it mean that my loveless life provoked my disease? Can solitude cause a fatal illness? I couldn't escape these thoughts for a long time.

"God," I sighed. "I'm so out of practice. I'm years behind all the interesting sex trends." I looked back to the screen. "Listen! Here's one who has just written to me. He calls himself Badboy53 and is apparently 'looking for fun'. He loves to give oral sex and is aroused by toys and anal sex. He *is* a bad boy, isn't he? I feel sick, yet a bit intrigued."

Ella didn't respond. I might have sounded too excited.

"Perverts!" I added, showing disapproval of the site's advertising. "What the fuck did I get myself into?"

"Don't be too fussy. You have a choice of guys, lucky you! Just get on with it."

"Wouldn't you want to try?" I asked, my defences prickling.

"You are joking! I'm not going to mix with those dirty bastards!"

There was a chill in the air. Ella understood that she had said something slightly discouraging to me. She continued to make amends, "For you, this is a necessity, it's your medicine. Otherwise, you'll stay trapped in this obsession. You need to fuck your doctor out of your head."

I could hear her light a cigarette trying to poison herself with smoke as penance for that slip, or perhaps Ella regretted not having the guts to do something with her own life.

To keep all my well-wishers satisfied, I hit the 'respond' button and embarked on my 'medical treatment', as prescribed by the top mental health healer.

An Epidemic of Celibate Marriages

5th December 2015
Mayfair, Central London

I parked my car just off Park Lane. Typically for early December, it was freezing and had just started to rain.

Fuck it! I thought. *My hair's going to be ruined.*

Saying the F-word always helped ease the stress and it didn't sound too bad in a foreign language. I had been brought up in a good Soviet family, and if I had heard this word in Russian from someone else, I wouldn't have had anything to do with that vulgar person.

I was worrying about too many things at the same time. I hadn't been on a blind date since my search for a husband more than twenty-five years ago.

My phone was buzzing and I struggled to locate it in that portable Prada 'house' of mine. It was my husband, which was an exceptional rarity. Sometimes I wouldn't hear from him for a whole week or even longer. I often thought if I died it'd take a while before he found out. Freddie probably felt that something was going on; perhaps it reached him through our energy connection. I decided not to answer his call, as time was pushing on. He had never apologised for his horrible behaviour at the 'Graduate' party. He would not accept that he'd done something wrong. In a way, my new adventure was a kind of revenge, and that gave me an injection of confidence. It was my first hi-tech rendezvous, worlds away from my handwritten search for a husband many years ago.

259

I looked at my watch. It was a Cartier, Gold Tank, of which there were only a few in the country. I had bought it for Andrew. But after his insulting letter, in which he called me 'a euphoric patient', I decided it would look better on my own 'euphoric' wrist. I hated the idea of Kovač looking at my present as an attempt to buy his love.

The guy I was set to meet was a South African from Cape Town. I didn't expect Raymond to be as young as Scott, my Australian pilot. *But, perhaps, he would be willing to fly me to the real landing!* My hopes were rising.

I was already twenty minutes late, and decided to walk in the rain without an umbrella. There it was – the huge neon letters drew attention to the proud name: 45 Park Lane. On the ground floor was The Cut, one of the best steak restaurants in town. I was about to meet my first date from the Ashley Madison dating app.

Amazingly, the guy looking for a fuck with a stranger had made a booking at this smart, exclusive place. That said a lot about him. I imagined that he must've been filthy rich to spend money on someone he had never met, or seen before. *Perhaps he does not go out too often and this evening is a very special for him. Even if the guy is shit,* I thought, *the steak should be good.*

To my disappointment, the restaurant was completely empty, though it was early for dinner – only 6.30 in the evening. The administrator, a girl between twenty and thirty, was staring at me and probably wondering why on earth anybody would invite this second-hand cow to such a glamorous place.

"Has anybody asked for me?" I interrupted her offensive eye-quiz.

"What's the guest's name?" The youngster made an effort to revert to her professional skills and went into neutral.

"Raymond . . ." I trailed off, realising that I had no idea what the guy's surname was. He most probably wasn't Raymond, either. I felt slightly embarrassed but quickly shook this feeling off.

"Someone is waiting for you upstairs in the bar," replied the girl, still looking at me with an evaluating expression. She was probably ageing me between 50 and 70. To someone of her age, anything in between would be equally ancient.

I turned my back to her with a spectacular twist of my broad hips and started to climb the stairs. I didn't walk, but virtually ran, trying to disguise my age. Tip top, tip top. *If someone is watching, they'll think I'm just 35, no – 30. At least from the back.*

Deep down, I knew that I was over-optimistic, verging on stupid, but I was trying hard to kill those thoughts with my positive thinking.

I spotted him straight away. Raymond had mentioned that he would be in a blue checked shirt and jeans. With his long curly hair and broad hairy chest protruding through his half-opened buttons, the guy looked like a biker. He was tall and strong, not the look you would expect to find in decadent surroundings of this sort. A powerful character shone through every inch of his well-formed, noticeably heavy body. I liked that kind of guy. It was only the short Kovač with his bald head who broke the pattern of my romantic preferences.

I was glad that I had chosen to dress down more than usual. I remembered from his message that he was coming in jeans, and I decided to clad myself in leather, to cover up the lies about my age, or at least to make it more believable. An olive-coloured leather jacket from MaxMara Weekend, and a yellow skirt and T-shirt from L K Bennett were brands available in John Lewis. I thought that a middle-class luxury saver shop would appeal to the guy. My striking yellow Tods were a bit out of season for the winter month, but they made me look sunny, cheerful and sexy. Van Gogh was right – yellow is the colour of life. I was happy with my arousing choices and hoped that the positive energy I was radiating would be detected.

Raymond turned around. He seemed to be older than fifty – the age he'd claimed to be. Just like me, he had chosen to forget about a few years of his life. I was unsure whether our chemistry would work well enough for immediate intimate relations, but he seemed to be an okay guy.

"Hello, Svetlana!" He addressed me with the name I'd given myself on that dating site.

"Nice to meet you, Raymond!" I was wondering what his real name was.

"Let's have a glass of wine."

I wasn't surprised he offered me a glass of South African, from his native land.

"Red or white?"

"Red, please."

"I recommend Bordeaux. Their blends are perhaps the Cape's strongest type, when it comes to reds."

"I prefer Syrah."

"South African Syrah it is. So you're partial to the strong robust cherry and blackcurrant flavour? We can share a bottle."

Within a minute, I was sipping delicious Syrah and thinking that it had been worth coming anyway, just to learn about South African wines. It was still rather frightening to be evaluated by a stranger and get a verdict as to whether you were still good for a fuck.

"What's your accent?" my generous host asked.

"I've lived in England for twenty-five years but never been able to get rid of my scary triple RRR. It's very Russian."

"I wondered!" He seemed to be intrigued.

"When I first arrived in this country in the nineties, it had been a positive feature. Everybody who heard my accent welcomed and embraced me: *Perestroika, Gorbachev, vodka, seledka.*"

"I recognised the first three words," the guy smiled, proud of his knowledge. "But the last one – *se-led-ka* – what's that?"

"It's Russian for herrings – a must with vodka. Unfortunately, after the events in Ukraine, in Crimea, being Russian made me kind of an outcast. Though my mum was Ukrainian, so I'm half-Ukrainian too." I giggled stupidly, happy with finding a solution.

"Don't be silly! It's not the Russian people; the leader is shit." He moved his right hand forward trying to take mine, but in the last moment changed his mind.

A fifteen-minute introduction to each other was enough for Raymond. He suggested we go down to the restaurant. It was already filling up: a couple of old farts in disgustingly extravagant hand-made suits were already chewing something deliciously expensive. Our dining table was near the window, which ticked another one of my boxes and added to the ambience of the evening. The well-mannered waiter brought over a steak demonstration board, decorated with all types of meat cuts made of plastic.

"It is nearly a Snyders," I remarked.

"I agree. I love his paintings with the wonderful displays of all sorts of delicious produce."

Not bad for the businessman. He knows something about art, even if only those pieces that are connected to his gourmet taste, I thought.

"The Japanese sirloin looks a bit fatty." Raymond gave his expertise.

"Have I heard you correctly? One hundred and eighty? That must be the price for half the cow." I said, unable to withhold my feelings of guilt being in this ridiculously expensive place.

"You are paying for the best-quality beef," Raymond tried to educate me.

Me? I nearly jumped out of the table, wondering for a minute whether we will go Dutch.

"The cow was fed an organic diet and massaged to achieve the quality of the steaks."

My date looked calm and relaxed, obviously accustomed to these sorts of surroundings and prices. I tried to keep my mind on the end goal, as our dinner was meant to be a prelude to something more exciting. I avoided getting into any argument. If Freddie was there, he'd have been very surprised.

I couldn't stop comparing Raymond to my husband, as there were many obvious similarities: both were successful businessmen, both were handsome and tall. Freddie used to treat me with expensive meals in smart places before our marriage. After the marriage he mostly downgraded our dining. I think it was a punishment for being pushed into our nuptials, as I was eager for a legal document and a son.

"Here's a menu. Have a browse," the waiter threw it at us, looking offended that he had not been understood.

I needed my glasses to read the menu, but no way was I willing to disclose my ageing blindness. Saving myself from this reveal, I very quickly announced I was going for a cheaper option, "New York steak will do."

Raymond took some time to choose what he wanted. He wasn't worried about using his glasses at all. I saw him as a clever, bossy businessman and imagined him selling and buying shares from his office, in big quantities of course. It was obvious – he loved good food. I could tell it from his rather bulky body. Another bottle of Syrah arrived on the table. Raymond wouldn't order by the glass. He enjoyed life and could afford the best of it.

"What made you decide to meet women online?" I asked, while waiting for my steak. I liked it medium and that always added a bit of extra time. "You're attractive, successful, and intelligent. The birds should be flocking around you."

He did not answer straight away. He picked up his glass, sniffed it and then sipped the contents slowly, thinking about what to say.

"My wife is a real beauty, but she doesn't talk to me at all. She has no interest in anything," he uttered. "But I still love her very much."

"You have chosen to meet with me because of my qualifications? You want to talk? Have I mentioned I have a PhD?"

"No. What was your subject?" The guy was impressed.

"Not in sex studies. I'm an art historian." I said. Our conversation went a bit dead after that. I simply couldn't mention anything about guiding in these smart surroundings. Guiding would be OK for the guys taking me to Carluccio's or Café Concerto.

"And what do you do besides arts?" Raymond tried to be polite.

"I fly," I replied and told him about my recent flying lessons. Raymond was very impressed when I showed him the photos of me in the plane, next to the young Australian tutor.

"Is it a Piper Warrior?" He was straight to the point.

"Yes."

"Why did you choose such an adventurous hobby?" He forgot to add that meeting him was a no less adventurous pursuit.

"When I was a young girl, I used to fly in my dreams, to whatever destination I chose; of course I would fly to my prince, who would rescue me from all the evils of the world and from my sadistic mother."

"Interesting, I also had very harsh parents who tortured me."

His sudden confession made me feel closer to him. I continued, "So you understand me. Everything is possible in your dreams – you are free there, gliding above the world and admiring God's creations. You can bend your fate the way you wish."

I was spilling my soul to Raymond, an unknown man. Raymond was listening with great attention.

"I had always wanted to achieve something even against all

reasons to prove my mother wrong, when she was telling me, as a young girl, that she regretted not aborting me." I paused. It was obvious that my words moved Raymond. He threw his body back into the chair, lifted his head up towards the celling, perhaps making a flight back into his own past.

"I can see you are still looking for a dream," he said.

Did he mean that I'm too old? But I sensed that he was looking too.

"I have a dream life. A beautiful wife. By the way, she is a model. Stunning. Two nice kids, wonderful house." He took a sip of wine to help with his revelations. "I'm doing well in business," he said, somewhat needlessly. "But I'm here…" he sighed and retreated into another glass.

The waiter interrupted our conversation. The smell of the expensive steaks was astonishing. I cut a little piece and put it gently into my mouth, trying to savour the taste. God, it was good. *You can buy heaven*, I thought, *at least for a few moments*. We both enjoyed our meal complemented with exquisite wine.

"Do you want one?" he asked, trying to persuade me into trying Grappa, a very strong grape-based brandy.

That's not what a happy man drinks, I thought.

Our conversation over dinner made me consider both of us as rather equal intellectual players. Each one was trying to impress the other with knowledge and sophistication, but we had both done it elegantly and joyfully. This little competition added a sparkle to the evening. We finished with coffee. I had a cappuccino – almost always my preference in spite of the big calorie count; Raymond had an Americano, sparing himself from a heavy load. The conversation began to wind down. We both knew the real reason we had met here today, but the natural thing did not follow.

Should I take the initiative myself? I thought. *But men hate being pushed. They are supposed to be predators.*

"Are you tired, jet-lagged perhaps?" I started from a distance, to have more space before reaching to the planned finale.

"A bit, but I have a lot of work tomorrow and need to do some Christmas shopping – presents for kids, family… you know, that sort of thing." He stopped himself pronouncing 'and wife'.

Raymond asked the waiter for the bill. He looked away from me, avoiding catching my eyes.

"I read that you're into tantric sex. Are you interested in the powers of energy?" I tried to turn out conversation to the important point.

"I have no idea. The website wrote that on my profile," he said apologetically.

"So all the blindfolding, experimentation, domination …"

"Sorry, I'm a family man. It appeared on the site automatically." Then he started laughing and I joined in.

It's not going to happen, I thought and accidentally announced it aloud.

"What are you talking about?" Raymond looked radiant after a good dinner. "I had a great time – fantastic meal, wonderful wine, strong Grappa, conversation with an intellectual lady and a good laugh. What a day!"

He more likely meant – that's enough for a day!

"Thanks for dinner." I found it hard to even produce a polite smile.

"Are you going?" That was an unexpected question from the South African.

"Do you want me to stay? Or perhaps we could have a cup of tea at my place?" I asked with my last shred of hope. At that point I tried to use manifestation.

I thought hard.

I knew I wanted it to happen and focused on it.

I told myself – I would get it!

After a short uncomfortable pause my guy mumbled, "No,

not today." As if he was prepared to do it tomorrow! "But it was lovely to meet you."

Dead end – it didn't work, I felt like rejected junk. *Noli Me Tangere* – do not touch! Again!

Raymond was hastily extricating himself from the table, seemingly afraid of being pushed into something he wasn't prepared for. This guy clearly preferred to keep himself in his celibate marriage.

I stood up and quipped, "Please, say 'hello' from me to your lovely wife." I turned my back and left, not quite sure whether to feel let down or pleased that there was no different ending to the night.

Christmas the British Way

25ᵗʰ December 2015
London – Cobham, Surrey

Christmas madness always started early in London. In November, one of my coach tours had passed the Natural History Museum and a tourist exclaimed, "Look! They have already put up the Christmas Tree!"

He was right – beside the magnificent Victorian building was the tall fir tree, extravagantly decorated with golden balls to vulgarly remind us that we needed to start spending and practicing our writing for the endless list of Christmas cards. Those 60 days of preparations took our attention off the real problems. There was also a large queue of events leading up to the big day.

The Christmas party for the tourist company I worked for looked splendid but wasn't much fun for me. Everybody had to come in costumes featuring characters from fairy tales. There were three Red Riding Hoods, a couple of Puss in Boots and a good number of kings and queens, including me. Most of the company's female employees looked like models – all young and slender – they were the princesses, selected according to how they look and not how many tours they were able to book. I felt the need to play the kind, motherly figure to avoid being laughed at by the others.

My husband's company Christmas gathering passed by without even a smile; no orangutans or guests from the Wild West were present. I managed to fit my attendance into fifteen minutes, no more. I felt lonely without my womb and love generally. By mid-December, I was far too distracted by the festivi-ties to look for another opportunity on the dating sites.

The best part of Christmas for me was decorating the fir tree. Fred-die would always choose the one that looked squashed and lopsid-ed. As if he especially went looking for ugly one to match me. It was ok – I learnt how to hide the balding parts with beautiful balls and garlands and, against the odds, would turn a heap of twigs into the most beautiful tree. The string of little lights was the last touch and I would switch them on and listen to their tune of *White Christmas* a hundred times. It was real magic. Despite this, I was plagued by the thought that imaging myself, Kovač and my husband all together around the Christmas tree made me a fucking monster.

The less enjoyable part of the festive season was buying gifts for the long list of Freddie's relatives, a few friends, and of course, for Freddie and my big boy Nick. I wasn't excited about receiv-ing Christmas gifts from friends, especially when it was clear that they were formerly unwanted presents to the senders simply re-addressed to me, as there was no way to return them. I always thought it was better to give something that people could make use of. A bottle or two of good wine, or brandy, or whisky, for example; the cost varying according to the recipient's importance in my life.

I hated wrapping presents. I tried to exclusively buy gifts that were already packed in a box. I could stick them into a nice-looking Christmas gift bag to avoid dealing with the rolls of paper. Occasionally, I was lucky, and some charity ladies did the wrapping for me in a local shopping mall – their services bought me five years' worth of relief.

***

In Soviet Russia, we never celebrated Christmas. It was a reli-gious holiday and religion was called 'opium for the people'. I was baptised by my granny in secret. My father could have lost his Communist party membership if this fact had been discovered, and without that membership he would have lost his job. We used to joke that in our country people were counted not by heads but by *members,* playing with this word's double meaning.

To my surprise, immediately after Perestroika all communists became extremely religious. They turned to God and fell in love with the church. Here in London, at the Russian Orthodox Church in Knightsbridge, I saw KGB officers watching and reporting those 'horrible immigrants', who had sold their souls to the 'rotting' West. Just a few years after Perestroika, the same individuals were queuing to baptise their children and offering heavy financial support to the church in exchange for God's blessing and forgiveness for the destruction of their own people.

We celebrated New Year's Eve instead. That was an all-night event, going from eight in the evening to six in the morning. We had it twice a year – on the first night of January and also, according to the old pre-Soviet calendar, on the thirteenth. The anti-communist aspect of this old-style celebration was somehow overlooked by the Soviet state.

New Year also signalled the start of the school holidays. People with money and connections would whisk their families away to warmer climates, away from the Russian cold that could sometimes reach minus forty degrees Celsius. Hardly anybody could dream of going abroad in those days. It was Sochi, Crimea or the other Black Sea resorts that they would choose. It was not a problem obtaining a travel visa to foreign countries; the problem was to getting permission from the Soviet government to travel abroad.

Festive events would be held all around the country; we'd call them 'Yelka', which translates to 'a fir tree'. All the parents used to come and watch their kids joyfully dancing and singing. I never looked for my mum in the crowd, either in kindergarten or later at school. Her presence would probably have made me wet my pants. Instead, I was always looking out for my granny. She would take me to her place after the events, and that modest residence would become my happy 'palace' for two weeks of the New Year holidays. She would treat me to duck stuffed with baked apples – still my favourite dish. Nobody could beat her cooking: her pancakes with homemade jam melted in the mouth and let me forget about all the horrible things that had happened to me. When I show *The Pikes* in Tate Modern to tourists – an installation by the French artist Annette Messager – it reminds me of all the pain I went through. Dolls' body parts, headless torsos and limbs in stockings would bring back memories of cruelty and childhood trauma.

***

"Nick will not be coming home for Christmas this year." Freddie delivered the 'news' to me a couple of weeks before the big day.

"I know. I told him not to. He only has three days off and flying across the pond for such a short time would be simply crazy. It wasn't that long ago, just a month, since we saw him."

I knew that my son's presence would add a lot of joy, and possibly some events would have taken a different turn, but I was sincerely worrying about my boy.

The one thing I wasn't worried about was the preparation of food for Christmas Day. That was my Chairman's territory and I wouldn't dare step on his toes. Freddie was an excellent cook when he could find time to spare. He had been in charge of our Christmas dinners every year since we met.

"I need to start getting on with the pudding," I would hear at least three weeks before the big day.

"But we are still in November!" I saw his hyper-enthusiasm towards the tradition as an obsession. Yet, Freddie would carry out everything according to the book.

"Where is my rope? I put it next to the stone." He would look around in panic. He needed his rope, his scales, his brick and raisins, of course, all to be in place before he could start. And his turkey! He always managed to turn this annual gift from the local farmers into a masterpiece of festive delights. Freddie would start at eight in the morning, aiming to be ready for the afternoon. After four hours in the oven, the turkey, nicely wrapped with bacon, would be loaded onto a beautiful tray and placed in the middle of the table. It would look provocatively juicy, and would be presented with its legs spread like a woman showing her best – in this case – the stuffing. Nicholas and I would be quick to dig the tastiest bits out of the turkey's valuable hole. We also adored Freddie's parsnips baked with cheese. I wouldn't miss sticking my fingers in the remains of the pudding's rum sauce for anything in the world. I would lick them one by one, not losing a drop, completely forgetting about my diet until the day ends.

As a good wife, I gave my husband complete freedom to do what he liked and he chose to play the housewife. Cooking was his therapy. Deep down I knew that if I cooked the dinner, it wouldn't be edible at all. Every time I attempted to cook, I burned a saucepan or two in the kitchen. I had to regularly raid John Lewis for extra pots and pans.

"Fuck! Again!" I would scream, running down the stairs and risking a great fall. But too late – it was always burnt beyond all salvation.

"I want to put all the ruined saucepans in the garden and use them as pots for plants to transform them into something beautiful." I nicked this idea from the Chelsea Flower Show.

"Russians don't have enough patience. That's not your virtue." My husband would shake his head and make himself a fast-track dinner: a toast with a piece of smoked salmon.

True – I was like Julius Caesar, handling many things at the same time but without his Roman success. Not in the kitchen, anyway.

***

I had hoped that my mind would be occupied by my work over the holidays, but as guides had to be paid double rates during Christmas, we were rarely booked. On Christmas Day, no one in this country would find any culture. Almost all museums, theatres and cinemas were shut. The exception being Charles Dickens House, which would experience the footfall of a rare species, those who want to get out and see something even on that sacred day of laziness.

Sports clubs, shops, railways – all are shut. If you don't drive a car, you can't see your friends and family. The country goes into hibernation. Whether you want to or not, you're left eating turkey, watching the TV and fattening up into a couch potato.

I spent my big day on the phone to Tamara.

"I wish I could be with Andrew during these festive days. I would love to do something special for him."

"I thought you were a bad girl now. You don't need that medical ghost anymore. He is just a part of your illness. The best you can do is to stay away. You'll make him quack in fear if you approach him now. He's with his family."

"Yes," I sighed. "How strange, that all the males from the dating sites have fallen quiet."

"They probably feel ashamed soliciting for sex during Christmas and gave it a break! I'm sure in the new year they will re-emerge and throw themselves into action." Tamara could always come up with a reasonable answer.

"Lay the table!" Freddie interrupted us. How fortunate that he had never learned Russian and couldn't understand a jot. For more than twenty years he had had only five words in his vocabulary – '*devochka*' – meaning a girl, '*krasivaya*' – beautiful, '*hui*' – the name for a male organ, and '*krot*' – identifying the main enemy in the garden – a mole. The culmination of his knowledge of Russian language was the word '*zayabal*' meaning 'overfucked' – that surely was an evaluation of his own actions. Whenever the Chairman saw my friends, he would demonstrate his linguistic talent by loudly proclaiming all 'big five', one by one.

It was four in the afternoon when the dinner was finally ready. The turkey, with my favourite stuffing stacked into her cunt, looked delicious and sexy. I needed a lot of willpower to resist the baked parsnips. Freddie made them so tasty that it was impossible to say no.

"Let's have a glass of wine," my Chairman announced, dropping into his chair for the first time since early morning.

"It's extra calories. I'll just have water." I needed to suffer for my look, even if it'd only keep me a few grams lighter and made me looking a few days younger. When it came to the food, I couldn't stop myself and finished the whole leg of the turkey with a few potatoes and parsnips. I hated myself for that.

"Did you try my bread crumble sauce? You want some gravy?" Freddie tried to break the pressing silence.

We sat at the table and we both had nothing more to say. I looked at the huge load of Christmas cards Freddie had received – they were all carefully placed around the house. They made me feel bad. It was a display of love and respect of so many people towards him, while my Russian friends just called, and no trace of their care was evident.

I could not avoid all of Freddie's commitments over the Christmas period. Every year, on the 26th of December, we traditionally drove to Dorset to see his older brother's family, always missing the Boxing Day sales. It was a big gathering – his four kids in their forties and their little ones made up the group of almost twenty. And they always had something beautifully wrapped for me. The wrapping was usually better than the contents.

It's the thought that counts. At least, these people remember I exist, I tried to stay positive.

The 27th of December was a free day where the Christmas sales were my savior. When I was about to escape from the house for a little retail therapy, my iPad bleeped. It kindly informed me that a fresh bunch of fuck-seekers had finished their turkey and were ready to restart the quest for birds of another sort.

A Big Misspelling

January 2016
Cobham, Surrey
February 2016
Venice

Now that Christmas was over, I was desperate to get a good return on my investments in nice underwear, autumn-shade clothes and the most precious part – my new slender look. I searched for new online agencies where I would be a complete 'fresher' and chose Lovestruck. The name sounded to the point – exactly what I wanted – to be struck by love, spiritually and physically. It claimed to help ignite real passion for those longing for sexual excitement.

I registered under the name Carly U.N. Taylor. I thought the English name would stand as a reasonable guarantee that I wasn't on the market for citizenship but for love with a sexy twist. For the most intelligent gents with some crossword experience or a talent for cracking codes it might hint at my aim and intentions. A discount was offered for signing up for several months. I loved a good deal, like my free Waitrose coffees and newspapers, and decided to multiply my joy by choosing a six-month membership. That seemed like a reasonable timeframe for finding someone who was prepared to fall in love with an ageing woman speaking with a Slavic accent; or at least would be brave enough to give her a decent fuck. I went to bed dreaming of forthcoming offers.

First thing the next morning I scanned my e-mails and noticed a welcome from the moderator of the dating site, 'Carly – a world of new discovery and exploration is waiting for you!'

Yep! That was a fair statement – I did feel like an explorer of new worlds. It was uncomfortable to receive messages from young men in their twenties or thirties, offering themselves up to me. I would reply, *You are too young, darling. I don't wish to be called 'mum'; I have a son at home.*

The elders in their late fifties and early sixties didn't feature in my fantasies either. I wanted to meet someone who could still touch his toes without getting a hernia or worse, piles. I deleted all the bodybuilders, too. They looked dodgy and overused. I also wouldn't consider anyone who asked for a photo of my tits or vagina, or those who kindly enclosed pictures of their mickies. They seemed a perverted, desperate or even dangerous lot.

I was intrigued when I came across a photo of a man in his late forties. With his shining, intelligent eyes charged with positive energy, the guy looked quite attractive. His profile read: *Successful European businessman.* Wow! *Six foot three* – that was a bonus! *Single, Caucasian and from London!* There were empty spaces under the scores that were supposed to illustrate his additional qualities: 'pursues fantasies', 'worth the time', 'better in person', 'hot to trot', 'popular' and 'salacious'. None were marked; obviously he hadn't much experience and must have been similarly new to the dating market. We began communicating online.

Daniel Cone: *Nice to have you here. Tell me more about yourself.*

Carly U.N. Taylor (me): *I've grown apart from my husband. My son's grown up – the empty nest has added to my loneliness.* (Something was true!)

Daniel Cone: *Sorry to hear that.*

Carly U.N. Taylor: *I'm ready to start a new chapter. What about you?*

Daniel Cone: *I was in a happy marriage until the last part of it became very sour... I met her at university. It was love at first sight. We got married and had one son. We lived happily until my best friend started an affair with my wife. I hired a special detective to investigate and was driven to such a state that I even thought of killing them both. But I gained self-control and finally got my divorce. I had a very hard time.*

Carly U.N. Taylor: *Oh my God! What a story!* (Unfortunately, I couldn't tell him mine, and had to invent some 'decent' crap.)

Daniel Cone: *That's in the past. I live an active life. I love every second given to me by God. I am very passionate about helping others. I've travelled and seen beautiful places. I want to take you with me.*

Carly U.N. Taylor: *How romantic! What a monologue! You sound like an actor!*

My heart started to pound quicker. At that moment, I knew what I had been missing – Daniel Cone next to me. I wished I could have reached through the screen and hugged him.

"I found him!" I screamed with excitement down the phone to my friend.

Tamara laughed, startled. "Calm down! Who?"

"He is just right for me. He's so emotional; he nearly killed his cheating wife and her boyfriend!"

"Are you talking about opera? It sounds like *Pagliacci* or *Cavalleria Rusticana.*"

She surprised me with her knowledge. *Perhaps she listens to classical music on her night shifts*, I thought.

"No! A man from the dating site. He prefers women close to his own age and wants to meet an intelligent person. God! Difficult to believe it's me he is interested in. He's going to whisk me away on a broom."

"Is that the new slang for dick?"

"Stop laughing! We have an energy connection; I think I've found the right man – substantial and romantic at the same time. His energy penetrates me."

"Stop this energy nonsense. You're just horny – whatever floats my pleasure boat, and the rest is your imagination. You need to think carefully about your reply – don't frighten him, you've been acting mad as a hatter for the last few months."

"I admit, after my op I was lost in a funny mixture of fantasies and illusions – I was sleepwalking through a fairy tale."

"And the wrong one. You need an audience, like in pantomimes, to shout at you all the time – *No, don't do it! Or yes, you should!* Grow up!"

"Yeah! And thank you for being my wonderful audience! I'm not sure I want to grow up yet – I want my fairy tale. This time it's the real thing! Don't worry! You don't need to shout any more. I know exactly what I need to do and what to write."

Be aware of my problems with spelling. I mentioned to Dan that I was dyslexic. I was worried that he wouldn't believe I had a PhD, judging by the number of mistakes I made. Sometimes the iPad would go mad, writing whatever it wanted. Fortunately, my dyslexia wasn't much of a problem in the bedroom.

Daniel replied, "*So is my son! I know all about dyslexia.*"

We clicked straight away – soulmates with similar problems. He told me that he was a jeweller who adored his twelve-year-old son. I told him that I was separated – the closest thing to the 'truth' I could produce. I was seriously considering how to juggle this lovely affair and my marital life. Letter by letter, twenty-two in a week – all my days were filled with reading and writing. I couldn't stop fantasising about this man I hadn't yet met.

"*Darling, how was your day?*" Daniel would ask that question every evening.

"At last someone cares!" I had to share this with Tamara. "He is so cultural. He loves art. He regularly goes to the Royal Academy!"

"So he said! He hasn't even mentioned opera yet to impress you." My friend didn't seem to suffer the same euphoria I did.

"Perhaps you're lucky and someone will talk to you about art instead of sex! Although I'm sure you can handle both well," she, the jolly virgin, laughed.

"Should I make the first move and invite him to my place?"

"Stop being ridiculous! The beauty of online dating is that you can start intense communication without even meeting in person. The initiative should come from the man."

"How would *you* know all that?" I was a bit rude to my spinster friend. "Jane Austen was too choosy about her fiancés, judging them on the basis of whether they had an impressive coach, like Mr Darcy. She kept waiting and waiting, until she was left to cover her head with a scarf and live the rest of her life with her sister Cassandra."

"That gave her time to establish her place in history with her novels." Tamara could not hide that she was hurt by my words.

"I'm not interested in making history. My waiting time expired years ago. Writing a novel is maybe not a bad idea. Thanks for the suggestion."

"It looks like you'll soon have enough material for a rather adventurous story. Let's hope it has a good ending."

"I told you not to leave your car in front of the house!" Freddie was screaming like a castrated ram. "Don't tempt the Devil!" I sensed that he had probably caught on to the energy flux and knew that I was ready to cheat on him, so he decided to hurt me in return.

"I had heavy bags. I was going to re-park but forgot!" I wasn't sure why I had to explain. "Is it worth getting so worked up over such a trivial issue?"

Freddie slammed the door to his room and settled in to watch the cricket and let off steam.

I immediately opened my iPad and there was a message from Daniel waiting for me.

I've been single for two years since my divorce. I am trying to find someone special and to see what the future holds for me… and I think it may be you.

His words were pathetic but electrifying. And more followed, *I am afraid to fall in love with you too soon. We should meet and have a nice time together without any great expectations and see what comes naturally.*

The handsome jeweller was expressing himself like a philosopher. I curled up in my bed, put Sinatra's love songs on the record player and hastily typed back: *I am in bed and thinking about you! You sound like a nice and gentle person, nearly unreal.*

Daniel did not make we wait for his response: *And I wake up with a smile on my face, knowing one day you'll wake up next to me. Let's go out next Tuesday. Where do you live? I'll pick you up. Let's make the world jealous! By the way, I am German!*

"Tamrico, it's happening," I squealed over the phone. I was already forgetting my doctor existed at all. Daniel kept me really busy. "You were saying he's a fake. He is German. I can't wait to meet him."

"For Christ's sake, don't even think of bringing him to your apartment. It could be dangerous. You said he is a jeweller? He may find a lot of nice pieces of jewellery at your place."

"Should I go to his place? What if someone else is hiding there?"

"Hire a neutral hotel room; that's more secure."

"You are talking as if you've been through this kind of thing yourself." I was truly surprised.

"I read a lot; and not only Jane Austen." Tamara didn't forget my snipe.

I needn't have planned it all out, as the date the following Tuesday never happened. Nor the meet-up after that. *Let's meet, dar-*

ling, my new friend said on repeat, but he always found some reason to delay the important date.

It has to wait, my Carly. I have to go to Kenya. It's business. As a jeweler, I have to travel a lot. I make designs for different companies. Hugs!

That was the proof – he was a man of repute in high demand. It made me dizzy.

I'll be back by the weekend and we'll see each other then. I feel like I already know you. Your letters have told me so much about your personality.

Dan promised to call and he kept his word, though it was bad news. His business trip had been extended. A few diamonds seemed to be in the way of my newly discovered happiness.

"The guy's voice sounds strange. Sometimes I found it difficult to understand him at all," I told Tamara later.

"You mentioned he was German. Some kind of accent?"

"He sounded like he had a speech problem."

"Perhaps he's had a stroke and is recovering? At this age, if a man is single and hasn't been snapped up by a lady, there's probably something wrong with him. You can't hope to find an ideal prince within his age group. If he's had a stroke, some of his precious parts may not function as you want them to," Tamara chuckled vulgarly at Dan's imaginary stroke-induced erectile dysfunction. She preferred me to stay a virgin to keep her company.

For five long days, my telephone didn't ring. My mind was conjuring images of Daniel falling ill. *Kenya is a dangerous country for a German man,* I thought. *What on Earth could make him disappear?*

At that moment, Freddie poked his head into my room, "If you still want to go to Venice, we can do. Go ahead and book it."

It was his apology that he never offered after screaming at me for parking my car outside the house. The Chairman spoke with his wallet.

My husband's anger issues ended up costing him a few thousand quid. I booked a five-star hotel and tickets for two to the Grand Carnival ball. I ordered expensive Venetian costumes for both of us. I didn't forget the smart Hunter's wellington boots, in case Venice flooded. I was so glad Freddie had shouted at me! To keep my husband happy, I booked economy flights, so he wouldn't feel like he had overspent. The Venetian trip emerged at the right time to help me manage Daniel's absence and tame my desire for his speedy return.

***

"Let's take a private water taxi." Freddie's generosity was an indication of how guilty he felt.

We landed at the private pier of the Venetian hotel. It looked like a royal palace. The building was in fact an old palazzo. In spite of my dyslexia, I managed not to mix anything up and chose the palace, not a simple place. Our room didn't disappoint – it was magnificent too. I jumped straight onto the enormous bed in my sexy boots and asked my husband to take a picture. I posted it on Facebook, sharing my happiness with the whole world. The comment followed: 'A queen, no less'. *If only I had Daniel next to me!*

The Carnival Ball was fun; it ought to be, considering the price we had paid. The evening started with a mystery walk through frightening, narrow streets trying to find the place. It seemed that the directions had been made especially complicated to engage us into the mystery of the play. We were greeted by vampires to keep us alert through the night. A whole bunch of Comedia del

Arte characters were performing for us in the beautifully decorated palatial hall. Casanova himself invited me for a dance. A five-course dinner followed, interrupted later by Italian music and a lesson in eighteenth-century minuet.

My husband took the stylised gestures as child's play. He had his own original dance style, including a mixture of rock and roll, twist and old-fashioned foxtrot. Yet, I noticed that he was really trying to learn new steps to keep up with me.

Freddie's white curly wig made him look like Casanova's father. He was trying too hard, and the huge head-nest was sliding around, failing to find much to attach itself to on his balding head. My Chairman fought with it as he danced, but eventually got pissed off and hung it on the back of the chair. That misfortune didn't ruin his intentions or the mood.

"Let's go for one more!"

Freddie pulled me out of the comfortable chair. I was wary of his heavy multipurpose Clarks, stomping around my delicate toes. With his Methodist upbringing and love of the low-key life, my husband had all of a sudden got a taste for the posh extravaganza. All he had hated or ignored turned out to be rather fantastic. He was trying to compensate by dancing the night away for the years of missed joy.

"Are you alright?" Freddie noticed me dashing to the lavatory rather often.

"I had too much wine," I lied. I was simply looking for a quiet place to check my e-mails, but there was nothing from Daniel, my king lost in Africa.

I returned to the table. I didn't want to dance anymore. Seeing my husband so happy at that party brought guilt to my soul. My mind started whirring.

Am I doing something wrong? For so many years, Freddie hasn't appreciated me. He has refused to do anything I liked. Even during our country walks, he has always chosen the steepest, most uneven road, as if waiting for me to fall. But now ... Has C changed him?

People around us were getting really drunk and their dancing appeared rather ugly. I wondered if we also looked odd, like two ageing people thirsty for joy and ready to spend lavishly for it. It all reminded me of the play *A Feast in Time of Plague*.

Early the next morning, the phone beeped and I sensed it was Dan. I rushed to the bathroom and turned the water on to disguise the sound. My Chairman was still asleep after the previous evening's excitement.

Darling, I have missed you so much. I wasn't even able to call you. My credit card was blocked. It's some kind of stupid mistake but until it's resolved, I'm not able to buy a return ticket. He didn't ask for anything, just stated that our lovely meeting had to wait.

The two days in Venice passed so fast. I enjoyed every minute of it – the spectacular parade on St Mark's Square, the gondola ride, the visit to Palazzo Ducale, the incredible collection at the Guggenheim Museum, and even Freddie's company. He had suddenly grown attentive, prepared to share my interests in art and music, never mentioning the cost. I realised that the trip was intended to be just for me, but was glad that he also shared the joy.

I'd stopped all my activity on the dating site due to a lack of time. Yet, I noticed briefly that Daniel was still searching through the love catalogue, logging into it quite a few times.

"Was he checking if I was still looking for lonely hearts?" I expressed my concerns to Tamara.

"He hasn't even met you yet. Why do you expect him to have any commitments?"

"You don't understand the close connection we've built. Don't try to ruin my feelings for this man."

But at the end, the 'jeweller' did it himself.

"Carly, I'm in trouble." Daniel confined to me during one of his few-and-far-between calls. "I promised my son I'd be back for his birthday. My bank is being useless. Can you lend me, darling, some money? Just six hundred pounds for the ticket to return to you."

I suddenly felt numb. I had read stories about these charming money extractors but never thought it could happen to me. I regained my senses fast and understood the breadth of it within a few seconds. I made an excuse to get off the phone and immediately called Tamara.

"He's probably an African man; that's where his accent comes from," I revealed my talent of deduction.

"And what about his surname – *Cone?*" Tamara spotted the con man puzzle.

"Shit! You're right! Take away the E and you can see the bare truth. How didn't I notice that earlier?"

"You believed all your fantasies. The guy's a classic fraudster, as so often described in newspapers. First, he becomes someone needed in a woman's life, complimenting her on her wonderful qualities and finding common interests. When he feels he has his victim on the hook, he asks for money."

"I thought you only read classical literature."

"Stop making me out to be some kind of nineteenth-century mistress. A money-grabbing crook is your Daniel. Surely part of an organised crime ring. They never meet face-to-face with the victim."

"He said he lives in London." I probably sounded stupid.

"He said, he said! I said that I am the Queen of Sheba! Are you thick or just pretending? It's typically older women who are duped."

"Are you saying I've lost my mind or developed dementia?"

"You were desperate for proof that you were still attractive and loveable. It's hard to recognise that you've fallen for a scam."

"Fuck! I can't believe it. He was so real. Everything seemed to be fitting so well, until he asked for the money. All these love letters, days of love games – just for 600 quid?"

"That would only be the start. Those guys are looking for women seeking any last remnant of love. Some ladies spend thousands, I read, even losing their houses. It's interesting – you were totally dormant and comatose. But you're a shrewd woman – you came to your sense as soon as he asked for money.

"I was blind. His letters were written in perfect English; John Evelyn, no less." I started laughing hysterically, so as to avoid weeping. Granny used to say, "If you feel like an idiot, laugh at yourself before others do."

"These letters were his golden investment. He probably paid some ex-Harvard guy to write them and then contacted many different women, just changing the name and address each time. His photo was probably cut from *The High Life* magazine." The spinster's knowledge on the subject was unbelievable.

"But my therapist was lucky – he met his wife through a dating site."

"A good woman, not a good man. There are plenty of good women around, trying desperately to find a suitable man." And she sighed deeply.

I decided to take a break from Lovestruck before someone successfully struck my bank account or even my head. I deleted all correspondence with the African freelance love-seeker, and moved on.

A Bedroom Robbery

With the arrival of spring, the search for love once again became a full-time job for me – spending hours looking through piles of letters, often full of rubbish.

Perhaps I should've knocked a few more years off my age and gone with 45 to attract more suitable profile visitors? This thought bothered me for a while.

Looking at the mirror, I realised that this would be an obvious lie, even with all the incarnations that I had been through. My face reflected the life I had lived, and the white lie of being 49-and-a-half was my absolute limit, to avoid becoming a laughing stock.

"Men can never grasp a woman's real age," my granny used to say. "Never confess. It's better to be a younger woman with a hard life behind her and a few extra lines on her face, than an old one looking after herself well, covering all traces of time with expensive efforts."

Unfortunately, my line-up of suitors did not overwhelm – balding men in their late fifties and sixties. Steve, an accountant from Epsom, didn't tick any boxes for me. He was divorced and, according to his profile, was clearly full of bitterness and anger. At five-foot-six, he was of Kovač's height, with the same moth-kissed bald scalp. What I used to consider a treasure on my doctor repulsed me on that guy.

It took me a few days before I spotted someone worth considering. I received a message from a man called Bruce, whose online username was Stevemaster. Five-ten, fit and English, an engineer from North London. Not too exciting but well-grounded, and in a skilful profession requiring the presence of a brain. Another plus point was his N1 postcode: the liberals' harbour. That was an indication he may enjoy going to the theatre from time to time. Married but unsatisfied with family life and sex – this statement appeared safe. Another comrade from a celibate marriage, trapped in his insecurities.

At 51, he seemed much too old for me. Whatever diagnoses I had had, at least I didn't suffer from gerontophobia: a kink for elderly men. Yet almost anything was better than loneliness. Numerous efforts without results had led me to lower my standards, calling for a speedy meeting.

Can you send me your photo, Carly? Bruce wrote to me with hope. His request was innocent enough – not looking for any features or measurements in particular - but still very worrying. I could once have offered a carefully maintained, wrinkle-free face, but those days were over. I was always aware of the aggressive army of fresh young ladies plastering their images online, keen to find a comfortable lifestyle by leaping into a marital bed.

I replied: *I don't believe in photos. They can be very misleading. Have a blind date and you won't regret it.*

I had learned how to answer, being now well-practiced from previous dates. I wanted my offer to sound intriguing, in comparison to his boring married life. The fuck-seeking engineer swallowed my hook.

Do you know Café Delaney in Aldwych? 7 pm, tonight. He was in more of a hurry than I was to find proof that the failed marriage wasn't solely his fault.

I'd never heard of that cafe. The name was obviously French, which explained why Freddie hadn't taken me there. But I knew the Aldwych area very well. This Anglo-Saxon word meant 'old settlement'. What a coincidence in choosing this place for two elderly DTF (down-to-fuck) settlers.

I chose a striking, Ralph Lauren red-and-yellow dress that one couldn't miss. It was very stretchy, so I wouldn't be reminded of my illusive waist. It showed off my best features – well, the best of the bad! Since my operation, I had started to like wearing a bra. It propped my tits up and created a larger bulge out of my modest cleavage, and also miraculously hid my stomach bump, improving the general topography of my 'delicate' body.

"You have to live in peace with yourself." Tamara was giving motherly instructions over the phone prior to my new adventure. She was a real gift. She was happiest when she could help others.

"There's a little pocket inside this dress. I can hide a couple of capote anglaises there. I don't think more will be needed."

"I pray that they'll be of use to you, though it's unlikely judging from your previous experiences." Even my closest friend was broken by jealousy.

Café Delaney spread itself over the ground floor of a huge Edwardian building. It looked very respectable, with two different parts - the restaurant for those who were prepared to pay generously for a meal and the café for the clients without much money or time. I couldn't hope for the option of a proper dinner – this would be no Raymond from South Africa. I was meeting a middle class Englishman. I looked around and couldn't see anyone matching the description.

"May I take this table near the window?" I turned to the waiter.

"Of course, madam, please do," he answered with a typically charming French accent. He was handsome – tall, with heavy dark hair nicely framing his high forehead; perhaps too lightly built to match my Rubensian look. My granny always used to calm me down when I, then a teenager, worried about being overweight. "Look at Rubens' Delilah or his Three Graces – you're as beautiful as them. Men like to feel a body, not just a skin." I was just twelve then.

Perhaps not so much of the flesh, I thought and sighed. I heard they didn't mind the older women in France. That was a positive discovery!

"Would madam like a drink?" The waiter paid attention to the lonely client.

I started thinking that the engineer may not even show up and it would be a pity to throw money away on expensive champagne.

"Half a bitter," I said, protecting my purse and illustrating my integration into British society. I was rather mean towards myself. It was the consequence of a Soviet upbringing. Bitter was a rubbish choice for the French luxury eatery. "*Life is too short to be a miser*", I remembered my granny's words.

"Excuse me, I changed my mind. Rosé, s'il vous plait," I said, and to limit my expenditure I added, "a small glass, le petit". These few words in French made me feel like a real polyglot and added to my self-esteem.

"Carly?" A gloom-looking man approached the table, as if he had heard about the champagne and wanted to share it with me for free. The guy from the dating site seemed to be slightly shapeless in his discoloured clothes, and was a little on the heavy side. He landed on the chair and ordered a pint to keep in with the Englishness, too. He obviously didn't have such a wise grandma as mine.

"Beer actually isn't good for sex," I said, making clear the reason for our meeting. "It relaxes all the muscles, not leaving anything tight." I had learnt this clever observation at the famous London Pride brewery, while researching for my pub tour.

"You sound like an expert. Tell me more about yourself."
Bruce screwed me with his little piglet eyes.

"There's nothing much to tell – stale sexless marriage, exactly what you've written about yourself. How many women have you met over the internet?"

"Just three."

I felt like he'd lied. He answered too fast. I thought: *He doesn't look like the type to cheat; perhaps he's just looking for the thrill of cheating.*

"Cheers!" Bruce nearly shouted to shut me up as soon as our drinks arrived. "I want to celebrate! You are a real woman!"

"What do you mean?"

"Oh! Online dating has so many ghosts. They make you pay a lot for the registration and access under the promise that you'll meet a number of women, but they don't have a big enough supply. All their dates turn out to be hookers or sugar-daddy-seekers, making their living from the site. It's not often you meet someone who actually exists and wants a normal relationship," he said, sipping his beer. By 'normal' I imagined he meant a free fuck, a 'quickie'.

His statement made me realise that I was still of some good value, though no daddy would be prepared to give me even a gram of sugar anymore.

"Would you like a piece of cake?" he asked – that was the only sweet on offer to me. Bruce didn't sound too generous; a fiver for a cake was clearly his limit.

"I've had all the cakes I could eat for the rest of my life." I knew perfectly well that being slim could prolong your youth and beauty. It was a rare occasion when I was able to resist offers like this one.

"When a woman starves herself, she often looks 18 from the back but 78 from the front." He was talking sense, the engineer. "Either face or arse", Brigitte Bardot once said in the interview.

"Still, the effort's needed to look a couple of inches less and a couple of weeks younger." I was flirting with this stranger, but I had enough of this small-talk foreplay.

"Let's get out of here." The time had come to launch my plan into action.

"Can we go to your place?" Bruce was well qualified.

"I suppose," I said absent-mindedly, the blood draining from my brain to my cunt. "Let's find a taxi." I had decided not to bring my Mercedes, as it might have revealed a connection to my husband's company.

"Maida Vale!" I felt uncomfortable giving a more precise address to the driver.

"Where exactly?"

"Head towards Little Venice, West 9, please. I'll direct you." I thought it would be less conspicuous if he dropped us off earlier along the way and we walked to my block. I was getting nervous and my pants became wet from fear and arousal. The driver smelt the delicate situation. Surely he was accustomed to this kind of customer, without a clear address but with clear intentions.

"Stop, stop here!" I was worried that he was driving up too close.

I jumped out of the car, leaving Bruce to settle the bill. I thought he could cough up a small amount as collateral for a fuck. We stayed silent all the way in the lift. It had been a very different silence when I had ridden it with the doc. I didn't feel like an achiever but after such a long quest, I was at last within reach of the shadow of desire.

Bruce's stony face didn't give much away, but I could tell that he was surprised by the lavishness of my apartment. All that I had created for Kovač – the paradise, the space for the lovers – that I had created for Kovač – was offered to a free-fuck-seeking engineer.

I walked straight into the bedroom. To guarantee a successful result, I had to initiate the sex, and literally take the matter into my own hands. He followed me like a robot. My bra flew into the air and landed on the back of the chair. I quietly removed my fat-holding Spanx and tucked them under the pillow. I left just tiny lacy knickers on, overwhelmed with the hope that Bruce could rip them off in his passion. I noticed that the Marks & Sparks protective wear had engraved ugly red lines across my stomach, where they were working hard to keep my waist in place. They looked like scars after a Caesarean section. I jumped onto the bed to cover my imperfections, without even a glance at Bruce or his wares.

I wanted safe sex, but couldn't work out how to fix the Durex, so I eventually forced myself to take a look. The engineer's dick wasn't massive at all; in fact, it was disappointingly small - an inch and a half at most. *Perhaps he'd had an accident on the construction site*, I thought sympathetically. No wonder his marriage was unhappy and sexless, as he had tearfully described it to me. I had him for one night, but his wife had to put up with his measurements for much longer! *The guy must've been born with the male menopause, stunting his dick's growth. He probably started online dating to find a doctor or a nurse to treat his sexual disability*, I thought as I watching the condom steadily engulf his little soldier.

Bruce climbed on top. Not a pervert, I noted. I desperately tried to open my legs enough to accommodate his big body. Unfortunately, my right hip, cramped with arthritis, limited my mobility, and wouldn't allow the 'Roman Emperor' a triumphant entrance through the archway into my deep halls. An approach from the back was way too long a route for the short-cut engineer. Bruce was aware of his shortcomings and as compensation slid down my body, offering a licking session.

"You have a nice cunt," the engineer purred, dipping into my pit. His tongue was much bigger than his penis. I couldn't share his excitement and muttered bitterly to myself, trying to embellish my experience, 'Invent your life and bend the truth, when you have to sleep with Bruce.' I was saying it all rather loudly, and the guy swimming between my legs probably caught me saying his name.

"Am I hurting you, darling?" he asked, very much like in the rabbit and she-elephant story from my colourful Soviet past. His wriggling tongue reminded me of a rabbit's tail. We must've looked worlds apart from the passionate lovers in the painting by Stanley Spencer *Artist and His Second Wife*, a double nude portrait. I thought how must have we looked worlds apart from the passionate lovers in that painting.

It was time to take the reins. I pulled the guy up out of my ocean and rolled him on his side to get acquainted with his male treasure. He had written on the dating app that he wanted a woman to be good with her hands. As a Good Samaritan, I gave him a few wanking thrusts. That was a hard job. I was sweating. His 'lollipop' didn't fancy standing to attention. Perhaps it needed to be activated by someone else, like a fairy, who could transform his dick into a wonder stick.

In spite of my ageing exterior, my old cave was still nice and juicy – no wrinkles, no warts and no vagina dentata. Yet, the guy couldn't show any virility. He was anorgasmic –unable to go to the end.

"Give me your lips." The bugger was trying to kiss me. I could open my legs for a fuck, but my lips were for love only.

"God! You smell like my pussy." I pushed him away. I didn't like the fishy flavour.

The little resistance excited Bruce; his member turned into a little warrior and he proceeded into me. The overexcited guy squeaked a few times - it looked as if he was praying. Possibly the arrival of the Messiah helped him to perform the act of ejaculating. I struggled not to laugh, but at the same time I was experiencing a cramp in my right calf. It nearly paralysed me. My future was clear - soon no sex without the presence of paramedics on the site would be possible. I produced a low-frequency howl that the engineer mistook for a sign of great pleasure.

"Did you like our lovemaking?" Bruce sounded satisfied with himself.

"That was truly spectacular!" I wanted to demonstrate my generosity and pretended that it was the best fuck of my life. The 'spectacular' shag was supposed to prove that I was still a woman, in spite of being robbed of a few features by Kovač's knife. It was great that my tits were still there, my dears. I loved to touch them from time to time to make sure they were still in place.

I threw on my silk Japanese kimono.

"It's time for you to go." A few lousy thrusts couldn't replace the emotional and physical connection I needed to help me heal. The 'healing experience' felt very shoddy.

I heard a lot of stories about one-night-stands that have gone wrong. Now it was my story. I hated this guy being in my house.

"Can you bring me a glass of water?" The engineer needed to regain his composure after such vigorous exercise.

"Sure," I said but didn't move anywhere. I didn't want to leave him alone in my bedroom filled with different treasures and memories. "I'll take you to the kitchen. Put your clothes on." His pale, shapeless body looked repulsive and out of place.

"It's ok. I'll leave. Go back to bed." Bruce got the message. He gave me a little peck on my cheek, trying to play at boyfriend. "I'll call you." He hopped to the entrance hall, helped himself with the door and quietly disappeared out of life, so I thought.

No more! I thought. *After him the bed looks disgusting and filthy as the confessional installation by Tracey Emin - My Bed.* Only the artistic comparison kept me calm and prevented me from throwing up. I felt like slamming the door behind him but did not want to risk revealing his presence to my neighbours.

I used a glass of whisky like a mouthwash and immediately rushed to the show, eager to get rid of any trace of the dating man. I stayed there for a few minutes under the hot water spray, sticking the shower-head deep into my cunt to cleanse my insides of this unfortunate affair.

What if Freddie had turned up? My swift return to the real world almost gave me whiplash. Luckily, I hadn't forgotten my granny's instructions. "You adapt to dishonesty. The more you cheat, the easier it becomes. Even if your husband catches you in bed with another man - never confess. Tell him you didn't feel well, and the guy was helping you recover." I wondered if she ever used this clever mantra for herself.

I dropped like a dead weight onto the bed, crushed in the aftermath of the disgusting sexual encounter. I cried a bit into the pillow, allowing myself some self-pity. I was upset not because I had cheated on my husband, I hadn't even considered that point at all, but because it was so inglorious. I despised the guy, and I despised myself even more. But what had been done couldn't be undone.

Early the next morning, I chose a simple orange dress for work, to encourage positivity into my day. Following the advice of those costly styling consultants, all my dresses and accessories had to contain some orange, red, yellow or gold. I simply needed to dress myself as Van Gogh's *Sunflowers* to conquer the world! I searched my apartment for my matching orange Mulberry bag, a new addition to my collection, but the bag was nowhere to be seen.

"I was robbed! The bloke took my new bag. Inside was my favourite gold chain," I sobbed on the phone to Tamara.

"Are you sure? You're just panicking."

"I went through all the cupboards, looked in all possible places. It's not a needle. If it's in the flat, I would have found it for sure."

"Calm down. What bloke? The one you went to meet yesterday evening?"

"Yes, the married engineer. I saw him leaving, and he had nothing in his hands."

"Well, he could have taken it earlier and left it behind your door."

"You're my Miss Marple. God has punished me for what I've done."

"Your life is like a story from Agatha Christie. Her novels don't end up well for some characters. Did you get your fuck, at least? It turned out to be a very expensive one."

"Don't mention it. I have to go. I'll try to find him and ask."

"The fuck? Are you still looking?"

"The guy. Stop laughing!" I felt like screaming.

"Be careful. If he was willing to steal, he could be capable of worse."

"Stop mothering. I'll ask our porters if they saw someone with my orange bag – it's pretty conspicuous."

They had seen nothing out of the ordinary. It was Sod's Law. The porters noticed only what they shouldn't have seen: Bruce and I together. I decided to contact him direct. On my commute to work, I took the number 139 bus. It was full. A young girl jumped off her seat, eagerly offering it to me. That was a shock. She was publicly saying, "You are an old cunt, this seat is for you." I took it, in spite of my anger, and immediately texted Bruce: *Return what you had taken.*

The response came straight away: *I didn't take anything. You weren't quite a virgin. You're a real cunt! Don't think I'm stupid!*

That wasn't very nice, but he was right. I'd lost the game to that little goblin. I could have been a model for those American 'Cunt' artists, like Betty Tompkins's *Cuntface* photorealistic paintings. They showed a vulva with teeth and eyes exploding. It was an accurate representation of my state of mind that was turning into *Vagina Dentata*. Like Betty's art last few months of my life had revolved around my partly damaged female organs. Her paintings were about women's rage, and my rage had reached its peak.

There was nothing I could do except call my confidante.

"He knows I'd never go to the police. I'm a married woman."

"Now you remember!" My sarcastic friend was laughing.

"But he's a married man."

"So he said. Perhaps he's a crook exactly like the jeweller. You pick them well; you have a great talent!"

I rolled my eyes. The overcrowded bus continued its journey through the streets of the city, and in the hot weather I felt as if I was riding in a mobile sauna. I checked a notification on my Facebook page and it made me shiver. There was a friend request, from Bruce!

"How did that bugger find out who I was? How did he do it? I'd used a fake name on the dating site!" I reported this black-mailing action to Tamara.

"If you know someone's e-mail address, you can trace them on the web." I'd never thought my virgin friend was an expert on such technical matters.

"He's posted his photo from his construction site on my profile. I wonder if he took one of us in bed." I noticed that passengers around me had taken a great interest in our conversation.

"Had that macho man much to show off?" My clever virgin made light of my trouble.

"I think you're safe. Judging by your description of his horrible looks and measurements, he wouldn't compromise himself with intimate photos. He has nothing to gain. But I'm so damn tired of hearing about your unfulfilled dreams; you've had a one-track mind for a while now. A few years, and you'll be getting a free bus pass!" Tamrico was mothering me.

"It's not yet tomorrow, my dear!" I looked around, hoping that nobody overheard this nonsense, and whispered into my phone: *If you don't use it you lose it.*" I saw some faces smiling at me. Our conversation was turning into a public domain. I hanged up.

My maddening sex drive, fuelled by post-operational hormone imbalance, added another twist to my already colourful life!

The Dancing Champion

"Dancing is a perpendicular expression
of a horizontal desire."

George Bernard Shaw

10ᵗʰ March 2016
West End, London
August 1988
Pitsunda, Georgia, USSR
24th April 2916
Central London

"They are so dangerous, your dating adventures. They could end badly, even tragically. Don't you read the newspapers?" Tamara was extremely concerned with my unfortunate romantic quest.

"I'm trying to survive a trauma. Nothing I've tried has worked out."

"What did you try? A fuck on the side? The mother of one of my pupils is taking dancing lessons. She told me that they are very therapeutic. Go to this studio and try ballroom dancing. You'll stop your mental sex obsession." Tamara was making a gigantic attempt to stop my dating pursuits. "You should know that scientific research has proven that ballroom dancing is very good for those over fifty. It improves your mood, posture, movements, balance, memory and even libido." That was incredible marketing for the ballroom business. I was impressed! The only

302

thing I didn't need from this long listing was improving my libi-do. I was desperate to diminish it.

"Yes, I read about it. There should be a huge queue for all those privileges. It's unlikely to improve my bank account though. I heard the prices are a killer. Only the mentally ill would pay that much for a dance. Dan's ticket from Kenya looks like pennies. It's probably true that it takes longer with dancing to become Ga-ga! After fifty, as scientists have established, women lose 5% or more of their memory power. And I am not sure if I want a better mem-ory. There aren't too many pleasant things to remember."

"Dancing with young guys is definitely safer than searching for another crook online. At least it'll provide a pair of male hands around your ... shoulders." Tamara stopped for a minute. She pos-sibly wanted to say – 'around your waist' but wasn't sure if I still had one. "Your body and soul will be far more in balance and harmony."

I was not born to dance. With my chubby body, one leg nearly an inch shorter that the other, with my nearly absent neck – just one piece of oval geometry was given to me by my unfor-tunate parents. I was a good match for Max Ernst's *Celebes* – a round body with a small head, short legs and complete madness inside it. "God had the flu when he created you," my Ukrainian mother used to say on a bad day. I was doubtful if I would ever be able to waltz but I kept those thoughts to myself,

***

"Natashka, come on, one more!" The Soviet dancing crowd adored ABBA's songs. *Money, Money, Money* was one of my fa-vourites. Its rhythm and lyrics would push any hips into action. Dancing to Western songs was in a way a protest against So-viet life – against the voting system which decided the winner before the campaign even started; against the empty shelves in the shops and neighbours talented in writing denunciations that destroyed the nation's best; against the use of newspapers for Soviet bums in the complete absence of toilet paper. It gave a chance for liberation, at least while the vodka still worked.

It was a hot summer day on the Black Sea at the holiday resort Pitsunda – a fantastic place, then part of Soviet Georgia. It was famous for its endless golden sandy beaches. Unfortunately, the splendid seaside views were ruined by six huge, plain concrete buildings. They looked very much like social housing blocks in the UK. They were called '*Pansionats*' – the most desirable hotels for holidays at that time. They were used mainly by the Soviet elite. If you were well connected, you could spend a month there full board for almost nothing – just for 130 roubles, the equivalent of $40. Two of these bleak buildings were special – they were only for foreigners. They had fantastic bars on the top floors with new western music and a good supply of Western-style drinks, and that was a real rarity during Soviet times. Most Russians were not allowed in there. With a few exceptions!

"Hande hoch! Ausweis!" I was talking to the security guard who would be always a KGB officer in those days. "Listen, my Dad fought the Germans during the war and now they seem to be the masters of the game over here." I was trying to push my way into this place for the privileged. I was sincerely upset that we, citizens of this country, were treated like second-rate people on our own land. I was twenty and very pretty, dressed in top fashion and possessed a huge confidence that had developed since I left my parents' home. My words and good looks did not work but a tenner did! And for this amount of money the dancing had to go on all night!

***

That evening, I walked into a small basement in central London and my life changed 180 degrees. There they were – three gorgeous guys. And each one of them wanted to lay his hands on me and keep me in a close hold. It wasn't about sex – it was strictly come dancing!

I had chosen the Armenian teacher, Tigran. He was just twenty five, a couple of years older than my son. The gorgeous guy was flown into the country from the Armenian battlefields to combat the depression of ageing British women, whose husbands had decommissioned their weapons too early.

The Dancer
- Gugokyan, Tigran
- An Armenian dancer/part-time chef
- Known as Tigrusha, the name given him by Natalia It stuck to him as if it was printed on his birth certificate
- Age 25 but it had been a hard life, and his beard made him look more like 30
- 5'9 – not too tall, not too slim, not too fat, not too clever just gorgeous and charming
- His smile could heal, his hysterics could kill
- Married to a Rumanian girl, a waitress, in a possession of a great dowry – a European Union passport. That helped him to withstand such a great burden as occasionally paying his own mobile phone bills
- Speaks poor English with an incredibly sweet accent
- It is not important what he says, it all sounds like love

"Excellent! You are very light on your feet and moving so elegantly." I couldn't believe these words were about me. Tigrusha was not a great specialist in ballroom – his main expertise was in Caucasian folklore dance, the Lezghinka. But he possessed an incredible talent in female rejuvenation and happiness recreation. He would look at me, as if I was the only one for him in the whole world. He would put his hands on the place where my waist was supposed to be. He would circle his beautiful black eyes and whisper with his hushed sexy voice,

"Natalia, you are becoming thinner and thinner every day."

Of course, it was a complete lie, but at my age a sweet lie was preferable to the bitter truth.

Possibly, it was a programmed tactic of the Dance Academy, telling their clients only the nice and positive things, the things they dreamed about. Any lie could throw some doubt into reality. After the lessons, I would spend hours looking into the mirror from all sides, trying to find any bit of my body that had become thinner.

Maybe he meant 'a sinner'? I thought. After my dating experience, that wouldn't be too far away from the truth.

Tigrusha was the new addition to the working forces of the Eastern European semi-slaves, recruited by this dancing sweatshop factory. Those hired guys were there to transform the tears of their clients into smiles by performing real magic for those who were ready to pay for it.

"Today we'll be learning the tango steps and tango passions," my dancing warrior announced. "Hold me firmer!" he ordered, pressing his masculine body to my tits. The Armenian dancer turned me around and swept along the room within the passionate sounds of the Tango, not letting his iron grip slip off my shoulders. The strong smell of cigarettes hit my nose, invading my brain already damaged by the strain of life.

"No smiling! Tango is about passion and drama. Show me your passion!" the dancer commanded, throwing me from one side to another in a demi-Corte – a rather tricky tango element.

"Don't be scared! Step straight into me, between my legs!" Tigrusha was dealing with me like a captain of a big boat. The words 'between my legs' has driven me into a completely wild state! After successfully performing demi-Corte three times, one after another, with a very close touch to whatever he had between his legs, I couldn't restrain myself anymore from orgasmic screaming. I thought everyone in the room would be astonished by my emotional reaction, but nobody seemed to mind at all. Rather the opposite – my lengthy lust sounds were an indication of business going well. I wasn't the only one screaming from happiness. 125 pounds for a 45minute lesson couldn't be wasted – love, passion and dance filled the studios!

"Camilla, I'm paying for ten lessons in advance. Can I have a discount, please?" I asked the receptionist. After that passionate Tango experience, I decided I'd give it a go, in spite of the heavy raid on my pocket. The way the girl looked at me, made me feel ashamed to ask for a discount for my happiness.

"Step from your heel. Heel, toe, toe, heel, toe, toe." It was time for the Viennese waltz. "Drag the foot back by the heel. Longer steps, please!" My gorgeous Armenian was supporting his vocal commands with his hands and vivid facial expressions.

A few weeks earlier, I wouldn't even think I'd be able to make one circle around the dance hall without getting dizzy. The cow had grown her wings!

***

"You should enter The World Championship in Paris, the category *Dancers of the Future*. A really glamorous event! You'll love it!" Khalid, the owner of the Dance Academy, suggested to me after watching my training session with the Armenian.

The Boss
- Khalid Algieri
- The owner of the Dance Academy
- A former tango Champion
- Age uncertain

- 5ft 9
- Looks like 1940s Hollywood star with some traces of former glory
- A unique specialist in a hard approach to everyone and everything
- Denies that money is much more important for him than the dance achievements of his clients

"Me? Competitions? With whom can I compete? Do you really think I can be anybody's future? What can I show except my fat arse?"

"Don't worry! You'll do well. You'll be judged according to your level and your age."

The word 'age' made me nervous and anxious.

Nothing in the world would make me compete in my age group together with the old pensioners. I would have to go for a younger group, even if this would deny me any chance of winning, I thought.

"You can perform in a different, younger age group as well," the pushy Khalid probably read my mind. He obviously had huge experience with dancing ladies of an uncertain age.

"That would be under 45?" My question gave an approximate orientation of the age I was comfortable to live with.

"Yes, but we need a few details," the ex-tango -champion mumbled, trying at the same time to evaluate what he was seeing in front of him. "How old are you?"

That was a shock! "That's not a very polite question for a gentleman." I felt really insulted.

"Seriously?" He tried to charm me with his $20.000 worth of white American dental work.

"I am 78," I joked.

"No! It can't be!" The former champion stared at me in disbelief.

It was upsetting seeing how Khalid was trying to judge me,

trying to find out if there could be any truth in what I'd just said. I'd expected him to take it as a joke and nothing more.

"I confess – I lied. Like every woman, I knocked down a few years. I am 83! You'll need to have an ambulance on standby, or I may fall dead while dancing!"

"Don't joke like that!" The former champion looked worried. He didn't want to upset me and diminish his income. *So he couldn't accept 83 but was hesitant with 78, the old peacock!* I couldn't stop thinking.

"If I win something, I'll take the medal to the grave and will make a provision in my will to put it on top of my chest as a great life achievement."

The guy was a bit confused. He wasn't quite sure if I was pulling his leg or I was using a superior Botox and fillers and the Never Ageing program, including the Vampire Facial rejuvenation with my own blood.

"Age doesn't matter, just dance." The school owner needed me to compete. He was counting how many lessons I would have to take in a preparation for the event and how much money would be entering his pockets!

"We want you to show yourself to the world. You can do it. You just need to stretch your abilities with extensive training in these coming weeks."

What the retired champion really meant was that I should stretch my pocket and ransack my bank account. Pro-am was supposed to mean 'professional and amateur', but it felt more like pro-amour to me. At least for the price. That, of course, was strictly a secret. The version for the customers was almost like a charity ad, 'We just love dancing.'

"All of my movements look like a parody. I'll be a laughing stock at the competitions."

"You are fishing for complements. You are a queen!"

It was probably the company trademark to label the female students 'a queen' as soon as they can no longer be called 'a princess'.

"If you are not confident in your routines, just copy your teacher. You're very expressive; you have a natural artistry and a great presentation. You'll do well. Believe me, there will be a lot of ladies much worse than you."

At last, he spat the truth! So I could possibly take a victory over a few limping pensioners. It sounded inspiring!

"If you want, we can start straight away. Slow waltz will be the best to begin with." The Armenian warrior was ready to conquer the world with me! His unconventional teaching brought me great success. Just a few months after we started training, I became the World Champion in International Ballroom dancing! It happened in Paris, in Disneyland. And it was not a part of the Disneyland show. It was a real world championship, but for some reason, I was the only one on the dance floor in my age group. I competed against myself.

And I won!

I stood there on all three steps of the pedestal and thought, '*Blimey! In one go, I won gold, silver and bronze all together.*'

But the most important thing – I felt like I won my life back.

After that, I could not stop – I danced, danced and danced away from my painful memories.

***

"Tamrico," I had to share my unexpected success with my friend. "I'm a champion. The world champion! Thank you for your recommendation. Dancing did me good. But … I wish I was dancing with Kovač."

"Then I do not know what else I can suggest other than you bury that ghost forever. Perhaps you need to focus on something different, something heroic. Go to the North Pole! You can thrust with polar bears. If the top of the world is far enough away from your doc – do it! Who knows, your next trip might be a ride on a spaceship!" Tamara obviously had had enough of my troubled mind. But there was something else I wanted to share with her.

"Wait. I saw an article in *The Mail* that the GMC would allow relations between a doctor and a patient two years after the end of their professional involvement. If I stop being his patient and give the safeguarding of my cunt to another consultant, in two years he may be free to embrace our love without fear of damaging his reputation." I was proud of how well I summarised why I had to leave Doctor Kovač.

"Our love?" Tamara teased me. "You probably slept with a winged goblin. For Kovač you were a nice, generous patient, but now you're the number one danger. Close the chapter on your doctor." My fairy hung up.

The Winner Takes It All

27th July 2016
Queen's Hospital, Central London

It had been several months since I had last seen Kovač. I stopped worrying about his 'betrayal'. In fact, I was triumphant – since had I arranged my trip to the North Pole, I had managed to shake off my emotional dependence on the doc. I booked an appointment to say goodbye, in case some *Titanic*-style fate awaited me during this adventurous journey and would leave me resting forever among the icebergs.

Kovač looked completely different – much older than before, dressed like he would be at home in a fluffy, checked grey shirt that did not require a tie. His paper cup was half filled with coffee, and the IKEA rubbish bin in the corner of his room was stuffed with the remains of his lunch and medical papers.

"How are you? I haven't seen you for a while. Is anything worrying you?"

He did not get up from his chair. He was obviously very tired – and just made a gesture for me to take a seat. He was smiling and seemed to be happy to see me again.

"Nothing is bothering me," I said, wanting to add 'even you'. "I've just been trying to catch up on life." I should have said *sex life,* but did not want to drag him through my 'distinguished' adventures.

"Why can't we become friends?" That came unexpectedly from Kovač. A minute of silence descended on the room. A few months ago that proposition probably would have made me very happy. But not anymore.

That's it, I thought. My granny used to say, "Men become your friends after, not before." She also used to teach me: "In case of a break-up, always be the first one to leave. Then it's you who left your partner. You're not a victim anymore."

"By the way, I became the world champion in ballroom dancing! And my dancing partner is twenty-five." I showed him a photo on my iPhone featuring me with Tigrusha on the top of the pedestal. That was my triumph! Kovač visibly shrunk in front of me. But I continued my revenge. "I'm leaving you. I'm off on an expedition." I loved the way I said it – so light, like Lady Windermere in Oscar Wilde's play would. My mind was already on the atomic icebreaker – I was ready to conquer the world. That exotic forthcoming affair gave me an incredible confidence.

"Where is it you're going?" The doc nearly choked hearing these words of mine.

"To the North Pole," I pronounced as casually as if I was talking about the Pizza Hut next door.

"Are you serious? Are you sure there isn't something else I need to know?" He looked astonished, desperate even, reaffirming my belief that I was right to end our game of Lovers' Chess.

"I have no time for jokes. And by the way…" I took a breath and I looked straight into his eyes, trying to get maximum satisfaction from his defeated expression. "And when I return, I'm going to move to another gynaecologist. I don't want to be your patient anymore."

Kovač looked crushed. He put his hands over his head and squeezed it, probably checking whether he was not asleep and having a nightmare. A long pause appeared to me as proof of his guilt.

"Let me do a check-up now at least," he practically whispered after a long pause.

He is trying to cover his real feelings with his professional duties. I haven't just shocked him; I've shot him, I thought. The famous ABBA's song *The Winner Takes It All* produced a triumphant resonance inside all parts of my body.

"No," I said quietly but firmly. I decided not to give him anymore access to my body. It was nice to be in control of my own sexual affairs at last.

I probably will miss his internal check-ups. My heart ached with this thought. *He always does it so fast without any pain or even discomfort – just squatting down into my pit and peeking through the peephole.* With his expert knowledge on women's private parts, Kovač could compete with the Australian artist Greg Taylor, who made one 152 life-size porcelain portrait sculptures of women's vaginas, modeled on ladies of different ages. I wondered what Kovač could actually see there with his eyes inside me? *Was cancer like insects crawling inside me or crabs, those arthropod body-eaters, or what?*

"Can you recommend someone else? I don't expect him to be as good as you, but it would be nice to find someone as close to your professional standards as possible," I wanted to end on good terms with the guy who saved my life.

There was a three-minute pause and then Kovač pulled himself together and articulated very officially, "I'll write to you with some names."

All of a sudden, I realised that I did not have any photos of him to remind me about my 'medical romance'. I nervously pulled out my iPad.

"Can I take a picture, please?" I was scared that he would refuse, but to my surprise Kovač only smiled. "No Facebook or other public media, agreed?" He looked rather flattered.

"Of course, Andrew. Just for myself." I knew where it would go – into a beautiful silver frame next to my bed, as a part of the collection of my men from the past.

Sanctuary on Top of the World

8th August 2016
The North Pole, 90 degrees N

"Wake up, wake up! In half an hour we will reach the North Pole!" The leader of the expedition, Jan Muller, announced on the radio at 6.30 in the morning. I had been waiting for these words all night, waking up every fifteen minutes. *Good Lord! I've reached the North Pole!*

There was no chance I was going to miss even a second of this remarkable event. I jumped like a teenager from the narrow bed in my cabin, dressed up like a fireman going to an emergency, and sprinted out onto the bow deck.

A crowd of over 100 people were already there, anxiously awaiting this moment of a lifetime. Some passengers didn't go to bed at all; 24 hours of day light and white nights made it easy to miss out on sleep. The boat had a misleading name: *50 Years of Victory*; it was less than 10 years old, but the name made it sound closer to my age.

The sun was shining as if we were approaching the Bahamas, casting its light on the ice and snow. If you saw it once, you would never say again that snow is just white. It's pink, blue and yellow too; it looked like a fairy tale setting.

It had taken four days on the atomic icebreaker, a huge ship the height of a nine-storey building, to reach the northernmost point of the planet. Barging its way through the endless frozen sea of ice, this powerful vessel made me feel more aroused than any man in my last twenty years of life. It was a storm of iron, powering through three-metre-thick ice, which surrendered under its weight.

When I told Freddie that I was going to the North Pole, his respond was rather disappointing, "What can you see there? Just miles of ice!"

How on Earth could he imagine that the experience could be so erotic? The polar bears, which Tamara had frightened me with, were unfortunately too far away to feel exciting. There was no chance for any contact. But the huge whales made me think about the volume of sperm they could produce, to the envy of the male population of Britain.

The breathtaking helicopter ride above the Franz Joseph Islands was so exciting that it almost made me forget about what had happened to me. Following the steps of Nansen's expedition, I felt like an Arctic explorer as well. When the small Zodiac boat approached a thirty-metre-tall glacier wall, the expedition team all turned into tiny dwarves launched onto an alien planet. I existed in a reduced gravity – floating in a wonderful world, hoping there was no need to return.

The official celebration for reaching the North Pole was due to start at seven in the morning, but some of the explorers had kicked off earlier. The vaporised scent of Scottish Johnnie Walker, French Martini and Russian Kremlevka hung above their heads and created a halo for those 'martyrs' of the Arctic.

"Champagne! Champagne is served!" the expedition leader shouted in English, and then in his native German. I could have only been as excited if I'd been celebrating my thirtieth birthday again. In fact, I felt and behaved like a stupid teenager.

"Hurrah!" I shouted – no, I sang with the power needed for the top C in *Nessun Dorma*. My opera training helped me fill the Arctic air with the incredible sound of pain interlaced with happiness. Like Prince Calaf from *Turandot*, I sang for my life. I needed to survive after everything that had happened to me, not only physically, but also emotionally.

It took some time for the crew to find a suitable place where all 80 explorers could be safely landed. "The ice is very thin," I was told by the worried deck officer. Eventually, in a couple of hours, we were able to leave the boat and step on the northernmost point of the world. Or very near to it – just two miles away from the real spot.

Someone handed me the North Pole marker, a wooden stick decorated with the magic words *North Pole, 90 degrees N*. This tall hard mast aroused me more than anything or anybody. I was hugging it and thrusting my body as if against the man of my life, even trying to breathe in its scent and exercise the sexuality that sprung out of me in this mysterious place. It was a pole dance on the ice.

A long-legged man rushed towards me with the speed of a rocket, screaming in a strong German accent,

"Madam, what the hell are you doing? Please, leave the North Pole sign in peace. It could crack under your heavy passions. Come back to the circle immediately! Ordnung!" This tirade of abuse came from Ulf Gratz, a six-foot-six member of our expedition nicknamed 'The Giraffe'. Although officially listed as a historian, he had so far demonstrated only two of his talents: a loud voice and long legs. His extremely high-pitched voice made me suspect that the word 'long' might not be applied to all parts of his body. As well as me, he had managed to catch a few other disobedient explorers of the North Pole, or, perhaps, just slightly extravagant tourists who liked the cold wind in their hair.

"In ten minutes, we need to film everybody walking around the circle holding hands. Join the rest and grab your neighbours' hand with the same eagerness as that pole. I said 'now!'" Ulf came across almost Bavarian with his strong commands.

Herr Gratz, of course, made a h-u-g-e mistake when he shouted and ordered me around. What did he know? The name Popov discloses my Slavic blood and, in spite of my British passport, I still act just as Slavs do. And for us, rules are there to be broken ; we favour the forbidden. Anyone, except Ulf Gratz, could see that nothing in the world would stop me carrying on doing exactly what I want to do.

"Roma, come on, let's ignore the Fritz. Take my photo with the sign. Hurry up!" Roma enjoyed taking on the role of my personal Sancho Panza on board. We'd met on the boat, and the guy had been following me everywhere. With his bulky body and a belly that stuck out under his jacket, he looked very much like Cervantes's character from *Don Quixote*.

"What's the pin code on your iPad? I'm not able to use it." Roma was ready to do as he was told. He was slow in his movements; his short, fat fingers could not function fast enough.

"It's… oh no!" I hiccupped and froze. The pin code was my year of birth and no way was I going to reveal it to anyone. "Give it to me. I'll do it myself."

I had to snatch the iPad from the astonished guy. I quickly unlocked it and almost burst with victorious joy that I'd managed to catch the situation in time without giving away my antiquity. Changing my pin code became a priority and I decided to give myself the gift of extra six years, to avoid having a heart attack next time someone asked for it. In fact, a few men would later think they were very smart, that they had figured out my 'real' age encrypted in my pin code! Ha-ha!

"Here we are!" I made a theatrical gesture and handed the device back to my companion.

"Smile. Cheese!" At such an important moment, he obviously

could not rely on my iPad's photo quality. He carried around his own equipment, worth at least £10.000. The guy was a successful businessman from Moscow. He had recorded most corners of our planet with his valuable lenses, which could transform any weary-looking blonde into a Hollywood glamour-puss with just one click. It was important to set everything up right.

"One moment, please. Let me turn sideways. In my big anorak, I look like a teddy bear."

"You look great! More like a well-maintained tigress." My new companion was a true gay guy: sweet and polite. I would've preferred being described as a bunny, but at least he noticed and admired the wild animal in me.

To Roma, I was a ballerina. As soon as I met him, I clocked that he weighed at least 120 kilograms, and his partner – whom he introduced as his cousin – weighed a hundred and thirty. To the best of my mathematical ability, which unfortunately was shrinking year by year, they were a quarter of a tonne in weight altogether. I felt guilty that I paid more attention to their frames than their souls. For a moment, it quelled the pride I felt in my own recently achieved lighter frame: I had managed to shave off more than twenty kilos in less than a year. Still, I preferred to keep the specifics of my real weight private, and continued skipping desserts; at least, every second one.

"Roma, may I borrow your hat for a picture? It looks like a prop from *Doctor Zhivago*."

I didn't wait for Roma's reply, and snatched his hat off his head. I placed it on mine like a crown: a queen with my quarter-of-a-ton squad. I quickly rushed over to the boat's anchor that was sticking out of the ice like a huge powerful penis. I climbed on top of it and lay spread-eagled across the anchor's phallic body, hugging and licking its 'dickery-sweet' top. The experience

319

felt like an extended orgasm, like I was thrusting with the whole crew. It was something I'd dream about. Often.

Very often.

Most of the time.

Poor Roma, I thought, *he must despise women after seeing an old hen screwing an anchor, shamelessly revealing all her dirty dreams in the purity of the Arctic wilderness.* Contrary to my worries, my personal paparazzo looked rather jolly and intrigued, snapping away on his camera and creating the rhythm of a decent fuck.

The flags of the twenty-six countries represented on board the ship were hanging on a line like a rainbow, stretched from the top mast of the icebreaker to the ground. Well, not the ground exactly, as the Arctic is just frozen water. To feel it in full and absorb it, one needed to take a dip.

"A swim in the Arctic ocean! The bravest explorers are invited to proceed to the polynya!" The radio was screaming in several languages, underlining the international importance of this event.

The polynya was a small black hole in the ice with stairs temporarily attached, provocatively inviting revellers into the most northerly waters. A few brave guys were ready to throw themselves into the water in spite of the temperature of minus two degrees Celsius. Most of them were clever dicks and had brought wetsuits to protect their manhood from completely freezing. Others were having a good sip – a bottle or more of vodka for Dutch courage before taking the plunge.

"Sergei, your bottle is nearly empty. Oh, God! This is your second one today, is it not?" I said to the handsome, tall, forty-something oilman from Siberia. He'd brought on board an impressive supply of traditional Russian healing drinks. Every morning, he would stuff his pockets with new bottles. Their volume would fairly reflect the state of his heart. Three months earlier, Sergei had lost his wife in very strange circumstances and was trying to find sanctuary in this mysterious frozen land. We were both on the run, both unsure of the direction – whether it was towards life or away from it. Vodka had saved many souls in times when nothing else was able to help. After a few bottles of this elixir of bravery, Russian soldiers laden with bombs used to throw themselves under the fascists' tanks during World War II.

"What about you?"

The oilman looked at me with what seemed like a great surprise, wondering why I wasn't grabbing this unique opportunity by the balls.

"I have a young son. I want to come back alive," I answered. I was flirting with him – I liked big, heavy guys, but the strong odour of vodka slowed down my eagerness. "At my uncertain age, I may have a spasm, collapse, and it might be goodbye forever to this world," I said, but in reality I simply wasn't that keen to reveal my second-hand body to the watching crowd of travellers and the crew.

"You'll be fine and will re-emerge a new person. Trust me: cold water purifies the body and soul and will open a door to you into a different world. I need it, too."

I could only guess at why he had a strong urge to be purified. Oil leaves dirty spots on both the soul and body. Yet, it makes money for just a few.

Did I actually say my thoughts out loud? Or did Sergei read my mind? Suddenly he quoted from St Luke, "Forgive and you will be forgiven." With this biblical prophecy he was off, jumping with his head down into the darkness of the Arctic Ocean.

Did he address it to me or to himself? I was hesitant and tried hard to make sense of his words. The door he mentioned, was it the same door the Saviour pointed at? The one you see on Frederic Leighton's paining *The Light of the World*? It had no handle and could be only opened from inside. The next move was now up to you.

Is that not why I'm here – to purify my body and soul? To shake off all that's happened to me? To forgive... and be forgiven.

At that moment, I knew what I had to do, and no other thoughts followed.

I took off my warm jacket,
pulled off my jumper,
got rid of the trousers.
And last in the queue
were my boots.
I did not feel the cold.
I took one step onto the ladder.

I was going to dip in slowly and test the water first with my toes, but some powerful wave of spiritual energy lifted me up and I jumped with great joy into the unknown waters, as if being newly baptized on top of the world.

Afterword

This book was supposed to come out three years ago, but my husband sent me a letter from his solicitors stating that he would divorce me if the book was published. So, after a lot of thoughts, I put it on a shelf, for the sake of a happy family.

The scary time of the pandemic brought me closer to my husband. Seeing that life can be so fragile made us appreciate it more. Using some parts of my novel, I made my first comedy gigs and I rediscovered a new adventure. It became a great substitute for everything that women of my age are missing out: attention, love and a new career.

Unexpectedly, my husband supported my beginnings in comedy. He promised though not see my shows based on my book and not to read the book, too. Only upon these conditions did I decide to go ahead with this publication. I am fully aware that there will be a few 'kind friends' who will try to upset my husband, and I dread that. My husband is proud of my new career, but never misses a chance to say, "When my wife asks for something, especially money, I know that she is a comedian. So it's all a joke."

I became a very good friend of my husband's girlfriend. Who is not a dog.

I know that Natalia is also doing well. Her relationship with her husband improved a lot. She regrets that her twisted mind – a result of her post operational trauma - didn't allow her to accept the friendship offered at the time by Kovač, her saviour.

I am grateful to have come across Natalia's story, and I am amazed at how much in common we have had in our lives.

Helen Prior

Artworks

1. Hans Memling – *Donne Triptych*, National Gallery, London
2. Alberto Giacometti – *Standing Woman*, Tate Modern, London
3. Hieronymus Bosch – *The Martyrdom of St Julia*, Palazzo Ducale, Venice
4. Max Ernst – *Man Shall Know Nothing of This*, Tate Modern, London
5. Mentioned works of Juan Miro, Tate Modern, London
6. Carlo Crivelli – The Annunciation, National Gallery, London
7. Sandro Botticelli - *Venus and Mars*, National Gallery, London
8. Jan Van Eyck – The Arnolfini Portrait, National Gallery, London
9. Quentin Matsys – *The Ugly Duchess*, National Gallery, London
10. Velasquez – The Rokeby Venus, National Gallery, London
11. William Hogarth – Marriage a la Mode, National Gallery, London
12. Thomas Gainsborough – The Morning Walk, National Gallery, London
13. Debuffet – *Busy Life*, Tate Modern
14. Cornelis van Haarlem – *Two Followers of Cadmus devoured by a Dragon*, National Gallery
15. Damien Hirst – *Pharmacy,* Tate Modern
16. Magda Cordell – *Figure (Woman),* Tate Modern
17. John Sargent – *Portrait of Consuelo Vanderbilt*, Blenheim Palace, Oxfordshire
18. Rebecca Horn – *Overflowing Blood Machine*, Tate Modern
19. Francis Bacon – *Three Studies at the Base of a Crucifixion,* Tate Britain
20. Germaine Richier – *Chessboard,* Tate Modern
21. Lucio Fontana – *Spatial Concept, Waiting* series, Tate Modern
22. Van Gogh – *Sunflowers* – National Gallery
23. Mark Gertler – *Carouse,* Tate Britain
24. Piero Manzoni – *Merda d'artista,* Tate Modern
25. John Sargent – *Portrait of Dr Samuel Jean de Pozzi*, Metropolitan Museum, NY

26. Louise Bourgeois – *Cell (Eyes and Mirrors,* Tate Modern
27. Rene Magritte – *Rape,* Metropolitan Museum, N Y
28. Lucian Freud – *The Fat Sue,* Private collection (exhibited at the National Portrait Gallery, London)
29. *The Venus of Willendorf,* Natural History Museum, Vienna
30. Damien Hirst – *Spot Paintgins,* World wide; 2012 Gagosian Gallery, London
33. Sheela Gowda – *Behold,* Tate Modern
34. Thomas Gainsborough – *Mr and Mrs Andrews,* National Gallery
35. Barnett Newman – *Zips, Museum of Modern Art,* NY, San Francisco, National Museum of Canada, Tate Modern
36. Sarah Lucas – *Pauline Bunny,* Tate Britain
37. Fragonard – *The Swing,* Wallace Collection, London
38. Carlo Crivelli – *Saint Michael,* National Gallery
39. Kazimir Malevich – *Black Square,* Russian Museum, St Petersburg
40. Pablo Picasso – *Nude, Green Leaves and Bust, Private collection (exhibited at Tate Modern)*
41. Pablo Picasso – *Nude Woman with Necklace,* Tate Modern
42. Salvador Dali – *The Persistence of Memory,* Museum of Modern Art (MOMA) NY
43. Rubens – *Samson and Dalilah,* National Gallery
44. Rembrandt – *Night Watch,* the Rijksmuseum, Amsterdam
45. Boris Kustodiev – Merchant's Wife at Tea, The Russian Museum, St Petersburg
46. Roy Lichtenstein – *Whaam!,* Tate Modern
47. Niki Saint Phalle – *Shooting Pictures,* Tate Modern, MOMA, others
48. William Firth – *The Derby Day,* Tate Britain
49. Titian – *Noli Me Tangere,* National Gallery
50. Guerrilla Girls – *Do women have to be naked to get into met Museum?,* Tate Modern
51. Raphael – *The Portrait of Pope Julius II,* National Gallery
52. Frans Snyders – *Still life with Grapes and Game,* National Gallery of Art, Washington D.C.
53. Annette Messager – *The Pikes,* Tate Modern
54. Stanley Spencer – *Artist and his Second Wife,* Tate Britain

55. Tracey Emin – *My Bed*, Tate Britain; private collection
56. Betty Tompkins – *Cuntface,* different exhibitions including Freeze London
57. Greg Taylor – *Cunts … and other Conversations* – serious of portrait sculptures, MONA Museum, Hobart, Australia
58. Frederic Leighton – *The Light of the World*, St Paul Cathedral, London